ST. CHARLES PUBLIC LIBRARY

3 0053 00638 8584

D1509555

ST. CHARLES PUBLIC LIBRARY
ONE SOUTH SIXTH AVENUE
ST. CHARLES, ILLINOIS 60174
(630) 584-0076

DEMCO

15Je04

FAMILY MATTERS

Books by Joel Rosenberg from Tom Doherty Associates

Home Front
Family Matters
Foreign Land

*Not Exactly the Three Musketeers**
*Not Quite Scaramouche**
*Not Really the Prisoner of Zenda**

*Fantasy

FAMILY
MATTERS

JOEL ROSENBERG

A Tom Doherty Associates Book
New York

This one is for David Gross.
He knows why.
So do I.

This is a work of fiction. All the characters and events portrayed in this novel are either fictitious or are used fictitiously.

FAMILY MATTERS

Copyright © 2004 by Joel Rosenberg

All rights reserved, including the right to reproduce this book, or portions thereof, in any form.

This book is printed on acid-free paper.

A Forge Book
Published by Tom Doherty Associates, LLC
175 Fifth Avenue
New York, NY 10010

www.tor.com

Forge® is a registered trademark of Tom Doherty Associates, LLC.

LIBRARY OF CONGRESS CATALOGING-IN-PUBLICATION DATA

Rosenberg, Joel, 1954–
    Family matters / Joel Rosenberg— 1st ed.
        p.   cm.
    "A Tom Doherty Associates book."
    ISBN 0-765-30499-6 (alk paper)
    EAN 978-0765-30499-5
    1. Editors—Fiction. 2. Sheriffs—Fiction. 3. North Dakota—Fiction. 4. African American teenage girls—Fiction. I. Title.
PS3568.O786F36 2004
813'.54—dc22

                                                    2004041161

First Edition: July 2004

Printed in the United States of America

0   9   8   7   6   5   4   3   2   1

FAMILY MATTERS

3 0053 00638 8584

1

Despite what my ex-wife would be more than willing to tell you, I've always been pretty good at leaving well enough alone. Where I fuck up is in not leaving bad enough alone.

But I'm learning.

Honest.

"The thing is, well, you committed a felony," he said.

"Oh."

It seemed like the thing to say, and probably would have seemed like the thing to say even if he wasn't holding a rifle at the time.

Which he was, although it wasn't pointed at or near me. And he was more holding *on* to the rifle than holding it, anyway; the barrel of Jeff's new Winchester .22–250 was resting on a pile of sandbags on my shooting bench.

Never shoot offhand when you can use a rest, as my old drill sergeant used to say, although not nearly as often as "Hemingway, yeah, *you*, Hemingway—you're a fucking disgrace to protoplasm."

"You arresting me?" I asked.

I thought it was a fair enough question under the circumstances, but Jeff Bjerke made a face, and for a moment he looked like the eight-year-old kid I remembered instead of the twenty-five-year-old kid he was.

But he didn't look over at me; he was still looking for the groundhog.

"Don't be stupid," he said. He bent back over his rifle, leaning his elbows on the shooting bench.

Well, I do try not to be stupid. Miracles do happen: Sometimes I'm even successful.

"Well, what do you think I did?" I asked.

"Hang on sec. I think I saw him again. Nervous little guy."

"Okay."

He leaned more heavily on his elbows and fitted his eye a bit tighter to the rubber socket of the ancient Leupold scope mounted on his brand-new Winchester Model 70.

A redwing blackbird perched on the bubble-gum rack on top of his blue Ford Bronco a dozen yards away just eyed the two of us skeptically, but didn't actually make any comment, unless you consider crapping, once again, on the Bronco's roof some sort of comment, which I didn't.

Birds usually know when to keep their beaks shut, not that this one was in any danger from either Jeff or me. For one thing, a rifle chambered in .22–250, equipped with high-powered scope, is an ideal tool for reaching out and hitting something small at, say, two or three or even four hundred yards, but an absolutely lousy choice for shooting at a bird a dozen yards away—the redwing would just be a big black blur that would cover the field of view.

For another, redwings are a protected species, and I do try to avoid violating the law, honest—Jeff's expressed opinion to the contrary.

More important, I don't believe in shooting something just because it's irritating. Which is just as well. I'm often told that I irritate easy, and always find being told that, well, you know: irritating.

The wind was light but in my face, so I shook a Camel filter out of the too-quickly-emptying pack on the shooting bench and fired it up with the battered Zippo that a friend had sent me.

Close to thirty years of being off cigarettes had, so to speak, gone up in smoke last winter.

I let my thumb rub against the inscription. One word: *Anytime*. Hard to decide whether it was a threat or a promise, although if it was a threat, it wasn't aimed at me.

The only threat that seemed pointed at me was what Jeff had just said, and while part of me wanted to take him by the shoulders and shake him, just to wipe the smile off of his face, that probably is just about the stupidest way to deal with somebody even if he isn't the town cop or a friend, and—common opinion to the contrary—I try to keep doing the stupidest thing to a minimum, thank you very much.

"I don't see him," Jeff said. "Think that last shot scared him underground?"

"No. Well, make that 'yeah, but not for long.' "

Woodchucks don't have great hearing. Or great eyesight. Or great brains. Or great personalities. What they do have is a great ability to breed, and to eat anything of value—sort of like rats with better-looking tails and a serious thyroid condition.

"Wait for it. He'll poke his head out in another minute or so."

I'd nailed a big fat one—fattened on some of the green sprouts that were going to be Jeff Thompsen's corn crop—just a minute or so before, just at the northwest corner of the field, and long before the time the shot finished ringing out the rest of them had gone to ground. We had already gotten half a dozen from this stand, and the woodchucks that remained were, relatively speaking, the wary ones.

But they'd be out again soon. That's the way it is with woodchucks. Not that they're particularly nervous critters; they're not. In fact, if you've got the patience for it, you can wear one of those camouflage netting hoods that hide your eyes although not much bother your vision and just stalk-and-walk to within maybe twenty-five, fifty yards of one, if you know what you're doing, and have the patience, and don't mind looking idiotic.

Me, I know what I'm doing, and I've got patience by the truckload, and I manifestly don't mind being thought of as an idiot . . . but still, I prefer the lazy man's way.

"Wish he'd hurry up," Jeff said.

"Patience, patience," I said. I'd been showing more than enough patience myself. "Now, can we get back to this felony you think I committed?"

"I don't think you committed it, Sparky—I helped you. Shit, I talked you into it, not that it took much talking."

Well, the truth was that, after more years than I cared to count of being a decent, law-abiding, and pretty dull citizen, I had, last winter, slipped the leash a little, or maybe more than a little.

For good reason, I had thought, and still thought. No regrets. And I'd also thought, to be honest, that we'd all gotten away with it.

Oops.

"Care to be more specific?"

His mouth twitched. "Remember that carful of dead gang-bangers out near Cole Creek last winter?"

"Is this a trick question?" I wasn't likely to forget. One of the many nice things about living on the East Dakota plains is not having to worry about things like inner-city gangsters. "Hey, I didn't kill them. Nobody did. They froze to death in the blizzard."

If you go over into the ditch in an East Dakota blizzard, staying with the car is a good idea, unless you're of a suicidal bent, but sitting in the car while running the engine until the carbon monoxide builds up to lethal levels is just a particularly silly way to commit suicide. It's amazing how warm a candle from the emergency kit can keep you, and in winter I try to remember to keep the emergency kit in my backseat, rather than the trunk, just in case.

Failing that, the only thing to do is just huddle into as small a ball as you can and crack the window about half an inch and run the engine for a short while every now and then just to get the heat going, then shut the window and kill the engine and wait for help. That's the only sensible thing to do, although not everybody does the sensible thing.

Happens, every winter, and you don't have to be some sort of city guy to let winter kill you, not on the East Dakota plains, you don't.

The folks who had gone off the road near Cole Creek hadn't done the sensible thing, and it had killed them. Which didn't bother me much, all in all, as they'd been on their way to Hardwood to kill Tenishia, and me, too, probably.

On a nice spring day, the sort of day when you wear a light jacket if you want to but don't miss it if you're walking, or, like we were doing, sitting out under the hot sun, it's hard to think about blizzards.

But it had been only a few months before that the snow was driving more sideways than down on the very spot where we were sitting in our shirtsleeves, icy fingers reaching for any crack to pry open, and the sun overhead had only dazzled the eyes, and didn't bring a trace of warmth with it.

"I didn't *say* you killed them. But when you went out with me to take a look at the scene, you were wearing that police badge, and that—"

"Which you gave me."

"Yeah. Which I gave you. And you were representing yourself as a police officer."

"You swore me in. Hell, it was your idea."

Jeff had, for good enough reasons, wanted me to take a close look at the trouble I had gotten not just myself but the whole fucking town into, and he had said it was a better idea to have me out at the scene as a reserve cop than as a civilian, as the cops were going to wonder what a civilian was doing poking around, and we didn't need a whole lot of official wondering going on at the time.

Surprisingly, we'd pulled it off without anybody looking me up and down and asking, "hey, what's that bald, middle-aged freelance copy editor with the strangely familiar name doing pretending to be a cop?"

"Yes, it was my idea," he said. "I'm not saying it wasn't. I was . . . distracted. As it turns out, I apparently don't have the authority to swear you in, not even temporarily." He shrugged, and then settles his eye back firmly into the rubber socket. "Live and learn, I always say."

"Yeah. I've heard you say that. Lots. So? What's going to happen?"

"Nothing, I hope," he said. "I wouldn't even bring it up, but . . . you remember that detective from the BCI? The bald guy?"

Vaguely. I had been paying more attention to the dead bodies and what they implied than to the cops. "Yeah. Franks?"

"No: Franz. Andrew J. Franz."

Yeah. That was him. A few years older than me, balding even worse than I am, a mustache halfway between walrus and Hitler, a beak of a nose, and a left eyelid that tended to sag. "Seemed to be a nice enough guy."

"Hmph. I always thought of him as something of an asshole, myself. He stopped by the office yesterday on some other business, and he asked about you."

"What sort of questions?"

"Nothing specific. Just how you were doing, being new and all. What sort of hours you were working. Like that."

"And?"

"And I sort of hemmed and hawed, and I don't think he liked that. He made a point of pulling down the *Century Code* from my bookshelf and looking it over, then left it open. He said he might be stopping by to talk with you at some point."

"Great. An investigation from a state cop. Just what I need."

"You've had enough official investigations lately, eh?"

"Well, yeah."

With all the paperwork and home visits from the CYS over Tenishia, I was seriously beginning to think about locking my front door and removing the knocker.

I had thought that was over. I don't have anything in particular against social workers—other than the belief that they're all reincarnations of people who were way too anal to get into the SS—but that doesn't mean I need one dropping by at random times to criticize my housekeeping, such as it is.

Which wasn't fair, but I'm not big on being fair, particularly not in the confines of my own house, or my own mind. Sue me.

"Well, he wasn't investigating," Jeff said. "Not officially. Just asking. But it got me to thinking, and I took a careful look at some of the laws—"

"You don't know the law?"

He snorted. "Shit, Sparky, you ever look at the Century Code?"

"I kinda doubt it. I don't even know what the hell a century code is."

"Hmph. It's the state laws, and it doesn't get any shorter every year, I'll tell you that. Our problem—"

"*Our* problem?"

"Shh. One problem starts with section 12-63-09, which is where Franz left the code open on my desk. Don't think it's a coincidence."

"And?"

"Performing peace officer duties without a license. That puts you into violation of 12-63-14, which is a class-B misdemeanor."

"Misdemeanor? You said felony." Not that I particularly thought the idea of being accused of a misdemeanor appealing. According to a book I once copyedited, all it means when a crime is a misdemeanor is that they can only put you in jail for a day less than a year.

"Patience, patience."

I could have argued that I didn't really perform any peace-officer duties—I was just walking around and looking at stuff, and had not, apparently, been sufficiently cursing myself as an idiot for taking Jeff Bjerke's word that his swearing me in had been good enough. I could also have said that I don't think of a criminal misdemeanor as something like a speeding ticket, either. I've gotten my share—or maybe more than my share—of those, given the combination of our good roads and our silly speed laws, but the only court I've ever had to show up in was traffic court, and that only twice.

But I didn't say anything.

He leaned back into the scope. "There he is."

You can always tell when somebody who knows what he's doing is about to shoot. Some of it's pretty obvious minor things—anybody I'm willing to hunt with, or plink with, will keep his finger the hell off the trigger until he's just about to make a loud bang, just as he'll be damn sure not to sweep the barrel across, say, me, even if the gun is unloaded.

But mainly it's the whole body attitude. You lock the rifle in, tight, to your shoulder, and your cheek against the stock, and you brace yourself for the recoil—particularly if you're used to heavier rounds than the little .22-250—and try to fit yourself to the rifle and the rifle to yourself in exactly the same way each and every time.

I didn't have to put my hands over my ears. I'm a traditionalist when it comes to most hunting equipment—the toys are for the boys—but the newfangled electronic earmuffs are neat. We'd been able to carry on a conversation without either of us having to shout even a little, or touch a dial when it came time to shoot—the electronics handled all that, and it understood the difference between a chat and a *bang*, although how it did it I don't really know.

"I see him," he said. He was trying hard to keep the excitement out of his voice, and only failing a little around the edges.

That's the thing about hunting, no matter what it is that's in your sights: It all gets real.

You can spend hours plinking away at paper targets and tin cans with a pair of foam-rubber earplugs covered by a clamped set of ear protectors, and the report of the rifle will still bother you. You'll still feel the butt of the rifle slam against your shoulder enough to notice it, even with a low-recoil round like a .22-250.

But put the sights on something breathing, something real, even something as unimportant as an oversized ground rat, and it gets all primal.

You don't need high-tech ear protection to filter out the sound, and you don't need a high-tech gel-filled pad on the butt of your rifle to dampen the recoil. Some primitive part of the lizard brain says, in effect, hey, asshole, let's pay attention to what's important, here and now, and it isn't noise.

I usually manage to get my deer each winter, and I can't begin to count the number of woodchucks I've nailed, even in the past few springs, and I've never once even noticed the report or felt the butt of the rifle slam into my shoulder.

Jeff's rifle barked, once. Thanks to the fancy super-electronic earmuffs, it was only a distant, muffled bang in my ears, although the shock of it sent the redwing blackbird fluttering into the air and made the ammo boxes momentarily dance on the shooting bench.

I brought my eye down to the spotting scope, and had to move it around only for a few seconds before I saw what was left of the woodchuck.

"Nice," I said. The shot had caught the chuck right in the head, blowing it clean off. Not that you have to be that careful with a .22-250, not on a woodchuck—a center-of-mass shot will nail it right away, blow out its chest and usually cut it in half, leaving just pieces. Even a .22 Stinger, if you place the shot right, will put it down before it can move an inch, and while the .22-250 is just about the same size as a Stinger, it's moving a *lot* faster.

People tell you that the bullet explodes, but that's horseshit, at least it is if you're using a decent bullet. I once copyedited a book by Martin Fackler, who knows about such things, and he explains that what really happens is that the "temporary wound cavity"—the temporary hole the bullet makes when it pushes tissue aside on its way through—is just too big. Make an eight-inch cavity in the chest of something, like a wood-chuck, that's six inches across—"temporary" cavity or not—and what you have is pieces of dead woodchuck spreading out over several square yards, and not some wounded animal crawling off in pain to die.

Which is the idea. I don't mind killing vermin that are fat-tening themselves on a friend's means of support, but I'm not into wounding them. I've made enough living creatures suffer for one lifetime, the way I figure it, and whatever your feelings are about woodchucks, they don't suffer, given that they're dead before they even know they've gotten a bullet through the chest or the brain.

Jeff was working his binoculars. "I don't see any more. You think we've cleaned the field out?"

"Unlikely. But we certainly made a dent. Can we get back to this felony thing? This thing *we* supposedly did?"

He smiled. "I thought that would get your attention."

"Yeah. You did. And it did."

Well, you don't look too fucking worried about it, I thought.

"Okay. We did the performing-peace-officer duties, and that

brings us to 12-63-14, Impersonating a Public Servant, and then we're into conspiracy—that's where you and I agreed that you would impersonate a public servant, and one of us performed an overt act in aid of that conspiracy, which makes both of us felons. Hell, both of us did—I handed you a badge, and you said you were the new part-time town cop."

"Great idea, eh?" I was surprised that my voice was developing a little heat, or maybe more than just a little heat.

Jeff hadn't come out to the Thompsen farm with me to arrest me after all. We were friends. Not close friends, but friends.

"Yeah, it was my idea," he said.

"You think we get to be cellmates?"

"Shit. Don't worry about that." He shrugged. "Hey. There's another one. Oh, shit—he just popped his head out and ducked back in."

Even woodchucks can take a hint.

"Let's leave him," I said. "So you didn't bring me out here just to arrest me, I take it."

"Nope. I came out here with you to shoot some woodchucks." He nodded. "Not exactly the best exercise in the world, but it's a lot of fun."

He hadn't shown any interest in woodchucks until a couple of weeks ago. Jeff Bjerke had always been a pretty serious hunter—he and his father-in-law and I have gone deer hunting every fall together for a good ten, fifteen years—but most of his hunting involved walking through the woods in search of rabbits and squirrels. He and his dad had spent a lot of spring, summer, and fall weekends—and the occasional stolen weekday—doing that, until his father had moved to Florida in January, officially to retire, but mainly to die of lung cancer in some hospital in Boca Raton. God's Waiting Room has good hospitals, I take it, or maybe they've just got cheap places to die. Or both.

This interest in varminting was a new one for Jeff, and my assumption was—well, it had been—that he just wanted me to show him the ropes, and maybe wanted to go hunting with me more often than we could for deer season.

It had seemed a safe assumption—he'd invited me along to shoot some rabbits and squirrels, but I'm not all that fond of walking through the woods with a .22, and I'm definitely not crazy about the taste of either rabbits or squirrels. And they're just too much work to clean. Yeah, a deer is a lot more work than a rabbit, but you can get a lot of meals out of even a small, one-point buck and just a bowl or two of stew out of a rabbit, and, as I've said, I don't go shooting animals just because I can. Squirrels are a problem in the city, but all they do in the woods is make annoying sounds, and there's lots better ways to get rid of rabbits than shooting them, if and when they become a problem.

Me, I'll shoot something that's causing enough of a problem, and I'll shoot things I want to eat, and if I really feel like shooting something just for fun, that's what tin cans are made for.

There are those, by the way, who say that woodchucks are edible; but I think the best way to handle them is to leave the carcasses for the crows—which works pretty well—and *pour encourager les autres*, which doesn't work at all.

He shrugged. "You want to set up on the other side of the field, or are we about done for the day?"

"Well, I think I'd better get home and get on the phone to my lawyer, eh?"

"Fred?" He shrugged.

"We got some other lawyer in town?" I asked, demonstrating my keen sense of the obvious.

"Yeah, you could call Fred and let him start the billing clock ticking," Jeff said, showing a suspicious concern for my bank account. "Or you could save yourself some money and just come on over to my father-in-law's tomorrow."

"Eh?"

"First Wednesday after the first Tuesday of the month. Town-council meeting."

Jeff's father-in-law, Bob Aarsted, has been the mayor of Hardwood for the past fifteen or so years, not that it shows, much; the only paid town employees, the school aside, were Jeff, old Emma Thompsen, the town clerk, and Ole Skoglund, the fire chief.

It's possible to find Bob in his office at town hall if you're willing to camp out, but you're much better off going across the street to Aarsted Hardware or—more likely—two doors down to the Dine-A-Mite, where endless Aarsted Hardware and town business is done over equally endless cups of weak coffee.

Hunting wasn't the only thing Jeff and I had in common. The Aarsted girls were another—although he had married his and mine had left for greener pastures, at least until recently.

"I've never been to a town-council meeting, and things have gotten busier lately."

Having a teenaged girl in the house had definitely added some demands on my time and attention, and then there was the matter of Bridget moving in. I wouldn't say that either Bridget or Tenishia were high-maintenances types, generally— not compared to my ex-wife, at least—but the whole dance with the Children and Youth Services people over Tenishia's status had chewed up a lot of time, and even more of my limited patience, and never mind that both Tenishia and Bridge were actually humans, with needs that involved some attention beyond a "good morning" and a "how's your day?"

It's not like having a dog.

I know; I have a dog.

Things had been so busy that I had just jumped at the chance to play hooky for a few hours when Jeff had suggested it, and not looked for the hook hidden in the bait.

"Make the time," he said, with a smile. "If you show up before seven, bring an appetite—better start fasting now, in fact. You know Bridget's mom."

"All too well."

Jeff looked me straight in the eye. "Hey, I'm sorry, Sparky. I didn't mean to scare you. Bob says we'll handle it; just relax."

"Yeah, sure." I glanced down at my wrist. "I'd better be getting home, though. Work to do, as much fucking fun as this has been."

He made a face. "Yeah. Sorry."

"Right."

Jeff helped me load the shooting bench and the accompanying gear into the backseat of my battered, dirt-colored Oldsmobile, then tossed his gun case into the backseat of his blue Bronco before he climbed in the front.

Then, with a wave, he set off at a slow enough pace to kick up only a little dust and rocks on the dirt road. I turned my back to protect my eyes, and only winced a little when a kicked-up pebble caught me just south of my left shoulder blade, where I couldn't even rub at it.

He slowed when he reached the county road about a quarter mile away, but then turned onto it and sped off—and I do mean sped off: He was easily doing seventy, maybe eighty, as he roared off into the distance.

Nothing wrong with that, not really.

It's different in the western part of the state, but East Dakota—North and South—was smashed flat as a pancake (the kind my mother used to make when she forgot to include the baking powder to make them rise) by the glaciers a geological eyeblink ago, and the roads are straight and wide, with enough visibility at intersections that you've got plenty of time to realize that it's safe, if not exactly legal, to speed through at eighty or better, and just about everybody does, accepting the occasional ticket as sort of a road tax.

I certainly did. Or at least I had. And that didn't make me unusual. Hell, even Dave Oppegaard, Hardwood's Lutheran minister, has been known to go to Grand Forks on a shopping trip and be back in under two hours, and the round-trip drive is a very solid ninety minutes if you obey the posted limits.

Then again, while I've often seen him in town without his clerical collar, I've never seen him drive out of town without it on, and I suspected he didn't get a whole lot of speeding tickets.

There's other ways out of it, too. I pulled the Reserve Officer badge, still in its battered leather wallet, out of my pants pocket.

I'd kept it—at Jeff's suggestion, the bastard—and it had gotten me out of a couple of speeding tickets since. Doctors aren't the only folks who practice professional courtesy, after all. I doubt it would have gotten me out of a drunk-driving charge, but since I don't drink and drive—we can discuss precisely what kind of idiot I am some other time, but it's not that kind—I hadn't been worried about that.

Spending time in prison on a felony seemed to be an awfully high price to pay for avoiding a few fifty-dollar speeding tickets, though, and even when I added in the costs that another dozen points on my license would add to my car insurance, it still didn't feel like anything resembling a bargain.

The redwing—I think it was the same one, although I could easily have been wrong—was now perched on a fencepost, looking at me.

Fencepost, as in "Ernest 'Sparky' Hemingway is dumb as a fencepost."

It cocked its head to one side.

"Yeah," I said.

Fucking bird was too smart for its own good.

2

Things at my house had gotten domestic, but not normal-domestic. Which, I guess, was only to be expected, all things considered.

When I came in from the garage, Bridget was in the kitchen, splitting her time and attention between the pot of spaghetti sauce simmering on the stove and the laptop computer busy doing laptop computer things on the kitchen table. In the kitchen, yes; barefoot, yes; but not, I was sure, pregnant. We were both getting a bit old to think of all of that, and if I'd had any doubt, Tenishia would have quickly persuaded me.

There was a time when I would have thought otherwise about me and Bridget—in fact, I did.

But while that was long ago, it wasn't in a country far away, and, thankfully, the wench wasn't dead.

I sniffed the air. At one time I'd have said she was using too much garlic—we were both brought up here in Hardwood, North Dakota, where even salt is considered an exotic spice—but I'd spent enough time away from Hardwood to realize one of the basic facts of life: There's no such thing as too much garlic.

Snake got up from his usual nap spot in front of the fridge and wagged over to be petted, nudging hard against my hand when I didn't pet him hard enough.

I pulled my hand away and towered over him.

"Snake, sit-stay," I said. He sat right away, and gave me an innocent look as I took a step back. Snake's a good dog, best one I've had, but you've got to be careful with German shepherds—they're very hierarchical, and always looking to move up the pecking order.

"Oh, Sparky," Bridget said, shaking her head. "He just missed you."

"He can just miss me just fine," I said, staring him right in the eyes until he looked away. "As long as he remembers just who the dog is."

"And that would be him?"

"That's my theory. I want to make sure it stays his theory, too."

I'd made him wait long enough; I beckoned to him and he came over, wagging again, and then accepted being petted without nudging.

With my dog, I'm always right, I'm always in charge, and I always must be obeyed. Not exactly the way the rest of my life works—more's the pity.

Coffee was burbling down into the pot of the coffeemaker, almost filling it, as though she'd started the pot when she had heard me drive in and had managed to get it going more quickly than I had put the shooting gear away.

A nice thing for her to do.

Not the nicest thing anybody's ever done for me, but if you stack up enough nice little things, you've got part of what Bridget is, and I'm kind of very fond of her, and thought things were starting to work out pretty well, despite some annoyances.

Very domestic, I guess, although there were some . . . idiosyncrasies.

For one: Bridget was wearing one of her old lab smocks as

an apron, her long legs bare beneath. The smock had gotten splattered with enough red sauce to make her look like an extra from a slasher movie, but the legs were still perfectly good legs without making allowances for her being in her forties, although I'd have been happy to make those allowances.

For another: A long piece of what looked to me like telephone wire but that Bridget insisted was a "cable" snaked its way from the computer on the kitchen table across the old linoleum, disappearing down the hall toward what had been my bedroom/office, but now was developing a serious personality disorder.

That was about the only kind of disorder that appeared to be tolerated *chez* Hemingway these days.

The county social worker had lots of opinions about how a house with a teenaged ward of the state was to be run. Ms. Hennessy—she insisted on the "Ms." rather than her first name; I assumed she had one—didn't quite say it out loud, but I think the theory is that dirty dishes in the sink cause middle-aged men to beat and/or molest teenaged girls, although I'm not sure what the underlying logic is. Dirty dishes don't make me either mad or horny. Neither do piles of laundry—dirty or clean—nor books spread out all over the floor of my office.

Becoming a foster father was basically a short, intensive course that might have been called Relaxing to the Inevitable 101. The only prereq consisted of a hole in the head, I think.

So: Dishes couldn't be left stacked up all over the kitchen counters and table until they became a problem, or even allowed to soak in the sink in soapy water for a few hours. Books were to be put on bookshelves when they weren't being used. Toilet paper was to be put on the toilet paper roll holder, and the roll not just left on top of the tank. Laundry was to be folded and put away in the hall closet or a dresser when it came

up from the basement; my days of throwing what I'd worn in—
well, mostly at—the dirty-clothes basket in my former bedroom and fishing for something clean in the clean-clothes
basket were over.

Shit, I couldn't even think of leaving an empty beer can on
the elbow table in front of the TV to use as an ashtray.

How much of all that was for the benefit of the social
worker checking up on Tenishia and how much of was for the
benefit of Bridget and Tenishia was an interesting question
that it wouldn't have been wise to ask, but none of it was for
my convenience.

"I like the outfit," I said. "What there is of it."

She smiled. "I thought you would." The smile broadened as
she parted the smock to reveal a T-shirt and shorts. She wasn't
wearing a bra. I'm not sure why the rest of the world thinks a
woman in her forties can't admit that time and life have
caused her breasts to sag some, but I had kind of worked that
out, and it didn't bother me even a little.

"I thought about adding a pair of high heels and getting rid
of the rest, but the kids are due shortly. Sorry."

"Not as sorry as I am."

I didn't ask about the smock. Aprons were in short supply in
my house, and not Bridget's style, anyway. It was one thing for
her to share kitchen duties with Tenishia and me—being a
good cook has a lot to do with practice, something to do with
innate talent, and very little to do with the shape of one's gen-
italia; everybody I know uses other parts of the body when
cooking—but it would have been another thing entirely to put
on one of Mom's old aprons.

Her hair was tied back in a simple ponytail that should have
looked too young for a woman in her forties, but didn't. Maybe
it was because of the way that some blond tendrils had escaped
the twisty-cloth-loop thing with the name that I'd have to

look up again, or maybe it was just that Bridget could always get away with doing what she wanted to.

I have a theory, myself.

She looked up at me and smiled. "New manuscript came in about an hour ago—it's not marked urgent. I'd have called you about it, but you don't have a phone," she said.

"I do have a phone," I said, pointing to the one hanging on the kitchen wall. "And several extensions. I installed them myself."

I'm notoriously cheap, but home-phone wiring is easy and inexpensive, and the best way to get an editor to call you is to take a shower; a bowel movement is a close second.

"You don't have a *cell* phone," she said pointedly.

"You said that pointedly," I said.

"Well, yes, I guess I did. I do want you to get a cell phone; it would make some things easier, like when it's your turn to do the grocery shopping and I remember that we need canola oil five minutes after you've left."

"I could wax poetic about the virtues of shopping lists. You know: What you do is you write down on paper the things you need, and then when you go to the store you buy them."

"Yeah. I think maybe I heard of those."

"Sarcasm ill becomes you."

Well, no; that wasn't quite true. It actually looked good on her.

Her eyes met mine. "But if the worst problem you and I ever have is you not wanting to carry—let me see if I have this straight—'a goddamn ringing plastic box on my fucking belt,' or, better, 'tied around my neck like an electronic dog collar'; is that about right?—we'll do just fine, you and me. If you can't take some good-natured complaining about it every now and then, we won't."

"I'll take the good-natured complaining, thanks." I had to smile. "But not always with the best of grace—I'm sort of set in my ways."

"I think I noticed that."

And, while I'm not complaining, adapting from years of solitude—how many depends on whether or not you include the last couple of years of my marriage—to living with two women did have its moments of frustration. While my ex-wife, Jennifer, had her share of flaws—including, if you care to count it, the inability to put up with living with me; opinions on that being a flaw vary widely—and had been known to alternate between nonstop complaining and endless cold silence, the subject of toilet seats had never come up, and these days I was spending far more of my life than I cared to discussing the mechanics of the operation of a simple hinge.

Okay, I lied: I am complaining, and if I didn't think that Ms. Hennessy from CYS was perfectly capable of bringing in a urine-sniffing dog, I'd probably have just taken up pissing in the bathroom sink.

"How'd it go?" she asked.

"Eh?"

"The shooting?"

"Interesting. Fun. Got a half dozen chucks, easy, although Jeff's new rifle bears out my theory that the peak of the riflemaker's art was 1963."

"Oh?"

"Yeah. His rifle's nice and all, but I wouldn't trade a dozen of them for my old pre-sixty-four Winchester."

"Is this discussion of guns supposed to get me all hot and bothered?" she asked, her smile taking any possible sting out of the words.

"Well, that wasn't its purpose, but it would be kind of nice."

"Maybe, but it'll have to wait for later." She glanced up at the clock. "The kids are studying here today. I told you that."

"Studying, or groping each other?"

She smiled. "I don't think there'll be any of that with you in your office, working. And I don't think Tenishia and Jeffie and Josh and Amy are into any sort of group thing, although I could be wrong."

"Probably not." Not that it was any of my business, as long as they played safe. Having a talk about that with Tenishia wasn't the most comfortable thing I've ever done, but you do what you have to, even though the mechanics of birth control was something, she explained quite clearly, she was familiar with.

Bridget cocked her head to one side. "Something else bothering you? Something I said?"

"Nah." I shook my head. "Nothing you said."

Bridget and I had set some ground rules when she moved in. Not many, but one of them was being up front with anything the other one did or said that was irritating.

I suspected she cheated more than I did. Which wasn't much, to be honest. I'm irritated with the universe most of the time, I think, and there was no reason to remind Bridget of that on a daily basis.

"But there's something else?" It wasn't a question, not really. It just sort of sounded like one.

"Well, yeah." I don't know why, but I was embarrassed. It had seemed reasonable at the time for me to pretend to be a cop, but in retrospect . . .

"And?"

"Jeff Bjerke says I appear to have committed a felony."

The smile vanished and she put the spoon down—on the stove itself, not on the ceramic spoon-rester thing.

"Tell me," she said.

It took a while to tell.

She shook her head and frowned. "It doesn't make any sense, Sparky."

"I had that thought, too."

"What do you think is going on?" She pursed her lips. "Dad's still feuding with Norstadt, and—"

"Norstadt?"

"Phil Norstadt. County commissioner—lives just outside Thompson. He and Dad have never exactly gotten along, and they haven't gotten any friendlier since Dad was able to push the school-bond issue through in ninety-nine, for one thing. Don't you follow politics?"

"As little as possible," I said. I hadn't grown up around the Aarsted family dinner table, either.

"Hmph."

"Besides, how would that involve me?"

"Not you—Dad. Any fuss in Hardwood would embarrass him, and it probably doesn't matter if the fuss is about something reasonable or not, not to Norstadt."

I shook my head. "That sounds too complicated and Machiavellian for me."

I didn't like the thought of how it also might embarrass Bob Aarsted if the fact that his daughter was living in sin with a man not her husband became the subject of more general county-wide gossip. I was certain it was a matter of some discussion in town—everything that happens is, in a small town, or at least in this small town—but I was also sure it wasn't a matter of particularly hostile discussion, or, at least, I hoped not.

Not that I gave a rat's ass about such things, but Bridget did.

"Like you say, you don't follow politics," she said.

No, I don't. I like to keep some things simple, and one of the things I like about life in Hardwood is how simple it all is. Or was, at least for me, at least until lately.

I shrugged. "My guess, if I had to make one, is that Franz is about as fond of Jeff Bjerke as Jeff Bjerke is of Franz, and he was just jerking his chain. Doesn't sound like the sort of thing anybody would want to make a real fuss over."

She pursed her lips. "I don't know. Conspiracy, that's pretty serious."

"Conspiracy, *bah*."

"Ah. The *Bah* Defense. How's that work in court?"

"I dunno. Hope I don't have to find out, and Jeff didn't seem to think I would."

"Yeah. And he got his law degree exactly where?"

"Same place you got yours and I got mine, I suppose. I could call Fred—and start the billable hours—or I can just wait until tomorrow night and see what's up."

"I still don't like it," she said.

"What's to like?" Ignoring her glare of disapproval, I shook the last of my cigarettes out of the pack and fired it up. I don't usually smoke in the kitchen, but I was under a bit of stress. "But probably nothing to worry about."

"Maybe." She walked over to the stove and turned the burner down a notch, then gave the spaghetti sauce a more vigorous stir than was absolutely necessary. "Can I trust you to keep an eye on the sauce?" she asked.

"Realistically, no, you can't." There was that manuscript that wasn't getting copyedited all by itself, and I like to concentrate on one thing at a time; the more involved I get, the better and quicker the job I do. Multitasking is for computers.

"Thought as much." She turned the burner down further, shook her head at it, and turned it off, but didn't make the usual comment about how she preferred electric stoves to gas as she walked over to the sink to wash her hands. I'm not sure I care, much, one way or the other, but I was used to the old gas stove, and the idea of replacing it with an electric one had no appeal at all, even forgetting the rather strong likelihood that a new electric stove would have a price tag on it.

"Going somewhere?" I asked.

"Yes. I think I'd better have a word with Dad and find out what's going on." She shrugged out of her smock and, instead of making for the laundry hamper in the hall, just folded it over the back of her chair.

I held up a hand as she started for the door.

"You walk down to Dine-A-Mite dressed in just a T-shirt and shorts, and what will be going on is every tongue in Hardwood wagging about how living with Sparky Hemingway has turned Bridget Honistead into some sort of loose woman who doesn't know how to dress decently in public."

"I'll change." Her lips pursed.

"I'd rather you didn't."

"Change?" She shrugged. "No problem."

"No. I'd rather you didn't go."

Things were awkward between me and Bridget's dad. Yes, her divorce from Frank was pending; no, Bridget wouldn't for a moment tolerate any discussion of her living arrangements, not in her presence, not from her father and not from anybody else, either, but that didn't mean he had to like it, and her taking him to task—in public, more than likely—over this wasn't liable to make things any easier between them, or between Bridget and me, or between Bridget and her father.

And any discussions with Bob Aarsted were likely to bring Bridget's mom, Emily, into it, and, even though she hadn't been my second-grade teacher four decades ago—and even though she had been half the age I was now—she was still old Lady Svensen to me, and she still scared me a lot more than any BCI cop did.

"Then you go," she said firmly. "You're going to have to face Dad—on more than this—and the sooner the better."

That's usually my philosophy—get a hassle over with rather than leaving it fester—but I'm not a slave to it. "I should get to work. There's that new manuscript—"

"Which isn't marked urgent." She got up from the table, retrieved it from the side table in the living room, and set it in front of me, grunting theatrically at its weight.

Another brick from Tor. Probably fantasy. Shit; I prefer skiffy, even. I tore the package open to get the bad news over with rather than spending a few minutes fantasizing about getting the new Donald E. Westlake.

Nope—another fantasy from one of the Minneapolis crowd. Oh, well. There's a reason why they call it work.

"Well, the sooner I get started on it, the sooner it's done."

"It's due in a week," Bridget said, tapping a fingernail on the cover letter. "Plenty of time."

"Only sneaky people read upside down."

"Don't change the subject."

"Besides, it gets easier to get another assignment when the present one is in."

"You're getting enough work, and you're still changing the subject."

Irresistible Bridget was getting ready to run into Immovable Ernest when the front door opened, sounds of laughter pouring in, and I headed into the living room, which cut off all the merriment.

I don't remember giggling so much when I was a teenager, although I do remember shutting up when a grownup appeared.

"Hi, Sparky," Jeffie Thompsen said, dropping his book bag on the couch, which earned him a glare from Tenishia, who carefully set her own book bag on the side table.

Sparky? I didn't give him a hard time about it, even though I felt every one of my years. How long had it been since he had stopped calling me "Uncle Sparky"?

He had inherited his father's bull neck and square chin, although the chin was covered with what should have been an embarrassingly thin fringe of dirty-blond beard, but which didn't seem to bother him much. More than a decade of farm work had built up his shoulders and upper arms better than lifting weights in a gym could have—farm kids start working young, and if you want to see them stop, you'd better get your-self a camera with a very fast shutter.

Jeffie disappeared in the direction of the bathroom, leaving me alone with Tenishia and Josh Ginsburg.

Tenishia was lanky rather than skinny, her skin the color of good coffee with only a little milk added, and high cheekbones that gave her face a vaguely oriental look. Her long hair was pulled back in a tight braid rather than the usual cornrows, and between that and the jeans-and-plaid-shirt combination, I was tempted to make some comment about her going native, but that wouldn't have gone over real well. She and I had moved from a ceasefire to something perhaps a bit warmer than détente, but part of that meant me being careful not to push when pushing wasn't necessary, as I figured it mostly wasn't. I tend toward being a control freak, sure—but what I want to control is my life, not other folks'.

"School go okay today?"

Tenishia shrugged—she was heavy on shrugging—but Joshua nodded and smiled.

"Great, Mr. Hemingway," He said. "Really terrific."

If he'd added "and a wonderful educational experience, Mrs. Cleaver," I'd have been even more reminded of Eddie Haskell—in his manner, if not his appearance.

You could see the father in the son: dark hair, a muddy brown just this side of black, and a weak chin that would be jowly in a few years, which didn't bother me; nobody mistakes me for Robert Redford, either.

His eyes always bothered me, though: too dark, too unwill-ing to meet anybody's. I'd have said he was a sullen kid, but that doesn't quite fit—he smiled far too much, even though the smile never seemed deep enough to hydroplane on—and I'd have called him introverted and a loner, but since his fam-ily had moved to Hardwood, he and Jeffie had been close to joined at the hip.

Until Tenishia had come along and messed that up. I'd have wondered how he felt about that, but, hey, it was none of my business.

"How're your folks?" It was the polite thing to say, although I didn't have much to do with Dr. Ginsburg; Doc Sherve has been my family doctor since before he delivered me, and like most folks in Hardwood, I'd rather deal with Doc, and I'm on good enough terms with both nurses to get away with it, most of the time, on the rare occasion I need to see a doctor, which is both not very often and too damn often for my taste.

"Fine," he said, the smile broadening until I was reminded of how the whole Ginsburg clan reminded me of the Brady Bunch, and how I really, really hated the Brady Bunch. "Really good."

"Well, say hi for me."

"Sure."

Tenishia gave him a look, and he walked off in the direction of her room, holding his own book bag close.

"Am I just paranoid today, or is something a bit off with the three of you?"

She shook her head. "Nothing. Amy'll be by a little later—she had to run some errands for her mother."

Hmph. Amy Larsen had recently turned the three-person after-school study group into four, and part of me was curious if that meant she was pairing off with the Ginsburg kid, but most of me knew it was none of my business.

"Fine. Check with Bridget before you make the offer, but I think there's enough spaghetti sauce for a dozen, and another two or three wouldn't be a problem for me."

She nodded. "Okay. Thanks." She gave me as little of a smile as she could get away with; the kid wasn't big on smiling, which was fine with me, particularly after a few moments with Joshua Ginsberg.

She headed for the kitchen, and I scooped up the manuscript and took it down the hall to my office/bedroom and spread it out on the desk.

I'd barely started to make my notes when I looked up to see Bridget standing in the kitchen doorway, her arms crossed over her chest.

"Are you going or am I?"

Back in college, I should have taken a course called "Relaxing to the Inevitable"; it would have been good preparation for dealing with Bridget.

"I'll go." I whistled for the dog. "Snake. Let's go take a walk."

He came quickly and wagging. Man is dog's best friend, at least when it's time to take a walk.

A gang of kids too young to go to school were chasing one another down the street, ducking between houses in the futile attempt to avoid the view of the faces occasionally peeking out of windows, and after a nod of permission from me, Snake galloped off, streaking across the lawns like a furry missile, for a quick game of dodge-kid, zipping in and out among them before orbiting back for another pass.

The only rule of dodge-kid, apparently, is for the dog to run as close to as many kids as possible without letting them touch him. After a few moments of watching a dozen shouting children try and fail to grab the dog's collar as he zipped in and out between them, in a sort of dog-style slalom—although what a, say, five-year-old would do with a German shepherd that was twice his weight if he caught Snake I couldn't guess—I started walking again, and Snake rejoined me, with an extra bounce in his step as though he'd proved something.

Between my tendency to spend most of my life in my house and the fact that it had only been a few months since I'd taken up smoking again, I didn't have all the fine points down, like being sure to keep a pack cigarettes in my pocket rather than on my desk, so I stopped off at Selmo Drugs on Main Street.

There are street names on the official town map, so I'm told, but Main Street is the only one there's a street sign for—it's right in front of the Post Awful—and it's the only street that anybody uses the name of.

Something I could never get used to in the city was houses and streets having numbers. I live in the Hemingway house, and if somebody wants to find me, they just come to my house, and I don't need a number—it's the Hemingway house, after all, like my next-door neighbors live in Bob Olson's house and Denny Olmodt's house.

Keeps things simple and personal, and I like simple and personal.

Snake and I crowded into the revolving door at Selmo's—a revolving door looks silly in spring, but it manages to keep the heat in during the winter and out during the summer—and pushed our way inside past the rack of comics and magazines.

From the back of the store, Wayne Berge waved from behind the pharmacy counter, then turned back to carefully explaining to old Minnie Hansen how to take the heart pills she had been popping six times daily since before he was fully toilet-trained—Wayne spent a few years in California, but the small-town boy hadn't rubbed off of him—while old Paul Berge set down the case of toothpaste he was placing on the shelves and came over.

"Good afternoon, young man," he said.

Subtract the wrinkles and the braces—don't ask; I didn't, either—and he hadn't changed in forty years: The old-style, stiff-collared pharmacist's tunic was buttoned up to the neck and looked like it had been freshly starched, which it probably had. To look at old Paul—to distinguish him from young Paul, who had moved away, as too many Hardwood kids did—you'd have never guessed that not only would he sell a kid comics on credit, but had strong opinions that he'd be happy to share about the latest *Avengers* lineup and Marvel not yet putting Chris Claremont, whoever he is, back on *X-Men*, where, apparently, God and everybody else except the owners of the company know he belongs.

He beckoned Snake to come around behind the counter and stooped to pet him and feed him a dog treat, then he looked up at me, his head level with the counter. "What can I get for you today?"

"Camel filters, please," I said. "Soft pack, if you've got it."

The smile didn't quite drop from his face, but the sincerity drained right out of it. He straightened slowly and pulled down a pack. "Three seventy-five," he said.

That was all the disapproval I'd get from old Paul for having taken up smoking again: a smaller smile and a request for cash, instead of just putting it on my account. Not because the account was overdue—it wasn't; having Bridget around had been good for me keeping current on check-writing as well as more important things—but because old Paul would be damned if he'd sell something unhealthy on credit.

I slid a five over; he cranked the register open and slid the change back.

Back when I was a kid, you'd have to go back to the pharmacist's counter and hang around for a while before stammering out a request for condoms. Now a rack of them stood on the front counter, in various colors and—no shit—flavors. Things do change.

Old Paul's smile became friendly again when he noticed me looking at the rack.

"You, er, need anything else, Sparky?" he asked. "Used to be it was, 'I'll take a pack of cigarettes,'" he said in a normal voice, and then, dropping to a whisper, "'and some condoms.' Nowadays it's 'hey, give me a dozen of those Trojans—the ones with the ribs,'" and, again in a whisper, "'and a pack of Marlboros.'"

"Times change, Mr. Berge," I said.

"That they do, young man—and for the better, probably, in a lot of ways." He slid over a couple of packs of matches without being asked. "How'd you do?"

"Eh?"

"Jeff Thompsen was in a couple of hours ago. Said you and Jeff Bjerke were having a fine time with woodchucks on his north field, from the sound of it."

"Well, we got a few. If you want to come along sometime . . ."

"No, I'm a pharmacist," he said. "I never kill anything or anybody on purpose."

Annoying—not the joke, although I'd heard it a thousand times before. What bothered me was I hadn't seen Jeff Thompsen drive by, and he hadn't stopped to say hi, even though he knew we were out there. My guess was that was because the farm road wasn't the way into town and he was in a hurry, but . . .

Nah. It was probably just that Barb, his wife, was utterly unthrilled with Tenishia as his son's girlfriend, but she knew better than to make a fuss about that, at least I hoped so. Turn the two of them into Romeo and Juliet, and some normal teenage sex that nobody officially knew about could turn into something a lot more serious, and quickly, given how stubborn the two kids were, and Jeff and I had talked that over at some length, and I'd left him to deal with Barb as best he could.

I didn't have much hopes of that being very well, but hadn't said that. There's only so much you can criticize a friend, even privately. Hardwood's not too small to have a few feuds going, but most people—me, included—try to keep them to a minimum, both in number and intensity. I don't even talk much about what an idiot Lars Hansen is, although there's a lot to talk about, and I could go on for hours; don't get me started.

I tucked the cigarettes into my pants pocket and went back to make my manners with Wayne Berge and Minnie Hansen, leaving Snake to get fed another dog treat by old Paul.

Wayne was sporting the handlebar Frito Bandito mustache that, along with a wife, he'd brought back from California, and he looked as Mexican as a pale blond norskie-type can—which isn't very much—as he grinned underneath it.

"Hey, Sparky," he said. "Need anything filled?"

"Well, I don't have any prescriptions, but if you're running a sale on oxycodone, I'll take a few dozen. I hear it's good for headaches."

He made a face. "Yeah, sure."

"How's Corinne?"

"Fine," he said, then broke into a frown.

"Problem?"

"Nah—I was just late with a delivery this morning." His chuckle sounded forced. "You'd think, after ten years in town, she'd have learned to leave the car keys on the visor, where they belong."

"Well, she is from California."

"I know." He rolled his eyes.

"Good afternoon, Ernest," Minnie Hansen said. Her voice was high and reedy.

I turned to her. "Good afternoon, Mrs. Hansen."

"How are you today?"

"Just fine, Mrs. Hansen."

"Are you sure?" She cocked her head to one side.

"Sure I'm sure."

She nodded. "I just wanted to check, so I don't have to worry about you making that sort of stupid comment about drugs in front of your foster daughter, as I hope you wouldn't. Drugs are nothing to joke about."

I could have said something about the time I was bringing Tenishia back from Minneapolis, when she had admitted to having an ounce of pot, and I made her pitch it out of the car, but that had a lot more to do with me being afraid of being stopped by the Minnesota State Patrol than it did with me disapproving of a bit of casual marijuana use.

A little bit of hypocrisy is a necessity in life.

But only a little: "I'm old enough, Mrs. Hansen, that I can remember when sex, drugs, and rock and roll were all fun things."

For a moment, I didn't know how it would go, but then her pursed expression broke into a smile. I guess you can find skinny old women with sharp eyes and pinched faces in just about any city, but the sort of impish smile that Mrs. Hansen has always had isn't common.

"Well, yes," she said. "I'm so old that I remember when only one of them was fun, and I'm not going to tell you which it was, Ernest Hemingway."

When Minnie Hansen uses your full name, you know you're dancing with danger, so I didn't say I had a good guess as to which it was. There are so many lovely times to keep your mouth shut.

"Stop by sometime soon," she said. "I've got some birch syrup for you and Bridget and Tenishia." I was looking for some trace of disapproval about Bridget and me living together, but didn't see any.

So I just nodded. "Sure, and thanks."

Yum. Only my well-known sense of fairness would impel me to share any of it with Tenishia and Bridget. Maple syrup is okay, but the birch syrup Minnie Hansen renders down every fall and spring is heaven. I would have politely asked if she was sure she could spare it—ask twice then accept gracefully is the rule—but I noticed Wayne setting a box of disposable syringes on the counter in front of her, and I'm perfectly capable of adding one and one and coming up with "diabetes," so I kept my mouth shut and made my escape.

Bob Aarsted was, unsurprisingly, in his usual booth at the Dine-A-Mite, papers scattered across the surface of the table in front of him, revealing only a sliver of red linoleum here and there.

The blue denim shirt with the two big red patches, one over each pocket, that said AARSTED HARDWARE on one side of his chest and BOB on the other side was probably to remind Bob who he was when he took it out of the dresser to put on in the morning.

He looked up at me. "Hey, Sparky."

"Hi, Bob."

At a nod from Ole—the state health inspector had done his annual checkup a month before, and things were back to normal at the Dine-A-Mite—Snake wagged his way behind the counter and began noisily munching on the dish of leftovers that had been set down for him.

With the way everybody in town fed that dog, it was just as well he got a lot of exercise playing dodge-kid.

I slid onto the bench opposite Bob and nodded when Ole, from behind the counter, lifted up the box of Red Rose tea invitingly. You can't keep many secrets in a small town, and telling lies is liable to get you talked about, but I'd managed to persuade Ole and both the regular waitresses that I'd turned into a tea drinker when I lived in the city, and managed to keep the lie working in the all the years I'd been back. Much better than having to put up with the weak coffee that seems to come with a Norskie heritage.

Tenishia, who worked weekends, knew better, of course, but she wasn't into ratting people out; when I stopped by the Dine-A-Mite on a Saturday morning, as I often did, she would serve me tea without so much as a wink while she poured coffee refills for other folks.

Aarsted raised a finger. "Hang on a sec; just got to finish making a coupla notes?" It wasn't a question; it just sounded that way. Runs in the family.

He scrawled something illegible on one of the letters in front of him—I don't read other folks' mail, not without a specific invitation—and then carefully laid it on the one neat pile in front of him, then did the same with a few others.

"Done," he said, looking up at me, resting his hands in his lap.

Here's the thing about Bob Aarsted: He pays attention. When he's doing things, as opposed to talking, he usually has several going at once, but when he listens to you, that's all he does.

He was a big man, and the years had taken a toll on him. His formerly massive torso had long ago lost the battle against weight and grew an equally massive stomach that wouldn't have fit behind any other booth in the Dine-A-Mite. What remained of his hair were dingy gray wisps around the crown of his head; but his smile was still the same as ever, revealing teeth far too white and even to be natural.

Vanity, thy name is Aarsted.

"I take it you talked to Jeff Bjerke," he said. "Which is why you're here?"

"Yeah."

His mouth twitched. "I'm surprised it's you—I was expecting Bridget."

"So was she."

He accepted that with a nod. "Everything going okay with the two of you?"

"Nothing to complain about. Particularly not to her father."

He didn't smile. "You'll want to go easy with her. She's had a hard time."

I didn't particularly want to discuss Bridget's marriage to Fred—with her father or with anybody else, including Bridget.

It was still a sore point, I guess, and while I tend to pick at sores, I'm trying to learn better.

"Then again," he said, "if the two of you are going to work things out, meddling from her old man probably won't help a whole lot, will it?"

I thought about it for a moment, then shrugged. "Everything's fine," I said. When in doubt, stick with the truth; it's easier to remember. "Fact is, Bob, I'm crazy about her."

"Makes two of us, eh?" He leaned back, as far back as he could, and cocked his head to one side. "Seems like just yesterday that I held this little baby in my arms, and . . . shit, I'm talking like an old man."

"You are an old man."

For a moment the smile vanished. "And I'm the old man who's put you in the way of some trouble, it seems."

"Huh?"

He frowned. "It's nonsense, that's what it is."

"You mean me having committed a felony?"

"Yeah, that. And some other stuff. It really has nothing to do with you. You can blame Norstadt if you like. I'd sure as hell like to."

Ole's timing was impeccable as usual—just when things were getting interesting, he walked up, my tea in one hand, the pot to refill Aarsted's cup in the other, and he and I made some quick small talk until Bob gave him a look and he went away.

I sipped at my tea. "Can you tell me why Phil Norstadt wants me in prison?"

He snorted. "Oh, relax, Sparky. You're not going to prison. Probably not even to jail."

Probably?

"It's just politics," he went on. "It's not even personal, not even between Phil and me."

"Eh?"

"You don't pay much attention to politics, do you?"

This was the second time an Aarsted had asked me that to-day—Bridget had taken Fred Honistead's name when had she married him, but she was still an Aarsted to me—and it was getting irritating.

"As little as humanly possible," I said. "I think there's a guy named Bush who's president, and if I remember right, he's been president for a long time, although I thought it was some other guy for a while." I shrugged. "Don't ask me who the governor is, though, or the secretary general of the UN. And isn't the mayor of Hardwood some guy named Aarsted?"

"Hmph." He tapped at the leftmost stack of papers in front of him. "Well, I guess you'd better start paying attention—you just got involved."

"Huh?"

"You been following the trauma-center stuff?"

"I don't even know what a trauma center is. Some sort of hospital?"

My mind is a junkheap, filled with piles of specialized and usually useless knowledge, usually gleaned from some book I'm copyediting, or doing the fact-checking necessary to do the job right. I've done more different kinds of books than I care to think about, but medical books are a very specialized niche, and it's not one of mine.

"Sort of," he said. "There's three kinds. Level One is the big guns—they can do anything from stopping bleeding to plugging in a new heart, burn care, reconstructive surgery—pretty much everything that somebody who's gotten chewed up might need. Think big hospital, in a big city—HCMC in Minneapolis, say. Level Two is a step down, but just a baby step—Altru, in Grand Forks, is a Level Two, and it's pretty big.

"Level Three is sort of an emergency room on steroids, running twenty-four–seven—emergency surgeons and surgical nurses, anesthetists, MRI and CAT scans, blood bank, ICU with at least one nurse for every two patients.

"Sounds like a MASH."

I'd been lucky enough to avoid any up-close and personal experience with a MASH in Nam; the closest I'd come was, once, helping load some poor bastard onto a dustoff after a mortar attack. The couple of times I got nicked, I was dusted off to a real military hospital.

He grinned. "Sure. The whole trauma-center movement came out of the MASHes. Used to be the theory was that a Level Three was just to stabilize the patient until you could transport him to a Level One or Two, but there's some mission creep. There's talk about doing what the folks in Mississippi have done—they've now got Level Four trauma centers. Much smaller deals.

"In any case, the deal is, when somebody's injured, the quicker you can get him to a trauma center the better chance he's got of surviving." He took a long pull on his coffee and slid an ashtray toward me while I was fumbling with the pack of Camel filters. "Remember when Big Steve Larson got his arm hacked off last summer?"

I nodded. Farmwork isn't just hard, it's dangerous. Jeff Thompsen says that if you forget, for just a moment, that the machinery really wants to eat you, it will.

"Well, he was able to get to the phone in the cab, and clinic records show that Arvie called in from the farm twelve minutes later—but the nearest trauma center is Altru in Grand Forks. Like I said, it's a Level Two—pretty big place."

Grand Forks is thirty miles away from Hardwood as the crow flies, just about forty-five miles driving. "Took them twenty-seven minutes to get a helicopter here, and he was lucky at that; average is a bit more."

"Hell, Arvie could have driven him in just about that." On a good day, you can easily hit a hundred on a county road. Different thing in winter, though.

"Yeah. He could have, and maybe he should have—I think

they overuse the helicopters at Altru, just to justify for the expense of having them. That's another issue. The point is, if you're hurt bad, the closer to a trauma center you are the faster you get to one, and the better your chances of surviving—and of recovering."

"How much better?"

"Well, the studies say about thirty percent better for survival, and I think they understate it. Hard to tell how much it affects stuff short of life-and-death, but shit, just the other week, some farmer outside of Grand Forks lost his hand— probably doing the same sort of damnfool thing Big Steve did—and the surgeons at Altru were able to sew it back on. Don't know how much good it's going to be, though."

"So you want a trauma center here."

"Want? Sure." He nodded. "There's going to be a Level Three trauma center somewhere in Grand Forks County—and not in Grand Forks, what with the Level Two there. The only question is where. I want it here."

I nodded. Bob Aarsted was, after all, a politician, and he'd want it as close to Hardwood as possible. It couldn't be closer than in Hardwood, after all.

"So the next time some idiot gets his arm ripped off, it gets sewed back on."

He made a face. "Yeah. That's part of it. Any idea how much money is involved?"

"Lots, I'd guess."

"Yeah. That's a good word, lots. A Level Three has a staff of at least four doctors—usually more, usually a lot more—plus at least a dozen nurses, and that's just the medical people. Add in clerks and technicians and everybody else, and you're talking about fifty people, minimum, before it even gets certified, and a lot more later. Figure an annual payroll of, oh, three, four million dollars."

"And who pays for it?"

"Oh, the state and county, and there's some money from the feds, for a start. Plus there's contracts from the HMOs—the quicker you can get somebody to a trauma center, the less money you have to spend on rehabilitation down the line. It'd be a good thing for the town. Let's not forget that the trauma center—the buildings, plural—would have to be built, and all those doctors and nurses and X-ray technicians will need houses, which would do something for the building trades hereabouts, just to pick one thing."

"And the houses would need plumbing supplies and all sorts of other stuff," I said.

I thought he might take offense at that, but he just nodded. "Sure. I'm getting by, but it's a bit tougher each year. Realistically, if we get the Level Three, some chain is going to want to buy me out, and at this point I'd be happy to let them do that."

"I thought you said chain stores are a tool of the devil."

"Well, maybe that's overstating it. But they're also a fact of life. But it's not about me getting a good deal on selling the store, understood?" He looked me straight in the eye. "It would be good for the town in a lot of ways. Certainly make for a bigger town—you've got to figure the population would grow by a couple hundred people at least, and that's just in the first couple of years. These sorts of thing have a way of growing."

"Make things more cosmopolitan," I said.

"Cosmopolitan." He laughed. "Yeah. You say that like it's a bad thing."

"Maybe." I like things the way that they are—that's one of the reasons I came back to town. Well, that and the utter failure of my brilliant career in New York publishing, which never went much of anywhere.

"So where does Norstadt come in?" I asked. "And me?"

"Well, Norstadt wants the Level Three for Thompson. Which makes sense in a lot of ways—it's on the interstate and we're not. Then again, it's only ten miles outside of Grand

Forks, and right up against the Minnesota border, and the lege in the People's Republic of Minnesota has decided, in its wisdom, that it doesn't want to participate in funding any Level Three across the border—the good folks in the People's Republic figure they've got enough hospitals already. I think Hardwood's a better location—hell, it *is* a better location, but . . ."

"There's always a but."

"Phil Norstadt's got some heavy hitters both in Grand Forks and in Bismarck, at the lege, batting for him on this."

"And when does it all go down?"

"The governor appointed a commission to study the matter last winter; it submits its report in a couple of months. Oh, they're doing surveying and land studies and all that, but there's plenty of land to be had pretty much everywhere, and one thing you can say for this state is that we've got good roads—it's going to come down to politics. It always does. It would be convenient for Phil Norstadt if there was some scandal in the news involving Hardwood."

"Which is where I come in?"

"Sure. Some sort of drug-crazed wife-swapping child-pornography Kool-Aid cult would be ideal, but I don't think anybody's going to oblige him there. Some crazy Vietnam vet being busted for playing cop would be fine with him, and if he happens to be living in sin with the mayor's daughter—and has some young black girl from Minnesota living with him, too—that would be even better." He smiled. "If Mike Wallace shows up on your lawn with a camera crew, stay inside."

"I'll try to remember that. You been working on this for a while, I take it."

"You don't pay much attention to a lot of things," he snorted. "Moshe Ginsburg"—he pronounced it like "mosh," as in "mosh pit," not "mo-*sheh*" or "*mo*-sheh"; even I knew that one of the last two was the right one, although I couldn't tell you which—"moved out here three years ago. You ever wonder what a board-certified member of the American Academy of Emergency Surgeons is doing playing country doctor?"

"I didn't know he was." I try to stay away from doctors, generally, and didn't know Doc Sherve's new—well, relatively new—partner well enough to have exchanged more than a few dozen words with him or his family. The only reason I really knew any of Ginsburg's kids was that Josh, of course, his oldest son, was very thick with Jeffie Thompsen, and Jeffie and Tenishia were what would have been called "going together" in my day.

"Well, he is. Cost the town a fair amount—I'd say it was more than I like to think about, but it's my job to think about things like that—to move him out here, and we were lucky to get him at that. If we get the Level Three, he'll be Chief of Emergency Services. If we don't get the Level Three, he'll be out of here within a couple of years."

"That be a bad thing? Sounds like he's overqualified if we don't get it."

"Don't be an idiot. Doc Sherve isn't going to last forever, and if we don't get the Level Three, I'll be back making my annual pilgrimage to Minneapolis, trying to talk some medical resident—any medical resident—into moving out onto the cold, snowy plains, or everybody will have to get used to driving into Grand Forks every time they've got to see a doctor." He tapped on his teeth. "Just like we do for the dentist."

"Sounds depressing."

It's one thing to think about that on a nice spring day, but two winters ago, I'd developed a real interesting abscess in a molar, or under it, and Jeff Thompsen had to drive me in to Grand Forks at about three in the morning, with me hopped off on enough Percocet that I barely screamed every time he hit a small bump in the road, and that forty-minute trip had taken two hours—and that only through a snowstorm, not a blizzard.

He nodded. "Betcher ass."

"You think if we get this Level Three, we might end up with a dentist in town?"

"Sure." He nodded. "Add in another fifty or so people with well-paying jobs and families, and Hardwood will look awfully attractive, what with no dentist in town. And don't just think dentist—like I said, this sort of thing is likely to have a lot of side benefits. So be at my house tomorrow night and we'll settle this part of it. I've got some ideas, but I need to bounce them off of Doc and Fred. See you tomorrow."

It was a dismissal.

I rose, dropping a dollar on the table for the tea.

He looked back down at his papers, then looked up again. "You and Bridget could come over for supper; Em'd be happy to have you—and since Doc's coming over, she'll probably do a roast, like usual. Tenishia's welcome, too, of course."

Yeah, sure. Bridget's mother would be delighted to have a couple of hours to glare at me, and probably drop a few comments about my table manners.

"Thanks, but I've got plans."

"Okay." He didn't ask what they were. When you live in a small town, you have to know when and how to mind your neighbor's business.

Still, what I'd said was true enough: I had immediately planned to be somewhere else.

3

Shooting woodchucks is fun; dealing with local politicians isn't. Neither activity pays the bills that support the lavish Hemingway lifestyle, even for very low values of "lavish."

Copyediting is what does that.

The romance of publishing has always been largely a lie, and gets to be more of a lie each year. For each Maxwell Perkins who sits in a high-backed leather chair in a spacious office and writes cryptic notes in the margins of a manuscript to instruct and inspire a small stable of writers, there's a division's worth of Amy Goldshlagers who spend their days in production meetings and cover-art meetings, and cover-copy meetings and back-cover-copy meetings and scheduling meetings, and spending lunchtime on the phone explaining, between chews and sips, to legions of unsympathetic agents why the latest advances in computer technology have caused semiannual royalty statements to be issued yet another month later, and where the delivery check is, when they're not explaining why they haven't returned the agent's preceding twenty phone calls, and where the hell's the book, anyway?

Agents are the least of their troubles, and angry writers are only a little worse—although I don't think it's an accident that

U.S. publishing is mainly based in New York City, which has the strictest gun laws in the country.

An art director who's having a bad day or a bad affair can sink a book quicker than you can say, "Hey, Captain, doesn't that look like an iceberg?" And, as far as I can tell, the only art directors who don't spend most of their time finding new and interesting ways to break their marriage vows with neurotic psychopaths are in between marriages to schizophrenic sociopaths.

And then there's the editor in chief who, like a Soviet-era Politburo bigshot, will—usually after a five-vodka-martini lunch—randomly ring in with his latest brilliant new idea, the equivalent of "Hey, let's invade Afghanistan: Look at all that wasteland filled with angry Pashtos, ripe for the plucking." The brilliant idea is usually something like oversized trade paperbacks, which combine the durability of a fall-apart-at-a-glance-mass-market paperback with the cost of a hardcover; sort of like Ford deciding to make the new Lexus out of Velveeta cheese—and cheerily insists that an editor's new pet book is the perfect test subject.

And never mind the new consultant that the company that owns the company that owns the publishing company has just hired, a twenty-four-year-old kid with a shiny new MBA who has some brand-new ideas about making things all fast and efficient that have only tried and failed a couple of thousand times before.

And then there's the publisher—the person, not the company. During my stint at never-mind-quite-where, the publisher used to spend most of *her* day—Ellen was always "her" or "she," at least behind her back—pacing halls, looking for somebody to fire, while assistant editors alternated between trying to seem busy while waiting for the next meeting and dodging the present phone call—when they weren't looking for a flask of lamb's blood to smear on the door frames, so that "she" would stalk on by without a word to them, or entertaining themselves with quiet riddles such as, "Why does she have only *one* child? Because there are some things even Satan won't do twice."

Or: "How many publishers does it take to screw in a lightbulb? Five—four to bend the writer over a desk, and one . . ."

Editing? Don't be silly. Editing is something editors do evenings and weekends, if they can fit it in.

Most of the time, editing doesn't get done, and the closest thing a writer comes to it is somebody like me.

I'm not an editor. I once thought I was going to be, but I'm not. I'm just a copy editor. My job is to go through a manuscript, find and correct blatant errors of spelling, grammar, and punctuation, do some fact-checking, and act like the continuity girl on a movie set—if a character has an eye patch on his right eye on page 13 and on his left eye on page 423, I bravely stick a Post-it note on the both pages 13 and 423, politely inquiring if the ~~talentless hack who churned this dog out in six weeks~~ talented writer who penned this immortal masterpiece really meant to do that.

"How many copy editors does it take to change a lightbulb?"

"None—copy editors can't make changes; they just query to see if the writer really wants it dark."

Or: "In the previous joke, it was a publisher rather than a copy editor who was changing the lightbulb; there's an inconsistency here that needs to be resolved."

I then send the manuscript back to an editor in NYC, who—at least in theory and sometimes in practice—gives it a quick once-over to make sure I actually did what I said I did, who then sends it to the talented writer who penned said immortal masterpiece, for said talented writer to scribble STET— manuscriptese for "leave this as I wrote it and ignore that idiot

of a copyeditor"—in the margin next to half of my corrections, and tear off and carefully ignore the carefully written
Post-it note inquiries I made.

Well, it pays the bills, as long as the bills are small enough.

Supper was finished—early, for once; it tends to run long in
my house—and the kids were gone. Tenishia had borrowed my
car to run Jeffie out to the farm, so I had taken Snake out for a
quick walk—that's dog-ownerese for "watching a dog take a
dump in the backyard, then kicking the shit into the
bushes"—wiped my feet on the grass outside, then gone in and
gotten to work.

I can work whatever hours I like, as long as I like to work a
lot of them.

I had just started my first pass on the latest skiffy book, making a list of character names that looked like they'd been read
off the surface of a bowl of Campbell's Alphabet Noodle soup,
while blue-penciling the obvious corrections—this joker's fingers thought there's a word spelled "teh", apparently, and the
notion of a spell-checking program was beyond him—and
making typesetting notations.

Forget everything you've heard about Ben Franklin and the
Gutenberg Bible—these days, typesetting is typically done on
a computer in some muggy, bug-infested sweatshop in Indone-
sia or Taiwan, often by people who don't speak English, who
just punch in the letters they see in front of them, obeying a
very short list of rules that include even less freedom than a
copy editor is allowed.

Just to take an example, when a writer submits a manuscript, he indicates an em-dash by using a pair of hyphens--like
that. Easy rule to follow, no? Even somebody who only speaks
Urdu could understand those instructions, if they were expressed in Urdu: When you're keying a book into the typesetting program, every time you see a pair of hyphens, just
substitute an em-dash and move on, right?

Well, yes and no.

While most dashes are em-dashes—so called because in the good olde days they used to be precisely the width of the letter m—en-dashes (guess what letter they're as wide as?) are also used for things like expressing a length of time, as in 2001–2003, and each and every em- or en-dash has to be marked, by a professional copyeditor, with a little "1" over it, and an "em" or "en" underneath it, like this:

$$\frac{1}{m}$$

Which is what they pay me the big money for, too.

Not exactly the most rewarding work in the world, but it lets me live in the house I inherited, feed myself and my dog, and the only time I take a drink, these days, is when I want one.

There are worse ways to live.

I'd just gotten to Chapter Two, where the characters had, through a remarkable coincidence, set out on a quest, just as they'd done in Chapter Two of the previous eleven novels in the series. I'd used a half-dozen Post-its to note that there really is a difference between a saber and a rapier—even if it's an "ancient elven blade" or a "sword of great antiquity and greater arcanity"—and that the author should really decide if Bleerp the Barbarian carries both and chooses one depending on which word fits better in the sentence, or if he'd prefer to simply pick one and stick with it.

So to speak.

There was a knock on the door.

"Yes?"

"Got a minute?" Tenishia walked in, tentatively, which wasn't like her—both the interrupting me when I'm working and the tentativeness.

I'd say it was hard to read her expression, but there wasn't any—she looked like a poker player.

Uh-oh. I was used to her glaring at me most of the time, and occasionally—rarely—smiling when she was absent-minded enough to let her guard down, but I wasn't used to the poker face, except at the family poker games.

"Sure."

No, I didn't have a minute. I'd been expecting to finish this dog of a manuscript Wednesday night, but it looked like I had other plans for Wednesday night, unfortunately. But that didn't seem like quite the right thing to say, and I don't always insist on saying and doing the stupid thing.

"What's up?"

"Nothing much," she said. "Just got something for you to sign."

Oh, great. Permission slip for an abortion clinic?

She must have read my expression—I'm not the one with a poker face—because she shook her head. "No. It's not *that.*"

"Well, good. Accidents do happen." Something that Jeffie's dad knew all too well, if it really had been an accident. Me, I'm not at all sure Barb Larsen hadn't decided that he'd been sampling the merchandise far too long and decided it was time to force a sale, but there are some things you don't even discuss with your friends, much less the girl who's dating your friend's son.

We were back to glaring, which was comfortable, if only because of its familiarity.

"Well, don't just stand there. Sit down, tell me about it."

I could have gone into my usual speech about how telling me about a problem wouldn't make it any worse and might make it better, but she'd already heard that, and apparently was taking it to heart. So rubbing it in didn't seem like a good idea at the moment.

She pulled a piece of paper out of her pocket and handed it to me.

MIDTERM REPORT CARD, it said. Back when I was a kid, a report card was, well, a *card*—this was a computer printout.
Damn computers take over everything, sooner or later.

After the hassle we'd had in February, with the midterm report card, I was expecting bad news, particularly given her expression, which wasn't happy. Two B-minuses, a D-plus, a D,
and an A. The D-plus was in English; the D was in social studies. The A was in metal shop.

"Well, it's better than the first one." There had been a bit of
an adjustment, I guess, and her grades had sucked rocks, and I
had heard more than I cared to from the social worker about
the necessity of Tenishia succeeding in school—and of me
making sure that she did her homework.

"You're supposed to sign this so I can take it back."

"Yeah—A in shop?" I hadn't known she was taking shop.

"Made one of those long forks for the barbecue," she said.

"Neat. I like those. But shop?"

"Better than Home Ec. I already know how to cook."

True enough. "Jeffie happen to be taking shop?"

She nodded. "Yeah. Him and Josh both," she said, as though
it was were challenge.

"But, shit, a D-plus in English? What are they having you
do? A neo-deconstructionist critique of *Jude the Obscure*?"

"Huh?"

"I could've sworn you and Josh and Jeffie were working on
some reports—I thought that they were for this English class,
and I know I heard the typewriter in your room over the past
couple of days."

She didn't say anything for a moment. "It'll be better next
time, honest."

"Tests?"

"Tests, shit." She shook her head. "I don't do good on
tests."

There was something wrong with all this, and I was starting to have a hunch.

"Yeah, sure." I reached over, pulled a book down from my bookshelf at random, and tossed it to her. "Read."

I thought she was going to put up a fuss, but she just opened it to the first page and started reading.

"He was born with a gift of laughter and a sense that the world was mad," she read.

Best damned opening line in all of literature.

"And that was all his patrimony. His very paternity was obscure, although the village of Gavrillac had long since dispelled the cloud of mystery that hung about it. Those simple Brittany folk were not so simple as to be deceived by a pretended relationship which did not even possess the virtue of originality. When a nobleman, for no apparent reason, announces himself the godfather of an infant fetched no man knew whence, and thereafter cares for the lad's rearing and education, the most unsophisticated of country folk perfectly understand the situation. And so the good people of Gavrillac permitted themselves no illusions on the score of the real relationship between André-Louis Moreau—"

"Okay—hold on. What's that mean?"

She shrugged. "I dunno."

"Yeah, yeah, we've played idunno before, and it's been a lot of fun. So much fun that, what the hell, let's save it for another time so we don't wear it out, okay? What's the stuff you just read mean?"

She glanced back down. "Well, it means that the guy had a sense of humor, and that some noble guy took him in and raised him from a kid, and that everybody thought that this noble guy was his father." She frowned. "You think I can't read?"

Well, so much for my hunch. She hadn't pronounced the names with a nice French accent, but you can't have everything. "Well, you can read and you can talk. So why the D?"

I thought she'd argue that it was a D-plus, but she didn't. "Told you, I'm handling it. I'm just not real good at writing. The words don't come out right. Josh and Jeffie just been helping me a little."

"Yeah, sure." She hadn't been in any danger of being named valedictorian at her old high school, but her grades had been solid Bs, leavened by the occasional As and more common Cs, and a D-minus in physical education that I had found more charming than irritating. I have a theory about gym teachers really being folks who are disqualified by lack of intelligence from flipping burgers or doing airport-security checks.

She shrugged again.

"Sit tight." I went and retrieved her book bag from the living room, then handed it to her. "Where are the papers you've done?"

"Didn't keep them," she said. "Only one I got is the one on for Monday." She handed over four nicely typed sheets of paper. "Knew you'd want to see it."

I gave it a quick glance. "Social Criticism in Literature as Found in George Orwell's *Animal Farm* and Charles Dickens's *A Tale of Two Cities*." I gave it a quick read-through.

"Not bad," I said, "except for the fact that you didn't write it."

She just gave me a blank stare. "Oh, come on. 'Both authors also endeavor to demonstrate that violence and the Machiavellian attitude of the ends justifying the means are deplorable.' That's not you."

"You think a nigger can't use big words?"

I started to say something stupid, but reined it in. I don't always insist on saying the stupidest thing possible. I needed a cigarette badly, and shaking one out of my pack and firing it up gave me a moment to calm down.

"I thought we had a deal about saying 'nigger' in this house. I haven't had any trouble keeping my part of the bargain, and

I'm not going to have you break your part of the deal just to get a leg up on me, so cool it."

She didn't say anything. We were back to that.

"As I was saying, you didn't write it. Download it off the Internet?"

An eyebrow lifted slightly. *Great, Sparky. Now you're giving her other ideas.*

"No," she finally said.

"Well, I know Jeffie, and while he's a bright kid, that's not the way he talks, and probably not the way he writes. So I'm guessing it's Joshua."

She didn't either admit it or deny it. "What are you going to do?" she asked.

"I dunno, not at the moment." I shook my head. "But I'm going to have to figure something out. Best thing is probably talk to his father."

"No." She shook her head. "You don't want to do that."

"Oh? Something I ought to know? Joshua's going to get hung on a meathook or have a bat shoved up his ass if his father finds out? Family tie him down to the dinner table and dance around, sticking forks in him?"

"No. I been over there, and they all seem nice, even that slow brother of his. His sister Debra's probably the nicest, and smarter'n Josh. And little Rivka is cute as shit."

The way I looked at it, Tenishia's arrival in town was a bonanza for the Ginsburg kids, who were probably sick and tired of being the only minorities in town. Not that there had been, as far as I'd heard, any persecution about that—you wanna beat up the doctor's kid?—but ethnic diversity was a relatively new concept here.

In a town that's almost exclusively Norski Lutherans, where somebody as exotic as being of Swedish stock is a rarity, a family of East Coast Jews had been a major novelty, and novelty takes a while to wear off. Given that Joshua and Deborah were widely rumored to be geniuses—if so, it didn't show in person, but maybe it did in class, or maybe it was just a relatively benign form of prejudice—some distraction would have had to be a Godsend from their point of view.

Tenishia shook her head. "He's just, he's just scared to hell of his father, and—"

"Well, he should be scared out of writing papers for other people," I said.

Lucky for me I don't choke on hypocrisy; when I was in college, I supplemented my GI Bill pittance and a weekend job doing typewriter repair by writing term papers for the rich kids, and goosed up the fee by 50 percent every time one of them chortled at having commissioned an original Ernest Hemingway. You do what you have to do to get by. If I'd gotten caught, I could have been kicked out of school, but I was smarter about it than Joshua Ginsburg seemed to be—reputation aside—and had always made a point of keeping the style plain and straightforward in everything except the social sciences, where I'd quickly picked up that the more trouble the teaching assistant who really graded the stuff had reading it, the higher the grade was. Which is probably true now, some, in college-level lit courses, too—these days, if I was doing it, I probably could start a paper with "To paraphrase Derrida," and then just hit random keys, run the thing through a spell-checker, accept all the choices, and be done with it.

"Can't you just leave it alone?" she asked. She was asking, not begging. Tenishia wasn't much on begging.

"Probably not." Then, again, Joshua wasn't any of my business, really. On the other hand, Tenishia was definitely my business, and if she were hiding some problem of hers with writing, what else was she hiding?

I'd promised her father I'd take care of her, and taking care of her didn't just include giving her a roof over her head and making sure nobody killed her.

There's not a lot I believe in, but I do believe in taking care of my own. The sensible, the reasonable thing to do would have been to make an appointment with her teachers and see what they had to say, but time had passed me by. I didn't really know any of them. Some of them were from out of town, and the rest were half my age, and I didn't know them, or trust them, particularly.

But there are people I trust.

"It's a nice spring evening. Let's take a walk."

I like porches.

In the winter, my porch is the outside freezer, and in November I can and always do cook a huge batch of mushroom-barley soup, dump it into the Tupperware, and set it out on the front porch swing to freeze, and then bring it in, container by container, as needed. It always works, as long as I manage to use it up by the end of February, and I do, although most years it can be safe well into March.

And in the summer, on a hot night, there's something luxurious about stretching out on the old daybed out there and letting the breeze do a better job of keeping me cool than any rattling piece of hardware could.

It's not just that I'm cheap, although I am; it's a family tradition. There used to be a story going around in town that if you found a penny that had a thumbprint embedded in it, it had definitely passed through my dad's hands.

But porches are nice, and not just because they save me money.

Come spring, some folks move out to their porches for dessert, sort of as a prelude to eating supper on the porch in summer, and doing that is considered an invitation to stop by and chat for a while. Privacy is easy to come by in Hardwood, and so is company, when you want it.

When we stepped down off the porch, Snake trotted off for a quick wag-and-bite with Arvie and Emma's terrier down the block, past the boarded-up Snyder house, and the two of them quickly disappeared into the fields beyond the Thorsen place.

The Olsons, next door, had moved their TV out to the porch earlier in the season than usual, and Bob and Osa and some friends were gathered around it, watching some million-aires hit a horsehide ball around. As I understand it, after a six-pack or so, enough brain cells get numbed that it all gets kind of interesting, which explains Bob. I'm not sure about Osa; she doesn't drink, and while I've never thought her to be the brightest person in the world—she does come from Hatton, af-ter all—she doesn't appear to be brain-damaged.

Their screen door slammed behind little Tommy as he launched himself off the porch like a semiguided missile.

"*Neesha!*"

The kid glowers at me all the time, with only a few pauses for sleep—and I'd better use her full first name; I still have boils up and down one side of my face from the glare she gave me the one and only time I called her "Neesha." But she was helpless in the face of a ballistic six-year-old, and she swept him up into the crook of a skinny arm that shouldn't have been able to support the kid as easily as it did.

"You babysit for me Friday?" he asked.

She nodded and returned a wave from Bob and Osa on the porch. "Yeah," she said. She ran her fingers through his very short hair. "New haircut."

"Yeah." He nodded and laid his head on her shoulder. "You like it?"

"Sure," she said, setting him down. "If they'd left a little more on top and faded it down the sides, you'd look just like Wesley Snipes."

He beamed. He didn't have the slightest idea who Wesley Snipes was, and probably was only a little less clear than I was what "fading it down the sides" might be, but he was utterly certain that Tenishia liked his new haircut, and that was all that mattered.

She made a shooing motion but softened it with a smile. "I'll see you Friday," she said. "We gotta go now."

He was going to ask where we were going, but Hardwood values get instilled young, and he just grinned and nodded and ran back to the porch and back inside, with another crash of the screen door as an exclamation point.

"Think he's got a crush on you," I said as we walked on.

"I kinda like him, too." The smile vanished.

"Problem?"

She shrugged. "Can I talk straight? Without you jumping up and down on me?"

"Probably. Take a chance."

She thought about it for a moment. "Lotsa black women take care of white folks' kids. Goes back to the slave days. Bet they liked the kids, too."

"You been watching *Gone With the Wind* again?" I asked, just for something stupid to say, then held up a hand. "Sorry. But you're not a lot of black women. Here you're not anything generic, at least not with anybody I've talked to. You're sure as hell not some generic black nanny to Tommy—you're Neesha, who's lived next door for four, five months, which to a five-year-old is just shy of eternity, and having you come over to watch TV with him is a treat."

"Could always quit babysitting if it bothered me, I guess. Weekends at the Dine-A-Mite pay more."

"Yeah, you could." I left out my usual comment about how Abe Lincoln had settled that issue some time ago. "You want to quit?"

"No. Don't think I do."

"Then don't quit. You want to complain about it to me some more, sometime?"

"Maybe."

"Well, that's fine, too."

We walked on.

Just dropping in always feels a little strange to me. I work at home, and, truth to tell, don't much like visiting with people in my house, so there's a double standard involved when I do unto others exactly the sort of thing that I want them to not do unto me, which only goes to show that there's something wrong with the Golden Rule, or with me, or with both.

Wan yellowy light filtered out through the old lace curtains at Minnie's front window, and a slim dark form quickly rose and walked to the door. It opened to reveal Minnie's smile.

"Why good evening, Ernest, Tenishia. Come in, please," she said. "Herschel, we have visitors."

Her living-room-cum-dining-room hadn't changed much in half a century. Still the same old-style furniture: overstuffed faded purplish couches and chairs that were always just a little overdue for reupholstering, and seemed to have always been faded; rows of fine cut-lead glasses and old china on display in her cabinets; rugs, not carpets, covering an ancient hardwood floor that had long since had any squeaks beaten or worn out of it.

There was one big difference: a modern and therefore junky-looking computer workstation-desk-thing stood against the wall where her late husband's gun case used to stand, with a preposterously large monitor on it, tuned—if that's the right word—to some screensaver that showed tropical fish swimming back and forth. None of them were floating belly-up on the virtual surface of the virtual fish tank, which made them different from the few times I'd seen a tank of local tropical fish.

Which makes them better than houseplants; you can't flush a ficus. I'm not good with houseplants, either.

Herschel Ginsburg was already shuffling to his feet. He and Minnie had been sitting at the dining room table, books and papers spread out.

"Hello, Mr. Hemingway, Tenishia," Herschel said. He was a younger edition of one of his brothers, and an older edition of another, with some variations on each.

His eyes didn't quite seem to focus on anything, and his jaw was ever so slightly slack. He wiped the back of his hand against a drop of spittle at the corner of his mouth before offering it to me in a far too formal and hideously damp shake, which I returned, forcing myself not to wipe my hand on my pants afterward.

Look: There's no sin in being retarded, or "having special needs," or whatever the politically correct term is these days. I know that. Really.

But Herschel Ginsburg still gave me the creeps, and there's no sin in that, either, as long as I let it be my problem and not his.

"Evening, Herschel," I said.

"Hi, Mr. Hemingway," he said again. His voice was too high-pitched, and there was just a trace of slurring around the edges. We probably could have spent the rest of the night saying hello if I wasn't willing to give up, which I was, and which I did.

I turned to Minnie. "Sorry about just stopping over—if this is a bad time, we can—"

"Don't be silly," she said. "Herschel and I had finished our work and we were just visiting."

"And doing a puzzle!" Herschel said, smiling.

Minnie ignored the interruption. "He should be going home about now or his parents will start to worry."

"I should go now?" he asked.

"Yes, Herschel."

He gave her a lopsided grin. "See you tomorrow afternoon, Minnie," he said.

"Right after lunch," she said, firmly. "No dawdling."

He picked up his book bag from the table—it had already been packed—and she ushered him out, then beckoned us into the living room.

She took a tentative step toward the kitchen. "Coffee—tea for you, I assume, Ernest—pop, or something stronger?" she asked Tenishia with a twinkle in her eye.

"Tea would be fine."

"I could use a double scotch," Tenishia said. "Been a long day."

The drinking age in North Dakota, like pretty much everywhere else, is twenty-one, but this was hardly the first time, or the thousand and first time, somebody had tested Minnie Hansen, and while it occurred to me that I could point out that Tenishia had been known to have an occasional half glass of wine or can of beer with dinner at home—Ms. Hennessy didn't drop by after working hours—it also occurred to me that I'd given up testing Minnie Hansen decades before, and that there was no reason to abandon that sane policy.

Minnie just nodded, and the two of us followed her into the kitchen, where she quickly lit the burner under the kettle with an old-fashioned wooden match and brought down a half-empty bottle of Pinch, its label yellowed and crinkled with age—the bottle should have been dusty, but wasn't—and a glass from a cupboard. She poured Tenishia a quick two fingers and set both the glass and the bottle on the kitchen table.

"So," she said, turning to Tenishia, "did you want to actually see and perhaps taste some of my birch syrup before you dared to let it in your house?" She put teabags in the two cups she had set on the counter.

"Excuse me? Birch syrup?"

"I didn't get around to telling her about that."

We'd had some other, more pressing issues, although, having had Minnie Hansen's birch syrup, I'm not sure that there should be more important issues; I'm a slave to my tastebuds.

"Then it's something else," she said, nodding, as she seated herself across the table from me.

I pulled Tenishia's report card out of my shirt pocket and reached into my pants pocket, where I'd put Joshua Ginsburg's observations on Orwell and Dickens, and set that in front of her, while Tenishia, looking as though she'd done it a thousand times before, sipped at the scotch.

"Hmph." Her mouth twitched as she glanced at the report card, then adjusted her glasses and picked it up. "A in metal shop, eh?"

"Yeah. We're awful proud of that," I said.

She gave a quick look at Tenishia, then eyed me levelly. "I can see that this after-school study group at your house has been a mixed success."

Tenishia didn't conceal her surprise, but I just smiled. It may or may not have had anything to do with their usual route home from school taking them right in front of her house. I'd long ago given up having any doubt that Minnie not only had eyes in the back of her head, but the sort of eyes that could see everything in town that wasn't covered in a lead sheath, and I'm not sure I'd bet a whole lot on the lead sheath, either.

"So," she said. "Let's deal with the obvious explanation first and get it out of the way. You're not stupid, so we can eliminate that." The kettle started whistling; she got up to pour the tea.

"What makes you think I'm not stupid?" Tenishia asked.

"Hmph. Well, for one thing, sad as it is to say, over the years I've dealt with children who were passed over when the good lord was doling out intelligence, and I should be able to spot one by now. For another thing, if it was just a matter of low intelligence, the school would have been able to pick up on that within a month. Or less." She made a face. "The quality of teachers isn't what it was when I was a girl, but they're trained to spot what they call 'special needs' children. Not nearly as good at spotting bright ones who can cover something up." She returned with the teacups and set one in front of me, then sat down and sipped at her own, made a face, and put it down to steep.

"I assume that if you could write a better paper than this piece of pompous tripe, you'd have done that instead of getting somebody else to write this piece of pompous tripe for you, so I assume you have some trouble with writing, and perhaps some reading difficulties?" She raised a palm. "No, don't bother admitting or denying it—you obviously have some difficulty with telling the truth. I've heard enough lies to last a lifetime, and don't care to hear any more at the moment just to reassure myself I can still tell the difference."

There was a pencil and a yellow legal notepad on the table; she tore off the top sheet, which had some of her own careful printing on it, and slid both notepad and pencil over toward Tenishia. "Please go into the living room and write down your class schedule, Jeffrey Thompsen's, and Joshua Ginsberg's."

"But—"

"If you don't know their exact schedule, there's an extension phone on the coffee table; you may use it. Now, Miss Washington," she said, "and you may leave the glass of scotch right here."

Surprising at least two of us, Tenishia just picked up the notepad and pencil and walked out of the room. "Please close the kitchen door behind you—there'll be no need to listen at the doorway, as Ernest and I will be talking very quietly about what to do about the three of you."

The door closed and the smile returned as she lowered her voice. "Difficult child, eh?"

"Well, yes and no."

She nodded. "That's fine. I like difficult children, and it appears I'm going to have three of them to deal with each afternoon."

"Three?" As usual, Mrs. Hansen was steps ahead of me.

"Three." Her mouth twitched. "Cheating is a serious matter. I don't take it lightly, and I'm sure Jeffrey Thompsen doesn't, either. Have you told him yet?"

I hadn't thought about it. On one hand, Jeff's just about my oldest friend. On the other hand, ratting out his kid over something like this didn't sit well with me.

She nodded. "I thought not. I never liked going to the parents, not if I didn't have to, and with these three I don't think I have to. You'll call him and explain the situation as you see fit; I'll handle Dr. Ginsburg; for some reason, he seems to be afraid of me."

"I can't imagine why," I said.

"You're not drinking your tea."

I sipped at my tea. It was too hot.

Tenishia returned from the living room and set the notepad in front of Minnie.

Minnie nodded. "Well, your handwriting is acceptable, although nothing to brag about." She glanced down at the paper. "Hmm. This shouldn't be a problem, although we'll have to take Joshua Ginsburg out of his AP biology class, which will no doubt not please his father."

"Huh?"

Minnie eyed her levelly, until Tenishia said, "Excuse me?"

Minnie gave an approving nod. "Better. I'll have some words with Dr. Henderson in the morning. What's going to happen is this: The three of you are going to be leaving school after seventh period, every day, and coming here for some tutoring during eighth—while, for a start, you're turning over the soil in my garden. I'm not too old to plant and weed and prune, but I'm getting on in years for moving much earth with a shovel, and three strong young backs will do fine."

I guess some sort of doubt showed in my face, because she gave me The Look. I never liked The Look. "It won't be a problem, Ernest. Tom Henderson is very grateful that he doesn't have to bus Herschel Ginsburg and Tim Lee into Grand Forks for special-ed classes, which would be a definite drain on his budget. Contract special-ed teachers are relatively cheap, but bus drivers are expensive." She sniffed.

"Special ed? You're a special-ed teacher?"

"Contract only; I'm too old to be on staff. It lets me keep my hand in, and, contrary to the opinions of some, I'm not an utterly useless old woman."

"Don't you need some sort of certification?"

"Yes," she said. "I understand one does—if one isn't grandfathered in, having been teaching school since Plato was a boy.

"Speaking of which." She turned back to Tenishia. "I'll see you three here tomorrow at two-thirty. Pick up the pen, please, and make a list. You'll need a copy each of *The Republic*—it may be listed as *Plato's Republic*—*Huckleberry Finn*, and a packet of tests that you can pick up from Mrs. McMurtry over lunchtime; she'll have them ready for you. Any editions of the books will be fine; it doesn't matter if they're not the same. Oh—and three sets of work gloves. Wear what you wish to school, but you'll need dungarees and shirts you don't mind getting very dirty; you may change in and out of them here. Oh, and work boots, please.

"You may finish your drink, Miss Washington, and then be heading home."

"I don't think I want it."

"Then you shouldn't have asked for it. Waste not, want not. Now, please, Miss Washington."

Tenishia drank it down in one gulp, but was too stubborn to choke on it.

Barely.

Work needs to get done, and I spent the whole morning plowing through the brick, letting Bridget pick up the phone,
which, even though I'd shut off the ringer of the extension in
my office, kept ringing. The only interruption was when Cat
scratched at the door, demanding to be let in. When I opened
the door, she stalked in, carefully climbed up onto the desk
while dislodging only an empty cup of coffee, another cup
filled with pencils, a stack of reference books, and my equa-
nimity before she took up her usual post on top of my computer monitor, graceful as—well, a cat.

I'm not much for computers, really, but the Internet is a fact
checker's friend, assuming that the fact checker is capable of
sorting out good information from bad reliably, or doesn't care
enough to be sure he's done just that.

Which am I? I'll never tell, but I was singing "Me and Bobby
McGee" under my breath, substituting "Freedom's just another
word for nothing left to lose" with "Freedom's just another
word for not caring about the quality of your work," even
though it didn't quite scan right.

Surprisingly, at one point, I actually got caught up in the
story, and read almost a dozen pages before I stopped myself,
turned back to the last page that had a Post-it on it, and got
back to work.

Happens, every now and then, even with skiffy. I'm a slut for words in a row.

Bridget looked up in irritation from her computer when I came into the kitchen to get another cup of coffee. Cigarettes are—were—optional, but copyediting runs on coffee as a fuel.

"Problem?"

"Nah," I said. "Busy?"

She gestured at the screen. "Well, yeah."

"The usual?"

"Yeah." She nodded. "But I can take a break." She rapped out a quick tattoo on her keyboard, consigning whatever she was working on to wherever she was consigning it.

Divorcing from a Wall Street lawyer—even a minor partner in as minor a firm as there is that has its own floor in a building on Wall Street—is, apparently, a business endeavor somewhat more complicated than a dotcom IPO, or maybe both are a lot more complicated than I have any idea about or any desire to know.

I'm not sure how much money was involved. It was, quite literally, none of my business, and all those zeros on her spreadsheets made me nervous.

Fred Honistead had done well for himself, apparently—other than the affair with the underwear model that had precipitated their breakup, although I guess you could say that was doing well, too—and I suspected that Bridget didn't entirely trust her own NYC lawyer to get all the details right, or thought that Fred's lawyer was smarter, or both.

Not that I asked. It was none of my business, in more ways than one.

She took a mug down from the cupboard—smiling at me when I smiled at the way her stretching pulled her T-shirt tight—and let me pour her a cup.

"So," she said, "how goes it?"

I shrugged. "About the usual. With removal of repeated

words, corrections of stupid typos, and notation of em-dashes is a copyeditor's fortune made."

"Yeah."

I pulled my pack of Camel filters out but desisted when she made a face. She had picked up one of those industrial-strength air-filter machines for the office/bedroom, but I tried to avoid stinking up the kitchen, at least most of the time.

So I offered a compromise. I was learning new skills all the time. "Want to step outside with me so I can grab a quick smoke?"

"Sure." She grabbed a light jacket. "Better than having to smell it when I make coffee in the morning."

The crows were out in force, three of them pecking at what remained of a squirrel down by the Olsons' mailbox while another squad waited its turn, and the west wind quieted the squeals of the kids playing out in the Thorsens' apple orchard.

"So?" she asked. "You nervous about tonight?"

"Eh?"

"Town-council meeting?"

I'd been able to blot it out of my mind for a while; I wasn't grateful to her for reminding me. "Nah. My heart is pure, and I'm sure your dad and Fred and the rest will handle it."

She sat down on the edge of the porch, and I sat down next to her.

"Anybody ever happen to tell you you're too trusting?" she asked.

I shook my head. "No. Particularly not my ex-wife. Why? You think your dad is trying to fix me up as the new blonde on the cellblock as a convenient way to end the scandal of his soon-to-be-divorced daughter living with a known ne'er-do-much-of-anything-well?"

She grinned. "I wouldn't say you don't do *anything* well, all in all. Maybe I should tell Dad in detail."

"Yes, Electra, that would be a great idea. But you're ducking the subject."

"Hmm. Maybe." She reached out and took the cigarette from my fingers and took a long drag on it, not coughing at all, before handing it back. "Trouble with you, Sparky, is you're full of on and off switches. The daughter of an old friend calls and says she's in trouble, and you don't just wire her a few bucks to take a bus out of town—no, you have to hare off to Minneapolis to see what kind of trouble you can get into."

That was true enough, at least in terms of the bald facts, although I'd been trying to get her out of trouble rather than get me or anybody else into it. "But—"

"And that's just one example." She blinked. "You want another?"

"Not particularly."

"Too bad. Shall we talk about Jennifer?"

"Could we just saw on my neck for a while with a rusty knife instead?"

"Okay. Skip your ex-wife, and let's talk about my dad. You've known him all your life, but to you he's just Bob Aarsted, the nice man who runs the hardware store and plays politician on the side. Simple guy, right?"

"Well, he's not stupid—Lars Larsen has that market pretty well cornered, at least on Main Street—but I wouldn't call your dad complicated." I shrugged.

"No, you wouldn't." She frowned. "But he's *not* a simple guy; he's just a guy who, for a lot of reasons, prefers to keep his life simple most of the time, except when he can see some advantage in doing otherwise." She shook her head. "This trauma-center thing is important to him—real important."

"Why?"

"How many people live in Hardwood?"

Someday, I'll learn how to change the subject in a heartbeat. "About two thousand or so."

"Close enough. And how many lived in town when you and I were kids?"

"Maybe three thousand."

"Just about that. Plot the trend lines out and play with the numbers. Or, if you don't want to, take a look at the graphs in Dad's notebooks—he's been making semiannual charts for years, right after he does his taxes in April, and again when he closes the store's books in October, and he switched it to computer last year. He's got a file on everybody in town: stuff like birthdates, number of children, his best guess at their income, like that, and he watches and charts the numbers obsessively. Town kids move out because there's no new jobs. Farm kids don't move into town, the way your dad did, because there's no new jobs.

"Definite downward trend here—another decade or so, and we'll be below a thousand, then down from there until it reaches the point everything falls apart in just a couple of years. Right now, the town's main industries are the school and the elevator. If we didn't have that mini–baby boom on the farms in the late eighties and early nineties, the school would be cutting back. And the elevator? Shit. Archer Daniels Midland could bump the Hardwood Cooperative Grain Elevator off the face of the planet without noticing, if it ever hiccuped. Hardwood needs a new industry, and Dad's been working on finding one."

"And the trauma center is the only possibility?"

"Nah." She shook her head. "Just the best possibility, probably. I've never known Dad to have only one iron in the fire when five or six would fit. Moshe Ginsburg has a cousin in Postville, Iowa, and—"

"Postville, Iowa?" I had to grin. "He doesn't look Iowan to me."

"Don't be an asshole." She snorted. "Postville got a big Jewish slaughterhouse a dozen or so years back—tremendous amount of jobs, and a huge influx of Lubavitchers."

"The black-hat guys? Look like cowboys?"

"Yeah, them. Dr. Ginsburg isn't one—the family's Conservative, which is a different deal—but he's got some Lubavitcher cousins, and a couple of them are in the slaughterhouse business in Postville. Lots of jobs—lots for locals, and lots for Mexican immigrants, too. Saved the town, but . . ." She shook her head. "I've got a book about it in storage—I'll show it to you when I finally get everything shipped out here. The slaughterhouse changed the town—not all for the worse, but not all for the better, either."

She reached for the cigarette and took another long drag on it. "If Dad had his choice, he'd probably pick the trauma center, and not worry about how a bunch more doctors and nurses and technicians is going to change the complexion of the town, and I don't think he's—and stop looking like that."

"Like what?"

"Like I've just put on a bedsheet and lit a burning cross on your front lawn, that's what." She glared at me. "Tenishia gets a few glares and sniffs—"

"From who?" My jaw was hurting, so I forced myself to stop clenching it.

"Oh, relax. It's just a bit of normal xenophobia."

"Big word, that."

"Shush. But it isn't only Barb Thompsen who'd be delighted if Tenishia's aunt in Chicago changed her mind and took her back, I can tell you that." She shook her head. "I'm not going to tell you who says what, but I will say I'm glad you figured out a way to handle this little cheating thing without making a public fuss about it."

"I still want to know who said what, and when."

"Why? So you can go break some bones or windows, or threaten to shoot up the Larsen house? And never mind which Larsens," she added with a glare, although I was already guessing Lars. "No, you're not going to do anything stupid, and there's nothing useful you can do, so just leave it be." She shook her head. "You've got a decent enough mind, but—"

"Gee, thanks."

"—but you sometimes don't notice things unless they stick you in the eye."

"Like what?"

"Like, for example, how badly Jeffie's knuckles were bruised around Valentine's Day, or that Josh was walking with a limp—you think his dad beats him? Or how about both Amy Larsen and her sister having taken up cornrows?"

I had noticed the last—I could hardly have missed it—and attributed it to Tenishia, which wasn't hard, since she had done up Amy's hair, and it looked good on Amy. Sort of a Bo Derek thing, and more than a little cute. I hadn't thought of it as a personal or political statement.

"Been missing a lot, apparently," I said.

She smiled. "That's what you have me around for, eh?"

"Among other things."

"Well, it's not to pay the bills," she said before she realized it was a mistake. "Sparky . . ."

I closed my eyes, opened them. "We can go over that again, if you'd like," I said slowly and carefully. "My house is paid for—Dad started paying it off, and I finished—and I've managed to live within my means for a number of years. I don't mind, much, that when it's your turn to make the grocery run into Grand Forks more porterhouse than hamburger always comes back, but whatever the hell I am, it's not a fucking kept man. Not in my dad's house. Not anywhere." It was my turn to give her a hard look. "I won't let Tenishia go hungry—or even Snake—but I'd swallow a lot of rice and beans a hell of a lot easier than I live off your alimony—temporary or otherwise—from Fred Honistead. Understood?"

"Sparky . . ."

I should have backed off; another man would have, but

I've got my limitations. "Do we have an understanding, Bridget?"

She made a furtive reach of her hand out to mine, but drew it back when I just sat there.

"Yes, Ernest," she said, quietly. "We have an understanding. You fucking stiff-necked bastard."

"Yeah; that's me." I nodded. "Yeah, I'll look for shades of gray when I can, although I can't promise I'll see them. But when I can't, you can either live with it or break my heart and leave me again."

She shook her head. "No, I don't think I want to do that. Either." She shook her head. "So? It's on your terms or not at all?"

I nodded, slowly. "Yeah, I guess it is."

"Part of the deal, eh? Like making spaghetti sauce instead of porterhouse when there's only ground beef in the freezer?"

"Yeah. Like that. I hope you can live with it," I said. "You wouldn't believe how much I hope you can live with it."

Her smile was weak and crooked. "Oh, I think I do. You love that spaghetti sauce, eh?"

"Or something."

On-and-off switch? Maybe. Maybe that's stiff-necked and proud of me, or maybe you decide what you live with and what you won't.

Or both. I dunno.

I took her free hand and pressed it to my lips for a moment. I probably should have looked to see if there were any eyes peeking out of neighboring windows; there probably were, but I didn't much care.

"Okay," she said quietly, covering my hand with hers. "If I screw things up with us again, it'll be over *us*, not over money."

Last time around had been more my fault than hers, no matter what I told her at the time, and told myself through a dozen years and a horrible marriage, and maybe it meant something that I could say: "No. It wasn't you. It was either just me or maybe just us."

"Not again," she said, quietly. "I promise." She ground out the cigarette under her sneaker and kicked it into the bushes, ignoring the way I lit up another.

"Just watch your ass," she said as she stalked back into the house.

"I'd rather watch yours," I said, just because I hadn't been enough of a jerk recently.

Well, that was one opinion.

Bob Aarsted banged a real gavel on what one writer I once did called a "little gavel thing"—honest. It's really called a "sound block."

"Okay, everybody, simmer down," he said, although there was no simmering down necessary.

In Hardwood, things tend to fit into well-worn grooves. The first Tuesday of the month is the sewing circle over at Bev Hansen's, a chance for women over forty—theoretically it's open to anybody, but only in theory—to pretend to exchange sewing tips while keeping up on the latest gossip. Poker night is every Friday at the firehouse, starting promptly at 7:30, and I've never heard of Ole failing to get the pitchers of Grain Belt there on time, except during the blizzard of '88, when he was all of five minutes late, a subject Bill Hansen still brings up with with a cheery, "Hey, Ole—you're on time for once", every damn Friday.

I'd never been to a town-council meeting before, but I could recognize the pattern: Bob Aarsted sat at the head of his dining-room table, with Emma Thompsen to his right, her notebook already open and pencils laid out in front of her. Fred Thompsen (a second or third cousin; I can never keep all the Thompsens straight), the only remaining lawyer in town, had neatly folded his suit jacket over the back of one of the spare chairs and opened an attaché case that looked more like something James Bond rather than a three-hundred-pound lawyer would use, then sat and folded his sausage-like fingers over where his vest was threatening to pop his remaining button.

Hardwood isn't much for formality, but it is much for individuality, I guess, and this was as informal as I'd ever seen Fred during working hours.

Doc Sherve, Reverend Oppegaard, and Minnie Hansen were already in their seats as well, Minnie in between the two men, being towered over by them, which wasn't hard to do. Oppegaard's full, mainly salt-with-increasingly-less-pepper-every-year beard was close-cropped in anticipation of summer, not hiding where his clerical collar was supposed to be and wasn't—but his easy smile was in place, as usual.

Doc looked bigger sitting down—even if he hadn't been next to Minnie Hansen—than he would have standing up. Nature had intended him to be a tall man, but nature had fucked up. His legs were about the right size for a man maybe five feet tall—if the man was built like a treetrunk.

He looked strange to me, dressed only, at least from the waist up, in a no-longer-clean white shirt—it didn't take a genius to guess he'd had very rare roast beef for dinner at the Aarsteds' rather than just come out of a messy surgery—instead of his doctor's white coat. He smelled of clinic astringents as much as of the violet-scented pomade that slicked back his thin gray hair, and with the five-o'clock shadow that covered his heavy jowls, he reminded me of Richard Nixon—in looks if in nothing else I could think of.

There were only three of us sitting on three of the eight folding chairs that had been neatly lined up at the junction of the dining room and living room.

Jeff Bjerke was in as much of a uniform as I'd ever seen him wear: a blue cop shirt over his jeans, with his badge prominently pinned to his chest. A thick Sam Browne belt, festooned with cop gear, was tightly buckled around his waist, but it had slipped up a bit, revealing the two-inch-thick belt that actually held his pants up—I didn't know whether he had to buy jeans with big belt loops or if Karen just sewed on the oversized ones.

"Hey, Batman," I said, gesturing at the belt.

He grinned as he stuck his earphone wire into the radio on his belt, then winced as he fiddled with the knob—he must have blasted himself with static or something.

It was heavily loaded down, from the handcuff case that kept rubbing against the chair's strut to the carefully shaped holders, one for I guessed was pepper spray, a boxy one I couldn't figure out, and what I was sure was for his radio, what with the wire running into it, as well as the pretty much ubiquitous cell-phone holder—although his was made of shiny leather instead of the usual black plastic. A small revolver in a holster rode high on his right side instead of the manly high-capacity automatics that most cops carry these days.

Dr. Ginsburg eyed us politely, having nodded a greeting but not said anything. If he was hostile or friendly, it didn't show. It sort of felt like being a bug under a microscope, maybe. His hair was black and slicked back like Doc's—I dunno; maybe it's a doctor thing—but he was still in his lab coat, with a little badge that said MOSHE GINSBURG, MD on it, just in case people needed to be told who he was.

"Let's get some stuff out of the way as quickly as we can," Bob said, gesturing at Ginsburg. "We don't want to keep Dr. Ginsburg any longer than necessary." Keeping Jeff and me longer than necessary was, apparently, not considered a problem.

There were nods from around the table.

"Fine. We'll skip the minutes," Doc said.

Minnie Hansen tapped a finger on the table in front of her. "Second."

"All in favor?" Bob didn't look up. "Approved. Okay: old business. We have one item of old business—as discussed last time, Dr. Ginsburg and I need to take a trip to Bismark on the . . . twenty-fifth and twenty-sixth, to meet with the Trauma Center Commission."

"Which should be meeting in Grand Forks," Doc Sherve said, frowning, "but—"

"Shh." Minnie Hansen tapped a finger on the table, and Doc shut up. "We don't need to hear about that again." She looked up at Bob. "I move we approve the costs."

"Discussion?"

Oppegaard cleared his throat. "Well, loath though I am to take up any more of Dr. Ginsburg's time than we have to, I would like to know what costs we're approving."

Aarsted nodded. "Yup. Emma?"

She leafed through her clipboard. "Two plane tickets, round-trip, at two hundred thirty dollars and seventy-five cents each; two hotel nights, at—"

"Please. Just the bottom line," Oppegaard said.

"One thousand eight hundred dollars and change," Aarsted said. "Best price we could get on the tickets, and I intend to get a couple of commissioners well-fed and maybe a little drunk. Further discussion? If none, the question is moved. In favor? Opposed? Unanimous." He beckoned to Dr. Ginsburg, who rose and walked over to where Emma already had turned to a page on her clipboard. I don't know whether or not he deliberately ignored the pen she offered, or didn't see it, but he had already pulled a pen out of his shirt pocket, clicked it with the distinctive sound only a Parker T-Ball Jotter makes, and quickly signed it.

Bob Aarsted gave him a salesman's smile. "Thanks for coming, Moshe," he said. "But I could have run by with this stuff myself tomorrow."

Ginsburg shook his head. "I didn't want to put you to any trouble," he said, his voice barely above a whisper, as though he were talking too loud in church rather than too quietly in Bob Aarsted's dining room. "And I did want to have a word with Mrs. Hansen, after you're done here."

Minnie Hansen got to her feet more easily than I thought she could have.

"No need for that, Dr. Ginsburg," she said. "These things tend to drag on for hours." She turned to Aarsted. "We can step outside if Bob won't let us use his study."

Aarsted chuckled. "My study is your study; I think it'll be a while before we have anything to vote on."

Ginsburg in tow, Minnie walked down the hall toward what had been Bridget's bedroom, way back when, and everybody sat quietly until the door closed behind them.

Oppegaard raised an eyebrow and Doc made a patting, leave-it-alone-for-now gesture. I guess Oppegaard hadn't heard about the new school arrangements. If he'd waited another few days, he wouldn't have had to ask Doc for a report—all the details would, no doubt, be gone over at great length in the basement of the church at the Sunday potluck, after services, and while I'd never known Reverend Oppegaard to gossip, his wife, Pamela, might have been a secret agent in another life, or at least seemed to have an ear permanently stuck to the ground in this one.

A nosy sort, Pamela, at least when compared to me. I'm not knocking her, though; as a dominatrix of my (nonprofessional) acquaintance used to say, different strokes for different folks.

"Okay," Aarsted said. "We're now in executive session, if I hear a motion to that effect."

He didn't, but Emma put her pencil down anyway, sat back in her chair, and sipped at her coffee.

"On to the Sparky problem," Bob said.

"Isn't that new business?" she asked.

"Nah." Doc smiled. "Sparky's always been a problem. Nothing new about that."

"Fred?"

"You want my carefully considered legal opinion about this impersonating an officer thing?"

"Yeah."

"It's bullshit," he said. "Yes, according to the *Century Code*, a person who performs peace-officer duties without a license violates NDCC section 12-63-14. Is showing up at a crime scene with a badge 'performing peace-officer duties'? Maybe, but probably not."

Well, that was fucking reassuring. I probably hadn't committed a crime, and I probably wasn't going to go to jail.

Yippee, skippy.

"Then again, look at 12-63-03.2," he said, glancing down at his notes—don't any of these legal folks actually know this stuff?—"which says, specifically, that 12-63-01 through 12-63-14 don't apply to unpaid reserve officers. As chief of police, Jeff has every right to swear Sparky in as a reserve officer—he just can't be a *paid* officer, not unless he passes the exam and goes before the board to get approved. For that, he needs to be 'of good moral character'—"

"So much for that," Doc said.

"Shut up, please," Oppegaard said.

". . . goes through a background investigation . . ."

"Who performs that?"

"The parent agency—the Hardwood Police Department."

Jeff gave me a smile, which I didn't return.

". . . passes a medical and psychological screening, and—here's the kicker—passes a training program as approved by the county police officer licensing board, which basically means POST training at the U in Grand Forks, unless he wants to spend a year in Bismarck."

"Excuse me?" I stood up. "What's all this talk about screening and training?"

"Sit for a sec," Aarsted said, waving at me.

"No, I'd rather not. The way you're talking, it sounds like I'm not in danger of being arrested as some sort of conspirator, since they can't arrest me for impersonating a cop. So why am

I here? And why are we talking about getting me paid as a police officer, and—"

"*Can't* be arrested?" Fred smiled. "Famous last words. They can *arrest* you for it, but they can't convict you of it; you've got a perfect defense. Black-letter law: You weren't impersonating an officer because you were legally sworn in as an unpaid reserve officer. I don't think Dave Norstadt would go for it no matter what his brother wants. It would be a slam-dunk defense as long as we could have Jeff to testify. He swore you in; that clinches it. Hell, Bob, as mayor, could swear you in as a reserve officer. For all I know—I carefully haven't asked—maybe he did years ago."

"So? What's the problem?"

"So," Bob Aarsted said, "it occurred to me that if, oh, I happen to be somewhere—say, across the state—and Jeff is somewhere—say, down in Florida with his dad—it might be a few days before we could prove it." He shook his head.

Oppegaard grunted. "I know this is politics that you and Phil Norstadt are going at it like cats and dogs, but do you think he'd really pull this sort of nonsense?"

"I wouldn't bet either way." Aarsted shrugged. "I think—no guarantee, but I *think*—we're more likely to get the Level Three than Thompsen is. I think Phil thinks so, too, although he doesn't know all that I know. Yeah, it might backfire on him, but we're playing for a lot of the marbles here—he might try it, and his brother is dumber'n he is."

Fred frowned. "I don't think Dave Norstadt is dumb—but, sure, he's loyal as a dog."

"Desperate men do desperate things," Oppegaard said, nodding. "It might be worth a try from his point of view."

"Ah." Aarsted raised a finger. "But not if we can put a license in Sparky's pocket."

"A *police* license?"

"Sure." Doc nodded. "That'd do it. Somebody with a police license in his pocket can do a lot of things, but he can't im-

personate a police officer. But I don't see how it's possible.
There's no problem with the background check and the medical screening—Jeff can write out a report tonight, and I
could run Sparky through the mill myself tomorrow—but I
don't see how you get around the training and testing." He
turned to look at me. "You take some cop courses I never
heard of?"

I shook my head. "Nope."

Jeff shrugged. "Well, like Fred said, they do offer POST
training at the U in Grand Forks, but that'd take a year, even
assuming you could get him into classes this fall." He furrowed
his brow. "I don't think there's summer courses, unless they're a
continuation of the spring classes."

"That could be arranged," Aarsted said. "Fairly easily, and I
think—"

The door to Aarsted's study creaked open, and Bob Aarsted
and the rest fell silent as Minnie Hansen followed Dr. Ginsburg back into the dining room.

"I'm sorry to interrupt again," Ginsburg said, addressing the
room, and then turned to me. "May I have a private word with
you, Mr. Hemingway?" he asked. "It won't take but a moment."

Behind his back, Bob Aarsted was nodding, as though I
needed to be persuaded of the necessity of keeping the relatively new town doctor happy when simple courtesy would
have been more than sufficient. You'd think he thought that I
was an uncouth—

Oh.

"Sure, Doctor," I said. "I'll walk you out to your car."

He picked up his bag and I followed him out.

The night was bright. Despite the dull glow of the streetlights,
it was easy to see that the sky was full of stars, and even make
out the Milky Way, although dimly. I didn't miss it much; a
five-minute walk out my back door and through the windbreak

and I could see the sky anytime I wanted to, which was fairly often.

He put his bag on the passenger seat of his Lexus and closed the door gently. Me, if I had an expensive car, I'd slam the door every time, just to hear the irreproducible, solid, high-priced ka-thunk. In my Olds it's more of a click-clang-shake-jingle.

"I believe my son owes you an apology," he said. "And so do I."

"Excuse me?"

"When I approved him coming over to your home with his friends in the afternoon, the understanding was that it was to study, but it appears he and his friends have been just listening to records or some such rather than buckling down and getting their work done. I'm disappointed in him."

"Approved"? What the fuck did that mean? Does the kid need your permission before he can take a dump, too?

But that wasn't quite the right thing to say, and I don't always insist on saying the wrong thing, public opinion to the contrary.

So I shrugged. "That's not the way I heard it."

"I'm sure you didn't. Children . . ." He frowned. "No, that wasn't quite the way Mrs. Hansen put it, either. She talked about Joshua doing well in school, but not achieving his full potential. As far as I'm concerned, that just means he's goofing off." He blinked, although what there was to blink about I don't know.

"His grades okay?"

He stiffened. He wanted to say something about how it wasn't any of my damned business, but that wouldn't go well with an apology. "Not entirely, no, they aren't. There's no reason whatsoever that he shouldn't be getting straight As, not in—not in high school."

You mean, not surrounded by a bunch of dumb Norskie farm kids? I don't know where city people get the idea that farmers are necessarily dumb, but that's not been my experience.

"I certainly got straight As at his age," he went on, "in a much more difficult environment, and without his advantages. His sister is managing it, and unless he pulls his average up—" He stopped himself. "He really should be doing better, and Mrs. Hansen has offered to take a hand, and predicted that he'll be able to finish out the year with much better grades if he works harder, and I assured her he will. I don't think he'll be bothering you anymore."

I shook my head. "No need to apologize; he hasn't been any trouble at all."

"That's very kind of you to say."

There's only so much politeness I'm capable of, even though I'd long ago gotten word that the new doctor had to be treated with kid gloves.

"He's been no bother at all," I said, forcing a smile. "Nice kid; he's welcome in my home anytime."

That's not the sort of thing I say lightly, and I really didn't know the kid well enough to mean it, but I did, anyway.

Ginsburg didn't say anything; he just walked around the car, got in, and drove off, slowly and carefully.

I was surprised that he could sit down to drive at all, what with that stick up his ass.

I finished my cigarette and had another before going back in, and tried to put the anal retentive Dr. Ginsburg out of my mind. I had other things to think about. It was starting to look like I wasn't going to be ending up in court, not exactly, but there was another sentence hanging over me.

I'm not sure what went on while I was out, but they were still deep in discussion. Bob Aarsted looked up, one thick eyebrow raised, but I ignored him.

"Yeah, but it doesn't do much of anything right now," Doc was saying.

Fred nodded. "So we need a waiver. 'Peace officers with experience *or* training outside the state before January 1, 1989, may qualify for exception from portions of the training requirement.' In practice, what that means is anybody with any kind of experience can get a waiver—as long as he's willing to agree to take the POST training."

Okay. Things were starting to get a little less murky. I still didn't like it, though.

Jeff nodded. "That's how Mikey Olson, over in Hatton, got the job; he was an MP in Vietnam." He shrugged. "Not that there was a lot of competition for the job. Pays less than here, even."

Aarsted gave him a look, and Jeff didn't press the pay issue.

"Well, fine," I said. "But I wasn't an MP in Vietnam—I was a tanker, tank you very much."

A weak joke, but everybody smiled.

Aarsted nodded. "Correct me if I'm wrong, but didn't you tell me, one time, about how you and the other three guys in your tank were seconded to the MPs for a while?"

"Well, yeah, but . . ." I shook my head. "It wasn't anything like that. Marino—a driver in another tank—went apeshit and tried to kill Captain Black with a shovel. Got in a good whack before Furball jumped him, and Prez and Horse and I and a bunch of other guys jumped in, too. Took six men to hold Marino down. Since Bosco was sidelined at the time, Captain Black had the four of us haul him down to the repair depot, and we just sat on him until the MPs finally showed up, and turned him over to them, then drove Bosco back, which gave us a chance to be sure that the new tranny really tranned." I shrugged. "Not exactly a lot of cop training, eh?"

"That's not the way I remember you telling the story," he said, raising a hand in what might have been a sincere apology when I glared. "Oh, relax, Sparky. Nobody's saying you were bragging."

"Good."

Look: There's not much I'm proud of, but I am proud to say I don't play the Vietnam War hero. I never was one. If I was to take my old Class A out of mothballs and put it on, I wouldn't even look like one, even if it did fit, which I doubt it would.

There's a lot of guys who have Bronze Stars—or heavier hardware—on their chest who deserve them, and a few who don't. I don't have any of that, which is fine with me, because I didn't earn any of it.

Yes, I got the Purple Heart and the CIB that came along with it, but there was nothing remotely heroic about it, or about the couple of clusters for the Purple Heart that came later. It was all small shit.

For the first one, I got clipped by some shrapnel while I was busy with an M79, playing flyswatter on Bosco's deck, but it was nothing. A little chunk of metal, about the size of a dime, just missed my balls as it caught me on the inner thigh—I was lucky it was a hot day, but, then again, it was always a fucking hot day—and I got bunged up a lot worse bouncing off sharp corners when I fell. Shit, the shots I had to take afterward were a lot more painful than the shrapnel.

I still have it in my dresser, somewhere. The shrapnel, that is. Yes, I kept the medals, too.

"Nor, for that matter," he went on, pulling out a sheet of paper, "is that what this notarized letter from Jonas Black, Esq., says. I quote: 'During the period of his service in 1969 in the Republic of Vietnam, as part of his duties in 1/77 Armor, Bravo Company, Specialist Fourth Class Ernest NMI Hemingway was seconded to the Military Police and received instruction and training in police procedures and practices from the undersigned. SpecFour Hemingway performed all assigned Military Police and other duties with courage, competence, diligence, and professionalism.'" He waved the letter at me. "Had to have him fax it twice—on the first try, he left on the Post-it note asking if there was anything else he could do to help you out, and I didn't want to run that by the commission. I faxed it to Harvey Hansen in Grand Forks a couple of hours ago. Hard copy arrives by FedEx tomorrow."

Gee, thanks, captain. Notarized, too?

It wasn't exactly a lie, not entirely; it was true only in the sense that you could call Cole Creek a raging river, and then, when challenged, insist that, well, a creek and a raging river are both wet.

The "training and instruction" had consisted of Captain Black telling the four of us to put on clean uniforms, get some MP brassards and a set of orders from Furball, and then haul Marino's crazy ass to Trieu Phong and turn him over to the MPs there. He also said not to take the fucking handcuffs off Marino even if he had to take a shit, then threw away the key to make it difficult for us to do anything else. Which made things interesting at Trieu Phong, because the handcuffs weren't regulation—I suspect Captain Black had them for, er, social purposes, although they weren't fur-lined or anything like that—and the MPs had to use a bolt cutter to get them off.

Well, he didn't say "extensive" training, but shit . . . it was like claiming Prez Washington was a medic because he used a pair of pliers to yank that hunk of shrapnel out of me.

Then again, we did perform the assigned duties. Got Marino there, after all, handed him over to the real MPs, and never mind that we spent the next day in the bars and hookshops in Trieu Phong, and caught shit for that when we got back, although not while there—Furball had, it seems, screwed up typing out our orders, which only cost us a couple of cases of beer, a gram of hash, and a look of disgust from the captain upon our belated—in his opinion—return.

"The war happened well before January 1, 1989," Fred said, nodding. "Twenty years before. And the Republic of Vietnam certainly qualifies as being outside North Dakota."

"Only one problem," Jeff said. "They're not going to make

an exception for a town that already has a POST-qualified cop, even if he promises to take the courses."

"Sure. Which is why I told Harvey we had to get moving on this, because you tendered your resignation last week, effective in another . . . lemme see, six days. We don't pay you enough, apparently, and there was this competing offer from some hardware store."

Jeff tried to look surprised, but I wasn't buying it.

Oppegaard shook his head. "You think the commission is going to rubber-stamp all this?"

"By about noon tomorrow," Aarsted said, nodding. "Norstadt isn't the only one with friends and relatives, and Harvey Hansen, the chairman of the licensing commission, is an old friend of mine. He's also thick as thieves with some of the Highway Patrol folks in Grand Forks. The captain there used to be a town cop himself—without any college degree, much less certification—and he doesn't like the idea of having to send out a trooper to Hardwood every time somebody runs over a deer."

"Yeah. Troopers like to stick to the interstate when they can." Jeff nodded. "Yeah. I can see it."

Minnie Hansen frowned. "Who pays for all this?" she asked. "If you don't mind such pedestrian sorts of questions about this no doubt brilliant scheme of yours."

"Already handled," Aarsted said. "COPs grant; Title I, 1994 Crime Act. It's nice to have a senator, eh?"

Doc nodded. "And it costs how much?"

"Nothing. We save money on the deal. COPs grant; I told you."

Jeff nodded. I raised an eyebrow.

"Cops?"

"Community-Oriented Policing, or something like that," Aarsted said. "The Feds will pay three quarters of the salary for a newly hired cop, up to some limits, with some restrictions and a lot of paperwork, all of which Fred and I have going already. Grand Forks went over their COPs quota last year, and there's still a few hundred thousand bucks in the county budget. So we give Sparky Jeff's job, and hire Jeff as a Community Oriented Policeman in a month or two—with enough of a boost in salary to make him and Karen happy. And the town still saves quite a few bucks, even if—I mean *after*—we pay for your POST courses at the U. Which don't start until fall, anyway."

By which time this would all be over. I've got nothing against school, mind, but the idea of sitting in a classroom with a bunch of kids whose idea of a good time was writing tickets for speeders didn't have very much appeal, and it was pretty clear Bob knew it, and that the whole POST training thing was just some more bullshit.

Which was fine. What wasn't fine was the rest of it.

I shrugged. "I don't like it much."

"Because?"

"Well, because, among other things, I've got my own work to do."

Jeff smiled. "I dunno, Officer Hemingway, but you just might find that Hardwood has a reserve officer pulling almost all of the load most of the time. We can work out some sort of, er, arrangement."

Translation: I'd be expected to kick back the salary—or at least most of it—to Jeff until he was back on the payroll, although he wouldn't say that in front of Fred.

He'd probably worked that part of it out with his father-in-law already. Or, more likely, Aarsted had explained it to him. I like Jeff and all, but I'm not entirely sure it's a great idea to have the town cop not just hireable and fireable by the mayor, but his son-in-law as well.

"And for another," I said, "I don't have the slightest idea what to do as a cop. Shit, I wouldn't even know how to write a ticket."

"That's not a problem." Jeff smiled. "It's pretty easy—you've been on the receiving end of it often enough. Just fill in the stuff the cop usually writes in and give it to the person you stopped to sign, instead of the other way around."

"Jeff'll show you," Aarsted said. "It's easy."

"I don't know what to do with it after, either."

Emma Thompsen had been sitting, listening quietly. "You turn it in to me at the end of the day, and I process it."

"Or if I have to make a real arrest?"

"Hey, this isn't the NYPD, you know," Jeff said. "If I'm not around, you hook up the perp, put him in the back of the car, and whistle for the staties, just like I do. Let them fill out the forms—they get the arrest anyway." He shrugged. "This isn't exactly a hotbed of crime, Sparky. The only time you're going to have to make an arrest is if you stop a DUI or a speeder who's got a warrant out, and we don't get bailed-out ax murderers out here—the warrants will just be things like unpaid traffic tickets. If you run into anything serious, like an accident, you do what I do: Get on the radio, or hit the big red button on your cell phone, and yell for help from the staties. As long as you handle the piddly shit, you won't have a problem."

I shook my head. "I don't know about any of this."

Aarsted pursed his lips. "Well, if you don't mind a personal observation . . ."

"Like I have a choice?"

"I've never thought of you as the brightest bulb on the tree, Sparky, but I've always thought of you as somebody pretty trustworthy, all in all. I'm disappointed you're not trying to help us out. We're trying to help you out, after all."

There was no answer to that.

Oppegaard might as well have been reading my mind. "That's about as unfair as I've ever heard you be, Bob," he said. "Sparky gets in trouble that he shouldn't have, mainly because of politics he's not been involved in, and you claim that when he hesitates over making a commitment—and I take oaths pretty seriously myself—you're going to accuse him of being untrustworthy?" He shrugged his massive shoulders. "That's just not right." He turned to me. "If you don't want to do this, Sparky, you don't have to."

Doc Sherve nodded. "Yeah. Sometimes you get all caught up in things, Bob."

I'd noticed that. Finally.

"Okay." Bob Aarsted nodded. "Phil Norstadt has scored off me before, and he'll probably do it again. Not your problem, after all, and if there's any hassle about this impersonating-an-officer crap, I'll cover for you, and make getting you out of jail my absolute top priority."

He was either trying to keep the disgust out of his voice and just barely failing, or trying to put just a trace of it in and succeeding admirably. I would have tried to guess which it was, but I'm not much for guessing.

I turned to Minnie, who had sat silent through all the discussion. "Mrs. Hansen?"

"Yes, Ernest?"

"I don't know about any of this. I feel like I'm in a room with a bunch of used-car salesmen, all of them explaining how that ping in the engine and the grinding sound from the transmission will both just go away if I ignore them—and I don't like any of it. What do you think I should do?"

She smiled. "And you want me to give you the answer?"

"Well, yes." That was why I'd asked the question, for God's sake.

"Well, *no*." She shook her head. "It's been forty years since you were my student, officially, Ernest."

It had been more than forty years, but I wasn't going to argue with her. "And your point is?"

She smiled. "My point is that I wouldn't give you answers to test questions then, and I'm not going to start now. Oh, I'll point out that this little good-cop-bad-cop routine from Bob and Doc and Dave was pretty clumsy, if you'd like, but you've already worked that out. I might even say it doesn't sound like a lot of work or a lot of trouble. I'll definitely say it sounds like a lot less trouble than worrying about being arrested, and I'll even go so far as to say I think you've always been a level-headed sort, and having you watch over the town when Jeff isn't around doesn't sound to me like the worst idea in the world; in fact, I think it's quite a good one." She shook her head. "But I'm not going to tell you what to do."

Yeah, right.

I nodded. "Okay. Let's do it."

"Let's do it," by the way, were Gary Gilmore's last words, just before he was executed.

Aarsted rapped his gavel on the block. "Okay, do we have a motion?"

I wasn't surprised when Minnie Hansen spoke up. "I move we accept Jeff Bjerke's resignation as chief of police, and appoint him as Community Police Officer, subject to funding approval. I further move that we appoint Ernest Hemingway as chief of police, subject to his being issued a provisional license by the county Police Officers' Licensing Board."

"Discussion? Hearing none, I call the question. All in favor?"

There was a chorus of ayes.

"Opposed?"

I probably should have said something.

5

Morning came, as mornings do: Every day, regular as clockwork, there's another one, whether or not you like it.

It was morning.

I was a day older, if not a day wiser, and my mouth, as was typical for mornings of late—ever since I took up smoking again—tasted like a bunch of pigs had wallowed in it all night. Which is about as philosophical or colorful as I can get until I've had a couple of cups of coffee.

The bedside clock said 8:13 in bright-red letters.

I'd slept in late enough to miss seeing Tenishia go off to school—as usual; the kid didn't need me to dress her or anything, after all—and Bridget leaving for some errands. I wasn't sure quite where she was going or what she was doing, but I didn't have any particular desire to call her on her cell phone to ask.

Leave well enough alone, I always say.

There are things I'm not overly fond of in my life, but it had taken a turn for the better of late, what with going to bed every night with a beautiful woman who would leave hot coffee behind when she went out in the morning, and messing all that up with constant questions of where-are-you-and-what-have-you-been-doing-and-with-who-have-you-been-doing-it was something I had happily given up after Jennifer walked out.

So while I downed a couple of cups and fired up the first couple of cigarettes of the day, I quickly fried up some bacon and eggs while I threw some Master English Muffin Toasting Bread in the toaster—I like it, but what it has to do with English muffins is a mystery—and took the breakfast into my office, leaving the fry pan to clear up later.

I had just finished mopping up the last of the egg yolks with the toast and was just settling down with the brick when there was a knock on the door. By the time I'd finished swearing at the interruption and made my way down the hall, Jeff Bjerke, Bob Aarsted, and Fred Thompsen had let themselves in.

"Hey, Sparky," Jeff said.

"Come on in," I said, not making the obvious comment about how they already were in.

Fred just nodded and sat down on the couch near the window, opening up his shiny metal attaché case. I wouldn't have been surprised if he'd pulled out some James Bond flying belt—well, maybe I would have, at least a little—but he just brought out some papers, and tapped them up and down on the old coffee table to straighten them out, then started arranging them into neat little piles.

All lawyers are anal compulsives, I guess.

"What's all this?"

"Just some paperwork," Aarsted said, with a smile. "Fred?"

"Let me see," Fred said. "Okay: Begin at the beginning. Application for your exemption from educational requirements for your police license because of previous training and experience outside the state of North Dakota and prior to January 1, 1989, referred to in Attachment A, notarized letter from Jonas Black, Esq., attached," he said, tapping on one sheet. "Application for your provisional police license—initial here where you say you've applied for the exemption as a matter of right, as per Century Code 12-63-08, in lieu of producing proof of testing and POST training, and here, where you refer to Attachment B, certification of medical and psychological fitness, as attested to by Robert Sherve, MD. Job application—Emma's filled it out; you can just sign it." Another tap. "Your letter of agreement to take the board-approved training course at the next opportunity, said training to commence no later than 15 September, said agreement to be null and void should you choose to surrender your license prior to September 15." Tap. "Waiver for search into your criminal and medical records, so we can see if you've been convicted for murdering anybody or been adjudged insane." He beckoned to Jeff. "You sign the successful completion of background screening form, carried out to the satisfaction and established standards of the Hardwood Police Department."

Despite Aarsted's glare and Fred's nod of approval, I read quickly through the papers—they said what Fred had said they'd said—and accepted Fred's Parker T-Ball Jotter to sign.

Jeff didn't even bother reading his letter; he just signed it.

Fred nodded and tucked the papers back into his briefcase, closed it, then rose.

"I'll get these out just as soon as I get the certification from Doc." He handed me a manila envelope. "You can drop this off with Emma after you go see Doc. You have a nice day, now." He left, shutting the door behind him.

Aarsted looked over at me. "Better get that thing with Doc taken care of soon as you can."

I nodded. "I'll give you a buzz in a while, and see if I can stop by later on."

Jeff shook his head. "Nope. He's waiting for you right now, and you know that Doc doesn't like waiting. I'd drop you off."

"Like I can't walk less than half a mile?" The clinic is on the other side of town, but that doesn't exactly make it a hike.

Aarsted just smiled. "Wouldn't want you to get lost on your way."

Normally, I'd have been embarrassed that I hadn't offered them so much as a cup of coffee, but I wasn't, and I didn't.

.   .   .

I had expected Doc's examination to be about as, er, thorough as Jeff's background check. Not that I'm complaining about Jeff's background check, and, for that matter, I don't think that Jeff really did need to do much of anything, and neither did Doc, having been my doctor ever since he pulled me out of my mother—screaming right away, so the family legend had it, without any necessity of slapping me on the butt, and then supposedly pissing right in his face.

Just goes to show I shouldn't assume.

Doc quickly had me out of my clothes—leaving the room so that I could do it wasn't his style; he just made helpful suggestions as I undressed—and into one of those backless hospital gowns that Doc always calls the "Garment of Indignity," and then had me stretch out on the examination table. He ran through the gamut of blood pressure, and listening to my heart, and putting one hand on my stomach while he tapped with his fingers on it—whatever that shows, other than that he's a doctor.

I'll give him this: He gave me enough warning to tuck the gown more thoroughly over my crotch—it had ridden up while he was doing all that tapping stuff—before he called Becky in.

She drew enough blood for a splatter film and then left, with nothing more than a smile, omitting the comments about my bony knees.

Then Doc had me sit up on the table and did the usual tapping the knee with a rubber hammer. He climbed up on his little footstool so that that he could peer into my ears with the little doctor-looking-into-the-ears thing that I'd have corrected to "otoscope" if I was working. Which I wasn't, so it was a little doctor-looking-into-the-ears thing, okay?

"Everything fine?"

"Yup." He nodded as he braced himself on the exam table to climb down off the stool. It was only a foot high or so, and the rubber tips gripped the floor just fine, but even a short fall can be dangerous at Doc's age. "So far, so good. Couldn't quite see through to the other side."

"We about done?"

"Well . . ." He shook his head. "No, not quite. A couple of things more."

"Like?"

"Like the psychological exam, which I'm about to certify having given."

I had, for some reason, thought all that would be bullshit as well, but Doc appeared to be taking it seriously. He grabbed a clipboard and a pencil off his desk and started into a whole bunch of questions, most of them about hearing voices and feeling like people were out to get me—I said no to the first kind, truthfully, and lied like hell about the second, which seemed only reasonable, under the circumstances, given that he was one of the people out to get me.

He checked off the answers as I gave them and didn't argue with me, for once—he just asked the questions, until he finally nodded and put the clipboard down on his desk, then used the little stool to climb up and sit on the top of the desk itself, his short legs hanging down. He beckoned me over to the chair next to him.

I tried to tuck the ends of the gown underneath me, but the vinyl instantly stuck to my butt.

The smile dropped from his face. "Okay, forget the silly questions," he said. "Got a real question for you."

"Yeah?"

"Yeah," He nodded, then pursed his lips. "You take this stuff seriously?"

"The not-going-to-jail part? Betcher ass, Doc."

"Nah. Not that. The rest of it." He pursed his lips and shook his head. "Bob Aarsted and I go too far back, maybe. Sometimes, he's, well . . ."

"A manipulative asshole?"

He snorted. "One way to put it, sure. He stampeded you into this with the threat of you getting handcuffed and thrown into a police car, and maybe even having to go to court if you didn't play ball. He's got his reasons, yes, and they make sense to me, all in all, but that doesn't mean he didn't railroad you." He shrugged. "There's some stuff he didn't tell you."

"Oh?"

He shook his head. "Nothing big or anything—unless he's keeping secrets from me."

"Always a possibility."

Doc nodded. "Yeah. But I asked him outright last night, and he denied it." He pursed his lips. "I've known Bob to play games, but I've never known him to straight-out lie to me when I've asked him a direct question.

"What he didn't happen to mention before, though, is that we've got one of the trauma-commission folks coming in next week to look over the town—and I don't think it's a coincidence that this is just before he and Moshe take their trip out to Bismarck. My guess is that one of the reasons Bob pushed this all along is that he'd rather show the guy a police chief who looks like a grownup rather than a kid who doesn't look old enough to shave." He raised a hand. "Hey, I like Jeff Bjerke just fine, and I think he's been doing a decent job ever since John Honistead retired—I thought he'd go speeding-ticket happy for a while, but he gave that up pretty quick. No, I'm not criticizing Jeff. Good kid." He frowned. "I worry about you, sometimes, Sparky."

"Gee, thanks."

"If you had to really do the job, the hard part of it—if, say, somebody started shooting up the Savings and Loan—you think you could?"

It was my turn to shrug. "Damned if I know, Doc." I could have made some stupid comment about how I'd never run away in Nam, But I was in a tank, and running away when things got interesting wouldn't have been cowardly, particularly—just difficult and suicidal, and never mind that it would have left the other three behind. "But I will say that while Effie Lindquist isn't particularly my favorite person in the world, or even in town, I wouldn't much like the idea of somebody sticking a gun in her face. Or Paul Berge. Or even that asshole Lars Larsen. Or you, for that matter."

"Thanks." He blinked. "Like I said last night, I think this is all a good idea, but . . . if you really don't want to do it, just tell me now, and I'll tear up the certificate instead of signing it. Bob won't like it, but I can take the heat, and I promise that you won't have to. Just a matter of you having flunked your physical—and Bob Aarsted knows better than to try to see how far he could push my notions about doctor-patient confidentiality to try to find out exactly why you flunked it." He looked me in the eye. "I'll cut corners here and there, Sparky."

"I noticed."

He shut me up with a glare. "But I've always taken being a doctor seriously. It's not just what I do for a living, Sparky. It's what I am. I'm a doctor, and you're my patient, and when I raised my hand and took the oath, I meant every word of it, not excluding 'first do no harm.' I wouldn't pass you if, say, I'd found some tachycardia I wasn't sure I could treat, but if you want to flunk your physical, you *will* flunk your physical."

"And if I don't want to?"

"Then you pass," he said. "You're in decent shape for a man your age. I'd like to see you give up the smoking and take up walking three, maybe four miles a day, sure, and from the smell of bacon all over you, you should probably cut back on the fried foods, too. But if there's something really wrong with you, I haven't found it, and probably won't—not unless you tell me I ought to."

I should have thought about it for a moment, but I was already in over my head, after all, and there was no sense in pretending otherwise.

"I'll do the job, Doc," I said. "Best I can."

Doc had known my dad all his life, and he'd known me all of mine, and he knew the magic phrase: "Do I have your word on that?"

"Yeah. You got my word on that."

"Well, your word's good enough for me, Sparky." The smile was back. "And I'm glad you said that. Although you won't be so glad, I think, in a minute." He was reaching for a box of latex gloves and a tube that looked like toothpaste. He slid on the glove and opened the tube.

"One more *leetle* part of the exam, and then we're done," he said, as he started squeezing a disturbingly thick, frighteningly clear, not particularly familiar liquid onto the glove's fingers. "As soon as the bloodwork comes back, you'll be all set, unless there's some surprises—and I'm not expecting any. So you're off—after this, that is."

"Oh, shit."

"Hey, I said I'd give you a full exam, and I will. You're not the only person in the world whose word is good, and you're over forty-five, so your full physical includes a digital exam, and I don't mean digital-in-the-computer sense. Lean forward, with your elbows on the table, and try to relax."

I guess I should have been glad to have finally found out why I had to wear the idiotic examination robe, but I've got to admit that it hadn't been my first thought.

"Maybe you should buy me dinner and tell me you love me first."

He didn't smile. "Maybe you should tell me a line I haven't heard a thousand times before."

"Doc—"

"You got a choice, Sparky. If I hear another word out of you right now, I might have to find a tube of Ben-Gay instead of using the KY."

There are many times in life where calling a bluff is a lose-a-lot-vs.-lose-a-lot-more proposition, so I walked over to the exam table and bent over.

Doc started humming that goddamn guitar-banjo duel theme from *Deliverance* as I tried to relax to the inevitable.

I seemed to be doing a lot of that of late.

I'd just gotten in the door when the phone rang. I thought about ignoring it—I usually think about ignoring a ringing phone—but picked it up anyway, as I usually do.

"Hey, Snake." I wouldn't have failed to recognize that voice on the worst day of my life.

It was Doc—not Sherve: Holliday.

Every once in a while I think about the other guys the combination of the U.S. Army Personnel Department put in the same company, and Jonas Black eventually put in the same tank—whether it was out of some hidden sense of humor that I never noticed in the captain, or because he wanted to put four bad apples in the same steel barrel, I dunno.

I'm always tempted to wonder about what sort of idiots would name a kid "James Holliday" or "George Washington" or "Crazy Horse", except that I'd have to have the same thoughts about George and Ethel Hemingway, who named their first son Ernest, and I try to avoid thinking about that. Doc's and Prez's and Horse's parents probably had their reasons, too.

Just not good ones.

Mom's father's name was Ernest Olmstead, but that doesn't seem to me to be a good excuse, and I don't like thinking about my late parents as idiots, so it's not right to criticize Doc's and Prez's and Horse's for doing the same sort of stupid thing, so I won't. Fair is fair.

Life isn't fair, I guess, but I try to be.

"Hey, Doc," I said.

Doc Holliday had, a couple of eons ago, been Bosco's tank

commander and one of the three guys I'd spent most of my time in Nam with. It wouldn't have quite been true that the three of us were all friends, and there were more than a few times during those months that I hated their fucking guts— sometimes for good reason, sometimes just because—but they were my . . .

I don't think there's have a word for it. I'd have settled on something like "blood brothers", but I know that Horse would have disapproved of a white man using the term, as he had every right to.

But it was something, and it meant something to me.

Short form: When Tenishia had gotten herself in trouble last winter and had called me up out of the blue—I had lost touch with Prez Washington, and didn't even know that he had a daughter—Doc and Horse and I had come running. Not particularly because we wanted to. But there's some things you don't have a choice about.

"Bad time?" he asked.

"Never a bad time to talk to you, Doc," I said, more or less honestly, although what I really wanted to do was get in the shower and wash what remained of the KY Jelly out of my ass, almost as much as I wanted to down a glass of whiskey and try to wash the memory of Doc Sherve feeling for lumps out of my mind. Well, at least he didn't find any, and he'd been thorough enough that if he's used toothpaste instead of the KY Jelly I'd have had preposterously fresh breath.

"How you doing?" I asked.

"Better than expected. Thanks for asking."

Depending how you looked at it, the years had either been very kind or very cruel to him. On one hand, he was a successful dermatologist in Indianapolis—I guess if you're going to go through life as "Doc Holliday", going to med school makes sense—and he making enough money that he could afford his own airplane, despite having to pay off two or three ex-wives.

On the other hand, he had those two or three ex-wives to support, as well as some sort of brain tumor.

Life sometimes sucks.

"Any news?"

"Some. One of my partners is taking retirement, and I'm having to break in a new one who started last week. Twenty-seven, right out of her IM residency, and cute as all hell. Which is making things, err, interesting in the office."

Which they would be. Doc's third or fourth wife had also been his medical assistant, and while I didn't ask about the details—although it would have been an interesting story, knowing Doc, and parts of it might even have been true—I had the impression she'd carefully worked her way up from medical assistant at Partners in Medical Services to being Mrs. Doctor Holliday, and stayed on in the office to make sure there were no similar future promotions.

"And?"

"Reminds me of Tenishia, actually. Black, skinny, although a lot less glowery, and a few more pounds, all of them in the right places. Cute as a bunny and smart as a whip—if you want some other clichés, I could probably come up with those, too."

"That wasn't what I was asking about." Doc and Horse had helped get Tenishia out of the trouble she'd been in the previous winter, and one of the arguments Doc had made about him taking the sharp end of it all, rather than me, was that he had a brain tumor.

I hadn't gone for it, by the way. Doc always had a suicidal streak, and I was never issued one of those.

"You weren't? Shit, boy, that's just because you haven't seen Masha. I'd send you pictures, but even if she'd go for it, I don't think Jodie would approve of—"

"Come on, Doc. Enough bullshit."

"You mean, am I going to die?"

"Well, yeah."

"Well, yeah, I'm going to die. Shit, Snake, everybody dies," he said.

"I'm sorry, Doc."

"Don't be. There's a but."

"Yeah?"

"*But*, if I'm going to die from this little brain tumor, it's going to have to grow back something fierce." If it had been me sharing such news, I'd have been jumping up and down, but he was just reporting it like he was talking about a wart. "I dunno if it was the chemo or the radiation, but it shrunk down to just about six millimeters and has remained encapsulated—that's a good thing. What's left of it is coming out next week—Monday or Tuesday. They're doing it at the Mayo, but that's just because I've got an old med-school classmate there and I'd rather get cut by somebody I know; it's not that big a deal."

"Doc, you're a fucking asshole," I said. I felt like jumping up and down and cheering, to tell the truth.

"Well, yeah, whenever possible. Sorry if I scared you."

"Sure you are."

"Not that I mind you giving me shit, or vice versa—fuck, Sparky, we're both entitled, all things considered—but I figure to be up and out of the hospital next Thursday, assuming everything goes right, and I was wondering if you wouldn't mind a houseguest that weekend."

"You going to be okay to travel?"

"Hope so. All this will probably be my one of last chances to fly—I'm due for my annual flight physical next month, and the odds are pretty good I'm not going to be able to cover this up, and basically zero of me getting a waiver. So I'm planning on spending every spare minute—up until the fucking FAA medic tells me my flying days are over—in the sky."

I could have said something about how I didn't particularly want to be under the flight path of some private pilot who had gone through brain surgery, or even one who was due for brain surgery, but I'm sure Doc had heard all that, and . . .

"Hey," he said, "don't make a big deal of it. It's just a pituitary tumor, okay, so getting it out isn't that complicated."

"Pituitary? Means nothing much to me, Doc."

"Well, it means a lot to me. They go in through the soft palate—you know, that thing at the back of your mouth?—and not the brain case. A day or so in bed, and that's mainly to recover from the anesthesia, and I just have to be careful about what I eat until the sutures heal. Easy as pie."

I didn't know if it was false bravado or real bravery, and there's no way to ask, and not much more of a way to tell, so I stuck to the obvious. "Hey, Doc, anytime you want to come out here, you know you're welcome."

"Yeah, Sparky," he said. "Thanks. I'll call you when I've got an ETA. Pick me up when I touch down?"

"Sure." It's a little less than a mile from the airstrip into town, but he probably oughtn't be walking, even forgetting the matter of luggage, and, besides . . .

"Give me your number?" he said.

"You just called my number."

"Hmm . . . no cell phone?"

"Nah. Bridget's got one, though." I had the number written down—whether my failure to have it memorized was advancing senility, stubbornness, or just me hating to call her on it weren't mutually exclusive explanations. But it was written on the pad next to the living room phone, so I read it off.

"Just one thing, though," I said.

"Yeah?"

"Last time you came out this way, you had enough guns in your plane to equip the Eighty-second Airborne."

"Pretty fucking wimpy outfit if all they've got is a few semiautos, a couple of Garands, and a twelve-gauge Mossberg shotgun."

"My point is—"

"Well, I'm glad you got one."

"—that you can put whatever you want in the plane, but don't go carrying anything around, not here."

Doc did have a carry permit in Indiana—although why I don't know; I guess Indianapolis is a tough city—but that was for there, not here. I've got one, too, but it's not the same thing.

Handgun-carry permits are easy to get in North Dakota—if you're over twenty-one, aren't a felon, and can pass a shooting test that does little more than show you can send thirty rounds downrange without hitting or scaring the instructor, you can get one.

I didn't know of many folks who either hunted or kept a varmint rifle in the car who didn't have a permit. Not that a lot of people hereabouts go around with a pistol stuck down the front of their pants, but if you've got the permit, you can keep a rifle in the cab of your car instead of locking it in the trunk, and not have to worry about having it taken away if you get stopped for speeding.

"Why? You think I'm some sort of brain-damaged Vietnam vet who's going to go around shooting up the place?"

It had taken him long enough to ask. I forced myself not to smile; Doc would be able to hear it. "Nah. But we're going to have a new town cop—chief of police, technically—in a couple of days, and word has it he's a real stiff-necked bastard."

"Hmm. Well, I'll play nice then, Sparky. Wouldn't want to embarrass you."

"Yeah, sure."

"See you." He hung up without saying good-bye or giving me a chance to tell him my own news.

Not sure that I would have, mind, although I was sort of leading up to deciding. Doc had jerked my chain a bit; it was only fair to pay him back.

I didn't think I'd exactly be doing a whole lot as town

cop/police chief, but if I could surprise Doc, that would be worth some of the trouble.

It's amazing how much work you can get done when you just sit down and do it. I wouldn't say I'm a perfectionist—well, I would, but I'd be lying through my teeth—but I do take a fair amount of pride in getting it right, "it" being "what a good copyeditor does", rather than "what a writer or an editor is supposed to be able to do but often doesn't bother doing."

Set your sights low enough, and you'll at least kick up some dirt.

I put my fantasies about copyediting another Westlake in the back of my mind—he's a fucking brilliant writer, and when he cares about factual matters, you only have to do fact-checking as a matter of professionalism; still, he seems to think that revolvers have safety switches, and has a typical New Yorker's knowledge of cars, which mainly seems to mean that he thinks it's something driven by a cab driver—and got to work on the brick.

I finished the first pass—blatant typos and grammar problems that screamed "FIX ME," as well as compiling the character list and making notes on continuity matters—and flipped the brick over to start again. I've done enough skiffy and fantasy that I can manage (translation: query; remember: I'm just a copy editor) the coarser problems you usually run into—broadswords being used like fencing foils and horses that gallop for miles without doing the obvious thing that would happen, assuming you could force a horse to gallop for miles: It would up and die on you.

There was a pretty nice scene that involved a fight in an alley—I admit it; I'm a sucker for fight scenes—but the talented writer who had penned this undoubted masterpiece hadn't put in street lamps, or even a full moon conveniently overhead, and I spent a few minutes thinking about why anybody would put street lamps in an alley or anywhere else next to the buildings of a low-technology city where all the wattle-and-daub and wooden structures would, sooner or later, give more than enough illumination for a really spiffy fight, at least until they fell into a pile of flames and ashes on the combatants.

Fuck it, I finally decided. "Fuck it" is my usual fallback position, after all.

I'll push the limits of what a copyeditor is supposed to do, but if they want me to play editor, they can start paying me for it. So I just put in a Post-it querying how it seemed odd that they all were be able to see to fight, there being no light and all, and noted that in the dark the normally blue eyes of the villain had become a frightening slate "grey"—which was corrected to "gray"; this is the US of A, not Jolly Olde England—left it at that, and plowed on.

Look: What I do is utterly devoid of romance and it doesn't pay particularly well. But there is a certain something to doing something you know how to do well, and then doing it as well as you can, and the rewards don't only come in the mail, with little pieces of paper that say those glorious words, "Pay to the Order Of." Sometimes they just come by plowing through a manuscript and thinking that if the guy who wrote it pays attention, he won't be embarrassed.

Not a major victory, but you take what victories you can in life. At least I do.

Still, there's only so much plowing you can do, whether you're a farmer or a copy editor, so around two I decided that I needed more of a break than a quick piss, or even a slow one, so I whistled for Snake and headed out the door.

My first thought was to head out to the Thompsen farm and see if I could nail a few chucks, but it was kind of late in the day for that, at least by present Hemingway household standards. When I lived alone, I could have come in after dark and eaten what supper I wanted when I wanted, but it was Tenishia's turn to cook, and the last time I'd been late for supper when she was cooking, she'd put the roast in the oven—on low, to be fair—and it had cooked until it chewed like shoe leather and didn't taste much better, and things had been a bit silent around the house for the next couple of days. Kind of reminiscent of my marriage.

My second thought had been to head down to the Dine-A-Mite for a cup of tea and maybe a quick chat with Bob Aarsted, but I'd been drinking enough tea lately, and dealing with Bridget's dad more than enough, so I just walked for a while. I wasn't sure how long Doc Sherve's advice to get more exercise would hold—I'm not much on resolutions, most of the time—but taking it a day at a time, as time and the day permitted, didn't sound like a bad idea.

There were the sounds of voices and some sort of relatively quiet clanging coming from behind Minnie Hansen's house, so Snake and I ducked around the side yard to the back, which was devoted to her garden.

It had fallen on hard times over the winter, as gardens tend to. The raspberry brambles that rimmed it and went on to grow wild in the woods beyond her house had grown enough to keep Sleeping Beauty safe from the semi-necrophiliac lusts of Prince Charming, although the haphazard brush pile over in the corner of the garden showed that the kids had made a start on cutting it all back.

Still, it looked like it had been done with a chainsaw wielded by somebody wearing a leather mask.

Not that it was all a disaster. The rose bushes were well-trimmed, although it looked likely that some of them hadn't made it through the winter. I guess they were getting old, too, or maybe Minnie hadn't covered quite all of them well enough with the those big plastic things that look like inverted garbage cans. An East Dakota winter isn't just hard on people—come spring, the windbreak stands of trees always contain a few that appear to have exploded during the cold, and Bill Aamodt makes a few extra bucks cutting them into foot-long splits and selling them by the cord to town folks with wood-stoves—we have a few of those; Yotl seems to be the most popular brand—too lazy to cut their own.

But mostly it just looked bare.

Minnie was never much for perennials—the roses and the thyme and sage aside; she wasn't a stickler for unreasonable consistency, either—and every spring she churned over the soil, stirred in fertilizer of various sorts like she was mixing a cake, and planted annuals in whatever combination suited her fancy that year. I don't know whether it was a matter of careful planning, natural talent, or if she was just consistently lucky, but the results seemed to bear out her methods, whatever they were.

The general Hardwood consensus is that Ephie Oppegaard has the nicest-looking garden, but it's always the same every year. I prefer Minnie's.

Almost before you could blink, the floor of the garden would be, say, an explosion of nasturtiums and daisies, pansies and dwarf snapdragons, with rows of geraniums and marigolds looming above them, topped only by the huge sunflowers that somehow always looked more impressive as they rimmed her garden than the endless fields of them out in the country did.

Not that a practical Hardwood woman like Minnie Hansen would grow only flowers. There would zucchini, of course, because gardeners always do have to make a point to plant vegetables nobody would want to eat. And cucumbers for pickles—it would be a shame not to grow something nobody would want to eat and then not do something with them if you could.

But there would also be be rows of different kinds of basil in shades of bright green and dark purple, and tomatoes, ranging in sizes from huge to tiny, and the bright green tops of carrots and onions . . . and the chives that she'd plant not just in the garden, but along the sidewalks out front, between the peonies—they supposedly chase some insects away—and that would spread out into the lawn the way chives do, and would make every Saturday morning smell like a cooking hamburger when the lawnmower ran.

I've got to say, it didn't look much like any classroom to me. Jeff and Joshua were swinging hoes to churn up the dirt, and Tenishia was down on her knees with a pair of pruning shears at the far end, snipping away at the raspberry bramble. Far as I could tell, a chainsaw would have been a better tool for that job, but I didn't notice Minnie asking me that, so I didn't mention it.

Minnie was sitting at the backyard table, drinking—coffee, I assume—out of an old china cup, book bags and books spread out on the table in front of her, papers held down with stones with what was probably excessive force, given the light breeze.

She smiled as she noticed me. "Good afternoon, Ernest. As you can see, work proceeds apace."

Well, "work" was one word for it. "Gardening" was a better one, and the gardening seemed to be proceeding apace, at that, but I couldn't see any other learning getting done.

I thought about making a comment to that effect, but only in the sense that I sometimes think about sticking a fork in my eye.

"You may sit and visit for a while," she said, "if you'd like, but we'll have to get back to work shortly."

"Yes, ma'am."

Jeffie gave me a smile as he worked his hoe. It's probably possible to work a farm kid hard enough to make it actually be punishment, but it would be a challenge to do that in a backyard garden. Jeffie spent more time than I care to think about loading hundred-pound bags of feed and seed and God knows what else on and off the back of his dad's pickup, and lifting fifty-pound cans of milk onto the bed of a Bobcat—when he wasn't hitching and unhitching various implements of destruction to the tractor or the combine.

Working a two-pound hoe on soft topsoil was more of a break than a punishment.

Joshua Ginsburg, on the other hand, was struggling to keep up, and was only lagging a little behind Jeffie. He had stripped down to his T-shirt and jeans, and, despite the coolness of the day, the T-shirt was darkened with sweat at the armpits and from neck to navel down the front.

"Children," Minnie said, raising her voice, although not much. They all perked up right away. "I think that's enough of a warmup for the day, and you've earned some classwork."

A pitcher of lemonade stood on the table, along with three glasses; Joshua Ginsburg dropped his hoe to the dirt and made for the table, while Tenishia and Jeffie just stood for a moment, breathing heavily.

"No, no, no," she said. "The tools get run through the hose first, and then put away in the toolshed," she said, not as though she was chastising them, but like she had read it off of some stone tablets that an early student of hers had brought to class. "And you'll want to wash your hands as well."

I got up to help—it's not impossible for me to sit when others are working, but it takes more effort than pitching in does. Rinsing off the spades and the hoes under the garden hose took only a minute or two, anyway, although I did manage to get my relatively clean shirt splashed with some muddy water all by myself.

I'm not sure, when Tenishia put her thumb over the end of the hose to blast a stubborn clump off of a shovel and the water caught me just below the belt, that it was deliberate or accidental.

Couldn't tell by looking at her, but that wasn't anything resembling unusual.

Still, only a few minutes later the five of us were sitting at the table. The three of them were pretty dirty except for their hands and faces, and I looked like I'd pissed myself, so I moved the chair a little closer to the table.

The three of them were already on their second glasses of lemonade while I was sipping at my first. Not enough sugar for my taste, but it wasn't bad.

Shirts and jeans were dirty enough to be part of the "before" section of a Tide commercial, but hands and faces had been tended to.

Minnie Hansen set her teacup down.

"We'll begin with *The Adventures of Huckleberry Finn*, by Mr. Samuel Langhorne Clemens," she said, "writing under the nom de plume of 'Mark Twain.' I take it that you have all read it before?"

Joshua nodded, but Jeffie shook his head, and, after a moment, Tenishia shook her head, too.

"Well, I guess I should be surprised as well as disappointed, but I'm not surprised—and you needn't look at me like that, Miss Washington; I was criticizing the schools, not you. Joshua, you'd oblige me if you'd begin reading it out loud from the beginning."

He shrugged as he picked up the book.

"We can do with a little less shrugging, if you please," she said. "If you've a comment to make, you can make it out loud."

He just opened the book.

Good choice, kid.

" 'You don't know about me, without you have read a book by the name of "The Adventures of Tom Sawyer," but that ain't no matter. That book—' "

"That's not the beginning," she said. "From the *beginning*, if you please, Joshua Ginsburg."

I was expecting to hear the copyright notice read out loud— it's what I would have done, probably—but he just flipped back a couple of pages.

"You mean this? 'Persons attempting to find a motive in this narrative will be prosecuted; persons attempting to find a moral in it will be banished; persons attempting to find a plot in it will be shot.

"'BY ORDER OF THE AUTHOR, Per G.G., CHIEF OF ORDNANCE.'"

"Yes, that's precisely what I mean." She turned to Tenishia. "Please continue."

Tenishia started to shrug but stopped herself, and read, "'Explanatory. In this book a number of dialects are used, to wit: the Missouri *negro* dialect; the extremest form of the backwoods Southwestern dialect; the ordinary "Pike County" dialect; and four modified varieties of this last. The shadings have not been done in a haphazard fashion, or by guesswork; but painstakingly, and with the trustworthy guidance and support of personal familiarity with these several forms of speech.'"

Snake was probably the only one present who had missed Tenishia's emphasis on the word "negro," and I'd have been perfectly happy to sit and sip my lemonade see what happened when they got to "nigger," which was going to be soon. It had been some years since I'd read Huck Finn, but there were more "niggers" in it than in a Quentin Tarantino monologue—but Minnie held up a finger, signaling for Tenishia to pause, and waited until she did just that before turning to me.

"Thank you for stopping by, Ernest," she said.

She might as well have said, "Go away, now, please, before you interfere any more."

Oh, well. You can't have everything. It's in the rule book.

Jeff Bjerke's big blue Bronco was just rolling up the street, heading in the direction of my house.

"Hey, Sparky—I was heading for your place. Get in."

I let Snake in the back and climbed in front.

"What's up? Some problem?"

"Nah," he said. "Bob just wants you and me down at town hall, and you weren't answering your phone."

"I wasn't in."

"Yeah. I figured that."

"So? What's going on?"

"Congratulations. Your police officer's license has been approved. Chief."

Shit.

Hardwood Town Hall, such as it is, is a small, one-story, flat-topped stucco building right next to the Post Awful and across from the bank. The front wall is mainly window, the inside protected by closed Venetian blinds, and with the rather pretentious words

HARDWOOD NORTH DAKOTA GOVERNMENT CENTER
435 SOUTH MAIN STREET
HARDWOOD ND 58267-4223

in gilt letters.

When the Post Awful went to those nine-digit zip codes to make sorting easier for the mail carriers, I guess they had to include Hardwood, too, but it does seem kind of silly. You need a nine-digit zip code in Hardwood about like you need a Global Positioning System in my bathroom to keep you pissing in the toilet instead of the sink.

Below the pretentious announcement was a peeling decal of the North Dakota state seal.

The seal shows a tree in the center, surrounded by three bundles of wheat, with a plow, an anvil, and a bow and arrow lying around nearby, and off to the side an Indian on horseback chasing a buffalo toward the setting sun, but the wheat bundles looked more like mushrooms, and time and sun had faded the details in the feathers in the Indian's headdress and made it look

like he had put on a knight's tilting helmet, which probably
wasn't going to help him catch the buffalo, all things considered.

Despite the fading, you could still read the state motto—
"Liberty and Union Now and Forever, One and Inseparable." I
guess it's a warning to any Confederate sympathizers that
might ride by, figuring the time was ripe for another attack on
Fort Sumter, but will maybe consider settling for the grain elevator if they're not scared out of it.

Despite the signage and all, to my eyes town hall looked like
it used to be a sewing shop, but that's maybe just because my
eyes know it used to be Swenson's Sewing Shop.

I opened the door, enjoying the gentle tinkle of the bell
mounted above it. It didn't look like a sewing shop anymore.

A folding screen hid all but the top of the jail cell built into
the far right corner, and rows of filing cabinets covered the rest
of the righthand wall.

Emma Thompsen's desk, complete with phones and computer terminal—you can't get away from computers these
days—was just behind the counter, facing it, and the big
gunmetal-gray office desk next to it held another computer
and an assortment of printers and copiers, and an old thermal
fax machine that was busy excreting a sheet of paper into a
metal basket that hung from the side of the desk.

The Triple-S had been a typical one-big-room-in-front-and-
storeroom-in-back sort of place, but the rear wall had been
knocked down and the left side of the entire floor been parti-
tioned off into three private offices with frosted-glass doors.

The one with the door that informed anybody who cared to
know that Ole K. Olson was the Chief of the Hardwood Fire
Department was open, revealing stacks of cardboard boxes. For
whatever reason, Ole apparently had been given an office here,
but, reasonably, spent most of his working hours at the fire station down the street—when he wasn't drinking weak coffee at
the Dine-A-Mite—and all the time with some some sort of

high-tech phone either on his belt or his nightstand or under his pillow, for all that I know. He bragged he didn't even know what the inside of the town hall looked like even more often than he bragged that, with the fancy phone, he could record a quick message, hit one button, and have it call the entire volunteer list all by itself.

The door that said ROBERT K. AARSTED under big black letters proclaiming him MAYOR stood closed.

The other door had a card table, covered with newspapers, in front of it, and Bob himself, his work shirt protected by a paint-spattered smock, was standing in front of the one that used to say JEFFREY J. BJERKE under CHIEF OF POLICE, but that now said ERNEST HEMIN, with Bob carefully daubing a little paintbrush to fill in the "g." It looked to me like it would end up a bit lopsided, even when he finished, but there are so many lovely times, in this life, to keep your mouth shut.

I couldn't quite see his legs under the smock, but my guess was that Bridget's were nicer, and, besides, he was wearing long pants.

Aarsted tapped the cover back on the paint can and set the paintbrush down on its edge, then wiped his hands on the smock before shrugging out of it and setting it down on the card table. He looked down at his big hands, made a face as though he was surprised not to find any paint on them, then gave a shrug.

He stooped to make his manners with Snake, then looked up at me. "Do me a favor?"

"Sure."

"When you stop by town hall in the future, please make sure we don't have visitors from out of town before you bring the dog in, okay?"

I nodded. "Okay." If these visitors—presumably the trauma-commission people—needed to have kept from them the deep, dark, dirty secret that there were actually dogs in the town of Hardwood, I'd do my best to keep it.

Maybe I could get Snake a disguise.

He looked me up and down. "I was going to get Bob Thompsen from the *Gleaner* to take a picture of me swearing you in, but I guess that had better wait until you look more like a police chief and less like a beachcomber." Yeah, sure. Like he'd ever seen a beachcomber. "Jeff?"

"We're working it, we're working on it." He was standing next to where Emma Thompsen was sitting in front of her desk, punching on her computer keyboard. He looked down at her screen, pointed, and muttered something. She nodded, punched a couple of keys, and the printer began to make printer noises.

Aarsted handed me a comb. "Run this through your hair, please."

I was disposed to argue, but just did what I was told as he picked up a Polaroid camera off Emma's desk.

"Jeff—out of the way," he said, stepping too close to me. "Sparky, lower your arms and look at the camera; I don't want to get the comb in the picture, okay?" There was a bright flash. "Okay—that's for your wallet ID."

He stalked over to Emma's desk and picked up a clipboard. "Here's a certified photocopy of your police license—Emma hangs on to the original. Fold it and keep it in your wallet until the plastic ID card arrives." He picked up a cell phone from the table, a plastic belt clip, and a manual, and handed them over. "Here's your phone; your radio's on order."

The phone was one of those flip-open types, so I pressed the little button on the side that flipped the cover up, and thought for a moment about saying, "Scotty, beam me up," but decided against it.

"Just clip it to your belt," he said, and stood there until I did.

Jeff nodded. "I'll run you through the basics on the phone—there's a couple of combinations you don't want to press unless you really need to. And leave that red button at the top alone—it dials the Highway Patrol internal emergency number."

Aarsted furrowed his brow and turned to Emma. "I know I'm forgetting something, and—"

She laughed as she pointed toward his office door. "I won't tell her if you don't."

"Oh." Aarsted walked over to his office door and opened it. "He's here."

Bridget walked out, tucking some makeup thingy into her purse. I'd have called it a "compact" if I was working, but it was a makeup thingy at the moment.

She was dressed more for church than for whatever we were doing here, in a cream-colored dress that was a little too tight at the bosom, but pleasantly so, even though it fell to below her knees and didn't even have a slit up the side to reveal a flash of leg. It did look a little strange, what with the sneakers instead of pumps.

She was definitely wearing too much makeup; I think her cheekbones always look just fine without some dark rouge to highlight them, and I've never figured out what genius figured that a woman's eyelids look better if they're colored blue, and, under the proper circumstances, I can find a woman's lips just fine without tiny brown lines drawn around them to guide me, thank you very much. Don't need landing lights, either.

"Hi there," she said. "Dad thought I should be here for this; hope you don't mind." She gave him a look, and he gestured at my dirty jeans. Apparently, she was supposed to be part of the picture he had wanted taken, even though that plan had gone by the boards.

I shook my head. "Not a problem."

"Well." Aarsted cleared his throat. "Okay, let's do this. Raise your right hand," he said. "Do you solemnly swear to uphold the laws and Constitution of the United States of America, the laws and Constitution of the Sovereign State of North Dakota, and, to the best of your ability, faithfully execute the position of Chief of Police in and of the town of Hardwood?"

We're all capable of being silly, me more so than most. I know this all was a put-up job, and there was no reason to take it seriously.

"I do," I said. But the truth is that there was a catch in my voice.

I lowered my hand.

"Congratulations, Chief," he said, shaking my hand. Jeff and Emma shook my hand, too, and then Bridget came over and leaned over not quite close enough to get her dress dirty as she simulated hugging me.

"Congratulations, Chief," she said, then whispered, "you sorry bastard."

Aarsted clapped his hands together. "Okay, okay, enough of this—Jeff?"

"Yup." He'd finished folding the piece of paper that Emma had printed out, and stuffed it into the back pocket of his jeans. "We'll be back when we get back."

Bridget nodded. "Have a good time storming the castle." She beckoned to Snake, who obediently wagged his way over. "I've got the dog, and I'll get Tenishia to hold your supper."

Yeah, have her hold it between her knees, came to mind—I had no illusions that Tenishia would find my being late for supper acceptable—but I just said, "Thanks."

Jeff picked up a briefcase from next to Emma's desk and beckoned to me. "Let's go."

"Go?"

"Grand Forks—and we'd better move it. Streicher's closes at six, and we'd better run by your house first so you can change."

"Huh?"

Aarsted nodded. "Shower, too. Use soap."

I just gave them a look.

Jeff made a face. "We're presenting you as a police chief, not some undercover cop playing migrant farm worker, so you need a shower and a change of clothes, and a shave wouldn't be a bad idea."

"Would the two of you please move it?" Aarsted was starting to get irritated.

Which made at least two of us. Well, three, if you counted Bridget, although I couldn't tell from looking who she was irritated at.

I'd probably find out later, whether or not I wanted to.

Jeff frowned when I lit up a cigarette, but didn't say anything, and I rolled down the window a crack to let it suck the smoke outside.

I was clean and freshly shaved, and in a fresh work shirt and clean jeans, and a light spring jacket over it all. At Jeff's insistence, I'd gotten Dad's old shub-nosed revolver out of the drawer and put it in the holster that Jeff had lent me last winter and I'd never gotten around to returning, and then the holster on my belt.

"So," I said, "anybody going to tell me what this Streicher's is, or why we're going there?"

"Police-supply store in East Grand Forks," he said. "You need a couple of uniforms, and some other things. Fair amount of other things." He thought about it for a moment. "And my guess is that it won't do any political harm if the word gets out in Grand Forks about all this, and about how pissed I am that you got my job. Cops gossip more than anybody else I know."

"You pissed?"

"That's the official story," he said. "I didn't do anything wrong, mind, but I'm officially not happy at officially taking a couple of months with no pay so that the town can qualify for the fed COPs money."

"You can pull that off?"

He smiled. "You should have seen me as Shylock in *Merchant of Venice*, senior year. 'If you prick a town cop, does he not bleed? If you take his job away and give it to some old guy, shall he not be avenged?' "

"Okay, forget the official story. You pissed?"

He sat silent for a while. "Maybe a little."

"At Bob or me?"

"Shit, I can't afford to be pissed at my father-in-law, and if I was, I sure as shit wouldn't tell you about it."

"Oh. I'm known to have a loose mouth?"

"I wouldn't say that. But you *are* known to have Bridget living with you, and she's just as much his daughter as Karen is, maybe more."

I couldn't let that pass. "Bob Aarsted, right about now, is not my favorite person in the world, but I think he'd cut off his tongue before saying a word that suggested that Karen's any less of his kid because she's adopted."

He gripped the wheel until his knuckles were white. It was his turn to get angry. "That wasn't what I was talking about, asshole—I was just saying that Bridget is more like Bob than Karen is, and that the two of them seem awfully close. That's all."

I didn't take a lot of time to think it over, although my first reaction was that it was bullshit. "I'm sorry, Jeff. No excuse, but I'm under a little strain, and my mouth is running off too much."

His laugh sounded only a little forced. "Apology accepted, Chief."

It was all I could do not to growl. "I wouldn't mind if you called me 'Chief' if it was as a show of the great respect and regard in which you hold me, but if it's just to jerk my chain some, could you find another way?"

"Maybe." He snorted. "We'll see how it goes. But when we've got those visitors from the trauma-center commission, if I use it a lot, I hope you won't get all twitchy about it."

That seemed reasonable, and I said so. Then: "You still didn't say whether or not you and I've got a problem, Jeff."

He was silent for a few moments. "Well, let me put it this way: I'll still drive deer toward you."

He took his eyes off the road only long enough to watch me nod.

That's a big deal, at least to me. Jeff and Bob and I mostly hunt from stands, rather than driving deer—personal preference, and as long as I can get my deer without a lot of work, I'll do it the lazy man's way. It's safer, in a lot of ways. You shoot down, rather than across, and while a bullet fired horizontally or higher can go for miles, one pointed down just doesn't go far—either into the deer or into the ground—but you've still got to know where the other hunters are, and you've got to know that they're not going to get carried away and jerk their triggers without considering, preferably in advance, where the bullet might go if they miss.

But there's a difference between "mostly" and "only"— we've never had a morning where all three of us have gotten a deer from the stands, and around ten or so we tend to meet back at camp so that we can work out a drive.

Driving deer is different. If I'm stomping through the woods making noise, I don't want to be walking in the direction of somebody I don't trust with my life, somebody who'll even think of raising a rifle to his shoulder, much less putting his finger anywhere near a trigger, just because his heart has started racing over some rustling sounds in the brush.

Hunting's not a real dangerous sport—it's not like skiing or football or anything risky—but it's like life: If somebody insists on being stupid, that somebody or another somebody is probably going to get hurt, and hurt bad, and I don't want to be any of the somebodies involved.

He was quiet for a while, and just drove.

"But I'm not sure 'pissed' is the right word," he finally said. "Concerned, maybe. I'm starting to think you're a trouble magnet, Sparky. If you hadn't brought Tenishia into town, we wouldn't have had to worry about those gangbanger assholes from Minneapolis coming out to get her."

His eyes didn't meet mine, and I don't think that was just because he was a good enough driver to watch the road.

Which he was.

Doc Holliday and Horse and I had come to terms with Sharif Harris and his little playmates, and I'd kept strictly to the terms of our agreement—staying out of Minneapolis wasn't exactly a major concession on my part—and there'd been no sign of any more of his thugs on the way out from there. The money Prez had skimmed from Harris, the money Harris believed Prez had frittered away, was safely resting in a lockbox in Tenishia's closet, and it would put her through college, just like her father wanted.

Case closed, as far as I could tell, although I had little doubt that the Minnesota Gang Strike Force, or whatever they called it, were still interested in Harris. But that wasn't my problem. Saving the world from the evils of drugs is somebody else's impossible mission, not mine.

"Yeah," I said. "But she's Prez's kid. Maybe I should have handled it some other way, but, shit, Jeff, I didn't think for a moment anybody would come looking for her here. I didn't have any reason to."

He nodded. "I didn't think so. But it sounds to me like you're making excuses, maybe, just a little."

"Maybe."

You take care of your own, I've always believed. But part of me taking care of Tenishia had put the rest of the town in harm's way, and if I said I didn't feel guilty about that I'd be lying. Those assholes Father Winter had done in for us wouldn't have known where to look for Tenishia, even though they knew she was staying with me, and undoubtedly had my street address—you can find it in the phone book, and some idiot police captain or lieutenant in Minneapolis had talked too much.

It wasn't just Tenishia and me who had been in danger. They could have gotten my address from the phone company, but my address wouldn't have done them any good—the phone company thinks it send its bills to me at 21 First Street, Hardwood ND 58267-4223, and since the accounting departments at the various publishers I work for are as anal as the phone company, they send their checks there, too.

I'm a human being, not a number, as somebody or other once said, and my house doesn't have a number; my street doesn't have a sign.

Would the gangbangers have just turned around and gone home? Maybe. But probably not. Harris wasn't the kind to take excuses real well.

They certainly wouldn't have spent a lot of time walking around town in daylight. Malik and his buddies would have been more than a little conspicuous.

Most likely they would've come back into town, say, after dark—and it gets dark awfully early in winter—and walked in somebody's door. They wouldn't even need to kick it in; we don't lock our doors in Hardwood like city folks do. Then they'd have asked where to find Tenishia, and probably not real politely.

And that would've been bad, real bad. A stubborn old biddy like Minnie Hansen wouldn't have told them anything, but I've had nightmares about her lying dead on her living-room floor, or one of those assholes sticking a gun in Tommy Olson's mouth and thinking about what Bob and Osa would have done, and what they would've *had* to have done would have been done to them.

How do you take care of the people when doing that endangers others you care about?

Answer: badly. A simple true answer and one that's utterly unsatisfactory.

"I'll do my best," I said.

"Good."

I nodded. "Okay. And if that means acting like a cop, I'll act like a cop."

"Yeah, you do that. You try to act like what you think a cop acts like and it'll work real, real well." He shook his head. "What you want to do in Streicher's—or anywhere else the two of us are on duty—is mainly talk as little as you can and ask me what I think. If I give you one choice, you take it. If I give you two, take the one I'm not recommending. That should hold us for now. The gun's a problem, though. Maybe."

"Oh? Yeah? But I'm legal." I would have patted at my wallet, which held my carry permit, but I was sitting on it.

"Yeah, you're legal, but . . ." He shrugged. "It's like this: If you're a cop on duty, you've got a gun. So you've got a gun. If you don't have a gun—"

"Folks will start to wonder how much of a phony I am?"

"Or, more likely, where you've hid it, and that'll draw a lot of attention. There's all sorts of rigs for carrying it under a shirt, or the good old ankle holster, which is about as useful as leaving it in the trunk, or maybe Thunderwear—"

"Thunderwear?"

"Kind of like a jockstrap that holds a gun."

"They way my dad used to say it, never point a gun at something you're not willing to shoot."

I've been around guns all my life, and don't remember ever thinking of them as some sort of magic wand or demonic death machine, but the idea of holstering a pistol by pointing it at even a less sensitive portion of my anatomy didn't have a lot of appeal to me.

"Yeah. 'Is that a gun in your pants or are you just happy to see me,' eh?" We were friends again, at least for the moment, it seemed. "Well, as I was saying, the snubby's a little unusual these days, but a lot of old-timers carry them, particularly plainclothes types—"

"So do you."

"Well, yeah." He patted at the right side of his waist. "Smith and Wesson Model 42 Airweight. Sixteen ounces. If I've got to carry stuff on my belt, I keep it as light as I can. You ever carry a gun, day to day?"

"Well, yeah, there was a time," I said, letting it rest there. Like I say, I don't play war hero.

"Oh, that," he nodded. "Yeah. M-16?"

"Well, that, too—but mainly it was a 1911A1 in a shoulder holster." Of course, during the times when I was detailed to Bosco's back deck—you can't see shit from inside a tank, except for a very narrow wedge of vision—I carried an M79 grenade launcher, too. Sort of like an oversized skeet gun for oversized skeet that are shooting at you.

"Well, the one absolute truth about a handgun on your belt is that they don't ever get lighter as the day goes by." He shrugged. "Nothing on your belt does. For anything short of setting up to do speeding stops—then I've got to put on that goddamn Sam Browne thing with all the other shit—you'll see, and"— his grin broadened—"since Hardwood PD regulations permit officers to carry a pistol of choice, I just carry this." He patted the shotgun mounted between us. "If I ever get nervous about something, the shotgun comes out real quick."

"Wait a minute. You said that this Streicher's place is in *East* Grand Forks."

"Yeah?"

I shook my head. "I don't think my carry permit is good in the People's Republic."

Grand Forks is in North Dakota; East Grand Forks is just barely across the river, in Minnesota.

Last winter, I had, in fact, carried a gun in the People's Republic of Minnesota a couple of times, during that Tenishia mess, but I hadn't had any illusions that it was even vaguely le-

gal, and had gone out of my way to avoid police—for that reason, among others. I'm not overly fond of cops.

Even though I was apparently one, at least sort of, at least at
the moment.

Walking into a cop store with a gun on my hip didn't sound
terribly sensible, and I started to unbuckle my belt.

"Oh, sit still. Your civilian carry permit isn't any good in
Minnesota, but your badge and license are, as long as you're on
official duty. Reciprocity; you carry on your badge."

I'd forgotten about the license.

"Is this official duty?"

Never be afraid to ask a stupid question, I always say.

He grinned. "You could ask the police chief of Hardwood if
this is official duty. Or, better, tell anybody who asks, and then
introduce yourself. Realistically, there won't be any questions."
He shook his head. "Just play it cool. We don't want anybody
doubting you're really in charge, and—oh, shit." He braked
the Bronco hard enough that I thought he'd lose it for a second, and I grabbed onto the grab handle at the juncture of
door and roof hard enough that it hurt. "Fucking *shit*."

I didn't see what he was pissed off about until I noticed the
snake of rubber skidmarks that terminated on the gravel shoulder. Some sort of accident?

He had punched the release on his seatbelt and was out of
the car fast; I followed.

I saw what he meant. There were bits of metal and glass
scattered on the road, and big splatter of what sure looked like
congealing blood.

He took a look up and down the ditch, then ran a few yards
ahead and quickly squatted in front of something, then
straightened slowly with something in his hand. If he looked
any more relaxed, he probably would've fallen right over.

"Well, thank God," he said, smiling broadly as he walked over.
He held out his palm, showing me the little chunk of antler.

Spring growth—it was still covered with a light gray fuzz. "Just a deer," he said, tossing the antler fragment off into the field.

Hard to tell, so early in the year, what the little green growths are, but I was guessing flax, or maybe chard.

"Thank you, Jesus." He was actually shaking, and sat himself down on the step of the Bronco.

"What did you think it was?"

"Well, being a *professional* police officer, I try to avoid having opinions until I've gathered and examined what evidence there is, but my first worry is that some driver hit somebody crossing the road, or maybe a hitchhiker." He pointed to the north, where a windbreak of trees stood at the far end of the field. "Big Steve's farm is just past there, and," he said, jerking his thumb over his shoulder, "Sammy Aamodt's just beyond there."

I guess I knew that, but I'd been paying attention to the conversation, and in the back of my mind enjoying not having to drive or worry about where we had to make the turnoff, so that I hadn't been paying attention to exactly where we were.

"And," he went on, "what with Giselle Larson and Bobby Aamodt having just discovered the joy of sex not long ago, I was half-worried we'd be finding a body." He shook his head. "Just a deer." He got to his feet and started to pull himself back up into the Bronco. "Well, shit, we could waste a few hours trying to find where it wandered off to die, but—"

"Nah." Maybe I shouldn't have opened my mouth, but I'd been reining it in a lot of late, and the feeling was getting old. "Check out the blood trail."

When I go for my deer, I'm a big believer in what they call the "poacher's shot"—aim for the spine, just at the back of the neck, and you either miss the deer entirely or drop it right where it stands. Worst case is you get it through the neck, and then you're no worse off than if you'd done what most hunters do.

Most hunters go for for the dinner-plate-sized target just aft of the front shoulder; you don't have to be near as accurate as with a neck shot, even though a shot through the spine will drop the deer instantly—and painlessly, I suspect, and certainly hope. The standard shot leaves you more room for error, and it'll eventually kill the deer.

But it's not like you see in the movies. They don't get thrown back a dozen feet, tumbling end on end. They don't just handily drop there, like with a poacher's shot. With a decent bullet, even if you're not lucky enough to hit the heart, you'll puncture enough arteries and veins and probably both lungs. Heart or lungs or both—it'll take off, but drown in its own blood and die pretty quick. Yet deer can move *fast*. More often than not, you've got to spiral out a fair distance before you pick up the first dark blood against the white snow, and I've known people to walk the better part of a mile to find it, even with a good, solid shot.

But a bullet is a tiny little thing, and this deer had been hit by a car, or, more likely, a truck—big and fast enough, if I was reading the marks on the road and in the gravel well enough, to throw the deer dozens of feet before it got to its feet and ran off, and I was surprised Jeff couldn't read the trail as well as I could.

"It went off that way," I said, pointing. There was a culvert a few hundred yards away where a farming road across one of big Steve's fields crossed the highway. "Fair chance it lay down in there to die."

"Yeah." He nodded. "Well, if that's the case, it's not likely to stagger back onto the highway, and we can just call the DNR to come find it and pick— Where are you going?"

There's lots of things I'll do, but leaving a wounded animal to die in misery isn't one of them.

"I'd better check it out." I patted the butt of my snubby. "If it's not dead, I'll put it down." A snubby revolver wouldn't be my first or second or twentieth choice to put down a wounded animal. The only thing I've ever used Dad's old snubby for is plinking away at cans out behind Jeff Thompsen's place and demonstrating to myself that it was about as accurate—in my hands, at least—as a thrown rock. But it was all I had.

Our eyes locked for a moment, and we weren't friends, or a real cop teaching an old man to play police chief. We were a couple of hunters, and the one who had been hunting deer for longer than the other had been alive was reminding the kid of one of the big rules: You don't leave a wounded animal to die in pain. You can talk about all the reasons for it all you want—and there's lots—but you just don't do it.

He finally nodded. "Sure." He leaned over to reach in through the door of the Bronco and punch a button, and the back hatch popped open.

He pulled the tattered old green blanket off the lockbox. The box was about the size of a footlocker, and he twirled the combination faster than my eye could follow, then flipped the top up and handed me out a lever rifle and took another one for himself. Not exactly high-tech police stuff—both were pretty ordinary-looking Winchester 94s.

I must have given him a surprised look. "Hey," he said, "it's not like this is the first wounded deer I've ever put down. Tube's full; chamber should be empty."

There's no way to check that without working the lever—which puts a round into the chamber—so I just made sure the safety catch was on and cradled the rifle in my arm, pointed off away from Jeff, then carefully made my way down the slope into the ditch. I figured it was better than fifty-fifty that I'd slip and fall—easy to do when your hands are full—but I made it to the bottom without more than a couple of scary moments.

Jeff, damn him, just ran down the side of the ditch, his rifle held in one hand, pointed skyward, his feet never seeming to slip or slide—like a fucking goat.

Color me jealous.

Following the blood trail wasn't a problem. It made, straight as an arrow, for the culvert.

It was lying inside there.

The thing about deer is that they seem to keep changing sizes from moment to moment. You see a big buck through a scope, and it looks like it could loom over a cow, but when you shoot it and drop it—and I'm a good enough shot and a lazy enough hunter that I'll usually pass up anything except a neck shot—and it'll look to be only about as big as a good-sized dog when it's lying there.

Of course, if you don't make the poacher's shot and have to go looking for the deer, then when you try to haul it out of whatever godforsaken brush it's managed to work itself in to die, it grows again and doesn't shrink an ounce when you field-dress it—which involves taking the guts out and leaving them behind, which should lower the weight, but doesn't—and then haul it up to the nearest road.

Utterly still, this one looked absolutely tiny, and, between the brightness of the late-afternoon sun and the darkness inside the culvert, I couldn't tell if its chest was moving up and down. It wasn't moving otherwise. One back leg was twisted up and around at such an angle that I couldn't have guessed whether it was the right or the left.

"You got a flashlight?" I asked.

"No. It's on that fucking Sam Browne belt back in the car, and I didn't think I'd need all that fucking shit," he said. His voice was level, but Jeff doesn't usually swear; my newly created professional opinion was that he was shook up and maybe a little embarrassed at having been more concerned with Bob Aarsted's timetable than with more important things. "Want me to go get it?" he asked.

It was at that moment that the deer twitched and opened its eyes. I guess I should report that its eyes were full of pain and agony, but they just looked like big deer eyes to me, so I'll leave it at that.

"Shit," he said.

"Yeah."

He just stood there for a moment, so I worked the lever—sure enough, the chamber had been empty—raised the Winchester to my shoulder, and took careful aim between the eyes, then laid my finger on the trigger and gradually increased its pressure until my finger was pulling so hard on the trigger that it hurt, and I realized that I'd forgotten to take the safety off.

"Oops," I explained.

I flicked the safety off, brought the rifle back up, taking aim between the eyes, and forced myself not to either hurry or stall. It wasn't the deer's fault, after all.

When you make a good shot, you increase the pressure on the trigger so gradually that the shot itself always comes as a surprise, and I wasn't used to this rifle's trigger anyway, so it bucked some in my hands as it roared, leaving behind a loud ringing in my ears and an unambiguously dead deer.

And one hell of a mess in the culvert.

Since I didn't have anything useful to do—and since it didn't seem likely that a bunch of wounded deer would spring out of the grass, needing to be put down—I worked the lever five times to clear the rest of the rounds from the Winchester, and Jeff did the same with his. Then we took a few moments to pick the rounds up off the ground, and I tucked mine in my pocket while he did the same with his. Just out of habit, we both worked our actions one more time to be sure that, yes, we each now had an empty rifle.

"Shit." He frowned as he looked at the mess we'd left in the culvert. "Normally I'd haul it back up to the shoulder for the DNR, but—if you don't mind, Sparky—let's just call them from the car and explain the situation."

I nodded. "Yeah." If we crawled around inside the culvert getting the carcass out, we'd be covered with enough blood and mud and shit that we'd look like a couple of ax murderers.

"Or maybe we should just get it out of there ourselves, head home, clean up, and go tomorrow."

He shook his head. "Better not. Bob seemed to be in a rush, and he called in to Streicher's—you want to explain to him how we had to miss it because of a deer? One we didn't even hit?"

Well, yes, I actually did want to explain it to him. But Jeff didn't, and I do try to get along, when I can, although I'd been doing far too much of that of late, at least for my own comfort.

"We can still make Streicher's before it closes, Chief, if I run the siren and flashers."

"You're allowed do that?" I asked, letting the "Chief" pass.

I'd thought that sort of thing was for emergencies. In the city, I always assumed sirens and lights meant things like a robbery or shooting in progress, or a hostage situation, or maybe a two-for-one at the local doughnut shop. The only time I'd ever heard a siren in Hardwood itself was on the rare occasions the fire truck was going out or Arvie was coming in or going out in the ambulance.

Oh, occasionally, if I happened to be outside, I could hear a distant siren off to the west, but I usually assumed it was Jeff or the Hatton town cop bringing down a speeder—the staties find better pickings for that sort of thing on the interstate, and tend to leave the hassles—and the added income from speeding tickets—to the locals, as Jeff had explained it.

He snorted. "Yeah. Unless the Chief of Police of the Hardwood Police Department decides to give me shit about it."

I nodded. "Just don't hit any deer, Officer Bjerke."

Shit, if he wasn't going to play nice, I wasn't going to play nice, either.

It's amazing how fast you can go on an East Dakota country road when you don't have to worry about being pulled over.

I kept a watch on the speedometer for a while, but soon gave it up. Ninety-five miles an hour down a county road sounds fast—hell, it *is* fast. But we had good clean roads, and Jeff was a good driver, and he managed to work his cell phone—I didn't ask why he didn't use the radio—to call the DNR to pick up the deer's carcass without taking his eyes off the road.

He was considerate or prudent enough—or both, I guess—to flip off the siren well before we went through Kempton and Larimore and went through each of those little towns at what felt like a slow walk before accelerating when we cleared them, flashers going back on quickly, the siren a few moments later.

Larimore's tiny, at about fifteen hundred people, compared to the hustle and bustle of Hardwood's two thousand-plus, and I'm sure somebody has a good explanation why there are five church steeples in Larimore as opposed to the one in Hardwood, but I don't know what the explanation is, and it's really none of my business.

He was quiet for a while, whether to fume or just to concentrate on his driving I don't know, but then, when he noticed me looking at the computer screen mounted on the dashboard—a big thing; it meant that I had to push the seat all the way back so I could stretch my legs out sort of diagonally—he just gestured toward the glove compartment.

"Manual's in there. You might want to start with the Quick Start section—it's pretty easy to use." He smiled. "On the way back, I'll show you how to run plates if you'd like—does state check and the NCICs check at the same time, unless you tell it not to. Not a bad place to start."

No "Chief." So I guess we were friends again.

"Sure."

"You don't mind some advice?" he asked.

"Shit no."

"You're probably itching to write your first speeding ticket—shit, you've gotten enough—but don't be in a rush."

"To be honest, I hadn't thought about it."

If I had, it wouldn't have been that I'd want to do a lot of

that. I think of getting speeding tickets as a minor natural disaster, not of giving them as a hobby.

"Then think about it. We've got truckers cruising through
on County Fifteen all the damn time, and if word gets out you
can put the pedal all the way down between Hatton and
Thompsen, somebody's going to get nailed turning. At least
that's what Bob says, and it make sense to me."

"And I'm going to have to handle that?"

"When I'm out of town." He swallowed heavily.

"Out of town." A nice euphemism for visiting his dying father. I had the selfish thought that it would be more convenient for everybody if Dave Bjerke just went ahead and died,
but while I'm not the brightest or most socially adept guy in
the world, saying it didn't seem like a good idea.

"Which the staties have been handling."

"Yeah. Up until now," he said, with more heat than I would
have liked. "Now that we've got a two-man department, if we
ask for a lot of routine coverage, we're going to be the little
boy who cried wolf real quick." He shook his head. "Highway
accident—sure, you yell for help. If Effie pushes the panic button at the bank, you don't even have to—the call goes out to
the staties just like it does to our cell phones.

"But do you really want to call up the staties and say, 'Hey,
this is Chief Hemingway, and I need you to send out a trooper
to help me write an ordinary ticket'?"

"Good point."

"Yeah. You've got to be able to do stuff like that, and it's
pretty simple. Or maybe I shouldn't say that." He shook his
head. "I don't want to make it sound too simple. It's nervous-
making. Or it should be." He tapped on the top of the computer screen. "Don't skip running the plates. Ninety times out
of a hundred, it's no big deal; every once in a while you hit a
jackpot."

"Like?"

"Outstanding unpaid tickets, most of the time. Stolen car's the usual real jackpot."

"That happen a lot?"

"Nah, I guess." He shook his head. "Depends what you mean by a lot. Happened a couple of times last fall—and no, they weren't out-of-state plates, either." He patted the computer the way I pat my dog. "Some of the time, you get some warrant out for unpaid speeding tickets—but don't get too eager about those; it could be the owner of the car, not the driver." He smiled. "Every once in a while, though, you do get a stolen-car report. *Then* you punch for the staties—and quick—and break the shotgun out," he said, patting the release gimmick on the shotgun rack mounted between the two seats, "and in as calm a voice as you can manage, you get on the loudspeaker and you tell the driver to get out of the car and just stand there."

"Pardon my ignorance, but what do I say?" It's not like I've never been stopped for speeding or anything, but the only time I've been ordered out of the car was the time I brought Tenishia to Hardwood, and that was by the Minnesota Highway Patrol— whatever they call themselves—and I'd been a bit too preoccupied, at the time, to take notes, what with the Minnesota State Trooper standing behind his car door with his shotgun out.

"Oh, try, 'Please shut off the engine, get out of the car, and stand by the side of the road so that you'll be safe from traffic. I'll be with you in a moment.'" He smiled. "Be sure to say please, at least the first time. And then you just sit there."

"They'll just stand there?"

He nodded. "Sometimes. Sometimes they'll take off the moment you tell them to get out. Most will try to talk their way out of it—and hey, sometimes it's a bad report or stale information at NCIC. Junior takes Dad's car but doesn't tell Dad, and Dad calls the car in as stolen, or the car *was* stolen, but the information at NCIC is stale . . . you don't want to be pointing a lot of guns at Junior, eh? So you let the staties handle it. Don't be a hero."

"Yeah. But if it's something serious—like a real stolen car— they're not going to hang around, are they?"

"Depends." He shrugged. "Sometimes they bolt, but that's okay. You just follow, flashers and sirens going—just keep him in sight; don't try to get too close or he'll just speed up—and then lag way back when the HP tells you they've got it. When they do the stop, be sure you lag *way* back—local cops make the staties nervous." He shrugged. "I did a double-trailer-semi stop in October, just about where we found that deer. Some criminal geniuses drove the truck right out of a meatpacker in Devil's Lake. I think they had a buyer for steaks in Aberdeen, given they were headed south—and they were smart enough not to get onto I-Twenty-Nine—but God knows what they could have done with a double-trailer-load of rennets."

"Rennets?"

"Yup. Rennets."

I had to laugh. A rennet is, to put it delicately, a cow's rectum. They're an essential ingredient in cheesemaking—after being thoroughly cleaned and chopped up, I'm sure—which exhausts my information on the subject. "The world's full of assholes, I guess, but . . ."

He laughed back. We were definitely friends again.

"Yeah. The staties stopped them at the turnoff at Blanchard—did the full felony stop. It was kind of . . . interesting for a few minutes. Then they put them in the back of the cruiser and laughed at them for a while before leaving them alone. The idiots had to have it explained what rennets were, and one of the troopers popped open a case and threw a couple of them in the backseat for the two idiots to talk over." He chuckled some more. "They wiggled a bit to get the them off the seat and onto the floor, and shit, they were pissed, and loud."

"With the camera running?"

He nodded and tapped at the spot on the roof of the cab where the camera was supposed to go, as soon as the federal money came through for it—those things are, so I'm told, expensive. "Yup. You should have heard them. They spent a good five, ten minutes cursing each other out about going to jail over a few tons of beef assholes."

I laughed. "Sounds like a good story. Surprised I hadn't heard it at the Dine-A-Mite, say, or on poker night." I don't always make poker night—particularly of late—but that was the sort of story that would bear repeating.

He shook his head. "People in this town talk too much, and I didn't want to tell the whole story." He wasn't smiling anymore. "What wasn't so funny is that they had themselves a couple of shotguns in the cab—they'd intended to hijack the truck, but got lucky. Well, sort of lucky.

"Just as well I didn't get all eager and walk right up to the cab, eh?" He shook his head. "No, I don't tell that story at the Dine-A-Mite. People talk, and I don't like the idea of Karen hearing that I could have gotten myself shot over twenty tons of beef assholes."

We zipped past the Air Force base in Grand Forks—which was quiet, unusually; most of the time I've been through, there's something taking off or landing, usually something big—and across the river into East Grand Forks without having to go through any sort of customs at the border.

Not that I'd expected it, not really, but, well, Minnesota is different. I've listened to Garrison Keillor on the radio, and he's a funny guy and all, but most of what little time I've had to spend of late in the People's Republic is in Minneapolis, which reminds me a lot more of the Bronx than it does of Lake Wobegon.

The only difference I could see once we passed the WEL-COME TO MINNESOTA, LAND OF 10,000 LAKES, AND AREN'T WE

SMUG ABOUT IT sign was that the roads weren't as good as they are in North Dakota. A collection of patched potholes does not a highway make.

There's no outside windows on the brick building in what I think they call the warehouse district at East Grand Forks—damned if I saw any real warehouses there; those all seemed to be at the outskirts of town.

There's just a few narrow slits in little insets in the bricks, sort of like arrow loops in a medieval castle, although the defenders inside would have to break the probably bulletproof glass in order to use them as such.

There were only a couple of bubble-gum-topped police cruisers parked in the lot outside Streicher's—one local-to-there, one state trooper. We parked next to an egg-blue Crown Victoria that might as well have had THEORETICALLY UNMARKED POLICE CAR emblazoned on its side, what with the inside-controlled spotlight next to the left sideview mirror, the extra antennas mounted on the trunk, and the computer console that took up all of where the front passenger's seat would have been—and the reinforced chickenwire divider between the front and the back that Jeff had informed me was "the cage," which was used to hold prisoners, unless police in the People's Republic transported a lot of giant mutant chickens from place to place.

We pushed in through the outside door, a huge polished steel-and-rivet thing that must have weighed a couple of tons and looked like it would be proof against a Hun invasion.

I stopped dead in my tracks.

The actual wall and door into the store itself were all glass, and while the display case on the right was empty, the other one held an awfully realistic dummy, dressed out in full cop-assault gear, with an awfully realistic-looking pistol clutched firmly in its hand, apparently pointing somewhere just to the right of my now rapidly-beating-heart.

Jeff laughed. "Everybody does that the first time."

"Thanks for the warning, Jeff."

We went inside. The dummy's eyes didn't follow me as we went in, but I wouldn't have been surprised if they did.

I don't know what I expected the place to be, but this wasn't quite it.

The best way I can describe Streicher's is that it's a sort of a Toys-R-Us for the police set, with a bit of Kmart, Lord & Taylors, and Waldenbooks thrown in. One side of the store was filled with shelves of shirts and trousers, mainly in blue and gray but with enough black that I was wondering if the Waffen SS occasionally stopped off to shop here, and shelves of shoes and boots and belts and such that made it look pretty much like the clothing section of any store, except that no belts in most stores appear to be about three inches wide, and at Wal-Mart you don't normally see light spring jackets with the word POLICE emblazoned in big white letters on the back.

The rest of the store, though, was the toy section. Besides an array of flashlights, ranging from tiny little things that fit on keychains to the huge, six D-cell Maglites that my suspicious mind suspects are more intended for clubbing somebody over the head than for illuminating them, there were rows of the bubble-gum racks that fit on the top of cop cars, and radios and nightsticks—I think you're supposed to call them "batons", as though a cop is some sort of cheerleader.

There was a whole book-and-video section filled with snappy little titles like *Advanced Concepts in Tactical Entry*, *Kill or Get Killed*, *A Tactical Guide to High-Risk Warrant Service*, and *An Inside Look at Motorcycle Gangs*. I could practically smell the testosterone in the binding glue.

The back wall was taken up with enough holsters of different colors and sizes and shapes to satisfy a leather freak.

The centerpiece of the whole back wall was another dummy—this headless, with its arms hanging down at its sides—dressed only in a POLICE T-shirt and shorts, but with a bunch of red plastic guns in a shoulder rig, a holster on each side of its wide belt, a little red plastic revolver in what I'm told is a "belly-band" rig—it looks like a girdle to me—and an ankle holster on each leg. Shit, the T-shirt itself had a couple of pockets sewn under the armpits and one of the red toy guns in each of them.

There was also a small but suspicious bulge in the front of the shorts, and I wondered for a moment if this meant the dummy was anatomically correct or one of those Thunderwear things Jeff had told me about, but I didn't pull down its pants to check. There are some things man isn't meant to know.

A portly, middle-aged salesman was helping a remarkably buxom young female cop, not quite leering at her, which felt strange. Not the leering part—she was pretty cute—but you know you're getting old when a woman cop looks like she isn't past the age of consent.

When he noticed Jeff and me, he gave a quick smile and raised a finger in a salesman's I'll-be-with-you-in-just-a-moment gesture that probably goes back to Grunt helping Ugh pick out his new bearskin.

Jeff was busy with the small batons, and took one down about the size of a Churchill cigar, and give it a practiced flip with his hand. The thing telescoped out to more than two feet. He gave it a few trial swings, then collapsed it back down by whamming it straight down on the carpeted floor, tip first. He then put it back.

Nobody seemed to pay any attention, although the sound would sure as shit have gotten mine.

There was a local cop and a trooper over by the gun case— no salesman present, although there were half a dozen various pistols laid out on a black-velvet sheet on the counter. They were, no doubt, causing Doctor Freud to smile from his grave as they discussed the virtues of the various sorts of handguns, although the one with the walrus mustache didn't quite stroke the barrel of the very shiny automatic he was holding. They noticed Jeff and me, and each gave us a quick, very masculine nod of greeting, and then went back to their sublimation.

The salesman left the female cop struggling with zipping the jacket up over her impressive breasts—you'd think that if they're going to have women cops, they'd actually make jackets that would fit them, or if they didn't, only hire flat-chested ones—and walked quickly over to us.

"Jeff Bjerke, isn't it?" he said, extending a hand. There was a trace of wheeze in his voice, as though he spent his life running up and down stairs in between asthmatic attacks, and his thinning hair was carefully combed over the bald spots on his head—not quite enough to look silly, yet. In a couple of years it would, if he was still doing it, and he would be.

"Yup." Jeff nodded. "Hi, Ralph."

He turned to me. "I'm Ralph Olson—and you must be the famous Chief Hemingway," he said, extending a hand. If there was any sarcasm, it was all in what he was saying and not the way he said it, and his handshake was just a handshake, without that clap-the-other-hand-over thing and the accompanying sense you get from a salesman that he's barely restraining himself from clutching you to his bosom and embracing you as a long-lost brother. "Got your license and the purchase order faxed in a while ago, and they said you were on your way—I was expecting you a little earlier." He glanced at his wristwatch. "We're supposed to close at six, but if we have to stretch it, we'll do it—just got to call the wife and tell her I'll be late for dinner again."

"Sorry to put you out."

He smiled. "No trouble at all. Full outfit, I assume?"

"I don't know as you need the full outfit, Chief," Jeff said. "You've still got your old belt gear. It's your choice, though."

"Yeah, I guess it is." I can follow instructions. "I think the town can afford to get me properly equipped. Don't you?"

"Yes, sir," he said, his face studiously blank.

Olson's face was even more blank as he gestured toward the clothes section. "You wouldn't happen to know your waist and shirt sizes, would you?"

"I can take a guess."

He smiled in approval. "Why don't you get started over there? I'll make that phone call and then we can fit you out. Changing room's in through there."

Pants and shirts are pants and shirts even if they're in blue and gray, with colored flaps over the pocket and stripes down the seams, and while I'm not used to having things altered—I normally live in jeans, and since I've got slightly short legs for my thirty-eight-inch waist, I tend to buy them in 38×30 and hack off an inch of the hem with a pair of scissors.

Ralph insisted I buy shirts that I thought were a size or two too big, as though my chest were going to expand with the pride of being named chief or my stomach with all the doughnuts—which, by the way, aren't given out free to *anybody* at the Dine-A-Mite. He added a light cotton blue spring jacket and a thicker one that reminded me of an old army field jacket, except that it ended at the belt, and took them into the back room. He came out a few minutes later with the same Hardwood Police Department patch that Jeff had presumably hot-pressed onto the breast.

Interestingly enough, they had jeans with the two-inch belt loops—another mystery solved. Jeff pulled a couple pairs off the shelf for himself and gestured for me to do the same.

I passed on the winter boots, despite the sale—Jeff recommended that we save the town some money by buying them now, again, so I didn't despite the temptation—and got a pretty ordinary pair of black shoes, plus some lace-up boots that you couldn't have told from ordinary work boots—and, given the label on them, probably were just that.

Ralph measured my inseam without quite asking me to turn

my head and cough, and marked up the trousers with that little chalk thing that looks like hotel soap.

"Pick these up on Friday, maybe?" he asked.

Jeff shook his head. "Nah. We'll take them with us and have my wife do it."

He was having fun. Sewing is a major hobby in Hardwood, but Karen Bjerke is famous for both being the most incompetent seamstress the town has ever seen and for having insisted on sewing her bridesmaids' dresses for her and Jeff's wedding, which had made even Bridget look silly. But there's no shortage of women in Hardwood who can do a hem— and, I suspect, no shortage of men who could do it, but wouldn't admit it except under duress, although I'm not one of them, and I had no doubt that that, too, had already been arranged.

But Olson just nodded. "On to gear." He fit me for one of those huge Sam Browne belts and sent Jeff out to the car to bring in his own so he could get the right pouches or holsters or whatever the hell they call them for the radio, as apparently the right radio was on backorder. My new cell phone went onto a little plastic gizmo that held the little plastic holder on the diagonal strap on the Sam Browne belt.

"Body armor next. Second Chance or Pro-Max?" he asked.

Before I could say anything—like, say, I'm impersonating a chief of police, not applying for knighthood—Jeff piped up. "Second Chance for the Two-A, I think," he said, patting himself on the chest, although what he had to pat himself on the chest or back about I didn't know.

"Two-A?" Olson nodded in approval. "Not Two?"

Jeff smiled. "Nah. The mayor's got the paperwork in, and we're approved for both Two- and Three-A."

The letters and numbers had gotten thick. I could have been approved for XYZB, for all I knew, but the best way to CYA (Cover Your Ass) is to KYFMSWP (Keep Your Fucking Mouth

Shut Whenever Possible), as well as RTFM (Please Read The Manual), or RTFMA (Please Read The Manual, Sir).

Olson just nodded again and pulled out a tape measure. "We'll need your shirt off to fit you for the Two-A."

The II-A turned out to be basically a sort of miniature white poncho that held one sheet of very flexible but still presumably bulletproof material in front and another in back. It had open sides, held closed by Velcro, and was only a little heavier, but no thicker, than a blanket. Olson had me try on several of them before he was satisfied with the fit.

He nodded as he helped me back into my new uniform shirt. "Feel comfortable?"

I'm not sure it would have been wise to complain if it did, but it wasn't uncomfortable, exactly, and it did explain why they wanted the shirts just a few sizes larger. "Sure."

He smiled. "Yup—er, you can throw the cover in the washer—gentle cycle—but make sure you take the liners out or you'll mess them up."

"Got it."

He set the box down on the counter and didn't suggest that I take off the little poncho thing. "For the Three-A?"

I didn't have an opinion, but Jeff just said, "Pro-Max SWAT," and they both smiled.

The Pro-Max SWAT vest reminded me of the body armor we'd had way back when—assuming it had gone through some serious steroid treatment—and between the "trauma plates" that fit into pouches in the front and the back and that were, so Olson explained, perfectly capable of stopping anything short of a hot .30-06. It weighed about a dozen pounds, more when he added the Kevlar helmet, complete with face shield.

I glanced at myself in the mirror. I looked like a fifty-plus-year-old man playing soldier, what with the camouflage design of the vest, which might have been useful in a triple-canopy jungle but that wouldn't exactly keep me inconspicuous anywhere in the East or West Dakotas unless I was trying to hide out in the clothing section of a military-surplus store.

I had no objection to taking it off and adding it to the pile on the counter.

The pile on the counter kept growing. In addition to the duty belt—and all the shit that went on it—I apparently needed a stiffer-than-usual dress belt, so we got one of those. We added all the pouches, and the flashlights—I apparently needed three, plus some charger gizmos—and a nightstick with a funny little stick sticking out of the side, and Jeff quietly went off to the book section and returned with an armload of books and VCR tapes.

He tapped at the top one. "This one's probably worth watching, Chief," he said. "There's been some new stuff on traffic stops in the past couple of years."

Well, he hadn't given me a choice, so I just nodded. "Yeah. Best brush up, what with all those truckers thinking that County Fifteen has become their private raceway lately." I glowered at him. I give a good glower.

Olson ignored it. "Well, you need a holster for your rig, and another for your dress belt, but we'll have to pick out your service piece, first."

Jeff shook his head. "You might as well just stick with your snubby, Chief, although I guess you could pick something else."

"Hardwood PD allows officers their choices of carry weapon, as I recall," I said. "Don't think I'm going to change that."

Olson chuckled. "Can I see the pistol?"

I took it out, swung the cylinder open, and handed it to him. I think he was surprised; maybe the cops he was used to didn't play safe with guns.

He handed it back. "Sure. Colt Cobra—same as the Detective Special. I think I've got a couple of Safariland holsters that'll fit it—one for the duty belt, one for your dress belt."

Well, as I say, I can obey orders, and Jeff had given me two choices, then recommended that I stick with the snubby.

"You got something in a 1911?" I don't know a lot about the Glocks and Sigs and the rest of the too-modern-looking guns that seemed to decorate the gun ase, but I do know the 1911.

His eyes lit up. "Sure."

The two cops—sorry, the *other* two cops—moved off to the side as we walked over to the display case. Ralph pulled a couple of guns out and laid them on the black velvet.

I don't tend to get sentimental about guns, not really, but I do tend to like tools that I know how to use, and I actually did own a 1911 that a friend had given me, and had carried one every day I'd spent in Vietfuckingnam.

These were both shiny, polished stainless steel instead of the dull gunmetal black we'd had in the old days, but still the same thing. I picked the nearest one up, dropped the mag and caught it with my free hand, then set it on the velvet, then carefully pointed the gun at the floor while I racked the slide to make sure it wasn't loaded—which, unsurprisingly, was the case. I gripped the hammer with my hand and pulled the trigger, slowly lowering it. Some things you never forget.

"Kimber Custom II," he said. "Night sights front and back. Firing-pin safety block, match-grade barrel, match trigger, full-length guide rod—and I think the walnut grips look pretty good, but we can put on a set of Pachmayrs for you, if you'd like."

Jeff was frowning, which I took as a good sign.

"Custom? That sounds expensive."

He gave a salesman's nod. "Well, yes and no. All the Kimbers are custom something or other—but, no, they're not the cheapest gun in the store. Seven forty-eight is the street price—SRP's higher—but department price is . . ." He paused, whether to remember what it was or to snatch a figure out of the air. "Six ninety-five, and I'll throw in a couple of extra mags. McCormicks."

I tried to wiggle the slide—it didn't wiggle—and he smiled. "Nah. Not like the old days—it's tight, but they make them right. Don't lubricate it before you put a couple boxes of PMC through it to get everything, just to give things a chance to settle in, then shoot a couple of boxes of the carry ammo and do a full cleaning and lube. After that, if you get as many as one-count-'em-one failures to feed in the next ten boxes you put through it, I'll take the gun back and refund the ammo."

I nodded. "I'll take it."

"Okay," he said, handing a clipboard with a pile of yellow sheets over to me. "You fill out the forty-four-seventy-three and sign it—I've got your department license, but I'll need your driver's license, and then it'll be just a couple of minutes," he said, not quite rubbing his hands together at the pile of gear on the counter. "And two belt holsters—Level Three for the duty belt?"

"Nah," Jeff shook his head. "A thumb break is just fine."

"Sure. You'll want a couple of cases of ammo—we've got PMC for the practice stuff." He thought for a moment. "All two-thirty-grain, I think. For the carry ammo—Federal or Winchester?"

"Winchester two-thirty-grain," I said, as I started in on the form. I hadn't bought a gun—in a store, that is; I've picked up a couple of things here and there unoficially—in more years than I cared to think about, and forced myself not to smile at the stupid questions.

No, I wasn't a fugitive from justice—well, not technically, anyway, although it felt like it at the moment—nor had I been adjudicated mentally defective. Maybe I should have been, but that's another matter. No, I wasn't a narcotic addict. Was I an illegal alien? I just wrote "no," since there wasn't enough space to write sometimes I feel like a stranger in a strange land, and that probably wouldn't have gone over real big, anyway.

Yes, I was buying the gun for myself, and yes, I was a U.S. citizen who hadn't relinquished his citizenship.

I put my driver's license on the form and slid it back to him.

"Take a couple of minutes to run the NICs check, ring this all up, and then you can sign the purchase order, and," he said, glancing up at the clock on the wall, "I even get out of here on time. Didn't mean to hurry you."

"No hurry at all. Appreciate it."

Jeff seemed to be twitchy, and I was getting twitchy myself, maybe just because I hadn't had a cigarette recently.

"I think we'll step outside and have a quick smoke while you do all that."

"You do that." He nodded. "I'll come get you."

Jeff waited until we were outside and I was lighting up before he started laying into me. "Shit, Sparky, why did you buy the gun?" He shook his head. "Bob's going to have a fucking shit fit over the bill, and—"

"Wait a minute. You said that if you gave me two choices, I was supposed to pick the one you were recommending against." I took a long drag on the Camel filter and forced my-self to turn my head and blow it in the opposite direction and rather than right in his face.

He opened his mouth and closed it. "Fuck. I forgot."

"Happens." I shrugged. "You want me to go back and tell Ralph I changed my mind?"

Jeff shook his head. "Nah. I'll explain to Bob that I fucked up and take the heat. It's my fault. But *seven hundred bucks*? Plus a case of ammo? Two cases. And two holsters?"

"Well, I'd have needed at least one, apparently—two-inch loops aren't going to go through this thing. And what was that about a Level Three?"

"Ah, it's a holster with a bunch of gimmicks in it. You've got to release two straps and rock it just the right way, before it'll let go of the gun. Great idea if you plan to wrestle with a lot of guys trying to take your gun away from you, but it takes a shitload of training to have a vague chance of remembering how to work it when the shit hits the fan." He shook his head. "And you're changing the subject."

I was doing sums in my head of all the other stuff we'd bought, and it didn't seem to me that another few hundred dollars was going to make that much of a difference.

"Shit, the radio was a couple of thousand, and the phone about that, and the body armor alone was twenty-five hundred—"

"Which we get the feds to reimburse us for." He shook his head. "The town's on the hook for the uniforms, and that's about all. We've got a grant for the expensive gear, sure—the radio, the phone, the body armor. But if the feds started paying for regular service weapons, every damn cop across the country would have something like a Wilson Combat or Les Baer custom job—and when the folks at Wilson Combat or Les Baer put the word 'custom' on a piece, they mean it, and you pay for it. Even the feds aren't stupid enough to write cops a blank check."

"They could just set a price limit."

"They aren't that smart."

Lot of that going around. "Well, I could go back in and tell him I changed my mind." Or, it occurred to me, I could somehow encounter a failure to feed right when I took the gun out to practice with it.

And I would do just that—practice, that is. I don't know much about this cop stuff, but I do know I'm not going to ever trust a gun to go bang when I pull the trigger until I've had it go bang when pulling the trigger a whole lot before.

"Yeah, you do that, and our careful little act where we made it clear that you're in charge goes all to shit," Jeff said.

I raised a palm in surrender. "Hey, I'll tell Bob it was my fault, okay?" I shrugged. "What's he going to do, fire me?"

"Thanks, Sparky, I owe you one."

Yeah, he did. I was about to make some comment to that effect when he looked over my shoulder. "You're not a big believer in coincidences, are you?"

"Never have been."

"That asshole Franz is pulling up next to where we parked. Just at closing time."

There's the old saying about how the first time is an accident, the second time is a coincidence, and the third time is enemy action. I read in some book about a guy saying that he didn't believe in coincidence, and he's suspicious about accidents, and it made a lot of sense to me.

I turned to see Andy Franz get out of another Crown Victoria, although this one was just plain brown, and could have been just a car.

I hadn't seen Franz since that snowy day out near Cole Creek and he hadn't changed much, which wasn't surprising, given that it had only been a few months. Felt like longer, though—things had been happening.

I'd say he looked older than me, but the truth is that he probably was just about my age and looked it, and the years hadn't treated him any more gently than they had me. You could take the position that he didn't have much of a chin, or maybe a couple too many; I'm neutral on the subject myself. His mouth was set in a permanent scowl, framed by a drooping mustache that was halfway between walrus and Hitler, and his left eyelid seemed to sag a little.

Both eyes looked tired. He looked more used up than anything else, and since I've seen that look in the mirror, I had some sympathy.

Except for the mustache, he was clean-shaven enough to make me wonder if he made a habit of running one of those portable shavers across his face while he drove, although he didn't look the type. He was balding, with just a rim of dark hair around the crown of his head, and while it touched his collar in the back, he had made no attempt to comb it over the top.

The one thing about him that looked all new and untouched was his slate-gray three-piece suit, which seemed far too expensive for what I think a cop's salary should support. The pleat down the middle of his trousers looked sharp enough to be scary, if you're capable of being scared by sharp trouser pleats. I'm a braver sort.

He nodded a greeting. "Hey, Jeff," he said, not bothering to give even a brief smile until he turned to me and offered his hand. It was a professional smile, without a trace of salesman or friend in it, and it only lasted while he said, "Can I still call you Ernest, or is it Chief Hemingway now?"

I wasn't particularly surprised that he'd heard.

"You Andy?" I asked.

He nodded.

"Then I'm Sparky."

"Why Sparky?"

I'd been asked question more than enough times, but once more didn't hurt. "If your name was Ernest Hemingway, wouldn't you want a nickname?" That wasn't the whole story, but I don't like to tell the whole story.

His smile was thin enough to hydroplane on. "Okay. I'm Andy; you're Sparky." He jerked his chin at the doorway. "Waiting for something?"

"They're just toting up my new gear and running the NICs check on my new service piece."

He nodded just a hair too eagerly. I had the feeling he knew all that.

"Well, I stopped by to pick up a couple of things, so I'd better get in before Ralph closes up for the day," he said, and started for the door, then stopped and turned. "Hey, you got time for a quick cup of coffee?"

"Sorry, Andy." Jeff shook his head. "My wife's already going to be just a little upset that I'm going to be late for supper—some other time, maybe?"

His mouth twitched. "Actually, I wanted to have little chat with your boss. Don't need to keep you."

"We came in the same car."

Franz turned to me. "I can run you back to Hardwood after, and I seem to recall you're not married."

I didn't want to get into my domestic arrangements with a stranger, so I just said, "I wouldn't want to be any trouble."

"No trouble at all." He shook his head. "Hell, Jeff—why don't you take off now, and I'll wait until . . . Sparky gets things settled, and I can haul his stuff back with him. That way you won't be late for dinner."

Jeff was trying to think of an objection, but a good one wasn't coming to mind.

I was having the same problem, if it was a problem; I was kind of curious as to what Franz was up to, and almost as curious as to what he'd have to say.

"Sure, Jeff," I said. "Head on back." I tapped on the idiotic plastic box at my waist. "If anything comes up, you know how to get hold of me."

Jeff didn't like it much—and, to tell the truth, neither did I, all in all—but he just nodded, said, "Sure, Chief. See you in the morning," and climbed into the Bronco, started it up, and took off, with just the barest screeching of tires.

Franz reached for the door, but Bob Olson was already pushing it open.

"Hey, Andy," he said. "How goes it?"

"Oh, pretty well. You closing up?"

"Well, yeah, in a few minutes. Just got to get Chief Hemingway to sign the purchase order, and then I'm done for the day. You need something?"

"Yeah. I stopped by to pick up a couple of things."

I believed that, of course. Along with the Easter Bunny, Santa Claus, and publishers sending out checks right away.

We went in.

While Franz picked up a couple of boxes of .38 PMC practice ammo, I signed the purchase order. It came to a preposterous amount, and I didn't have the expertise or the time to try to figure out which of it the town was going to end up paying for and which part would be picked up by the feds.

I expected I'd be hearing about that, though, in some great detail. But that could wait for tomorrow, or, if possible, forever.

I let Franz and Olson help me load the boxes and bags into the trunk of Franz's car. I hefted the blue plastic case with the 1911 in it for a moment, not quite willing to put it in there. While I wouldn't worry about what I left in my car in Hardwood—kids do the darndest things, but breaking into the trunk of a car isn't among them—this was the city, after all.

Franz smiled. "It's okay; we'll grab coffee at Starbucks, and there's always cruisers in the lot—mainly GFPD, but some EGF. Not a lot of breakins, honest."

Because I was a professional law-enforcement officer, I immediately concluded that GFPD was Grand Forks Police Department and EGF was East Grand Forks. I could quite figure out what they did to lose their P or D, though.

He sipped at his coffee and made a face. "Fucking decaf. Doesn't quite taste the same, eh?" How he had managed to down half the cup in one gulp without either burning his mouth or wetting his mustache was something I probably wasn't going to figure out. Maybe they teach it in POST training or something.

"I wouldn't know," I said. "If I'm going to drink coffee, I drink coffee." I sipped at my cup. Not bad. The very pretty girl behind the counter didn't remind me of Tenishia at all, except for being black—she was much more the buxom, burgeoning type, with an easy smile, instead of no smile—and I wondered again if the inability to make decent coffee is one of those things, like eating lutefisk, that comes with a Norskie heritage.

He snorted. "If I have more than a couple of cups of the real stuff, I'm up all night." He sipped some more.

"Different strokes, eh?"

"Yeah."

I let things go silent for a while, although what I really wanted was a cigarette.

"You seem a bit twitchy," he said. "Too much coffee? Guilty conscience?"

"Nah, to both. Conscience got shot off in the war."

His face went blank. "Yeah. War hero, so I hear."

Fuck him. "Then you heard wrong."

"Oh?"

I try to get along with people, but there are limits, and that war-hero shit is beyond them.

"I guess there must be some people who'll tell folks they were some big-time Vietnam war hero, and maybe not quite all of them are full of shit."

"Maybe."

"And then there's folks who talk modestly about how, hell, they just went and served, but really think they were something more, or maybe want you to think they're just modest fucking big-time Vietnam war heroes."

"Yeah. I heard a few of those."

"That's not me. I was there, and I did my job, and there wasn't anything even vaguely heroic about it.

"Not that I don't know what a war hero looks like, mind. On the seven-oh-seven that brought me back to the world, I happened to walk past the seat where Fred Zabitoski was sitting, and did the double take that everybody apparently gets when they see that little blue ribbon with the five stars on it."

"Yeah. I saw one of those once." He nodded. "Kind of leaps out at you."

It does that. There's only one medal that the U.S. armed services give out that hangs around the neck, but Medal of

Honor winners don't tend to walk around with it. I don't know if most of them wear the ribbon—which is just five little white stars on a blue background. It's entirely possible to go through more than a tour or two without ever seeing one.

"Fred Zabitoski? Green weenie? SFC or something?"

I shrugged. "Yeah."

"I think I heard the story. Something about hauling a pilot out of a burning helicopter under fire?"

"Something like that." I'd looked up the details once, but they weren't the point. "I spoke to him, on the flight when we were waiting in line at the head. I said, 'How you doing?' and he said, 'Fine.'

"That's my brush with greatness.

"You want to talk about war hero, you talk about people like Zabitoski. Me, I was just a guy in the 1/77 Armor—tank gunner on an M48. No hero at all, and if you heard otherwise, you heard wrong, and you didn't hear it from me, cause it just ain't so."

"Just asking," he said, like he really meant to say "Just testing," and like I'd passed the test.

"You there?" He was about the right age, and he'd shown the usual, er, respect for the U.S. Army Special Forces.

"Sixty-eight." He nodded. "716th MPs."

"Tet?"

"Yeah."

"I was lucky enough to miss that."

"Good choice." A ghost of a smile. "Nobody hung a medal around my neck either, and I didn't deserve one either." His mouth twitched. "You forgot to duck a couple of times, though, as I understand it."

"Yeah. You?"

"Once." He shrugged and started to move his hand toward his belly, then stopped himself. "Not a big deal. That how you got your CIB?"

"Well, yeah." I sipped at my coffee. "Okay, now that we've

beaten our chests and each other and performed some manly bonding, any chance you can tell me what's really on your mind?"

He snorted. "You about done with your coffee?"

"Why?"

"Let's talk in the car while I run you home. It's getting late."

I could have asked why he'd wanted to go out for coffee at all, except that it was obvious—he'd wanted to get rid of Jeff, for whatever reason, and that had been the easiest way to do it.

"Mind if I smoke?" I asked.

"Fuck, I don't care if you burn."

He waited until we were out on the interstate before he said much of anything. I just cracked the window a little and blew smoke. Blowing smoke, after all, seemed to be the theme of the day, and far be it from me to ruin a good theme.

"Looks like you got some interesting politics going on," he said, just as we passed the sign that said THOMPSON 8 MILES.

"That whole Level Three trauma-center thing?"

"Yeah. You been following it real close?"

I shook my head. "Not until recently."

He nodded. "I don't follow politics much myself. Not unless I have to."

"And there's some reason you have to? About this stuff?"

He didn't answer right away. "What I have to do is my job," he said. "Got things I think I need to be doing that are more important than chasing down a whole bunch of bullshit reports."

"Which you can't just ignore when then come from Phil Norstadt."

"Nope. County commissioner thinks there's a problem, or says he thinks just maybe there's a problem, BCI doesn't ignore it, or my boss's phone starts ringing, and he doesn't much like that." He shook his head. "Some town weirdo in Hardwood playing cop sounded like a problem. My guess was that's just what it was: something that *sounded* like a problem."

"Which it wasn't, apparently."

He grunted. "Depends on how much of a pain in the ass the new chief of police is, I guess. But since you're all qualified and licensed and all, and a professional peace officer, I hope we're not going to have a lot of trouble, you and me."

"I don't see why we should."

A snort. With a nose like that, he should have been more careful about snorting. "Yeah. Always thought of Hardwood as a quiet little town." He gestured down the road. "Had a lot more trouble in Thompson, really."

"Oh?"

"Yeah. Right on the interstate, and every so often—too damn often—we get some clown who thinks that the Super-America just off the highway is the ideal stop-and-rob. But, no, I spend most of my time in Grand Forks, and that gives me plenty to do."

"Oh?"

"Not as bad as it used to be, when the air base had a lot more going on, but there's always shit." He frowned. "And a fair amount of different kinds of shit and shitheads moving in and out. Don't get a lot of choice about what I have to do, but I'd rather not have to spend a whole lot of fucking time chasing down complaints about how there's a whole hotbed of crime in Hardwood, and that the town cop is more interested in keeping the mayor happy than he is in doing his job."

"All this over this impersonating-an-officer thing?"

"Nah." Another snort. "Mostly it's a lot of piddly shit—you know a guy named Steve Larson?"

"Big Steve? Yeah."

"Well, he's due for a visit from the DNR about using illegal insecticides. DDT." He shrugged. "Which I kind of doubt he's doing, but there's been this report. Anonymous. If it was up to me, I'd say fuck it, but I don't think the DNR looks at things quite the way I do."

"Oh."

"As for you, well . . ." He looked over at me. "You, you're a lucky man."

"Not sure I always feel that way, truth to tell."

"Well, you should. If you hadn't just gone through all that shit with Children's and Youth Services over the foster-parent thing . . ."

"Yeah?"

"Well, another anonymous report—came in last week—about you were living in sin with some underage girl. Under other circumstances, would have earned you a real serious, real fast visit from the Ministry of Love."

"Ministry of Love?"

"CYS," he said.

"I've dealt with them." I didn't much like the social worker, but I don't like a lot of people. "Pains in the ass, but not real scary."

"Yeah, but you haven't seen them when they're investigating an abuse report. Different bunch; different attitudes. Imagine a bunch of folks who gave what little charm they had to the IRS, the DEA, and me."

"That bad, eh?" I hadn't exactly liked the surprise visits from Ms. Murphy, but . . .

He nodded. "Or worse. Fortunately for you, they already screened you, and the investigation, such as it is, is going to be pro forma. Matter of fact, if I can have a few words with Tenishia Washington, I might be able to put in a report myself, and you might—not promising anything, you understand—you might not hear from CYS much at all about this."

"Why'd you want to do that?"

He shrugged. "Because I don't want to be spending the next

couple of months driving out to fucking Hardwood and fucking Thompsen over this shit."

"Understandable."

"You know the nice thing about working a homicide?" He'd apparently been taking changing-the-subject lessons, too.

"Nah."

"It's unambiguous is what it is, at least most of the time. You got a dead body, and nobody, and nobody wonders if it's really dead, and when you don't have the asshole boyfriend or the asshole husband or the asshole wife standing over the body with a baseball bat or a kitchen knife, you've got the witnesses in the bar who'll tell you who did what, and it doesn't matter if they don't all tell quite the same story. All you gotta do is hook somebody up, read the fucking Miranda card, take a confession, and then you're done.

"Or maybe you've got one car that smashed into another car, and a dead guy in one, and a guy with a blood-alcohol level of, oh, two-point-three still stuck in the other, and all you got to do is take some pictures while the firemen pry the live one out, make some sketches, and write that one up, too, and read him his rights and let him blubber for a while in front of a camera how he's sorry and all, and then you turn that over to the prosecutor's office and just fucking go home." He made a face. "Or you get a bunch of guys who froze to death in car in the middle of winter, and the ME comes back to tell you that, yeah, they died of carbon-monoxide poisoning, and you figure that they just got stuck out in the middle of nowhere and did something stupid."

"Simple."

"Yeah. I like simple. A couple of politicians seeing if they can find some embarrassing thing in another town, something that'll make the papers and impress some other bunch of politicians, that's not simple."

"Wouldn't imagine it would be. I also don't think Bob

Aarsted would do that kind of thing." I realized how stupid
that sounded after it came out of my mouth.

"Oh, no," he said. "Nobody ever would, right?"

I let that pass, having used up my saying-something-stupid
quota for the minute.

"The thing I wanted to say to you," he said, choosing his
words slowly, and possibly carefully, "is that I want all this shit
to stop. Both sides."

"I can understand that. You always get what you want?"

"Shit, no. But if you try sometimes, yeah, sometimes you get
what you need." He didn't look much like Mick Jagger, and at
least he didn't try to sing it. "I don't think you're much in
charge of anything. Not expecting miracles." He looked over
at me. "What I want from you is knowing that you're doing
your best to keep a lid on it from your side. Or you and I aren't
going to be the good friends that we'd both like to be, eh?"

"Yeah." We rode quietly for another minute or two. "This
what you stopped by to talk to Jeff about the other day?"

"What do you think?" He shook his head. "Don't know as I
got through to him, though, the mayor being his father-in-law
and all."

"Well," I said, "Bob may end up being my father-in-law,
sooner or later, too."

"Oh?"

"His oldest daughter, Bridget, lives with me."

"Divorce from Fred Honistead taking some time?"

Which pretty much meant he already knew about Bridget
and me—and shit, if he'd seen the CYS report, he certainly
did. I'd have felt like I was playing chess with the other guy
about three, four moves ahead, if I knew how to play chess.

"Yeah," I said.

"That mean that when he takes a sharp right, you break
your nose?"

"Probably not." And probably not for Jeff, either, but . . .

But Jeff was in his twenties, and I'd had a few more decades' practice being stubborn, and could probably manage it for a few months until the commission made its decision. Bob would know that, and Franz knew that he'd know that.

Shit.

I lit up another cigarette and thought about it for a minute, pulled the goddamn cell phone off my belt and opened it, and punched in my home number.

It took a couple of rings for Tenishia to pick up.

"*What?*"

I don't know where she got her phone manners. "Hey, Tenishia," I said. "I thought we had a deal about answering the phone."

"I thought we had a deal about people being ready, and sitting at the table for supper at suppertime when it's my turn to cook," she said. "Particularly after I spent half the afternoon digging up a garden, and the other half—"

"Can we save that for later, please?" I asked.

"You calling from a car?"

"Yeah. My official new chief-of-police cell phone."

"You just trying it out, or you got something particular on your mind?"

"Well, I was wondering if we've got enough of whatever it is for you to set another place."

She probably would have made some snappy answer—she was good at that—but then she remembered that this was a food thing, and Tenishia and I have always gotten along well on matters of the stomach.

"Yeah," she said. "No big deal. Throw in a bit more rice, and I can boil a few more carrots, and it'll stretch. Shouldn't take too long. The pot roast is done, and unless you're bringing along a real food hound, we should be okay."

Which probably meant she'd made enough of everything to leave leftovers for the next day again. Which was fine.

"I'll be home in about . . ." I hadn't been watching the road. "Twenty minutes?"

Franz nodded.

"Yeah," I said. "Twenty or so. Bringing a detective—BCI guy out of Grand Forks—with me. He wants a quick chat with you."

"What about?" She sounded nervous, and I didn't blame her. There was the matter of that seventy thousand dollars in the lockbox in her closet.

"He wants to know if I've been . . . touching you inappropriately."

"You mean he wants to know if you've been fucking me?" She laughed loud enough that even Franz grinned when I held up the phone so he could hear it.

"Well, yeah, I suppose that's another way to put it."

"And I suppose I oughta tell him the truth?"

"Well, yeah, I suppose you ought to tell him the truth. I think he's being straight with me, so, just for the fun of it, let's just be straight with him. If it turns out he's interested in all sorts of Minneapolis gang stuff you don't know anything about, well, then you might want to talk to your lawyer about it. I don't know. But about this? I don't see a problem. My heart is pure, and my conscience is clean."

"I wouldn't go that far. But, shit . . . he there in the car with you?"

"Well, yeah."

"Okay. You maybe explain this all to me sometime? Sometime soon?"

"Possibly."

"Then I'd better get back to cooking, 'cause I've got a shit-load of reading to do for that Mrs. Hansen tonight, and you and Bridge got the dishes. You wanna talk to her?"

"Not at the moment."

She hung up without saying good-bye, and I closed the phone and tucked it back in its little holder on my belt.

"Gang stuff in Minneapolis?" Franz shook his head. "I heard some stuff about that last winter. Sort of like to know what those Minneapolis gangbangers were doing out in the middle of nowhere when they froze themselves to death, but, shit, ME ruled it an accident—and it sure looked to me like an accident." He looked over at me. "You were there."

"Looked that way to me, too."

"And it's none of my business."

"None of mine, either," I said, lying through my teeth.

I'd been expecting a who-the-hell-do-you-think-you're-fooling look, but I didn't get one, and we just rode quietly for a while. That was okay. I don't mind quiet.

"I didn't ask if you had dinner plans," I finally said.

"Nothing special. I could eat," he said, nodding.

Both Tenishia and Bridget were in the kitchen when we walked in, and the table had been set with Mom's best table-cloth and silver. Not the usual Thursday dinner, but hey, a guest is a guest.

Bridget walked over with a hand out, and Franz shook it and introduced himself, then stooped to make his manners with the dog. Snake liked him, which, given Snake, meant roughly nothing—anybody who'll pet him is Snake's new best friend. Cat was nowhere to be seen; the only thing that meant was that if Franz was allergic to cats or just plain didn't like them, Cat didn't know it yet, or she'd have been buzzing around his ankles.

Tenishia just scowled at him and pointed her chin at a seat. "Supper's ready. You can wash your hands in the sink, or the bathroom."

Franz nodded and quickly washed his hands in the kitchen sink, then dried them on a paper towel, while Bridget and I

helped Tenishia get the food from the oven and the stove over
to the table, and then showily washed our hands, too.

Franz nodded as he pulled out the chair that Tenishia
pointed at. "Thanks for inviting me."

"I didn't invite you," she said as he seated himself. She
walked over and looked down at him. "He did. His house; his
rules." She looked at me, then back at him. "So we get this
straight right off: He don't fuck me. He don't ever *try* to fuck
me, and he don't walk around the house with his dick hanging
out. He don't come into the bathroom when I'm in there, and
he knocks and waits for me to say 'Come in' when I'm in my
room with the door closed, and even when it's open, and the
only time he ever put his hands on me is when once or twice he
hugged me," she said. She jerked her chin toward Bridget. "She
put her hand on my shoulder a few times, but she don't try to
fuck me, either. You got all that, or you want to ask him and
her to step outside so that you can take out your little notebook
and write it down while I tell it to you again in private?"

Bridget wasn't even trying to stifle a smile.

"Yeah," Franz said, nodding. "I got all that."

"Good. I probably wouldn'ta been so polite about it in private." There was a crack of a smile. "We about done with the
bullshit, then?" Tenishia's glare was still firmly in place.

"Probably," he nodded. "I think so."

"Then we can eat." She dropped the glare and cocked her
head to one side as she sat. "You ever read a book called *Huckleberry Finn*?"

"Yeah."

"Good. Then we got something to talk about."

6

The phone was ringing. Well, not really ringing, beeping—it was, of course, the goddamn cell phone—and it was beeping louder and louder, and Bridget was shaking me.

"The phone."

I forced myself to open my eyes. The alarm clock on the nightstand redly blinked 5:32, then turned to 5:33 while I was fumbling around on the floor for my pants and the goddamn cell phone. I found it.

"*What?*"

"Just me, Sparky," Jeff Bjerke's voice said in my ear. "Can you be ready in about fifteen, maybe twenty minutes? I'll pick you up."

"Some emergency?"

"Nah. Just ordinary police business," he said. "Bank delivery—I just got the call."

"And what do we have to do?"

"I'll tell you in the car. Nothing much, but I thought, you being the new chief and all, you'd want to get started right away."

Yeah. Sure. Just what I wanted to do at 5:33 in the goddamn morning. "Okay. See you in fifteen. I'll be waiting outside." No need to wake everybody in the house at this godforsaken hour. It's not like I'm a farmer, after all.

"If you can pull the cars out of your garage and park them

on the street, it'll be better if I can pull in there. Particularly if you leave the door open."

He hung up before I could decide if I wanted to ask why, much less ask.

Bridge rolled over and looked up at me. I couldn't make out her expression in what little light there was leaking in from the hall. I reached over and patted at the swell of her hip to tell her to go back to sleep.

"Some problem?" she asked.

"Nah. Jeff's just started playing Let's Jerk Sparky's Chain early today."

I stepped into my pants—yes, I know, I should have put them in the clothes hamper the night before, but I hadn't.

CYS, do your fucking worst.

A quick run to the bathroom, and I put on a T-shirt and stepped into my shoes before I went into the garage to move the cars.

Bridget's keys were, thankfully, on the visor where they belonged, so I didn't have to go back into the house to search for the copies she'd had her dad make for me at the store—although God knows why I'd need copies of her car keys; I don't—and moved my Olds out before I came back and got her black Mercedes and parked it behind my car, then walked back up to the driveway to the house.

The world was waking up too early, as it usually does. Across where the hedge between our houses used to be, Osa peered out through her kitchen window—Bob starts early in the morning—then gave me a quick, friendly wave before getting back to whatever she was doing. The hedge and I had had a dispute during the winter, and the first backyard cookout of the spring had been at the end of a work party to tear it out.

There was the distant whoosh of something, probably a truck, moving down the county road, although the windbreak prevented me from seeing it, and a distant train whistle proclaimed that the regular 445 Soo Line was coming through about as late as usual. There was some movement going on in Betty Lundgren's kitchen window, and if I listened real hard I could probably have heard clucking coming from her chicken coop—Betty's always been of the opinion that nobody else knows quite what to feed a chicken, or maybe it's just what remains of the farm girl in her; I dunno—and if she had a rooster it would have been crowing, no doubt.

No rooster, though, which was fine by me. Except when you're actually out on a farm, and far enough away that it won't bother the neighbors, roosters that insist on extensive greetings of the dawn seem to frequently die of the disorder known as "neck spasms," which doesn't affect the taste at all, as far as I can tell.

Another couple of million years, and anything more than a quick, quiet chirp will be all evolved out of them. Evolution in action.

I went in to get dressed, which would have all gone quicker if Snake hadn't taken me getting up to mean I was getting up, which meant that it was time for his morning piss and dump, and he kept wagging in anticipation as I got dressed for real. It was less bother to walk him than it was to argue the matter, so we were in the backyard when I saw the lights of Jeff's Bronco, then heard it pull up the driveway.

"Go play, Snake," I said. It was important to the dog that I witness him relieving himself, but there were cats and dogs and soon there'd be kids walking to school to play with, and he was off in a quick scamper.

Jeff was coming in through the garage doorway at the same time that I came in the back.

I'd tried to be as quiet as I could, but both Bridget and Tenishia were up, still sleepy-eyed in their robes, gathered around the coffeemaker like it was a campfire.

"What the fuck is that?" Tenishia asked, turning to Jeff.

I would have asked, roughly, the same question, except I sort of knew the answer. Jeff had on his Level III-A body armor over his usual semicop clothes.

He shook his head. "Not a big deal. It just looks like a big deal, which is why I came in through the garage." He frowned at me. "I thought you were going to be ready."

"Ready for what?"

"Bank delivery." He raised a palm. "Nothing exciting, honest. We just sit out in the car while the armored truck pulls up, and watch them go in and then come out."

"We expecting General Cinque and the whole SLA, the James Gang, or just John Dillinger?"

"Hey, relax." He glanced down at his wrist. "It's just part of the job, and not a big deal."

"You could have mentioned this last night."

"I would have if I'd known." He looked at his watch again. "If you can get dressed quickly, we've got enough time for a quick cup of coffee—then I'll help you into your gear."

Bridget smiled. "You get to look like a pretend soldier, too?" Tenishia brought another cup down from the shelf and poured four.

"Oh, yeah," Jeff said. "It's part of the fun."

Jeff already had one of the Winchesters out, resting on the back of the passenger's seat, and he handed me a box of ammo. "Load it up," he said. "I haven't had a chance since yesterday."

I nodded and worked the action—yes, it was empty—and then pushed one cartridge after another into it before getting into the car.

He frowned at me. "You don't really want to hold it up like that. We don't exactly want to scare anybody."

"Yeah." I set the gun down, propped up next to my leg, muzzle down, and then tried to fasten the seatbelt, but it wouldn't fit around the combination of me and the body armor, although Jeff didn't have the same trouble.

He started the car and punched the little release gizmo on the shotgun. It didn't pop up into the air or anything; it just sat there.

"Any chance you can tell me what's going on? Just for the fun of it."

He watched the mirror carefully as he backed the Bronco out of the garage. "Really, it's not a big deal." He shrugged. "About once a week I get a call from the armored-car folks that they're making a delivery, and I—er, we—just sit out in the street and watch, and then we're done."

If we'd had a bank or armored-car robbery in Hardwood recently, I think I'd have remembered it. The bank had been robbed once, when I was in the City. It hadn't made the national news or anything—a couple of guys had come in, showed some guns, taken some cash, and then driven off and got stopped by the Highway Patrol out on I-29. Talk of the town for years—we're not exactly the Wild West out here, or even the more-wild-but-with-less-of-a-reputation-for-it East.

He drove down Main Street and parked the car across from the bank, leaving the engine running. The lights in the bank were on, and so were the lights at Selmo's, although Paul Berge opens promptly at seven.

"And you do this all the time?"

"Well, yeah. Just part of the service." He shrugged again. "The thing to remember, though, is that the armored-car guards aren't exactly what you'd want to call rocket scientists, so unless anything gets interesting, we don't get out of the car until they're all done."

"Fine with me. And if it does get interesting?"

"Try to do something useful, I guess." He shrugged.

Both our phones rang at the same time. He raised a palm. "I'll get it." He pulled his phone out. "Officer Bjerke, HPD," he said, sounding all businesslike and official. Then: "Yes" and "Blue Bronco," and then he read off short a number/letter combination that was probably his license plate, then hung up.

The armored car rumbled up the street and parked in front of Selmo's, and two uniformed men got out the back door, one with what looked like a metal case in his hand. They were both wearing uniform jackets, not the silly-looking stuff we were in, and they quickly walked to the door of Selmo's.

"ATM machine," Jeff said.

"I figured that out."

Paul met them at the front door, and they made their way inside. About a minute later that they came out, again with one of them carrying a metal box, and climbed back into the armored car, which drove all of a couple hundred feet down to the bank, where roughly the same thing happened, except it was a full canvas bag that went in and a less-than-full one that came out.

Jeff sagged back into his seat. "Well. That was easy."

"That's it?" I asked.

"Yup," he said, smiling. "That's it." He made a face. "A few things to remember, though."

"Yeah?"

"Most robberies involving armored cars are inside jobs, one way or another. Maybe one of the guards is involved, although usually not. But sometimes guards talk too much, and sometimes they have friends, and if some of the guys from Berns Security were to talk too much, I think it would be a good idea if he might mention that when they make their stops in Hardwood, the local cop—in that expensive battle gear that the feds bought for him—is sitting outside, as well as the sniper on top of the building across the street."

"Sniper?"

He smiled. "Well, I've been known to embellish the story a touch."

"Everybody else do this?"

"Nah." He shook his head. "A couple do. Most don't bother. Most probably think I'm being paranoid, although they probably wouldn't come out and say it."

"How about the guy in Thompson?"

"Phil Jennings?" He shook his head. "Nah. He's got the staties cruising by all the time, and he's a lazy sort." He pointed with his chin at where the armored car had parked in front of the Dine-A-Mite. "If they're running ahead of schedule, they sometimes grab breakfast here."

"After all that trouble, they just get out of the car?"

"Nah. There's three of them. One always stays locked in. They take turns. The time to worry, so I understand it, is when somebody is out of the car with money, or the door is open."

Which sort of made sense.

"And if somebody comes up behind one of the guys while he's out of the car and sticks a gun in his ear? What do they do then?"

"I dunno. I know what they're *supposed* to do—which is just punch the panic button and not open the door—and I do know that they keep switching the teams around, and that part of their training is to show them the same pictures I saw in POST training of three dead guys in the back of an armored car, after just that sort of thing happened, but . . ." He shrugged. "Like I said, I dunno." He shoved the shotgun down into the bracket, then locked it back into place.

Jeff drove into the alley behind the Dine-A-Mite, and I unloaded the rifle while he got out of his armor, and then he stashed the rifle and his rig in the lockbox while I got out of mine. I felt more than twelve or so pounds lighter for some reason.

"And now we have breakfast," he said, slamming the hatch shut. He gave me a quick look up and down. "You'll do," he said, frowning at my raggedly nonhemmed jeans. "But just barely."

"Well, you said Kathy was going to hem my uniform pants."

"Yeah." He smiled. "Bob said he'd take care of it. We probably should have thrown all that stuff in the car and dropped it off."

"Visitors soon?"

"I expect."

I shrugged. "I can ask Osa; she won't mind." Quite the opposite; Osa Olson is always looking for chances to do a favor for Tenishia or Bridget or me, for some reason or other.

"Sooner the better."

I guess I shouldn't have been surprised to see Bob Aarsted in the Dine-A-Mite, sitting in his usual booth. But I was. It's one thing for him not to walk home for lunch from the hardware store, but taking breakfast in a restaurant, even the Dine-A-Mite, seemed awfully uncharacteristic.

"Hey, Sparky," he said as he sprinkled enough salt on his eggs-over-easy to melt ice. "Pull up a seat. You, too, Jeff." He looked over at Jeff, not at me. "Everything go okay?"

"Mainly," Jeff said, nodding. "The first thing we've got to see about is getting Sparky's uniform pants hemmed."

Oh. He was talking about the Streicher's trip, not the little business with the bank delivery.

Jeff shrugged. "Not that I mind," he said, patting at his own denim-clad thigh, but . . ."

Aarsted snorted. "Yeah, Sparky looks like a proper chief of police—from the waist up. There'll be some surveyors in today, and I won't be surprised, one way or another, if there's a commission guy with them. You'll see to it? Emily says she'll do it, assuming she doesn't have to measure him."

Fine with me. The thought of Emily Aarsted measuring my inseam was more frightening than embarrassing.

"Nope. All marked up." Jeff nodded.

"And what's next on the schedule?"

Jeff thought about it for a moment. "Got to spend some

time on radio procedure and with the computer, and do a couple of speeding stops."

"Speeding stops. Yup. A nice, progressive town with a Level Three doesn't have a raceway on the county road. Good." Aarsted nodded. "Sounds about right, and the town can certainly use the money."

I didn't know what the town's share of a a fifty-buck speeding ticket is, but even if it's 100 percent—and it could have been, for all I knew—it would take a hell of a lot to make any sort of difference to any budget bigger than my own personal one. "Set that up for this afternoon," he said. He turned to me. "If that's okay with you, Chief."

Yeah, you Chief me, too.

"I'll fit it in. Got to head out to Jeff Thompson's place this morning, though, and put a few rounds through my new service piece."

He furrowed his brow. "You bought a gun?"

"No, the *town* bought me a gun. We can talk about it in a minute," I said.

"No, we can talk about it now," he said.

"Okay. If you'd rather talk about that than talk about how and why I had that BCI detective over for dinner last night, we can do that. Your choice, Bob. You're the mayor, after all; I'm just a town employee."

That got him to blink.

"Jeff," he finally said, looking at me, not Jeff, "why don't you swing by Sparky's and pick up those pants and get them over to my house?"

Jeff nodded and made his escape.

Ole sent Becka Hansen over with my tea—I was beginning to hate him—and Becka raised an eyebrow. How she managed to keep her light-gray pullover sweater clean while working was one of those mysteries I'd probably never figure out. She'd been on since six, but, as always, she still looked like she had just walked, freshly scrubbed, out of the shower.

"Good morning, Chief," she said, with only a hint of a smile. The word had apparently gone out.

"Morning. It's okay to smile. Laugh if you want."

"At what?" She gave a little shrug, and I forced myself not to let my eyes follow the way it made her breasts move under the sweater.

"Not like I've never seen a cop before," she said. "Hash and eggs? Over easy or basted?"

I don't often eat out—and breakfast out usually involves hunting season—but it's not hard for somebody to pick up on your habits after a few years, even if those habits are exercised rarely.

"Basted. If you think Ole can manage it."

Her mouth twitched. "Basted's easy. White or wheat?"

"White. As unhealthy as possible."

She nodded and walked off, after giving a quick glance at my cup to make sure there was still plenty of tea in it. I would have paid attention to her walking away—yes, I like girls; sue me—but Aarsted had been waiting patiently long enough.

"Any chance you can tell me what's going on?" he asked.

"I was going to ask you about that." I reached for my cigarette pack, then remembered that I'd tucked it into the pocket of my supercop getup, which was in Jeff's Bronco. Shit. "Interesting coincidence, Andy Franz showing up at Streicher's yesterday."

"Coincidence. Sure." He didn't ask who Franz was. "Is he going to make trouble?"

"How could he?" I asked. "After all, there's nothing illegal about a licensed, qualified police officer–type like me being appointed chief of police. Hell of a lot less fuss than me maybe being arrested for molesting Tenishia."

"*What?*"

"Yeah. Some anonymous report to CYS. But I think Franz is going to step on it. Not hard, maybe."

"Shit."

My turn to shrug. "Well, I've got two reasons not to worry on that score. For one, I don't mess with the kid. For another, well, you should have heard Tenishia straighten Franz out. She isn't shy about that sort of thing."

"And Franz said he'd fix it."

"No, he just said he'd put in a word." I wasn't sure whether I'd have preferred that he repeat what Tenishia had said, word by word, or left it as a special surprise if a social worker asked her the obvious sorts of questions, but I hadn't asked him; we'd just made small talk when I'd walked him out to his car after dinner.

I was still fidgeting for the nonexistent cigarette when Becka walked by and flashed a smile as she dropped three of them on the table next to me.

"Thanks."

"Well, you were looking twitchy. You want to wait on your eggs until the hash is ready?" she asked.

"Please."

"No problem."

I picked one up. A Marlboro, not a Camel filter, but any port in a storm, I always say.

"That's low, even for Norstadt," Aarsted said.

"Yeah," I said. "Yeah, it is. Sounds like there's been a lot of anonymous reporting going on. You and Norstadt are beginning to sound to me like a couple of schoolkids playing Johnny's Copying Off Me."

"Me?" He was the picture of offended innocence. "I haven't done anything."

"Well, good," I said. "And it would be best for all concerned—me in particular—if you stop doing whatever it is you haven't been doing."

"It sounds to me, Sparky, like there's some sort of or else in there."

"Hell, yes, there's some sort of or else. I'm not sure what the law is—although I can find out—but I've got a hunch that making false police reports, anonymously or not, is officially naughty."

"And you'd try to arrest me?"

I liked the "try." I shook my head. "No, you'd fire me before I could."

"Well, if it came down to that, I'd need to get at least one vote from the town council," he said. "I think I could."

"Oh?"

"Yeah. Four of us—Fred and Emma don't vote—and the mayor breaks ties. Not sure about Minnie, but I could probably get either Doc or Dave Oppegaard. Dave never much liked this whole idea."

That hadn't showed at the time; they seemed to run things by unanimous consensus. Then again, one town council meeting was probably not exactly what you'd call a representative sample. "But you could do it."

"Sure."

"Well, under the circumstances, wouldn't bother me a whole lot. But you've painted a real pretty picture here—an up-and-coming town that could use but isn't desperate for the Level Three, with a two-man police force that keeps things quiet and a brand-new, experienced-looking chief of police who can reassure important visitors by his presence and appearance that things will stay nice and quiet. Plus, you've managed to get one up on Norstadt. I assume there's going to be a nice story in the *Gleaner* about my appointment?"

He nodded. "You mind copyediting it?"

"Nah; always can use the work. I can bill you at my regular rates, or I can do it on company—on Town of Hardwood time. Dealer's choice."

"I thought maybe you'd want to do it as a favor."

I just looked at him.

"Do it on town time," he finally said. "I know what you bill."

"Not all that much, and I'm worth it." I shrugged. "But my point is, it'd be a shame to ruin this pretty picture by firing me, with the commission about to be snooping around. Or, for that matter, have the staties get all irritated with you when Jeff's out of town—by you throwing away a perfectly good second cop, and all. He's going to have to go to visit his dad again soon, and you solved that problem by hiring me. Betcha Thompsen doesn't have double coverage."

"Which will look good to the siting committee, sure." He shook his head. "I thought you'd think it more important that all this got you out of some embarrassment, or spending a few days in a Grand Forks jail."

"Which wouldn't have been a possibility in the first place without your politics."

"Politics, shit. I'm talking about the town's goddamn survival here."

"Yeah, Bridget told me all about your charts and graphs, and I'd like to see them sometime. And, truth to tell, I'd like there to still be a town here ten, twenty years from now. I like this place. I like my neighbors. I like living in the same house that Mom and Dad bought; when I go down to the basement to pull some cans of soup off the rack, I like that it was the rack Dad and I built ourselves." I shook my head. "But I'm with Franz on this one. People are getting hurt over this, and it's not just me, and if it doesn't stop, it'll get worse before it gets better. Big Steve's about to get a visit from the DNR inspectors—somebody said he's been using DDT or something."

He didn't say anything, so I did.

"Sounds to me like this could get real, real ugly, and maybe the commission will decide to put the Level Three in Hatton or Larimore, where there aren't so many games being played.

Didn't somebody mention to me, just the other day, about how there's lots of land around?"

"And there might be county-level problems with zoning for any other site except here and there."

"Oh." I should have figured that he'd have worked that part of it out.

"Besides, there's too many churches in Larimore," he said. "Lots of hassles there. Quieter here."

"Right now it is. If you two little scamps don't stop playing around, it won't be."

"I heard you the first time."

"Yeah, and you probably should have heard this from Jeff months ago, when it all started up." It felt disloyal to say that, although I don't know why.

"Jeff does what he's told. And doesn't do what he isn't. That's his job. Now, what's this about you buying a gun? I don't see it."

"That's because it isn't here. Just this." I patted at the butt of my snubby. "For all I know, my brand-new firearm doesn't have a firing pin, or there's some other reason that it won't go bang when I pull the trigger. Going to fix that this morning. As to buying the gun, it was an honest mistake. Jeff and I got our signals crossed—hell, I misunderstood him. Blame me, if you need to blame somebody."

He almost smiled. "Okay. I can always deduct it from your salary."

I shook my head. "Nope. I don't need another 1911-style semiauto. Already got one. Then again, it'd probably be a good thing if the new chief of police has a shiny new handgun to go with his shiny new badge, and shiny new uniforms, and shiny new battle armor. With all the millions involved in this Level Three thing, you want to quibble about a few hundred bucks?"

"Sounds like a thousand, all said."

"Yeah?"

"But we'll let it slide," he decided. "I wouldn't want you to feel . . . inadequate."

I could tell he was upset. That sort of dig wasn't usually his style.

"Well, when it comes to this sort of stuff, about the only thing I feel *is* inadequate."

Inadequate, as well as irritated, pissed off, out of my depth, frightened, and a few other things I didn't feel like mentioning at the time. Only a fool is an utter slave to truth. "And, if it matters, I like tools that I know, and I know the 1911. The only thing I know about the snubby is that it'll make a bang when I pull the trigger, and that I can throw a baseball more accurately than I can shoot it. So I'm keeping it as long as I'm keeping the job."

"You don't seem to have a lot of give in you, these days," he said.

"Your daughter can get a whole lot of give out of me," I said, lying only a little. "But she plays straight with me. Doesn't bullshit me, doesn't try to manipulate me—or when she does, she comes right out and says it, and doesn't play games. Bridge and I, well, we stay honest with each other." I took another pull on the Marlboro. "I'd like it to be that way with you and me, but I'm beginning to have my doubts if it's possible. So: We have a deal? No more phony complaints?"

"Yeah," he said. "I'll stop if he stops."

"No, you'll stop even if he doesn't, and if he doesn't, you'll try to see that the fact he's the one—the only one—playing games gets pointed out to the right people." I shrugged. "I might even be able to help a little there. Unless you don't listen to me, in which case it'll all get as ugly as I can manage to make it."

"Bridget put you up to this?"

"Up to what? Being straight and up-front with you?" I shook my head. "Nah. She doesn't need to. I'm capable of working that out myself, thank you much."

Aarsted thought for a while, then nodded. "Yeah, I suppose

you are. Always thought she should have married you instead of Fred Honistead."

"I thought we'd agree'd you'd stop lying."

He didn't quite know how to take that, and I was beginning to realize I didn't give a shit how he took it.

About an eon, or a geological age, or some other large unit of time ago, I'd thought of Bob Aarsted as not just a good guy, but a simple one, and I missed that ancient time. I missed it more than I would've thought I could. I didn't quite know what I thought about him right now.

"Okay," he said. "No more games. And if that loses the town the Level Three—"

"Then it never was ours, anyway."

He blinked. "Maybe so."

"You got other irons in the fire, I suspect. Maybe it's time for you to think about heating them up."

"Maybe," he said, his eyes never leaving mine. "Maybe not. We'll see."

"Yeah, that's a safe bet: We'll see."

He looked over at me. "Come this winter, you still willing to go hunting with me, Sparky?"

I shouldn't have been surprised at the question. Like I said, Bob Aarsted pays attention.

"I don't know. I'll have to think about it. Jeff Bjerke, yes. You're a maybe right now. I'm not sure I trust you, Bob," I said.

No, I didn't think Bob would, even if he thought it was convenient, decide to mistake me for a deer. But I'm particular about who I go hunting with.

"Maybe you've got good reason." He nodded. "Or maybe you're overreacting just a little?"

"There's always that possibility."

Becka arrived with my hash and eggs. And we just looked at each other over the table, and didn't say more than a few words while I ate.

I don't expect a world-class meal at the Dine-A-Mite, and I didn't get one. But I managed to chew all the food and swallow it down, so it wasn't a total waste.

I think.

Well, not all salesmen are liars, I guess. The Kimber worked just fine. Not everything else did, but that's kind of the way life works.

Jeff Thompsen—not Jeffie; his dad—was out behind the shed, next to the barn, when I got out there. Things around the Thompsen farm tend to take the definite article, a legacy from Jeff's father.

"The shed" is what it's called, although it's a big corrugated metal building, painted an awful lime green, capable of holding both tractors, the combine, and the various things that get hitched up to both, as well as all three cars and various other bits of machinery, like the Bobcat. It looks more like an airplane hanger than anything else.

He'd taken the old tractor out—the green John Deere that his father had bought new, when the world was young—and spread out a bunch of tools on a dirty old blanket, and gotten underneath it, but he slid out and was on his feet before I was out of the car.

"Hey, Sparky," he said, wiping his hands on a rag. "And don't you look semirespectable in your new cop suit."

Farmers seem to follow the law of the excluded middle: Either they're skinny and ropy-muscled—the sort you'd think couldn't possibly lift up and haul around everything a farmer hauls around, although they do—or built like a wrestler. Jeff, like his son, was the second type: big and square and blocky, with thigh muscles bulging hard enough to threaten to split the seams of his filthy overalls.

He was still wearing his winter beard—which was unusual; Jeff usually shaved it off early in the spring, either in anticipation of how hot summer days get out this way, or as part of some sort of preplanting ritual; I dunno.

He wiped his hands on the rag some more and made a point of looking down at them, and didn't offer me the usual handshake. "Social visit, or have you come to arrest me for using DDT?"

"You're using DDT?"

I don't keep up with the chemicals they use on the farms—other than RoundUp, as you can't avoid the commercials for it, every spring, if you watch even a little bit of TV. But DDT has long been illegal, and I don't even know where you'd get it if you wanted to—besides, so I understand, there's a lot of perfectly good pesticides that a farmer can use without violating half a zillion state and federal laws, and DDT isn't one of them.

"Nah. Neither is Big Steve." He made a face. "But there's a bunch of DNR folks over there right now, taking samples. He called. Been wondering if I was going to get a visit."

"I heard last night it might happen—there. Didn't think it was on today's agenda."

His face darkened. "And you didn't think to tell him about it?"

"Well, no, it hadn't occurred to me to head over to Big Steve's and tell him not to do something that I was damned sure he wasn't doing anyway. Maybe it should have."

"Maybe."

"Shit, Jeff, cut me a fucking break, eh?"

He smiled. "Okay, Sparky. You playing hooky to kill some chucks for me today?"

"I'd love to, but it seems I don't run my own schedule at the moment." I jerked my thumb toward the car. "Wanted to know if I could use the hill to try out my brand-new chief-of-police-type pistol."

"Sure."

"And maybe if you felt like playing a bit?"

"I better not . . ." He started to shake his head, then stopped himself. "Shit, the old tractor can wait a few minutes. Yeah, let's do it."

"Problem with the tractor?" Like everybody else, Jeff does most of his maintenance during the winter. It's possible, I suppose, to be a farmer without being a good jackleg mechanic, but I don't know any. It probably takes Jeff longer to put a new transmission in his combine than it would at the John Deere dealership in Grand Forks, and if it broke down during the harvest, he'd do just that—but, shit, he only works about six, seven hours a day during winter, and God forbid he should waste his time sitting around.

"Nah. Just an oil change," he said. "Regular maintenance is the key to the farm's survival, like my dad used to say."

Yeah. Most things his father used to say ended with "is the key to the farm's survival," whether he was talking about getting up early in the morning, reading the latest DNR brochures, raising your own meat and butchering it yourself, and probably washing your ass with your right hand in the shower.

I don't know how Jeff turned out so well.

We got the shooting gear out of the car and headed around behind the house, and while I got the pistol out and loaded up the mags with practice ammo, Jeff went into the house to let Barb known what was going on.

The hill—it had always been called "the hill"—had started life as a twenty-foot-high, hundred-foot-long berm of earth on the west edge of the yard that Jeff's dad had plowed into place back when we were kids. It was a little more complicated than it looked—there were a couple of drainage pipes buried under it that emptied out in the field beyond, to prevent the backyard and therefore the basement from being flooded during the spring melt—but basically it was just a berm.

The official reason for it was to protect the house from the

winter wind and snow that had, for the previous decades, an-
nually been driven all the way across the plains to stack up
against the side of the house, and it certainly did that.

I think Jeff's dad's suspicions about Weasel Larsen spying on
the family across the field had more to do with making the hill,
although what joy anybody would have had had from spying on
kids playing in a backyard or the Thompsens having a barbecue
escapes me, and more than likely escaped Weasel Larsen as well.

He could, of course, have built a fence, like anybody else
would have, but I guess you had to know Jeff's dad. A simple
fence just wouldn't have been his style.

The remains of our old fort were still on top of the hill,
mostly overgrown. A stand of two-inch birches crested the
hill, and the grass was already long and destined never to be
mowed, and mostly hid the half-buried logs there.

Jeff came out of the house with a cardboard box under each
arm and a machete belted around his waist, and he chopped
away at the grass to clear the top of the third log up. I set up a
line of cans as he cleared, then dumped what remained of one
box in the other and set it down. I took the empty box and set
it on the log, putting a few rocks inside to hold it in place.

"What's the matter?" he asked, smiling, as we walked back
to the picnic table. "Don't you think you can hit a can from
twenty feet?"

"I dunno. For all I know, this newfangled supergun might
boomerang right back on me."

"Yeah, sure."

I slammed the magazine home, hard, remembering a red-
faced drill sergeant screaming, "It's perhaps best to be gentle
with your girlfriend when you wish to engage in sexual inter-
course with her, but I do wish you wouldn't be quite so gentle
with the semiautomatic pistol the government has been kind
enough to issue you, since it's unlikely to break if handled with
firmness"—or something to that effect—then racked the slide.

"Ears, Sparky," Jeff said, tapping on his own hearing protectors.

Oops. I set the pistol down on the table and put my hearing protection on, then flicked the switch, getting the familiar ears-blocked feeling, sort of like when they don't pop in a plane.

I took aim at the center of the box, ignoring Jeff's knowing smile, and squeezed.

Wham.

Jeff nodded. The hole was about six inches left of center.

"I was shooting left," I lied.

"Sure you were. Aim for the hole," he said.

I did, and tried another few, and they grouped nicely just about six inches to the left of the first hole.

Bob Olson had been right, though; no lubrication, save what came from the factory, and the gun pointed just fine. I'm not fond of pistols—reaching out from a couple of hundred yards with a .22-250 is more my style—but there was something satisfying about shooting it.

The slide locked back and I handed the gun and a mag to Jeff. He let the slide drop, squeezed off two shots—dead center on the box, about an inch apart—and then started trying to drop cans, missing a couple, hitting a couple, sending them tumbling down the hill's side, or the hillside, or whatever you want to call it.

"Not bad," he said. "Shoots straight for me."

"Well, maybe my eyes are on crooked."

"Or maybe it's pointing right and I'm overcompensating." He raised his head and his voice. "Hey, Barb?"

"Yeah?" sounded from the window.

"Can you grab your ears and come out here? I wanna try an experiment."

Barb Thompsen came down the steps a few moments later, with her own hearing protectors—fancy and electronic, like mine, not the plain sort that Jeff had—in one hand and a flat-bottomed wicker basked loaded down with goodies in the other.

There was a lot to like about Barb. Looks for one. She was slim but rounded in all the right places, emphasized by both her jeans and the way she had her plaid chambray shirt tucked in tightly at the waist. If there was any sign of whatever four decades, three late-term miscarriages, and one full-term pregnancy had done to her figure, I'd never been able to see it. Her blond hair was tied back, and there was nothing particularly unattractive about the dirty smudge on her right cheek; it would wash up just fine, and her full lips never needed any lipstick.

And it's not just looks.

She's good at a lot of things—more so than even the usual farm wife, who has to be a jack of most trades and an expert in all of them. She keeps the farm's books, and beat the IRS the three years they compliance-audited them, and can head out to the chicken coop and the garden with that wicker basket, and, in more time it takes to tell about it but a lot less than it should to do it, turn raw ingredients into the best ten-course coq-au-vin dinner for a dozen you'd ever want to have. Over the past few years, in her copious free time, she'd torn the kitchen and all the bathrooms down to bare studs and put them back together better than new, and built and installed the solar-water-heater array that had basically taken over the south roof of the house single-handed. She's also a trap and skeet shooter of some local repute—she prefers Humiliation to more standard forms of competition—and has been known to embarrass even the Coulters in a friendly little match.

But I don't like her, and she doesn't have much more use for me.

"Hi, Sparky," she said, with a smile that she didn't much mean, any more than she meant, "Good to see you, looking all official." She didn't mention the pants.

"Hi, Barb. Sorry about all the noise."

"Not a problem." Her smile broadened.

She set the basket down on the table. There were a couple of big plastic two-liter bottles of pop, and three glasses filled with ice, and a plate piled high with sandwiches. Thick slices of home-baked bread, not store-bought. "Ham okay? Got some roast beef in the fridge."

I could have said that I wasn't hungry, which was true enough, but Barb and I have never much liked each other, something that Jeff carefully pretended to ignore, most of the time, and refusing food wasn't in the program.

"Ham's fine," I said.

"You mind taking this for a quick spin?" Jeff asked, hefting the .45.

She eyed the cardboard box. "Shooting left?"

"That's one theory."

"Sure." She set her earmuffs on her ears, switched them on, then accepted the gun from Jeff, dropped the mag, racked the slide, and took up a stance, then squeezed off first one shot, then two, then emptied the mag.

Bang. Bang-bang. Bang-bang-bang-bang.

The shots all made a tight little group, roughly where mine were. "Yup. Shoots left," she said. "A little drift right on the rear sight should probably do it, but try just point-shooting it."

"Eh?"

She made a gimme gesture to Jeff, and dropped and replaced the magazine before handing the gun back to me, not seeming to go to any effort at all to be sure that the pistol, loaded or empty, always continued to point downrange.

"Don't use the sights this time," she said, mimicking having a gun in her hand as she stretched her two hands straight out at chest level. "Just hold it level. Point it, don't aim it."

I did as she instructed, and squeezed off a shot. Just about center of the box.

"Again. Empty it." Same thing, repeated seven more times.

She nodded. "Yup. Gun fits your hand fine; just drift the sights—click the sights," she said, correcting herself, "a couple notches to the right, and it'll be dead on." She helped herself to my gear bag, pulled out the screwdriver set, then held out her hand for the gun, which I locked open and handed over.

A couple quick clicks, and it worked just fine.

At twenty or so feet, the bullets went where I thought they were supposed to, and I amused myself by knocking down the cans that Jeff had missed.

She grinned as she put the screwdriver back in the kit, then the kit back in the gear bag. "Yeah. That'll do." She looked back at the house, as though thinking she should be getting back to work. "New gun? You going to put a few dozen boxes through it, I suspect."

"If you don't mind. Sorry about the noise," I said again.

"Mind?" she smiled. "*Please*. With those DNR assholes over at Big Steve's, some gunfire coming from here wouldn't bother me at all." She gave a grin. "I was thinking about shooting a little skeet myself, if maybe I could get somebody to throw for me."

Oh, great.

"Yeah, sure," I said, "the DNR would absolutely, unconditionally refuse to think about investigating a complaint if they thought that it might result in somebody threatening to shoot at them."

What the fuck was she thinking? The DNR folks confront hunters—both legit and poachers—all the damn time. That's part of their *job*. "Naturally they'd just give up and go home, and wouldn't think to send for reinforcements if they were at all concerned."

"But—"

"But nothing." I don't know who I was madder at, her or me.

I grabbed the goddamn cellphone off my belt and in punched Jeff Bjerke's number.

"Hello."

"It's me," I said.

"I can tell from the caller ID," he said. "What's up?"

"You've got numbers for the DNR folks handy?"

"Yeah."

"Well, get on the phone to somebody there, and make sure the people taking samples out at Big Steve's place know that the sound of shots they're hearing from Jeff Thompsen's farm is just me breaking in my new service piece. If they're planning a visit here, they can head on over anytime—and they can call you or me if they'd prefer to have somebody local around, although there won't be any trouble. Tell them that. Wouldn't want them to get the wrong idea."

"Got it. I guess it makes sense."

What do you mean, guess? I thought.

"We still on for noon?" he asked.

"Yeah. I'll meet you at my house."

He hung up.

Barb was glaring at me, and I was glaring at her, and Jeff was trying to look the other way.

"Well," she finally said, and turned off and walked to the house without a look back, closing the door behind her very gently, too angry to show weakness by slamming it.

Jeff sighed. "Well, I see I still don't have to worry about the two of you sneaking around behind my back," he said, too lightly, as he seated himself at the table, took a quick look at his hands, which were filthy, and grabbed himself a sandwich anyway. "The two of you are like a couple of schoolkids pretending not to like each other, except I don't think either of you is pretending."

"Your wife—" I stopped myself. There would probably come a day when I had to say out loud to my oldest friend what he knew damn well I thought of the manipulative bitch he married, but today certainly wasn't it. "Barb probably didn't think that through as much as she should have," I finally settled on.

"Yeah, maybe." He cocked his head to one side. "Pull up a seat and eat something."

I did, and yes, the bread was fresh and homemade, and the crust had a nice, meaty crunch, and the ham was sliced paper-thin and piled high, and the mustard was eye-tearingly wonderful, and it all went down just fine with a glass of icy pop.

"She's a good woman, Sparky," he finally said.

"Yeah."

"You don't sound convinced."

"I am. She's kept you happy, and, hey, the two of you produced one hell of a kid. Good enough for Tenishia, in my opinion—not that either of them is asking my opinion."

"Nobody else's, either," he said. "I kinda like Tenishia, but I don't think it's a secret that she's not Barb's favorite person in the world. Then again, there's a fair number of people I like that Barb doesn't have a lot of use for."

"I think I may have noticed that from time to time over the years."

He smiled. "Now, what is it you want to tell me about this after-school program at Minnie Larsen's?"

I'd been putting that off—I'd preferred to have put it off forever. Jeff's father would have taken out the belt over any hint of being involved in cheating in school, and while I didn't think that was a live possibility here, I didn't know as to how he needed to know what the kids had been up to.

I'd say that when the issue had gone from some hypothetical DNR agents showing up with drawn guns to the kids actually cheating on their papers, it shook me—and that's true enough, silly as it sounds—but the truth is that I hadn't wanted to get into it at all.

"Nothing much. Tenishia needs a bit of extra tutoring, and

I figured it would be easy on everybody if she doesn't get sin-gled out. Hope that's okay with you."

He nodded. "Yeah, that's fine by me." He looked me straight in the eye. "I'm not sure I entirely believe that's all there is to it, mind you, but there's this question of trust, Sparky."

I probably should have said something, but I didn't quite know what to say.

"Not sure I can trust you to tell me the truth, and my guess is that I can't trust you to tattle on my kid, but I don't know as that that's all important. Think I can trust you to keep my kid out of trouble?"

"Yeah."

"Good." He nodded. "I think he should do four years at the U, if only to give him something to fall back on if the farm goes under. He thinks he should just work full-time on the farm after he graduates high school. Him, say, getting expelled for cheating would mean he gets his way—the wrong way. That wouldn't be good. I'm willing to lose the argument if I have to, but not that way."

"No, it wouldn't be good. But I don't think that's going to happen." I didn't ask how he knew what he knew. The fact that I'd lied to him was bad enough. Did him knowing it make it better or worse?

Good question; wish I had a good answer.

I'd have been tempted to blame Aarsted and Norstadt, but I'd been prepared to dance around the truth on this before I'd been up to my nose in politics, with the sewer water rising.

"Fuck," I said. "Truth is that Josh Ginsburg's been writing Tenishia's papers for her, probably at Jeffie's instigation. Not that any of them will admit any of it, quite."

He nodded slowly. "Yeah. Friends cover for friends from time to time." He smiled. We'd spent most of our boyhood covering for each other over various things. I think the balance was mostly in my favor, but that's largely because my father was just imperfect, while his was an asshole. "I don't hold with cheating, but I do have this thing about loyalty."

"Yeah, but—"

" 'Yeah, but,' right. So you're saying I shouldn't officially know anything about it?"

"Sounds right to me."

He nodded slowly. "And I sure as shit can't say anything to Barb about it, can I?"

You're a fucking asshole, Hemingway. First I'd lied to a friend—if only by omission—and then I'd put him in the position of having to lie to his wife, again if only by omission.

"Probably not. And I'd probably better get going." I wrote down my new chief-of-police cell phone number in my official chief-of-police notepad, tore it out, and handed it to him. "If there's any problem—if the DNR folks show up—call me. And, for Christ's sake, keep Barb from playing games with guns."

"Yeah." He stared down at the paper long enough to memorize it, then tucked it in his shirt pocket.

Well, writing speeding tickets isn't the most difficult thing in the world. I'd been aware that it was a pain in the ass from the, er, receiving end, but . . .

"Okay," Jeff said. "The first thing we do is to calibrate the gun."

We were sitting in the Bronco, parked behind Brian Gisslequist's field shed, just off the county road, and Jeff had the radar gun—which looked more like an overgrown *Star Trek* phaser gun than anything else—plugged in, and turned on.

"See this button that says 'Calibrate'?" he asked.

"Yup. Just press it?"

"Go ahead."

I did, and the little LED screen lit up to say OK.

"Well, that's easy enough."

"Yeah, and totally useless. Legally speaking, all it says is that the machine thinks the machine is okay. Grab the log and the bags out of the glove compartment."

I did. The log was just a notebook, with RADAR LOG written on the cover in bold block letters.

There were two plastic bags; each contained a tuning fork—I mean, a real tuning fork, like I used to use to tune my violin back when I was a kid.

"Take either one out; doesn't matter." I pulled out the bigger one, which had 33.2 inscribed on it.

"Now, hit that on your knee, point the gun at it, then pull the trigger."

I did, and after a moment of wavering, it settled on 33 for a second or two, then displayed 9999.

"That's thirty-three point two megahertz?"

"Nah. It vibrates at thirty-three point two miles per hour. We're calibrating a radar here, not tuning a banjo. And plus or minus five percent is the standard—let's try the other."

The reading from that one, which said 77.6, was 77.

"Okay. Now we're calibrated, and you can put the forks away." He set the radar gun down on the floor rather than in his lap and beckoned at me to open the log. "Note the date, your name, and the calibration numbers, and we're ready to rock."

"What's this all about?"

"Rules of evidence. We can now provide evidence that today, at . . . twelve-thirty-one P.M.—write while I talk—two certified tuning forks—certificates in that manilla folder in the glove compartment—showed that the radar was accurate well within the five-percent standard." He smiled. "And now we just wait."

"And shoot any car that passes?"

"Uh-huh. Well, okay—shoot the next car," he said.

"Going east?"

"Either way."

Have I mentioned that East Dakota is flat-flat-flat-flat? The

Gisslequist shed blocked any view to the west—we wouldn't
see an eastbound car until it passed by the shed—but County
15 runs utterly straight for easily forty miles from Thompson to
McVille, with just a little right-angled jog at Cole Creek about
ten miles in.

I couldn't see anything headed our way, but it didn't take
long before a little blue Toyota whizzed by, and I managed to
get it square in the sights and pull the trigger, and immediately,
73 MPH appeared in the display, and just about that time the
brake lights of the Toyota came on.

Well, only an idiot drives without a radar detector.

Jeff just sat there. I'd been expecting him to throw the
Bronco into drive, and peel out, lights flashing and siren wail-
ing, but he just sat there.

"Am I missing something?"

"Yup. Couple of things. For one thing," he said, gesturing at
where I'd set the radar gun down on the seat between my legs,
"you really don't want to do that. Even when it's off, the gizmo
gives off some radiation—"

I snatched the radar gun up quickly.

"And while a couple of minutes isn't going to do much
harm to you, I don't really think you want to find out what it'll
do to your gonads, not in the long run."

"You might have mentioned that before."

"You might have read the manual."

"Well, yeah." I was eying the radar gun suspiciously—he just
gestured at the dashboard.

"Just set it up there; it should be okay. And, like I said, a
couple of minutes in your lap probably isn't going to make your
balls shrivel up and fall off. Just don't make a habit of it."

"So we didn't go after this guy because I put the radar gun in
my lap?"

"Nah. Different matter." He drew himself up straight. "Mr.
Hemingway," he said, doing what I think he thought was a

Perry Mason imitation, "what first suggested to you that the car in question, on the date and time in question, was traveling in excess of the posted speed limit?"

"Well, there was the fact that this here certified radar gizmo that fries your balls if you leave it in your lap said so, and—"

"By 'radar gizmo,' you mean the Genesis Handheld Corded Stationary Traffic Safety Radar Gun?"

"Yeah."

"So it was the radar device that made you think my client might be going too fast."

"Well, he looked like he was going fast."

"After you had already checked his speed with the Genesis Handheld Corded Stationary Traffic Safety Radar Gun?"

"Well, yes."

"Is it possible that your opinion about my client's speed just might have been influenced by the reading on the Genesis Handheld Corded Stationary Traffic Safety Radar Gun?"

"I don't think so?"

"It's utterly impossible? You couldn't possibly have been influenced."

"Well, maybe."

"Hmm . . . so, if the device were defective, your training and expertise possibly wouldn't have been able to tell you that, given the possible influence on your opinion?"

"Well, yes, that's possible."

"And what training did you receive in the use of this particular device?"

I grunted. "I received my training from Officer Jeff Bjerke of the Hardwood Police Department."

"And this Officer Bjerke—is he a certified instructor in the use of radar speed-detecting devices in general and the Genesis Handheld Corded Stationary Traffic Safety Radar Gun in particular?"

"I don't know."

"Hmm . . . and how many hours of instruction did this training consist of?"

"Er . . . five or six?"

Jeff dropped the Perry Mason and said, "Yeah, it'll be about that." He cleared his throat. "And are you aware, Chief Hemingway—it is Chief Hemingway, isn't it?—that many departments have adopted the National Highway Traffic Safety Administration standards of not less than twenty-four hours of classroom instruction and not less than sixteen hours of supervised field experience?"

"Well," I said, improvising, "the Hardwood PD hasn't adopted that standard."

He nodded. "Yeah. You'd—you'll get that in POST classes, though." Yeah, sure. Like that was ever going to happen. Who did he think he was fooling?

"Harrumph." He looked up at an imaginary judge. "Your honor, given that this officer's training is substandard, and that he didn't observe my client traveling at an excessive speed before trusting to this . . . this *device* to do his observing for him, I submit there's reasonable doubt that my client was, in fact, traveling at an excessive speed, and ask that you dismiss the case." He shrugged and again dropped the Perry Mason act. "And it depends on who you get, but he probably would."

"So why are we bothering?"

"Well, for one, after you take your POST classes in the fall, you can give different answers." Yeah, assuming I wouldn't be out of this before then, which was an assumption I sure as shit wasn't making, and nobody but Jeff was much pretending to. Once the Level III committee made its decision, either way, I'd be back to my life.

"Secondly," he went on, "if you had already noticed that the car appeared to be traveling too fast, and the radar just confirmed and quantified it, the judge may not care about your training. It's a training standard, not the law. Thirdly—how often have you fought a speeding ticket?"

"Well, never. Never got quite enough points on my license that I needed to take a day off and spend it at a courthouse in Grand Forks, and probably lose anyway—easier just to pay the ticket."

There'd been a couple of years when points had done a real serious number on my insurance rates, but then I'd been careful for a year or so, and one had come off every three months I'd managed to avoid getting a ticket, and eventually they'd dropped down to what the insurance company calls "safe-driver" rates, as though there's something unsafe traveling at eighty down a flat country road where the visibility goes on forever, and you probably should be able to do a hundred or better if you've got the car for it.

I don't think I'm quite the first person to notice that the law is an ass or that insurance companies are goats.

He nodded. "Yup. That's one of the reasons that the lege keeps fines low—and why there's no points at all for one to ten miles an hour over the speed limit. And I bet that most of the time you've been ticketed, the ticket hasn't read more than fifteen above the limit. Ten to fifteen above is only one point."

"True enough."

"Now try the next one."

A distant blot grew closer, and it seemed, at least to me, to be doing so awfully quickly, and by the time that I could tell that it was some sort of station wagon, I was pretty sure it was moving quickly.

"That vee-hicle," I said, "appears to me to be moving at something in excess of the posted speed limit."

Jeff smiled. "Well, then, perhaps you should verify your impression with the Genesis Handheld Corded Stationary Traffic Safety Radar Gun."

I did, and the LED quickly settled on 88. Perfectly reason-able speed, under the circumstances, but . . .

Jeff flicked on the bubble-gum lights and threw the Bronco into gear, rolling slowly down the slight incline of the dirt road.

I shot the radar gun at the car again.

"Don't bother. It isn't certified for when we're moving."

I carefully ignored the 73 MPH readout as I set the radar gun down. On the dashboard.

It was a new-looking Ford station wagon, with that idiotic phony wood siding I've never quite understood, and it flashed by at what appeared to be a decreasing speed as Jeff turned sharply onto the highway and stepped on it, not bothering with the siren.

"No reason to get all noisy if he plays nice," Jeff said.

It took a couple of seconds that felt longer than that for the driver to either notice or decide to notice that he was being followed by something with flashing lights on top, and he quickly slowed and pulled over onto the shoulder. Jeff fol-lowed, and stopped the Bronco about twenty feet back of the station wagon's rear bumper.

"Safety tip—leave plenty of room. If somebody comes along while we're out and smacks into this car, it'd be nice to have a little warning so we can maybe think about jumping out of the way," he said, while his fingers were already punching buttons on the computer. "When we get out, you take up a position at the right rear of the car, and just stand there, okay?"

"Sure."

He unclipped the microphone from the dashboard and flicked the loudspeaker switch. "Please just sit there for a mo-ment, and I'll be right with you," he said, not sounding either threatening or friendly, just professional.

Computers can be complicated, but this was all menu-driven and looked easy enough. In a few seconds a name and address popped up, along with a table of information below that Jeff quickly scanned, then nodded.

"Should be fine," he said. "Let's go."

Jeff set his cap on his head and patted at his ticket clipboard, then gestured at me to get out of the car, which I did. He took his funny-looking nightstick from where he'd stuck it into the seat and slid it into the metal loop on his belt, then marched over to the car.

"Hello," he said as he approached the rolled-down window. "License, registration, and insurance card, please."

"Yes, officer, but—"

"Hang on. We'll get to that in a minute. You're Nils Kupperman?"

"Yes, sir."

"Still live at thirteen-fifty-four Columbia Street in Grand Forks?"

"Yes."

"Okay. Do you know why I stopped you?"

"Probably because I was speeding?"

"Well, yeah." Jeff smiled and gave me a reassuring nod. "My boss here clocked you at eighty-eight. Speed limit is sixty-five in daytime here. I'm going to make a little mistake on the ticket and only show you as going seventy-five. Fifty-dollar fine; no points. You'll get a notice as to your court date, and if you don't show up in court, you'll be found guilty and they'll send you a bill."

"Could I just pay the fine now and get it over with?"

"Sure," he said. "MasterCard or Visa?"

"Cash okay?" he asked, maybe too casually.

"Nope. If we go the cash route, I've got to find the judge, or I'll have to stay up late at night worrying that somebody might think you bribed me to forget about the ticket, and I hate staying up late. You got a Visa or MasterCard?"

"Well, yes." He passed over a credit card, and Jeff gave him a friendly nod.

"Okay. Just sit tight and I'll be back in a minute."

As he walked back to the car, he gestured at me to get in.

"What was that all about?"

Jeff shrugged as he made some marks on his ticket pad, then punched a few buttons on the computer, and slid—I think you're supposed to say "swiped"—the credit card through the slot on the side. "Nice enough guy; no attitude, and since he lives in Grand Forks, I don't particularly want him to get interested or irritated enough to fight the ticket. Hell, he didn't even get out of the car. Tends to make me nervous when they do."

"And if he did?"

"Well, if he just gets out of the car when he stops and just stands there next to it, no problem—particularly if the plates say he's from down South. That's the SOP in some states there. Or if he's a trucker—hard to hand down the stuff from up there; most just climb down out of the cab with their paperwork already out.

"But if he starts marching toward the car, then I tell him to stop again, a little more firmly—but I'm still in the Bronco, not having yet run the plates. What makes me nervous are the ones that get out of the car *after* I've gotten out. Then I give him one of these"—he stretched his left hand out, fingers spread—"and if that doesn't stop him, the stick comes out real, real quick." He patted at where he had the funny-looking nightstick tucked back into the seat next to him. "At that point, you're into I-don't-know-what-the-fuck-he's-going-to-do-next territory."

"Wait a minute. How do you get the license if you're not going to let him get close?"

"It's not a getting-close thing; it's a compliance thing. If he doesn't comply with something as straightforward as not coming at me, I don't know what the hell he's going to do, and I'd rather find out before he maybe has his hands on me. A loud word and a big stick get you farther than just a soft word, and the only time I actually had to use the stick, the guy was so drunk that he fell right over."

"How often do you have to do that? Take the stick out?"

"Not often, thankfully." He shook his head. "Maybe six, seven times, total." He pointed his chin at Kupperman's car. "This guy's no problem here, and he's probably not going to be a problem in court."

"Well, yeah. Lot of work to go through for whatever the town's share of a fifty-dollar ticket is. Half?"

He snorted. "Nah. State fine for ten-miles-over is ten bucks; the other forty is violating the town ordinance against speeding. Got the schedule on the clipboard," he said, not looking as he tapped at it.

"And they let us get away with that?" It didn't seem quite right.

"Well, given that Bismarck's local ordinance starts at a thirty-six-buck fine, Fargo's at forty, and Grand Forks's at fifty-one, and all of them go up from there, I don't think we'll have a problem, particularly as long as we don't have a lot of folks fighting the tickets. Again: Take a look at our schedule. It's the same as Grand Forks's up until you get to twenty-five or so, and then we use the same as Bismarck. And—ah: Bingo." He gestured at the screen. "And his credit card's good." He quickly finished out the ticket form, and printed the numbers on a very ordinary-looking credit-card slip, then pointed at the little comments line on the ticket. "We enter the secret message that says that guy wasn't a problem here."

"Oh."

"Yup. We leave it blank. Anything else and the prosecutor knows I think some attitude adjustment is necessary, and don't want him to think about a CCD. Whether he *does* anything about it is another matter. Now, technically, what Kupperman's doing is posting a bond, that, through a miraculous coincidence, just happens to be exactly the same amount as the fine. Makes it easy for him to just stay home and forget about it, which saves you and me the trouble of going into Grand Forks if he decides to fight it."

"Which we would do?"

"Nah." He shook his head. "Not unless we get a whole batch of folks fighting them—which does happen. Different for truckers—they pass the word around, and anytime any of them fights the ticket, I show up, even if it's the only one on the docket that day. But Kupperman here's just a salesman for ADM, and—"

"How did you know that?"

"His briefcase is open on the seat, and I'm a professional police officer. But as I was saying before I was so rudely interrupted," he went on, "I don't want him to fight it, and I don't particularly need to give the guy an attitude adjustment—he was just speeding, after all, and didn't give me shit. He's just doing his job and trying to keep his travel time down; I'm just doing mine and getting him to slow down along this stretch, and the pause while we're filling out the forms is as much a part of making the point as the ticket is."

"Okay."

"Do me a favor?"

"Possibly."

"Don't mention that under-ticket to Bob. I think it makes sense, but I don't know what he'd say." He finished with the form and signed it. "Okay, listen close while I finish up with him."

We both got out of the car, and he walked over and handed over the clipboard first. "Sign here on the credit slip, please; and here on the ticket. Signing the ticket is not an admission that you were speeding—you already did that—but just an admission that I gave you the ticket, so we don't have to get you in front of a witness for me to serve it on you."

Kupperman signed and handed the clipboard back, and Jeff handed over his license, registration, and insurance card.

"You have a nice day," he said, "but do keep the speed down, at least for this stretch, okay?"

"Okay. Thanks, officer. You have a nice day, too."

Jeff and I went back to the car and waited until he pulled away.

"Well, that didn't go quite the way I wanted it to."

"Oh? I thought it wasn't a problem."

"Yeah. That's kind of my point," he said, putting the Bronco back into drive. He carefully checked his mirror before pulling a quick U-turn and heading back toward our spot in front of Brian Gisslequist's shed. "Might give you a sense of confidence you shouldn't have. Just about everything that could go right went right—no attitude, no problems with his license and registration, no problem with his credit card going through."

"Shit—it sounded like you weren't even going to insist on that."

He nodded. "Sure. He'd pay—and if his credit card happened to be maxed out, I wasn't going to make an issue of it. But I don't want you to think it's always this easy."

"Okay, noted: It's not always this easy. Is that I'm-going-to-make-a-mistake-on-the-speeding-ticket thing usual?"

"For me? Sure. For somebody with no attitude, who lives in Grand Forks, just about half a mile from the courthouse, it's standard. I just want him to slow down a little around here and pay the fifty bucks. Don't particularly want to run his insurance up or add another couple of points to the eight he's already got on his license," he said, patting the top of the computer screen.

"You have to go to court often?"

He shrugged. "Every couple of months. Got a dozen or so

cases stacked up for a week from Friday in Grand Forks. Some of them will show up; if I don't, the tickets get tossed." His mouth twitched. "Which is why it's either you or me who does the whole thing—from observing the car to shooting the radar gun to writing the ticket. If we're both involved, both of us have to show up. If they contest it."

"You want me to take the next one?"

He chuckled. "Well, I was going to have you watch a couple, but let's see. If that's okay with you, Chief."

We were back to that again.

I didn't end up taking the next one—it was a big tractor-trailer job, and Jeff got nervous and decided to take it himself when the driver came down out of the cab, as Jeff said that most truckers do.

He was a big guy, and he had a permanent glare on his face, but the only thing he had in his hands was his clipboard, with his license, registration, and insurance information above his manifest, and he was actually no trouble at all, unless you consider glaring to be trouble; when Jeff beckoned him back to the side of the road next to the Bronco, he just tamely handed out his cards without being asked.

"I've made a little mistake on the ticket," Jeff said, after the usual ritual. "Seems you were only going nine miles an hour over the posted limits—I'd take it as a favor, though, if that part of it doesn't get out over one-nine."

The big guy just nodded. "Yes, sir," he said.

Jeff smiled as he took the ticket clipboard back. "Much rather hear over the CB"—he jerked his thumb in the general direction of the Bronco—"that the town clown in Hardwood is a hardass, and maybe the folks who want to make up some time should think about swinging south and picking up I-94 instead of trying to cut time this way, eh?"

He slowly nodded. "You got it."

He didn't say thanks as he climbed back up into the cab, and didn't wait until Jeff and I were back in the Bronco before he was rolling.

"Any particular reason for that one?"

Jeff shook his head. "Nah." He turned on the CB, which was already set to channel 19. "I checked his manifest; he's coming from Devil's Lake. If he was one of those guys using the county roads to cut time on an interstate run, though, I wouldn't have cut him a break at all." He frowned. "That's what the interstates are for."

"Can't say as I blame them for trying, though."

An extra five or ten miles an hour doesn't mean much if you're cruising around a city and suburbs—who cares if the trip is twenty-two minutes or twenty?—but when you're going long distances, it adds up pretty quickly.

"Not into the blaming thing, Sparky."

Oh, I didn't say. *I hadn't noticed that*, I didn't add.

We had just gotten back into position when a silver Volvo station wagon zipped by, and my carefully trained police eyes noted that it appeared to be traveling at a high rate of speed; the Genesis Handheld Corded Stationary Traffic Safety Radar Gun pegged at eighty-three.

"Can I take this one, Mr. Bjerke, can I, huh, please, huh?" I asked. "Since I was the one—I mean, the *police officer* who used the radar gun and all?"

He cracked a smile. "Sure, Sparky," he said. He flipped on the flashers and threw the Bronco into gear, moving slowly until he was clear enough of the shed to throw a look to the right and see that there was nothing coming in that direction, either.

The Volvo was small blot in the distance by the time we got moving, and it felt like it took longer to catch up with than it should have, and even when we pulled up to a hundred or so feet behind it, it didn't slow down. Without taking his eyes off the road, Jeff punched the license plate numbers into the computer, which I found fairly impressive, then brought his hand back to the steering wheel to give a few quick blasts on the siren.

For a moment, I could have sworn that the Volvo was accelerating, but then the turn signal went on, and the brake lights flashed on suddenly enough that when Jeff hit the brakes, I was glad that I had the seat belt on.

The Volvo pulled onto the shoulder and we braked behind it.

"Well, look at that," Jeff said, gesturing at the computer screen.

The car was registered to one Philip K. Norstadt, 12 First Street, Thompsen, ND.

There were, unsurprisingly, no warrants out on his driver's license nor a theft notice on the car. No points on his license, either.

"Well, I know I said you could take this one, Sparky," Jeff said, "but . . ."

"Yeah, you did," I said, already getting out of the car.

I hated Norstadt at first sight. Not that it mattered.

He had already rolled down his window, and was just sitting there, his hands folded in his lap.

He was a big man; he looked to be in his early sixties or so, with a good head of politician's hair, all full and well-combed, and a nice, luxurious gray. His suit jacket lay neatly folded on the seat next to him, and his tie had been loosened, revealing a bull neck.

He gave me a quick nod. "Something I can help you with?" he asked.

"License, registration, and insurance card, please," I said.

He didn't make a move. "Is there some sort of problem?"

"Nah. Other than you just sitting there when you need to be giving me your license, registration, and insurance card. Now, please."

He barely nodded. "Okay, okay. No problem." He reached two long, elegant fingers into his shirt pocket and pulled out his wallet and opened it, then pulled out all three cards and passed them over.

I more felt than saw Jeff beside me; I handed them over. "Go run these, Jeff, please," I said, reaching them out and taking the ticket clipboard back from him. "Take your time; do it right."

"Okay, Chief," he said. He backed up a few steps, like he was going to say something, but thought better of it and turned and walked back to the Bronco.

Norstadt was silent for a moment. "So, you're this Ernest Hemingway I've been hearing so much about."

"Not *the* Ernest Hemingway," I said. "He stood in the doorway of his house, stuck a shotgun in his mouth, and scattered his brains all over the walls when I was a kid."

"That wasn't what I meant."

"Then, sure. Yeah, I'm me."

"How's the new job going?"

"Just fine. Still got a lot to learn, but I think I can manage it."

"I wouldn't doubt that."

"I've been hearing a lot about you, too, of late."

He nodded. "I'd guess that'd be so." He eyed me levelly. "This would be where you try to throw a scare into me?"

I shook my head. "No, this is where I give you a speeding ticket. That's all," I said. "I clocked you at eighty-three. Eighteen miles an hour above the speed limit. Three points on your license."

"Hmm." He nodded. "I think you were mistaken, but we can talk about that in court."

"Sure," I said. I'd finished writing out the ticket, and carefully printed VERY POLITE; NO TROUBLE AT ALL on the comments line, and showed it to him.

He smiled as he signed it. "Thanks for the kind words, but I was only going sixty-five, I'm sure."

"I'm sure you were going eighty-three. So is the radar gun." I shrugged. "But, like you said, we can argue about that in court."

"Guess we'll have to. Unless you'd consider just letting me off with a warning?"

"Nah." I shook my head. "I think what I need to do is just play things by the book. The radar gun says eighty-three. That's what I'll write down here. Not seventy-three, and not a hundred and three, either."

"But you could. Do either, that is."

"Yeah." I nodded, then shook my head. "But I won't. I was just saying to Bob Aarsted today, about how I think there's been a little too much . . . creativity going on around here lately—like whoever it is that got the DNR to take a close look at Big Steve's farm."

His lips tightened just a little. "I hadn't heard about that."

Okay, fine. I could play that game, too. "Somebody called into the DNR tip line and said he was using DDT. Which sounded kind of strange to me, given that DDT is illegal as all hell, and probably hard to get, too. You'd think that the DNR would have better things to do than chase down stupid anonymous calls."

He nodded. "Yeah. I'd think so." It was his turn to shrug, and he took it. "Then again," he said, his voice low and casual, "I would have thought they have better things to do than go stomping through the woods behind my cousin Ralph's house, looking for deer guts. Seems that somebody called the DNR and said he'd been poaching."

My turn to shrug. "Sounds like a shitty thing to do. Just a little less shitty than calling up the Ministry of Love and claiming I'm molesting the kid who's living with me."

He nodded. "Yeah, just a little, maybe."

"I hope all that shit stops," I said. "Told Bob that just this morning. I don't remember anybody asking me, but I think it's a bad idea. Matter of fact, if somebody from that Level Three commission were to ask me about it, I'd probably send them to Andy Franz in Grand Forks, and I bet he'd tell them he thinks maybe they ought to pick a town that's full of grownups instead of either Hardwood or Thompsen."

"Like Solomon and the baby?"

It took me a moment to get the reference. "Yeah. Except I don't think Franz would give a fuck if he had to slice the baby in half. Not his baby, after all."

"And not yours, either?"

"Maybe. Some people I know think the Level Three would be good for the town. I'm not sure, but I'm willing to be convinced. I'm pretty damn sure I don't like the idea of you two playing spin the bottle, with me and Big Steve and your cousin Ralph and God knows who else taking turns as the bottle."

"And you said this to Bob?"

"In pretty much those words."

"Think he'll listen?"

"Oh, yeah," I said. "Be pretty embarrassing if a public official got arrested for making false reports. Any public official."

He nodded. "Yeah, I can see that. I'm sure you could arrange for that to happen . . . in Hardwood." His brow wrinkled. "But I'm not sure you could make anything like that happen anywhere else—doesn't your authority end at the town limits?"

How the hell would I know? "Probably. If I thought that was happening, I'd probably have to talk to the staties or the prosecutor or the papers or somebody, wouldn't I?" I cocked my head to one side. "I seem to remember something about how you need a subpeona to get phone records, don't you?"

"I don't know," he said. "I guess I could ask my brother the prosecutor about it."

"Yeah. You do that." I nodded. "Maybe I could drop him a line and ask him about it, too."

"With copies to . . . ?"

"Anybody interested. Lots of people might be."

"I . . . I think that won't be necessary."

"You'll stop if he stops, eh?"

His smile seemed genuine. "Well, I wouldn't say that—I haven't done anything. I'm just saying that I think there won't be any more trouble unless Bob makes it."

"That'd be good," I said. I handed over the clipboard for him to sign the ticket. "Sign here, please. Signing is not an admission that you were speeding; it's just an admission that I gave you the ticket, so we don't have to get you in front of a witness for me to serve it on you."

He signed and handed it back. "You want me to post a bond?"

"Nah. Not if you tell me you'll either show up in court or pay."

"You got my word."

"Good enough. Be worth fifty bucks to find out if your word isn't worth shit." I tore off his copy and handed it back to him. "Keep the speed down, at least on this stretch, please," I said, turning away.

"Hey—my license, registration? The insurance card? You keeping those?"

Shit. "Hold on." I walked over to the Bronco and got the three cards back from Jeff, who didn't seem to have decided whether he was going to smile tolerantly at me or glare at me, then walked back and handed them over to Norstadt. "Sorry about that. I'm kind of new at this."

"You seem to be picking it up just fine so far," he said, then looked down at the cards in his hand. "Well, some of it, anyway."

7

There is, it turns out, a little more to being a cop than eating doughnuts.

Jeff put me through radio procedure, which was necessary if I needed to talk to the staties without embarrassing myself, although he said they tend to assume local cops don't know shit—a fair assumption, in my case—then went through the short course on evidence preservation. Apparently, the legal theory is that if you leave an open can of beer you've taken off somebody out of your sight on the seat of the car for a second, gnomes will sneak in and replace the mineral water that otherwise invariably comes in cans of Bud with actual beer.

After that, we went into drunk-driving stops and the like, and more on the damn radio procedures until I had combinations of numbers and letters coming out my goddamn ears, and had to beg for mercy, but the only mercy I got was a walk into the woods to a clearing for an hour with the hard-rubber training version of that funny-looking nightstick, and then a quick course on handcuffing techniques that left me with a twisted ankle, Jeff with a scrape across his browline that barely missed his eye, and both of us wisely deciding that picking things up on Monday made more sense than beating each other up any more.

So I took Friday off playing cop and got back to work, and finally got the brick ready, and called FedEx to pick it up before noon.

Two more manuscripts had come in, although, thankfully, neither were rush jobs nor skiffy—a bathroom-remodeling how-to and a thin self-improvement so earnest and sweet that just looking at the first page had me wondering if I needed to start checking my blood sugar.

On the grounds of both do-the-shorter-one-first and get-it-the-fuck-over-with, I dove into the self-improvement, which was pretty bad, and just for amusement I decided to take a sip of coffee every time I ran into the words "empowerment," "actualization," "self-esteem," or "foundation," and pretty quickly found that I was so overcaffeinated that I not only had to stop playing the game, but needed to take a break to settle my nerves.

Took maybe ten, twelve pages.

You know—maybe there is something to this decaf thing after all.

Well, Saturday was my turn to fix supper, and marinating takes time, so I got the leg of lamb out of the fridge—surely a chief of police can afford an occasional expensive cut of meat—and gave my knife a few quick strokes on the sharpening steel, carefully ignoring the custom twenty-piece teak block set of equally custom David Boye knives that had moved in along with Bridget.

It wasn't just that they were too pretty to use, although that probably was part of it: The damn things were engraved with pastoral scenes, except for the big cleaver—that one had an engraving of Bridget on one side and Fred on the other.

The cleaver alone had probably cost more than my car was worth—which wasn't much, now, but shit, it probably was worth more than my car had been worth new. David Boye is a craftsman, and his wife, who does the engraving, is an artist, and neither art nor craft of that level come cheap. It's not like it's writing or copyediting or something.

It wasn't that I would have felt kind of silly boning a lamb with a knife with a bunch of rabbits frolicking in a meadow on one side of it and a slack-shouldered wolf leering from a rock down from the other—although I would have.

Mainly it's a matter of using the tools I like. My dad had won a matched set of Bob Loveless hunting knives back when I was a kid, and while my crazy baby brother had stolen and then lost the five-inch straightback—I shouldn't have turned my back on the little shit—I'd been able to keep the drop-point hunter with the three-inch blade, and, like they say, size isn't all that important anyway.

You can keep your Sabatiers and Messermeisters and Bokers and Wüsthofs; just give me my Loveless hunting knife. In about five minutes I had the skin off the leg, had dissected out the kneebone, and, after that, it was just a matter of a couple of minutes of getting the rest of the bone out, wasting no more than a fistful of meat—which could have been less, but there was this eager-looking dog patiently waiting, so I set the bone and the scraps in his food dish and got back to work.

The butterflied leg—yes, I know that loin is the better cut, but a human being can afford a leg; lamb loins are, apparently, mined by deBeers—went into the big glass baking dish, and I threw in a handful of black peppercorns and a sprinkle of thyme and rosemary before heading down to the basement to get a bottle of wine.

I'm not much for wine—I'm more of a beer and whiskey guy—but I'd found a buy on a case of cheap lambrusco in Grand Forks, and it's great for marinating meat. I twisted off the cap and poured most of the bottle in the baking dish, then realized I'd forgotten the garlic.

Ooops.

Not a problem. I got two bulbs down from on top of the fridge—bulbs, not cloves; there's no such thing, again, as too much garlic—and had barely separated the second one into cloves when I heard the garage door open. I went out to help Bridget with the groceries.

She had the trunk of the Mercedes already open, handed me a couple of bags of groceries, then followed me into the kitchen, carrying three bags herself.

"You look kind of tired," she said as she began to unpack.

"More wired than tired, I think. Too much coffee." I didn't go into my silly little coffee-drinking game. There are some things man is not meant to admit.

"I think you've been working too hard," she said. She opened the fridge and pointed at one of the bags. "Meat for the fridge is in here—meat for the freezer is on the chair. I hauled it in; you haul it to the basement."

"Deal." I pulled out a white paper-wrapped package from the meat-for-the-fridge bag and tossed it to her, then quickly followed it with another. Snake sat up, his head moving back and forth as he watched the goodies fly.

"You know," Bridget said, "maybe you should have a word with some of these editors?"

"About what?"

"About maybe them asking if you're available instead of just sending you the manuscript and a due date."

"Nah." I shook my head. "I start doing that, they start re-membering that there are folks in the city who'll pick up and deliver manuscripts themselves."

"Not as good as you, maybe?"

"Maybe not."

"Modesty?"

"Okay: probably not. And maybe some small number of ed-itors care, from time to time, about the quality of the work as well as the speed and predictability of the turnaround." I shook my head. "Me, I can't afford to be fussy."

"Always the cynic, eh?" she asked with a smile.

"Not quite always," I said. "I haven't started making book on when you go back to Frank."

The smile went where a popped soap bubble does. She bit her lip and didn't say anything.

"Shit, Bridge, I'm sorry," I said. "Sometimes I talk too much."

She nodded. "Yes, you do," she said. "That door's closed. Do you want to close another one?"

I don't respond well to threats usually. "No," I said, deciding it was time to make an exception, which didn't take anything beyond a fraction of a second, even with my apparently room-temperature IQ. "I'd rather just stop acting like an asshole, if that's okay."

"Is that possible?" Her smile was weak and forced, but it was a smile.

"Probably not entirely. But I'll give it the old college try, eh?"

"Okay." Her body had clenched like a fist. She let herself relax into a kitchen chair—another talent I'd like to learn.

"We could always kiss and make up, you know," I said.

"Or more than kiss?" She cocked her head to one side.

"I'm old, but I'm not dead yet."

"Nah. You'd take that as a reward, and encouragement to act like an asshole again."

Fair enough. I didn't much feel like it, anyway. I'm not saying that coffee and arguing and sex don't mix at all, but it's not an obvious sort of combination.

She was silent for a while, and I just stood there and looked like an idiot rather than opening my mouth and saying something that would have added talking like an idiot to the look.

"Tell you something," she said. "If five, six years from now you're still giving me shit about Frank, we'll probably not still be together."

"I got that long to straighten out?"

"Rome wasn't built in a day."

"Thanks."

"But don't push it. You're not Rome."

"Okay. I'd better get back to work then." The coffee hadn't worked its way out of my system. The easy way to settle my nerves could be found in a glass bottle with a cork stopper, but I'd given that up when I'd given up my editorial career, and hadn't even taken it up too often when Jennifer used to scream at me—which was, all in all, far worse than a caffeine overdose. Coffee won't leave you if you scream back, after all.

"Shit, Sparky—maybe I'm a little oversensitive," she said, getting up and out of the chair.

No shit. "We probably both are. It'll work itself out," I said, as she stood in front of me, waiting for me to make the next move. My idiocy and stubbornness do have limits; I slid my arms around her waist and gently pulled her close. "Just give it time. Just give me time."

She smiled. "Now, if you're trying to get me all aroused, that's a much better plan than bringing up Frank."

"Well, good, I—"

The goddamn fucking phone had to pick that fucking moment to goddamn fucking start fucking goddamn ringing. With a sigh, I let go of her the moment she let go of me and grabbed the receiver off the wall.

"*What?*"

"Hey, Sparky, you not getting laid often enough?" Doc Holliday's voice was barely audible over the engine noise. "Or it is just too much coffee?"

"Well, I definitely had too much coffee this morning, Doc," I said. "Where are you?"

Holliday? She mouthed. I nodded.

"About fifteen, twenty minutes out." You're not supposed to use a cell phone from an airplane—although I don't know why, and until a few days before hadn't had to think about such things, except theoretically—but Doc Holliday had never been much for rules.

"I thought you were hoping to come tomorrow," I said, trying to keep the irritation out of my voice, "but I shouldn't worry if it was Saturday."

"I made my escape early. If that's okay with you."

"Just fine."

"Can you do a pickup? Or should I call a cab?"

"You heard of some cabs in this town that I don't know about?"

"Then you'd better come out to the airport. See you." He hung up.

Bridget was smiling. "I thought he was due in tomorrow."

"Hey, me, too. Ten, fifteen minutes," I said, "not quite enough time for anything interesting."

She smiled. "Sure it is."

"Oh?"

"Yeah—get into your chief-of-police suit so you can give him a shock." Her grin was only a little condescending, but in a friendly way.

"The body armor and all?"

"I think that would be a bit much," she said. "But it'd be kind of fun if you show up wearing the rest of the outfit."

"I hadn't even thought of that," I said, lying through my teeth.

She grinned.

Honesty is only occasionally a tool of domestic felicity.

What both the hand-painted sign and the local twisted sense of humor refers to as "Hardwood International Airport" is just a landing strip outside town on the east edge of Orphie Honistead's farm, with the combination office-and-hangar on the side of the strip at the south end, and two lonely-looking pumps a dozen or so yards in front of them. The strip itself is asphalt, but I think you're supposed to call it tarmac, and runs about two thousand feet.

On a winter afternoon you'll often find some kid out on it, skidding a car around, in theory to learn how to handle a skid but mainly for fun, a practice that's officially frowned on but generally ignored—and is, by the way, one hell of a lot of fun, as well as a way to teach your hindbrain that stomping on the brakes is a losing proposition.

The airport, such as it is, is a side business for Orphie, who has a fair amount of time on his hands, as he went to renting out most of his fields and sold off all the livestock and related equipment when the last of the boys moved away.

Not exactly the busiest airport you'd ever want to see; other than the occasional private plane on a cross-country trip that prefers to stay out of Grand Forks AFB airspace, the traffic consists almost entirely of the two crop dusters that the Coulson boys run from there. There's a fair amount of work for them between planting and harvest, and both of their bright-yellow biplanes were tied down outside rather than hangared.

Still, nobody was in the office when I parked next to it and let Snake out of the car while I rapped on the window.

Not a lot of business, which wasn't unusual, but, so I understand it, there are some tax advantages to the operation, and God knows any farmer will do anything possible to gain an edge on the feds, who appear to be actively hostile to independent farmers—although, rumors to the contrary, neither the U.S. Department of Agriculture nor the Internal Revenue Service are wholly owned subdivisions of ADM; I looked it up.

I had hurriedly dressed in my cop suit, with all the bells and whistles save for the body armor, and borrowed Bridget's car, just to impress Doc—yes, I'm an asshole—although I told myself it was because she had more room in her trunk.

But I hadn't hustled the Mercedes across town to the field. Squashing a kid on the way would be liable to get me talked about, after all.

Snake had just trotted over and pissed against the side of the hangar, then trotted back, manifestly very pleased with himself for some doggy reason, when I first heard the distant drone of the plane.

I wasn't sure, for a moment, if it was Doc's Beech Baron— I'm sure I can still tell the whoop-whoop-whoop of a Huey from the loud drone of a Jolly Green just fine, but I haven't ever spent enough time around prop planes to tell you anything by the sound other than that they're not jets—but then it got close enough so I could make out it was a white twin-engine job, and didn't figure that was a coincidence.

The plane swung wide to the east and circled around, as though Doc hadn't quite liked his first approach, and it was a couple of minutes before it came into sight again, low over the far windbreak beyond the end of the field.

Engines making enough noise to rattle my fillings and make me regret I'd left the electronic earmuffs at home, it touched down on the big white-striped end of the field, bouncing just a little before it settled down.

He taxied over to what looked to me to be too close to the nearest of the biplanes, and didn't spin the plane around like I'd expected him to, but just cut the engines.

I hurried through the deafening silence over to the plane, the dog close behind me.

Doc Holliday was just climbing down from the doorway, with Horse right behind him.

Doc looked like shit. His hair was gone, leaving his scalp naked and blotchy, and the mustache had gone with the hair, too. He'd visibly lost weight—and he was skinny to begin with—and his jeans were belted up tightly enough that they were sort of crinkled under the waistline, and his shirt hung loosely enough on his bony shoulders to make me think of a scarecrow.

He hesitated before taking my hand, then carefully set one foot on the mounting peg and lowered himself to the ground, turning my grip on his hand into a handshake.

"Doc, you look like shit," I said.

"And you look like a cop, Snake," he said. The eyes were still the same. Doc's eyes were always the same; they never quite settled on anything, but swept across me until they locked on Snake, and Doc broke into a smile.

"Hey, Dog," he said, bending slowly, painfully, like an old man, to give the dog a pat. He kept doing it for a moment too long, and I took a step forward to give him a hand straightening up, but he shot me a look and I turned the move into me offering a shake, and he gripped my hand too hard.

"Good to see you, too, Snake," he said.

Horse paused in the doorway to give us a chance to move out of the way. He hadn't changed since the winter. Under a thick shock of ink-black hair, his face was deeply lined, like good old leather, with a nose that looked like a flattened beak. He hadn't bothered to take the hedge trimmer to his eyebrows, like somebody or other might without any social graces might well have suggested he do at some time or another.

He took a quick glance at Doc's back and held up both palms, fingers spread wide, and gave me a smile and a nod, then quietly mouthed, "It's okay."

"Yeah," he said. "He does look like shit. But at least *he* doesn't look like he's dressed up for Halloween, so maybe you shouldn't be throwing stones."

He levered himself out of the door and dropped easily to the ground.

To be honest, he looked great. His T-shirt was easily a size too small, revealing a broad chest and thick shoulders and arms. I could almost make out the ripples in his stomach muscles. My own stomach ripples kind of differently.

He caught me looking and patted his belly, grinning. His teeth were too even and too white.

"Amazing what a little bit of cosmetic surgery and a few million sit-ups can do, eh?"

"Vanity, thy name is Crazy Horse," I said.

He chuckled. "Nah. Business expense. Gotta look good if you want to get killed by Ah-nold."

Doc straightened—too slowly—and jerked his chin at the Mercedes. "Looks like this police impersonation stuff pays pretty well," he said. "If that's yours."

"Nah. It's Bridget's. Figured I'd impress you with it, and with my new uniform."

"Very impressive," Doc said. "I'll take three boxes of cookies, little girl. You still have thin mints?"

"Give him him a break, Doc," Horse said, grinning. "You want to get the car while Sparky helps me with the bags?"

"Plane needs to be tied down."

"We can manage," Horse said.

I turned to Doc and held out the keys. "Assuming you can handle a standard."

He gave me a puzzled look. "Is there some other kind of transmission?"

I handed him the keys. He looked like he was going to say something, but he just turned and walked away toward the car, Snake trotting along beside him.

Horse opened the side doors and started handing out bags. "You can stop looking like you're at a funeral anytime you want to. Not as bad as it looks, not nearly," he said quietly, handing me a big suitcase that seemed to claim it belonged to somebody named "Louis Vuitton." "He just got out of surgery night before last, and that turned out to be not a big deal.

Mostly it's the chemo and shit, and that'll take a while to work its way through his system."

I nodded. "Which explains the landing."

"Nah." Horse grinned. "That was me; he's a still a bit shaky. I think he'll be okay," he said, punctuating it with a shrug. "Assuming that they got out everything they were supposed to get out." He handed me another bag.

"He let you fly his baby?"

"The flying part of flying is no big deal, Snake; you just set the autopilot and sit back—but yeah, he let me do the takeoff and the landing. He's not quite as reckless as he used to be, maybe."

"So he called you to fly him out."

Horse didn't answer for a moment. "That was part of it, sure. I have a bit of free time, at least until next month—I'm getting killed by Mel Gibson on the fifteenth, and then I think I get killed by Ah-nold, again, first week of May. Doc's going to fly me back home after we leave here, and then spend a couple weeks with May and the kids and me."

Horse had taken retirement a few years before, out in LA. Well, somebody's got to live there.

He supplemented his retirement pay—which can't be all that much; he got out after twenty-five, even though he was CW3 by then, with about the same retirement pay as a major, which isn't exactly generous—by doing bit parts in Hollywood. Usually, for obvious reasons, he played an Indian, although for the last few years it's been mainly playing-the-dispensable-but-noble-minor-Indian-character in war flicks.

"You ever in a movie where you don't get killed?" I asked. "Or get killed by somebody other than the star?"

"Well, yeah, every now and then." He shrugged. "And I don't really get killed by Mel this time—it's some chick actor

I'm trying to rape. Even got a good line: 'Hey, baby, anybody ever tell you better red than dead?' "

"Oh. And the good line would be exactly what?"

He grinned and handed me down another bag. "Well, after that I get to grunt a bit when she pulls my knife out of my belt and stabs it into my back, me being a dogshit-stupid Indian rapist and all. Unless the director changes his mind, or Mel changes his mind for him." He shrugged. "It's not an adventure; it's just a job, eh?"

The car started moving.

"So how is he?"

"I'm not shitting you, Snake," he said. "It went a lot better than he was worried about, and if I had to guess, I'd say he'll do just fine."

"You said that was part of it."

Horse nodded. "Well, yeah. Doc tell you how this surgery was no big deal, too, right?"

"Yes."

"Well, turned out he was right, apparently. But he had some worries about it."

"Understandable. I don't care how peripheral it's supposed to be—somebody carving on my brain would make me more than a little nervous."

"Yeah. So, well . . . you know Doc." Horse patted one of the suitcases. "Just in case it didn't work out all right, he wanted to cover his bets. Don't think he entirely trusts Jodie to believe his living will, just in case he ended up between Karen Anne Quinlan and broccoli, you know?"

"Shit. And the asshole put you in that position?"

"Fuck you, Sparky," Horse said. "He had it covered. Not quite sure what was in the syringe, but he gave me some specific instructions as to where to put the needle just in case he wasn't in any condition to take the pills he also gave me. Said it would take about two days, and I should get myself gone if I had to do it." He made a face. "And, in case you're wondering, he gave me gloves, and his fingerprints—not mine—were all over both the bottle and the syringe, and we dumped the Baggie with it into the garbage at the hospital, so give me a break, too."

Doc pulled up; Snake hopped over into the back while Doc popped the trunk. He started to get out, but Horse made a sit-down patting motion, and for once Doc didn't argue, but just sat there.

We made him wait while we pushed the plane over to the tie-downs—it's amazing how light and easy those things are to push—and Horse took his time hooking up the bungee cords just right before he and I loaded the gear in and I slammed the trunk closed. It made that nice Mercedes ka-thunk. I don't know how they do it, but they do—shit, the cigarette lighter makes a nice little ka-thunk when you push it in.

Doc wasn't making an effort to get out of the driver's seat, so I climbed in the back with the dog and let Horse ride shotgun.

"You remember where my house is?"

He smiled. "Well, if I get lost in this huge metropolis of yours, you be sure tell me where to go, okay?"

Not that the house is ever really messy these days, but by the time we got back, what little clutter there was had disappeared, as had what remained of the scraps from the lamb, and Bridget was just finishing up getting the garlic into the marinade—using the flat of the flashy Boye cleaver to smash Fred's face into the garlic on the cutting board with probably just a little more force than was absolutely necessary.

She dumped the rest of the garlic in the baking dish, stirred it around with her fingers, quickly rinsed her hands off in the sink, and then wiped them on her lab smock, coming over to give a hug first to Horse and then to Doc.

Doc, being Doc, had to cup his hand on her ass, but she just reached back and held it in place, and gave him a little hip-grind to, er, rub it in.

"Good to see the two of you," she said, letting him struggle for a moment before she released his hand. "Coffee?"

Horse nodded and went to pour himself a cup. "Sure." He looked down at the lamb leg, still marinating on the counter. "This supper?"

"That's the theory," I said when Bridget gave me a nod. It was her turn to cook tonight, but the two of us switching off wasn't a problem. I took a fork and flipped the meat over, careful not to splash any marinade on my fancy cop clothes, and swished it around a little. "I'll fire up the charcoal in a little while."

"Why does everybody in the midwest say 'coffee' instead of 'hello'?" Doc asked.

" 'Coffee' *is* the Norski word for hello," she said with a grin, and then grinned some more. "So what do you think about Sparky's new suit?"

Doc shrugged. "Didn't know they made Cub Scout uniforms that size. You the den mother?"

"If you'll excuse me," I said, "I think I'll go change into something maybe a little more comfortable and maybe a little less amusing."

"Yeah," Doc said. "I don't think you're going to need that bulletproof vest around me or Horse. We're peaceable types these days."

"I'm not wearing a bulletproof vest."

"Then maybe you should lay off the doughnuts for a while, Officer Hemingway," he said.

"That's *Chief* Hemingway."

"I sense a story there."

"Yeah. Let me get out of this stuff and we'll talk. Sounds like we've got a lot of catching up to do."

. . .

"Problem is me," Tenishia said. Her voice was starting to slur a bit, at least to my ears, although that may have had a lot more to do with the six-pack I'd washed the lamb down with than with the one glass of wine she'd had.

She had been sitting too close to the fire, maybe, and her face was shiny in its light. It was a nice enough night out, and after we'd finished cooking I'd thrown some wood baulks on the big brick barbecue, both to keep the bugs away and so that we could do some marshmallows.

Horse took another pull on his beer. "Nah," he said.

"Got the three of you in shit before."

Doc chuckled. "Most fun I had in thirty years," he said, then chuckled again. He was doing a lot of that, and Tenishia and Bridge and Horse and I had carefully managed to not notice the hand-rolled cigarette he'd gone over to the edge of the back yard to smoke before dinner.

It apparently had the desired effect: He wasn't drinking, but he had managed to eat at least a pound of lamb, plus several helpings of assorted sides, and then wolfed down two huge slices of the raspberry pie Osa had brought over—"I made an extra," she'd said.

"Yeah, sure," Tenishia said.

"Besides," Horse said, "it doesn't sound like such a big deal." He looked over at me. "They're going to pick the site for this super-emergency-room thing before fall, right?"

"Yup."

"Immediately after which, unless I'm missing something, you get yourself fired or quit."

"That's the plan," I said. "Not that anybody's quite saying it out loud, mind you, and I think it would be better the idea doesn't come up when we've got other folks over, say, tomorrow or something, but . . ."

Horse shrugged. "So? Doesn't sound like that big a deal to me." He turned back to Tenishia. "Doesn't seem to bother Chief Hemingway much—"

"Fuck you very much," I said.

"—so don't worry about it, Ten."

She glared at him, but didn't correct him. I guess it wouldn't have gone down better with a mea culpa, but I didn't want to experiment to see if I'd been given an amnesty as well.

"Me being here gives some asshole something to complain about," she said.

"Yeah." Horse tossed the beer can one-handed toward the garbage bag and missed, then muttered under his breath as he got up to retrieve it. It wasn't my beery eyes that made him look wobbly, I think. "But so what? Assholes always got something to complain about."

"Not always the same something," she said, pointedly fiddling with her cornrows.

"Shit. Try being an Indian for a while." He opened another beer. "Sounds to me like you got it pretty good here, all in all. If you don't think so, you got another option. My second-oldest is off to Cornell in the fall, and we got a room."

Doc looked miserable. "Yeah. Two other choices. At least." Horse started to say something, but Doc shook his head. "But not if you don't want to."

Tenishia grinned. "I'm starting to feel awful popular. With some people."

"Well, good," Doc said. "Might be good for you to get out of this . . . nice little town."

"I like it here."

"She likes it here," Bridget repeated, then smiled a warning at me. We'd mentioned Jeffie Thompsen to Doc and Horse before Tenishia got home, but going into that in front of her would only embarrass her. Or maybe it wouldn't; I'm not sure which possibility bothered me more. Teenagers are supposed to be twitchy about that stuff.

"There's things she likes about it," I said carefully. "The school's decent, and she's got one of the best teachers I ever had tutoring her."

"Yeah." Doc made a face. "Which doesn't overimpress me, Snake. Why should she need extra tutoring?"

"Leave him *alone*," Tenishia said. "I got myself into trouble, not him."

"You're sixteen."

"Seventeen."

"And you're supposed to get into trouble, more or less. We're the grownups; we're supposed to think ahead." He turned back to me. "Gotta start thinking about schools. College."

I nodded. "Yup."

"I get a vote?" Tenishia asked.

"Nope." Horse shook his head. "Nah. You get a choice, not a vote. You take the SATs yet?"

"Not until May."

He nodded. "That sounds about right. Do any pretests?"

"Pretests?"

"Yeah. Trial tests. Courses. Show you how to beat the system a little."

"I think," I said, "there's been a more than enough beating of the system going on around here. The system isn't a drum."

"Oh, ease up, Snake," Horse said. "It's not cheating to get ready for the SATs. George—my younger kid—took a course that brought his scores up a hundred-odd points for his second try. That's how he got his fourteen-thirty, which is what got him into Cornell, although maybe their diversity program helped some."

"Don't need no fourteen-thirty to get into the U."

"University of North Dakota?"

"Yeah?"

Doc cocked his head to one side and snorted. "Why the fuck would you want to go there?"

"Well, for one thing, it's about three grand a year tuition," she said. "I've got that."

She had rather more than that in the lockbox in her closet. That seventy or so was probably something less than half what she'd need to get through four years at a private college, but could put her through the U and still leave her with a nice five figures unspent.

"Bullshit," Horse said. "You score well enough on your SATs and get decent grades, and you can write your ticket anywhere, outside of maybe California and Florida."

"Marian, say," Doc said. "You might do better at a small college than a big university. I could talk to some people there."

"Sure; always good to have an option." Horse nodded. "Or maybe she should roll the dice and see if she can get into Hudson High."

"Huh?" Tenishia's brow wrinkled.

"West Point. Or Annapolis, or maybe Colorado Springs. Just an idea. Not pushing it."

"You ever know a fucking asshole of a ring-knocker worth pissing on if he was on fire?" Doc asked.

"Yeah," Horse said. "I was in a lot longer than you, Doc. I know quite a few."

"Name one."

"Well, we can start with First Lieutenant James McKittery Crazy Horse, Company B, Tenth Mountain," he said quietly. "First Brigade, 1-32 Infantry. I'm kind of fond of that particular fucking asshole of a ring-knocker, truth be told." His voice was too quiet, too level, too calm. "Not just because he made me promise that if it should turn out we ever have to go back and finish with those shitheads in Minneapolis, he's in."

Things got awful quiet for a moment. I was wondering just what threat it would have taken to make Horse promise if he didn't want to—and his expression made it clear that he hadn't wanted to—and the obvious possibility probably should have scared the shit out of me, or made me disgusted with the Crazy Horse family's disregard for human life, but it didn't.

"You might have mentioned that before I shot my fool mouth off," Doc said.

"Sure. And you might have asked. Before you shot your fool mouth off." He let that sit for a moment, then took a deep breath, let it out, and turned back to Tenishia. "Army's not a bad life," he said, his voice normal again, "even as an NCO— better as a warrant, and if I had to do it all over again, I'd probably have hit the reserves for a few years and picked up a commission. No regrets, though." He turned back to Tenishia. "Since it's just us, I'm not going to bullshit you. You're going to take a lot of shit in life because you're black."

"I kinda worked that out already."

"Nah," he said, shaking his head. "You don't have a fucking clue. You had it easy. You and your dad lived in the the north end of Minneapolis, and now you're here. But you haven't lived in LA, or Georgia, or Mississippi, or New York, or Dago. I have, and most of the time I've taken less shit when I was in uniform than out."

Her lips tightened. She gave me a look, then looked back at Horse. "You ever walk into Dayton's or Target with black skin and have dozens of people watching you, just waiting for you to steal something?"

"Nah," he said. "Just red." He shrugged. "All Indians are drunks and thieves, you know?" He took a long look at the beer in his hand and set it carefully down on the ground. "I don't know as how the white folks are gonna understand this. No offense meant, Bridget, Doc, Snake—but you don't have to live with this shit. Ten and I do." He turned back to her.

"Snake says you got a boyfriend here, and unless Snake's been holding out on us, he's a white kid, yeah?"

"You got a problem with that?"

"Shit, no. I married a white girl, remember? Got two half-breed kids, and yeah, some people find that whole biracial thing real, real cute, but a lot fucking don't." He shook his head, then made a face at me. "Oh, stop flinching, Snake—it's not just white folks. I hear a fucking lot of muttering about FBIs when I go back to Rosebud, and May switches off between not going with me and not letting me go without her."

Bridge's brow wrinkled. "FBI?"

"Full-Blooded Indian. Something neither George nor James are." He shook his head. "But I want to get back to the point. Ten, you—"

"Tenishia," she said.

"Tenishia, you have to take the shit; you may as well get the benefits that come with the shit, too." He gave Doc a pointed look. "You want to think that our congressman got Hudson High to let James in because they didn't have enough Indians, that's okay with me. You want to think that fourteen-thirty wouldn't have been good enough for a white kid to get into Cornell, well—"

"Okay, Horse," Doc said, raising both hands in surrender. "I get the fucking point."

"Well, good. No reason I can see for Tenishia to go to the Unifuckingversity of North Dakota when she can get into someplace better, and I—"

My phone rang. Horse gave me a look.

"Shit. Sorry." I got up from my chair and took a few steps away before answering.

"Hello."

"Hi, Sparky. It's me."

"What is it, Jeff? Time for a crash course in how to read parking meters?" Not that we even *have* a parking meter in

Hardwood, mind you, but it was the kind of bullshit I'd been putting up with lately.

"No," he said.

"Okay, then I guess I've got to get into all my battle gear, load up a rifle, and go watch the garbage get taken out behind the Dine-A-Mite?"

"No," he said. "I . . ." His voice broke. "I'm sorry, Sparky. I need to come over for a minute, talk to you about me being out of town for a while."

My timing is always impeccable. "Your dad?"

"Yeah. He's not doing well. I need to, I need to—"

"Easy, Jeff," I said. "Come on over."

"Thanks."

Fuck me. I pushed the "off" button on the phone and looked at it for a minute.

"Sparky?" Bridget's hand was on my shoulder.

"Jeff Bjerke's on his way over. Probably bringing your sister, too."

Doc grunted. "Good. Like to give the little shit a piece of my mind about—"

"Shut up, Doc," I said. "His dad's busy dying of cancer in Florida, and Jeff's got to go watch it happen."

Things got awfully quiet for a moment. "Well, I put my fucking foot in it, didn't I?"

"Yeah, you did," I said. "But there's a lot of that going around."

"I really hate to dump all this on you right now, Sparky," Jeff said.

"Not a problem," I said, lying through my teeth.

He had set a clipboard down on my kitchen table, and was busy adding things to the end of the list faster than we were making it down the list. We'd gotten through the emergency and other phone numbers, the combination to the lockbox in

the trunk of the Bronco, the Olsen-Hansen fence problem—
not digressing into why both Lars and Einar were idiots; even
the short form of that would have taken longer than we had—
and the calls I'd have to make to Grand Forks to get a contin-
uance for Jeff's speeding ticket cases scheduled for next Friday.

I wanted to ask him how long he'd be, and kept turning over
phrases in my mind that wouldn't amount to "So, when do you
think your father is actually going to up and croak?"

Shit.

"When's your plane?" I finally settled on.

"Just after seven P.M. tomorrow, out of Chicago. We're going
to leave around five, I think, just to make sure we have enough
time."

"Chicago?"

"Yeah." He shrugged. "We've got to fly out of Chicago. Only
thing we could book on such short notice. Nothing open on
Northwest from Minneapolis to Sarasota for a week, and I
didn't want to tell Mom I was going to have to sit around in
Minneapolis and wait for them to have an open seat or two.
Got a flight out of Chicago; change in Atlanta, and then we're
there at about two in the morning. By the time we bounce
around from Grand Forks to Minneapolis to Chicago, we
might as well drive—and if we miss a connection, we're
fucked. So as soon as we finish here, Karen and I are going to
call it a night and see if we can get some sleep. Long day tomorrow."

"Shit." Chicago is a good twelve hours from Hardwood. Not
the worst drive in the world, but it's a long, long day, even
switching off.

"Not a big deal," he said.

Fuck.

I walked to the kitchen window and tried to look out into the
backyard, but the only thing I saw was the reflection of a guy in
his fifties glaring back at me, his eyes bleary and tired-looking.

"Okay," Jeff said. "Let's talk about—"

"Nah," I said, holding up a hand. "Think about it for a sec. You got anything for me to do that the town'll burn down if I don't?"

He started to object, then stopped himself. "Nah. Guess I'm just spinning my wheels so I don't think about other things."

Understandable. "Yeah. So let's go get Karen, and I'll run you two back home and you can get some sleep."

One of the first things we'd settled was that I was going to take Jeff's Bronco while he was gone—the new radio and computer gear for me was waiting in the storeroom at town hall until Bob Aarsted finally came to terms with the fact I wasn't going to buy a new car to play cop with, and he'd either spend the money to have the gear put into my old Olds or up and spend the serious money on buying a real cop car for the town.

"You could probably use a drink," I said.

"Yeah. I could, at that."

I took a couple of glasses down, then opened the cupboard above the fridge and took a look. "What do you feel like?" Our hunting tradition, Jeff and Bob and me, is that we bring along a new bottle of Crown Royal to open at the end of the day or whenever the last of us has gotten his deer—whichever comes first. But I didn't have Crown Royal.

"Anything," he said.

"Scotch?"

"Sure."

I brought down a half-empty—or half-full, if you insist on being an optimist, like the bottle is going to get any more full, ever—bottle of Famous Grouse and poured each of us a slug. We brought the drinks out into the back.

Doc and Horse and Tenishia were still sitting around the fire, but Bridget and her sister Karen were off down the slope, toward where the windbreak of birches marks the end of my backyard. Bridget had her arm around Karen's shoulder, and Karen's body shook.

I wasn't sure what that was all about, not really. Norskis tend to be stolid folks, and I know for a fact that Karen never had much use for her father-in-law. I dunno; maybe she was doing Jeff's crying for him.

Jeff pasted a smile on his face as he grabbed the free chair next to Tenishia and sat down more suddenly than he probably intended. "I'm sorry to interrupt your evening," he said.

"Yeah," she said. "I'm more sorry about your dad." Her hand fluttered out toward him, withdrew, then gripped his arm. "I miss mine," she said.

Jeff looked down at her hand on his arm like he'd never seen a hand before, and just let it lie there. "Yeah." He looked over at Horse and Doc. "Sorry about interrupting your visit."

"Shit." Doc smiled. "Not as sorry as I am—"

"*Doc.*"

"—'cause I was looking forward to giving you some shit about the shit you put Sparky through," Doc said, ignoring me. "Which doesn't seem quite right. I mean, raking your ass over the coals about making him dress up in the Girl Scout uniform doesn't seem quite fair under the circumstances, does it?"

Horse made a face. "You know, Doc, you're being more of an asshole than usual tonight."

"Thanks."

"Just thought you ought to know, in case you hadn't worked it out for yourself yet."

"Probably." Doc shrugged. "And I'm just warming up. What's this about driving to Chicago?" He jerked his chin over to where Bridget and Karen were.

"Only flight out of Grand Forks is the Northwest feeder to Minneapolis, and we can't get a Northwest flight from there to

Sarasota until at least next Wednesday without going through Chicago—and getting on the same flight that we'll be on to-morrow night anyway. Assuming we don't miss the connec-tion."

"Okay." Doc looked over at Horse. "You mind?"

"Not a problem." Horse shook his head. "I can use the hours. I'll get the Jepp charts." He rose and walked toward the house, not wobbling at all.

Huh? I thought.

"Huh?" Jeff said.

"We'll run you down in the Baron," Doc said. "Holliday Air to the rescue, eh?"

"All the way to Chicago?"

Doc made a decidedly impolite sound with his lips. "Hey, in for a penny, in for a pound—it's only something like nine hours from here to Sarasota, and I'm not going to be able to do this much longer, anyway." He tapped at the side of his head. "Flight physical coming up, and they're going to take my li-cense away. Flight from Sarasota to LA should be fun—we get to take the shortcut across the Gulf part of the way if we go VFR." His grin wasn't entirely friendly. He picked his drink up and downed it, then glanced at his watch. "Not that I'm heavy into rules or anything, but the FAA says eight hours bottle-to-throttle, and you being a cop and all, let's just obey them. See you out at the airport at, say, seven-thirty or so, okay? Pack as heavy as you want to; we won't be near maximum with just four of us."

"Sure, but—"

"And you and your wife take some Dramamine first thing when you get up—at least an hour before we take off, even if you have to set your alarm. The stuff doesn't work after you get airsick, and it sometimes gets a little bouncy up there." He rose and walked off toward the house.

Tenishia got up and followed him.

Jeff was silent. "What should I say?" he finally said.

"Oh, something like, 'Sparky, you got some pretty decent friends,' maybe."

He nodded. "Yeah, you do." He looked over at the house. "But I think I already knew that."

8

Monday was, basically, a nonstop pain in the ass.

Literally and figuratively.

At Bob Aarsted's insistence, I started the morning off at eight sharp by setting up shop in my new office at town hall, and hauled both the manuscripts over—which was no big deal—and my reference shelf. Carrying the boxes in threatened to break my back.

Just because I was playing cop didn't mean the work didn't have to get done.

Which meant that instead of maybe meeting Bridget in the kitchen when I wanted to take a break, I had Emma popping her head in every few minutes to see if I needed anything, and the honest answer—"yes, I need to be fucking left alone"—didn't seem to be right, and she didn't take my repeatedly saying "No, I'm fine" as a suggestion that maybe I wasn't in need of something, even when I changed it to, "No, I'm still fine," or even, "No, I'm *still* fine."

Some people can't take a hint.

The impressive-looking leather chair behind Jeff's—*my*—desk would probably have been just fine for a chairman of the board, but apparently had been made during a day when they needed to get rid of some excess springs in the chair factory, and got rid of most of the surplus in the part of the chair where my right buttock wanted to rest. Besides, when I sat down the butt of my pistol pressed into the seat of the chair, causing the pistol itself to press up and into my side.

Sitting around the office in my chief-of-police costume—complete with with nicely hemmed trousers—was bad enough, but sitting around with a couple of extra pounds of steel on my belt was something I'd been willing to do for about two, maybe three minutes, and when I'd tried to hang the Sam Browne belt on the back of the chair from hell, it had fallen to the floor with a clunk. So I'd hung the belt, with all its accompanying gear, on the coat hook by the door.

Except that, of course, the damn Sam Browne belt wouldn't hang quite right, and the only thing that appeared to keep the gun from falling out and clattering to the floor was the little thumb-break retainer gimmick on the holster. While the front of my mind knew that it wouldn't fall out, I kept watching it out of the corner of my eye, expecting it to, so I just said "fuck it"—quietly enough, I hoped, not to be heard by whichever busybody had just rung the damn bell mounted over the door again—and took the the gun out of the holster and set it down on the desk out of the way.

And tried to get back to work.

Except, of course, every time I started to begin to make a dent on the bathroom-remodeling how-to, somebody would come in or go out through the front door, sending the bell jingling, and while I kept the door closed, the sounds were a constant interruption; every time that goddamned bell over the front door jingled, I thought I'd jump out of my skin.

The only break in it all was going across the open side of the open area to use the bathroom.

Since I've long had it trained into my lizard brain that you don't ever leave a loaded gun lying around—not that I was terribly worried about a bunch of kids coming in to play cops and robbers in the office—I tucked it into the back of my pants, gave a quick and phony smile to Emma, who was busy actually getting work done, and set the thing down on the back of the toilet while I used the facilities, then tucked the pistol back in after I washed my hands, and walked past Emma again.

"No, thanks, I'm *still* fine, really."

And back to the office to set the pistol down, then listen to phones ring and bells chime while I tried to work.

Not a whole lot of work was getting done.

My mother used to say something about how, when you're upset or angry, a good way to deal with it was to make a list of your blessings, so I sat back down in the chair from hell and started making a list of the good things about the situation. I got as far as:

1. Don't need to pay for own toilet paper.
2. Don't need to pay for slimy bathroom soap.
3. Don't need to pay for paper towels.
4. No longer considering *ever* buying a bell to hang on my front door, thereby saving something like $1.98.

Then I gave it up as a lost cause and tried to get back to the how-to.

At which point, of course, the bell over the front door jingled again, and then the phone rang, and I lit up a cigarette more in frustration than because I really needed another nicotine fix at the moment.

There was a knock on the door.

"*What?*"

Bob Aarsted's round face peered in. "You're not smoking in here, are you?" he asked, as though the cigarette burning in the ashtray in front of me wasn't a hint. I guess he wasn't a keen-eyed professional police officer and all.

"If you mean crack cocaine or marijuana," I said, holding up the cigarette between thumb and forefinger, "no. If you mean this, yes."

"No." He shook his head. "You can't do that. Clean Indoor Air Act."

I rolled my eyes. "Come *on*, Bob."

"No, seriously—if you need to take a cigarette break, just step outside and do it there. Preferably out back, or just go over to the Dine—" His eyes got wide. "And what's *that* doing on your desk?"

"*That*," I said, as I crushed the cigarette out, probably with slightly more force than was absolutely necessary, "is my brand-new chief-of-police Kimber Custom Two semiautomatic pistol. And as far as I can tell, it's not doing anything. The gun has, according to the manual, three different safeties in it, and it's unlikely to spring up off the desk and start shooting up the room all by itself."

"Well, don't just leave it on your desk."

I pulled open the nearest drawer and put the gun inside, then carefully closed it. "Better?"

"Yeah. Thanks. Mind if I come in for a minute?" he asked, not meaning it, since he didn't wait for an answer before stepping all the way in and closing the door behind him.

"My time is your time," I said.

He raised his hands in surrender. "Okay, okay. Enough. Can we call a truce? Or are you going to see if you can make yourself enough of a pain in the ass that I'll decide this whole thing was a bad idea?"

He was smiling, but he didn't mean it.

"Now there's an idea." I think I meant my smile.

"Yeah. Not a good one." He shook his head. "You said something the other day about how we've painted a pretty picture here and it would be a shame to spoil it. So if you're going to have a tantrum over it, could you do it now and just get it over with?"

"Sure." I took the ashtray off the desk and dropped it to the floor. It shattered with a satisfying sound. "Okay. I'm done. What do you want?"

He carefully moved the manuscript away from the edge of the desk and threw a hip over it. "I just got the word. We're getting a couple of commissioners in day after tomorrow. Finally."

There was a knock on the door and Emma stuck her face in. "Everything okay?"

I raised my palms. "No problem. I just broke an ashtray."

"An *ashtray?*" Her forehead furrowed; she pronounced the word like it was vaguely obscene. "You're smoking in here?"

"Nah. Clean Air Act. Can't do that. It just slipped off the desk."

"I'll get the broom."

"Nah. I can clean up my own mess," I said pointedly.

Bob gave her a look. "We're almost done here," he said, also pointedly.

"Okay, okay," she said, unsmiling. "I can take a hint." Maybe I would have argued the point, but she left, closing the door behind her.

"And?" I asked, turning back to Aarsted.

"And what?"

"And what do you want me to do with these commission folks? Make sure not to ticket them if they speed in?"

He rolled his eyes. "I want you to help me show them around, talk about the law-enforcement concerns . . ."

"Law-enforcement concerns?"

"Yeah. Like what we're going to do to increase the police coverage after we get the Level Three."

"Oh. Sure. One problem, though."

"You don't have the slightest idea what we're going to do to increase the police coverage after we get the Level Three."

"Yeah. There is that."

He pulled a couple of folded sheets of paper out of his pocket and set them on the desk. "It's pretty straightforward— schedule, budget, you know."

"And, let me guess, a lot of it'll be paid for by fed COPs money?"

He grinned. "If at all possible." The grin vanished. "Now, what's your schedule look like for the rest of the day?"

"Well, since getting my own work done isn't exactly optional, I figured I'd put in another couple of hours on it here, then head out to County Fifteen and see about doing a few speed stops." I cleared my throat and put on my best cop-voice. "Can't have all them there truckers thinkin' County Fifteen is their private speedway and all. Unless there's something serious you think I should be doing?"

He shook his head. "Nah. That'll be fine." He slid his hip off the desk. "By the way, Kathy called me from Sarasota a couple hours ago."

"How're things going?"

He shook his head. "Pretty bad, all in all. Dave could hang on for another couple of days, maybe, or maybe another couple of weeks. She told me about how you had your friend fly them out, though. Thanks."

I was going to say something to the effect that it hadn't occurred to me, that I'd had nothing to do with it, that it was Doc Holliday being himself, doing somebody a favor because it amused him, or for his own reasons, or maybe just because it seemed like a clever thing to do.

But he just gave me a nod and left.

Shit.

I got the broom and dustpan from the utility closet, swept up the glass and safely stowed it in the trash can, then stepped out back for a quick cigarette. I was just sitting down again on the same sharp spring when the intercom beeped.

"Call for you, Sparky," Emma's voice said. "A . . . Detective France? From Grand Forks?"

"Franz," I said. "Thanks."

"No problem."

One button on the phone was flashing; I took a wild guess that that was it.

"Hemingway," I said. Answering my official chief-of-police phone with my usual "What?" didn't seem quite right.

"Hi, Sparky," Franz said. "How's it going?"

"Well, you know, Andy—the usual. Bank robberies, wife swapping, drug smuggling, riots, child molestation, DDT, and I think we've got some Satanists scheduled to be holding a black sabbath in the back room of the firehouse."

He snorted. "Yeah. Seriously?"

"Seriously, it's quiet."

"Too quiet, *kemo sabe?*"

"Nah. Just quiet. Which is just as well—we're down to a one-man department for a while; Jeff's off in Sarasota, watching his dad die."

"Shit. Sorry."

"Yeah, me, too." I realized he couldn't see me, so I stopped in mid-shrug. "Is there anything in particular I can do for you? Or did you call just to chat?" Yeah, sure.

"Well . . . I thought the bullshit was over, but we got another complaint."

"So? Who gets rousted this time? And where?"

"Nobody, I hope. I'm getting pretty fucking sick of this myself."

"You and me both," I said, probably with more heat than I'd intended. "I had words with Aarsted."

"And with Norstadt, too, so I hear."

Why wasn't I surprised? "Hey, it was a good ticket."

"Yeah. And a real nice speech, too."

"Huh?"

"He had a tape recorder running, and he played it for me. He said it showed that you were threatening to harass him—give him a ticket for going a hundred and three or something."

I didn't say anything.

"Fuck that," he went on, "I heard what you said. Hard to construe it that way, it seems to me. Seems to me that you were just telling him that you'll play it straight and want everybody else to."

"That's what I *thought* I was saying."

"Yeah. And that's what I told him it sounded like, and what I told him I'd tell you it's what it better *be* like."

"Gee," I said. "I'm pretty intimidated. Glad I didn't pretend he was going, say, one fifty-five."

"You should be," he said. "I also told him that I thought it was a pretty fucking good idea—all the bullshit stopping. I sort of thought he was listening, but . . ."

"But he wasn't. Shit. So, what is it that I supposedly did now?"

"It's not you. I think that well went pretty dry. You got a kid named Herschel Ginsburg in town?"

"Yeah. One of the new—well, relatively new—doctor's kids."

"Retarded kid?"

"Yeah. But I think you're supposed to call them 'special needs children.'"

"Well, Betty Ingstrand from CYS called me this morning and says that she got an anonymous call on their tipline that this *retarded* kid named Herschel Ginsburg is supposedly molesting little boys in the bathroom at your school."

"Oh, *fuck*."

"Can't just ignore this shit, Sparky."

"Yeah, but . . . shit."

"Shit is right. So I'm not ignoring it. I told her I'm referring it to the chief of police of Hardwood to investigate. She's fine with that; I think she's got enough real work to do, too. I was going to ask you to have Jeff do it, but, shit, I don't think we really want to sit on it for a couple of weeks."

And what am I supposed to do? I didn't quite ask.

"Think you're up to doing an investigation and writing up a report?" he asked.

"Andy . . . I, er, I don't exactly have a hell of a lot of experience with . . . this particular kind of police investigation, you know."

"I kind of figured that out," he said, not quite chuckling. "On the other hand, you've apparently got a lot of experience with bullshit—both giving and receiving. So just go talk to whoever you think you need to talk to, which probably doesn't include every kid in town. Write it up as best you can—names, dates, the whole bit—and send me a draft in a few days. I can knock it into official report-bullshit language send it back to you. You sign off on it, I approve it and hand it over to CYS, we mark the fucking file closed."

"Talk to whom? I start going around the school asking all the kids 'Hey, did Herschel Ginsburg try to molest you,' and somebody's likely to notice, and word will get around, and get a lot of people pissed off, starting with Bob Aarsted."

"So don't do that. Just go down to the school and ask around if there's been any problems—like you're looking to see if there's anything going on that the brand-new chief of police should be looking into."

"Which would make me look like somebody playing cop, who didn't have any business—oh."

He chuckled. "Yeah, it would, at that. Can you live with that?"

"I guess I kind of have to, all things considered."

There was a pregnant pause. "Yeah. So you do the report, I go to my boss, and he and I try to decide if this is Norstadt playing more games or Aarsted trying to make me think that Norstadt is playing games."

"For what it's worth, I don't really believe Bob's that smart, or—particularly—that stupid."

"Well, I was thinking that, too. Likely to piss off this Dr. Ginsburg a little, unless it's handled just right," he said, his tone of voice making it clear that was going to be my problem, not his, if it happened. We weren't friends; we just, at least for the moment, had a common interest.

"Yeah," I said. "More than a little likely. And Dr. Ginsburg pisses off pretty easy. Besides, how would Bob know it was going to be handled just right?" I asked. I mean, if I were Bob, I wouldn't have been counting on his new police chief's personal loyalty, not at the moment.

"Yeah."

"Which makes me think it isn't Bob."

"You vouching for him?"

"I'm not doing a whole lot of vouching these days, Andy. Just playing it straight." Besides, I had the feeling that me vouching for Bob Aarsted wouldn't have a whole lot of weight. Andy Franz and I weren't buddies—we were just a couple of guys whose interests seemed to intersect, at the moment, something that would change the second he thought of me as helping cover for Bob rather than trying to ride herd on him.

"Yeah," he said. "So: Talk to some of the kids and teachers, write it up, and then I think my captain and I sit down with Norstadt, or maybe just his brother the prosecutor, and explain to him that some *other* prosecutor gets to handle this bullshit, and that his asshole brother maybe gets to hire himself a lawyer. Unless you fuck it up."

"Huh?"

"Not the investigation part. But if you don't mind a little friendly advice . . ."

"You got another kind in stock?"

"Don't tell Aarsted anything if you don't have to."

"I was just thinking about that."

"Let me know how it goes."

"Yeah."

"I mean it—you let me know how it goes. Understood?"

"Yeah, I'm afraid I do."

The obvious thing to do was start at the school, so instead of doing that I headed over to Minnie Hansen's house, driving home only to change out of my chief-of-police suit and into something human, like jeans and a work shirt, stashing my cop gear in the lockbox in the back of the Bronco.

It felt kind of silly to be driving instead of taking the ten-minute walk home, and half that over to Minnie's, but that was part of the deal: A cop is supposed to be able to get somewhere quickly if he has to.

Pain in the ass. I'm not big on walking, but driving just to get home from downtown and then over to Minnie's?

Still, going to Minnie's wasn't the obvious thing do to.

The *obvious* thing was to turn in the damn cell phone, and my keys, and my brand-new chief-of-police semiauto and particularly my fucking combat gear, and let Aarsted and Norstadt play their fucking little games by themselves without my help.

But I wasn't going to do the obvious thing, not at the moment, so, like I said, I headed for Minnie Hansen's house, stopping off only to change and pick up the dog, who'd been waiting for me at the back door.

She was out in the back in her gardening clothes, on her hands and knees, working her way down a row of what was clearly going to be peas. My keen analytical mind was perfectly capable of noticing the picture of a split-open pea pod on the seed envelope she had thrust in the ground on a little stick at the beginning of the row.

Snake went over and took a quick sniff at her butt, desisting at her instant glare. I wish dogs would just learn how to shake hands and say hello.

"Hello, Ernest," she said, ignoring the dog. "Is everything okay?"

"Hardly. But what else is new?"

She gave a quick smirk. "I suppose you want to know how the children are doing."

"Well, yeah," I said, not quite having worked out how I wanted to handle the Herschel matter. "Working miracles yet?"

She shook her head. "I don't think I look like Ann Bancroft, and Tenishia is no Patty Duke. Then again, I don't think miracles are needed. She's a very bright young lady, if you put any stock in either IQ tests or an old woman's opinion." She grinned. "I'm not one for telling children their IQ scores, since it's asking for trouble, but she's ten points ahead of Joshua's rather impressive score, and rather more than that ahead of Jeffie Thompsen."

"So? Are her grades going to go up?"

She nodded. "Certainly. Just a matter of some work, I suspect, and careful attention to study habits. Have her show you the paper she's working on."

"I will."

She'd made her way down the row as we'd been talking, and slowly, laboriously got to her feet, rubbing her filthy hands on her already filthy shirt. "Herschel is due here in . . ." She glanced toward the porch. "Just about fifteen minutes, and I should shower and finish getting ready for that."

"You don't make him help out in the garden?"

She grinned. "No. With him, I've got to actually work. With your three—"

"My three?"

"—the main trick is to get Tenishia irritated enough over doing garden work that she'll settle down and keep at her schoolwork, and then let her and Joshua argue about the fine points of *Huck Finn* or *The Republic*. They have lovely arguments." She cocked her head to one side. "So, if you'll excuse me . . ."

"Well, I'd like to, but there's another matter."

"Yes?"

I hemmed and hawed for a moment until she interrupted. "Ernest, you usually aren't this reticent."

"And I usually don't get a call from a state cop saying somebody's made an anonymous complaint that Herschel Ginsburg is molesting little boys in the bathroom at the school, either."

I'd never seen Minnie Hansen speechless before. It took a good five seconds before she said anything, and then it was, "Oh."

"Yeah: Oh. That's roughly what I said."

"And what did Bob Aarsted say?"

"Nothing. I haven't told him yet, and I don't think I'm going to, not if I can stomp this out before he does something stupid by way of retaliating."

She nodded. "You'd prefer I don't say anything to him, either, I take it."

"I'd prefer you tell me it's impossible that Herschel Ginsburg is buggering little boys in the bathroom."

She gave a snort. "I think it might have been cause for more than some anonymous report, if it had happened. And I'm sure I'd have heard about it." Her expression darkened. "There's a fair amount of prejudice against the retarded on such matters, you know."

"Molesting little boys? I'm prejudiced against retarded kids molesting little boys and little girls, and probably sheep, for that matter."

She gave me a look of disgust. "That's not what I meant, and I suspect you know that as well as I do. The prejudice is about the likelihood of retarded people being molesters."

"Well . . . I hadn't thought much about it."

"Well, you don't have to, I'd imagine." She shook her head. "How closely did you follow the Burt Snyder matter?"

"Too damn closely. Just not early enough."

Look: I like my town. I like my neighbors, by and large, and not just because—most of the time, and by and large—they leave me alone. But I'm not the sort of idiot who thinks it can't happen here, for most values of "it," and every time I walk by the Snyder house, I wonder how it was that Burt Snyder had been molesting his daughter for years without somebody notic-ing something, without somebody saying something, until she turned up in Doc Sherve's office and something she'd said or done—or had; I dunno, and Doc won't say—had gotten Doc suspicious enough to ask some pointed questions, and stubborn enough to insist on answers.

Burt Snyder had gone to prison, and Elizabeth and Glory and Amelia had moved away, and the house stood empty and boarded-up beside the old Honistead place, as a reminder that it very much can happen here, and that I live in Hardwood, North Dakota, not Shangri-fucking-la.

"You were hardly the only one," she said gently. "But that's the typical picture of molestation—an adult, in a position of authority. A stepfather, more often than not, or a relative, or a priest or minister. I'm not saying that stranger-molestations don't happen, but they're rare, and if you read up on the subject, you'd find that sexual predators are intelligent, and clever, and a whole bunch of other things—that's how they can get away with it at all." She pursed her lips. "A retarded molester?" She shook her head. "Almost certainly not. The closest thing you're likely to see—other than some inappropriate hugging— is inappropriate masturbation, and yes, there were some problems with that for both Herschel and Tim. But that's easy to redirect, and—"

"Redirect?"

"Yes, redirect. It's just a matter of education. You don't try to get them to stop, just to do it in private. There's nothing wrong with a young man being sexual, and it's likely that masturbation is the only sexual gratification Herschel will ever get." She gave me a stern look. "If you think you have to talk to Herschel, I want you to do it in my presence."

"His parents?" I asked, although I knew what the answer would be.

"His parents would have a fit. They had enough difficulty with him masturbating in his room and forgetting to close the door."

I nodded. "I hadn't really wanted to talk to Moshe Ginsburg about it."

She grinned. "I can imagine not." She thought for a moment. "Very well. Then that's over with." She glanced at the clock on the porch again. "And now I'd really better get into the shower."

"Hi, Mr. Hemingway," Herschel said. "Minnie says you need to ask me some stuff." We were sitting in her dining room, at the table, books and papers already set out in preparation for his lessons.

He tried to push Snake away, but the dog just nuzzled his hand some more and didn't desist until I looked down at him, and said, "Snake, *down*. Stay."

The dog dropped to the floor, while Herschel's eyes got very wide.

Minnie reached over and patted his hand. Her hair was still damp from her shower and pulled back tightly, giving her face even a more stern look than was usual, which is a lot.

"It's okay, Herschel," she said. "That's just the way you have to talk to a dog."

"I don't like it," he said.

"Okay. You don't have to like it," she said, nodding. "But the dog doesn't mind. It's just how he understands. Look at him—does he look upset?"

He didn't look convinced; he just kept looking at Snake, whose tail was still wagging.

"Well, Herschel," I said, "how are things going in school for you?"

"Great!" he said. "We had tuna-noodle hot-dish for lunch today."

I repressed a shudder. "I mean, have you had any problems with the other kids?"

He frowned. "Becka called me a stupid retard when I knocked her books over by accident. I didn't mean to, honest." The frown deepened. "I don't like her much."

"I don't blame you." And, to be honest, I didn't blame her much, not at the moment.

"Herschel," Minnie asked, "remember when we talked about good touching and bad touching?"

He seemed to have trouble focusing his eyes for a moment, then looked down and said, "Yes, Minnie. I've been closing the door, every time, just like you said."

"Good!" she said enthusiastically. "But that wasn't what Mr. Hemingway was asking you about, and it's not what I was asking about. Have you been touching anybody else? Anywhere a bathing suit covers?"

"No, Minnie," he said. "I don't do that." He looked like he was about to cry. "Except when I help change Rivka." He brightened. "Sometimes she giggles when I wipe her."

"Okay, then," she said. "I just wanted to ask. You don't mind me asking you questions, do you?"

"I don't *like* that kind of question. I like questions about food and puzzles and stuff." He turned to Minnie. "Can we do a puzzle now?"

"Certainly—in just a minute. I've got to finish talking with Mr. Hemingway, and then we can do a puzzle—*one* puzzle—before we get to the lessons."

"Okay."

"You go pick out a puzzle—not the ones we did yesterday, please—and I'll walk Mr. Hemingway out."

He slid his chair back, went over to the bookshelf, and started going through the stack of boxed puzzles.

I got up and beckoned Snake to follow me, and Minnie walked us out the front door.

"Well?" she said.

"Well what?" I shrugged. "You got a built-in lie detector?"

"You're not taking this seriously, are you?"

"Not really. But—"

"But you don't like Herschel."

"No, I don't." I raised a hand. "I'm not going to throw handcuffs on him and shove him in the back of the Bronco because I'm uncomfortable around a retarded kid, okay? But he gives me the creeps. I didn't know that it showed. I'll try to hide it from you better; best I can."

"He knows you don't like him, too. You look at him as though you think retardation is contagious," she said.

"On some level, I probably do." I lifted up a shoe. "Want to check my feet for clay?"

She chuckled. "I think not. So: What do you do now?"

"I think I go to the school and ask around, although I don't quite know what I'm going to ask. And then, I think, I write up my report and wait for the next shoe to fall."

"What are you going to say at the school? Who are you going to talk to?"

"I haven't worked that part out yet."

She didn't look terribly impressed by my clever plan. Which was fair enough. I wasn't terribly impressed by my clever plan, either.

"Do you mind a suggestion?" she asked.

I just gave her look.

"Giving a couple of classes a lecture on good touching and bad touching wouldn't be a bad idea," she said. "I could set that up with the school."

"Principal Henderson would take a suggestion, I'd guess."

"I think he might."

"Well, that's great, but who's going to do it? I don't know much about the subject."

And, to be honest, I was getting pretty damned tired of doing things I didn't know a damn thing about, and the idea of standing up in front of a bunch of schoolkids and saying, "Hey, if some asshole sticks his hand down your pants or tells you to suck his dick, call a cop"—or however you're supposed to put it—didn't have a lot of appeal for me.

"I'm qualified," she said. "I keep up on my reading, you know. Let me think about it, and maybe make a few calls, and I may be able to come up with another idea," she said. "If you don't mind putting off going over to the school until tomorrow, at least."

"That'd be okay, I guess." I also wouldn't mind putting off giving myself a ground-glass enema until tomorrow, at least, either.

"And now, if you'll excuse me, I do have a *current* student to attend to."

"Yes, Minnie," I said.

. . .

Bridget was at the kitchen table when the dog and I walked in from the garage—my Olds was spending its time parked on the street in front of the house to leave space for the Bronco—her fingers beating on the keyboard of her computer with more force than I would have thought was needed. I almost tripped over the wire—the "cable"—to the connection down the hall in the bedroom/office as I headed over to the pot for some coffee.

"Divorce stuff?" I asked as I poured.

"Yeah." She nodded, sitting back and looking at her handiwork, not taking her eyes from the keyboard as she reached down to idly pet the dog. I glanced at the screen and read as far as "I shouldn't have to explain the basics of accountancy to a fucking accountant" before remembering I was staying out of this for good reason.

"I'm thinking I need to get another accountant to take a look at the books," she said. "I'm beginning to wonder if Fred got to the real estate appraiser . . . and this idiot of a so-called accountant seems to think the NPV of rental property is less than the appraised market value, and Arthur is making noises about letting him get away with it, and never mind the idiocy about the stock portfolio and the stuff that's conveniently made its way into Fred's private account."

"Well, silly him."

The two of them seemed to be spending enough time and money on lawyers and accountants and appraisers to choke a horse, and I didn't think a choked horse would solve their problem. I would have made an obvious suggestion—put everything the two of them owned up for sale and split the proceeds according to whatever either the law is or the lawyers could work out. Or, alternatively, let Fred split everything they owned into two piles—stocks, property, whatever—and let Bridget pick whichever pile she wanted.

But I had the more than vague impression that that
wouldn't have gone over real well on either side. Bring in the
lawyers, and common sense goes out the window.

Works with politicians, too, apparently, as I'd been learning
too much about lately.

And, yeah, it also occurred to me that as long as they were
fighting over money, patching things up personally wouldn't
occur to either of them as a possibility, and, selfish bastard that
I am, the idea of her permanently hating Fred and stacking up
a few more grievances on the already-large pile of them didn't
exactly militate toward some sort of reconciliation.

Insecure? Me? Well, yeah.

Then again, the prospect of losing a huge pile of money on
lawyers in the interim, and even more on their settlement
eventually—as well as whatever drain the temporary alimony
was, which I didn't know; I don't open other folks' mail—
might well result in Fred thinking that an appearance here in
Hardwood, with flowers in hand, a hangdog look on his face,
and a private resolution to keep future affairs private wouldn't
be a better deal, all in all.

Shit.

"You know," she said, too idly, "at some point I really should
have my own office, and not just camp out in the kitchen or
living room."

Which was true enough. She hadn't just spent her time in
the city being Mrs. Fred Honistead. Bridget had put her business degree to good use, managing the family investments, and
I suspected the zeros in the account books had a lot to do with
her being good at it, as well as Fred running up the billable
hours, first as an associate, and then as a partner.

Just about the only thing I know about working the stock
market—when I think "stock", I think of the sort of stuff that
moos or oinks—is that it takes a lot of work, and probably a lot
of luck, and her subscriptions to the *Wall Street Journal* and

more than two dozen business magazines every month were only part of the work.

"Well, yeah," I finally said. "I was sort of figuring that when Tenishia goes off to college, you'd get her room as an office." Well, no, I hadn't been thinking much about that. I'd been thinking, sexist pig I am, that it was nice to walk into the kitchen and often find her there. Yeah, it's a double standard, what with me hating to be interrupted when I'm working—I don't insist on consistency; I just have to surrender to it from time to time. "But, yeah, that's something like a year and a half away. Can you wait that long?"

"I can wait," she said. "But I'd rather not. And, besides, I don't like that idea. Ten'll be coming home on vacations, and I think you need to keep her room for her. Don't you?"

Well, I hadn't thought about it much, actually—par for the course—but she did have a point. This was Tenishia's home, and a home is a place where you've got a room that's yours. You might have to share it with a brother or a sister or more— but sharing it with Bridget's office was something else, maybe.

"It sounds like you've got something in mind."

"Well . . . any chance I can talk you into thinking about the old Snyder place? You wouldn't believe how little they're asking for it right now, and when Dad gets us the Level Three, the price is going to go up to something reasonable, and quickly."

"No," I said. "There's no chance you can talk me into living in the old Snyder place, even if you buy it."

"I was thinking we'd go in on it together," she said. "It's in good shape—I was just over there the other day, and went through it, attic to basement. Oh, I'd want to put in new carpeting, and the kitchen is from the Stone Age, but it's sound. If you don't like the bad juju of the Snyder place, there's the Hansen house, or—"

"Assuming that I'd go for it, what precisely would I do for the money?"

She shrugged. "Once we get the Level Three, this house will be worth a lot more than the Snyder place is now."

My heart did a flip-flop. "You're assuming we'll get it."

"Assuming? No. Betting? Yes—and I've made riskier investments. Not recently," she said, frowning. As I understood it, since the split, the guy who had been their stockbroker was magically converted into some sort of trustee, and most changes needed approval by both her and Fred, and Fred wasn't cooperating. She had her own private portfolio, too, as I understood it, but the bulk of their investments were in the joint one, and she probably felt handicapped by not being able to move the whole thing around, like she probably used to, and there are economies of scale in stock trading, so I understand, that make moving small amounts of money around a real loser of a bet.

Which left Bridget spinning her wheels, something I'm sure didn't displease Fred a whole lot.

"So? What do you think?" she asked.

"I'm thinking that this is my home." I tapped my fist against the wall. It was solid—good lath-and-plaster construction that's not quite a lost art, not the shitrock that you can put your head through if you stumble into it. "It's always been; always will be—that's what I think."

"And if," she said, choosing her words slowly and carefully, "*if*—I'm just saying *if*—it were a choice between this house and me?"

When in doubt, go with the truth. "I'd choose you in a fucking heartbeat," I said. "But I don't think you'd ask me to make that choice, knowing how I feel about this place. And I think that if you did, I'd find that hard to forgive and forget, and I think you know that, too."

"Yes, I'd worked that out," she said. "And no, I wouldn't." Her smile seemed kind of strange. "But a girl likes to know where she stands."

"And if I'd said I'd choose the house? I lose?"

She shook her head. "If a few stupid words were going to screw things up with you and me again, I'd have left you three times this week, and you'd probably have kicked me out, oh, once every couple of months."

"The ratio's as bad as that?"

"I was being generous." She smiled, then shrugged. "We're not the same, you and me. To me, a house—even my mom and dad's—is just a house. I know it's different for you, at least right now. But things have gotten crowded, and maybe you should think about a little more elbow room."

"I'll think about it," I said. But there's not as much give in me as maybe there should be; that's all I said.

"I thought you'd say that," she said. She glanced at the back door. "You know, we could enclose the back porch."

"Well, that'd be pretty expensive." Electricity wouldn't be a problem, even if I didn't already have a weatherproof outlet on the outside wall—running electrical cable is only a little more trouble than running telephone wire. "Putting up walls would be easy if we used Sheetrock—but roofing it over would be a bitch, and an expensive one. Probably have to rip off the half the roof, and accept a shallower slope, and then have to worry about ice dams every spring."

"The money isn't a problem," she said. "Unless it is for you. But there's another possibility," she added quickly, before I could point out that yes, spending her money on changing my house *was* a problem for me. "I was looking around the basement," she said, "and if we move a few things around, I could put in a small office there. Southwest corner, next to the stairs? We could move the washer and dryer over closer to the boiler, and the rest of what's there is just boxes, and that slanted funny little space under the stairs would work fine for bookshelves. I don't need a window; just some room."

"I could live with that," I said, although I didn't like the idea, for reasons I couldn't quite explain, not even to myself.

But it made sense. Bridget should have some space of her own, if this was to be her home, too, and the kitchen table just didn't cut it.

Moving the washer and dryer wouldn't be tough. Just a matter of cutting some pipe—measure twice, cut once—as the daughter of Bob Aarsted of Aarsted's Hardware would know.

"Ceiling's low enough as it is, though," I said. "If I put in a floor, you're going to be banging your head every time you stand up."

"But the basement floor's been dry for a million years. Put down a vapor barrier—maybe just some floor paint—and carpet it over, and it'd be fine. Some paneling on the walls wouldn't hurt any, though. And I could mount some track lighting up on the joists."

"I could live with that. Screw it—I could take the basement office myself, and let you have my desk in the bedroom."

"I'd rather have the basement."

"Fine with me."

She nodded. "Okay. And how were things at the office, dear?" she asked.

"Oh, wonderful. Bells and phones and Emma driving me bugfuck crazy, and another anonymous complaint."

"What did you do now?" she asked, smiling. "You been beating me, maybe?"

"Not that I recall. But I think the chief of police should check you thoroughly for marks," I said, beckoning her to rise.

"You're changing the subject again."

"Not successfully, apparently."

"Nope. So?"

"If you believe the latest anonymous call, Herschel Ginsburg has been molesting little boys at school."

Her lips tightened. "I'm starting to get more than a little angry over this."

"Welcome to the fucking club." I lit up a cigarette and opened the liquor cabinet over the fridge, then thought better of it. Too early in the day, really. I closed the cabinet.

"So? What are you going to do?"

"Well, I talked to Minnie Hansen about it. Basically, I'm going to sit on my hands until she gets back to me. And then do whatever sort of asking around I have to, then write up that I don't think there's a problem. Andy Franz says he'll knock my notes into what he called 'official bullshit' and pass it along to CYS, and mark the case closed. He says he's getting about as sick and tired of this as I am, but I don't think he has any better idea of how to turn it off than I do."

Well, that wasn't quite true. Right now, enough leaning on Norstadt just might help—particularly if the leaning involved him getting a ride in the cage—but I didn't exactly remember Franz promising to do that, and I don't think it was because he forgot.

As I've been reminded both too often and apparently not often enough, I have this bad tendency to sort people into friends and others, and putting Franz in the friends category would be a bit of a reach.

Besides, there's the whole matter of corroboration. I don't know much about this stuff, but my understanding is that you have to have something we cop types call "evidence" to convict somebody—did Franz have enough even to arrest Norstadt?

"And what are you going to do right now?"

"Go play cop for a while, I suppose."

I stripped off my work shirt and picked up my cop shirt, which still hung on the back of the kitchen chair, then stopped myself and went and got my underwear-style body armor out of the bedroom and put that on, along with the rest of the gear from the Bronco. Unsurprisingly, gnomes hadn't crept into the lockbox and unloaded the .45—when I pulled the slide back to check, the brass of the chambered round was still there.

I thumbed back the hammer, made damn sure the safety was on, holstered the pistol, clicked the little retainer strap over it, then stopped worrying about it.

"Well, as my father used to say, when you don't know what to do, do what you do know how to do. He used to add something like, 'And you know how to clean your room,' or 'You know how to walk downtown to the barbershop for a haircut.'"

"Doesn't make much sense."

"That's what I used to think. I'm beginning to think the old man had a point."

"And what do you know how to do?" she asked, maybe leering a little. "Besides turn a girl on with that spiffy uniform?"

"As a cop, just about the only thing I know how to do is give speeding tickets. I'll go hand out a few." I glanced down at my watch. "When Ten gets home, have her give me a call on the cell phone, eh?"

"The cell phone?"

I patted at where it was clipped to the strap across my waist. "Yeah. The cell phone."

She cocked her head to one side. "You sure you don't you mean the goddamn ringing plastic box on your fucking belt, or, better, tied around your neck like an electronic dog collar?"

"Yeah, that, too." I gave her a look. "You're thinking that I'm capable of changing, aren't you?"

"It had occurred to me."

"Come on, Snake," I said. His ears perked up and he got to his feet. "Let's go for a ride." He wagged.

I'm a slave to my bladder—who isn't?—and years of having my bathroom twelve paces down the hall most of the workday had tended to make me not plan much about such things, and I started getting about-*now*-would-be-fine-Sparky messages south of my belt when I was on the road out of town, heading toward the same spot that Jeff and I had used just a few days before, so I pulled off County 15 at the windbreak outside Weasel Larsen's place and walked a decorous distance into the woods to do the business.

Which I did. Snake, of course, used the opportunity to mark whatever was could.

"Hey—I think you missed a blade of grass there," I said. "Or something else."

There was a patch of a familiar stalky-green plant with long, pointy leaves growing there, already waist-high.

You see them all over the place in this part of the world, and it doesn't mean much of anything—cannabis is a weed, after all, and the only relationship between the wild stuff and Maui Kazowie or whatever is appearance and genetics. As kids we'd all tried to smoke the wild stuff and had gotten nothing more than a funny taste and a cough for our trouble. There's only a trace of THC in it, apparently, as opposed to the real stuff grown by serious growers, which has been bred to be something more potent than even the green we used to pick up for preposterously small amounts of scrip on just about any street in Vietnam.

Well, that's not the only similarity. It's just as illegal, at least technically, as the real stuff. Theoretically—I've never heard of it happening out here, but it has happened, in other places—you can be in just as much trouble for not getting rid of the weeds as you can for actually growing the stuff yourself although it's a matter of what they call "prosecutorial discretion." There was also this thing called "jury nullification" that I'd read about when copyediting David Gross's book.

Neither of which is something I'd want to count on, not with what Washington calls the "War on Drugs," Bridget calls the "War on Some Drugs," and I call a slow-motion witch hunt. Beer and whiskey are fine with me when I need a buzz, but if you want to get your high from smoking marijuana or snorting cocaine or shooting up heroin, shit, it's your lungs, your nose, and your arm.

But, as the song says, paranoia strikes deep.

Jeff Thompsen wasn't the only farmer I knew who would take a sprayer bottle of Round-Up along when he took an occasional walk through the strip of woods bordering his fields. Round-Up is not technically a herbicide, as I understand it—it's a hormone that just gives any plant it touches a bad case of cancer, and then breaks down into harmless components while the plant busily dies. Hit any weed with it, and the weed goes—unless you get sloppy, it'll leave the plants next to it doing just fine.

Paranoid? Maybe. But distrust of the gubmint isn't vaguely unusual for farmers, or unique to them. Even paranoids have enemies, after all.

Unless things had changed a lot since I was a kid, there probably were patches of nonwild stuff growing here and there, and it was probably the duty of the Chief of Police of Hardwood, ND, to try to figure out where those secret growing places were and arrest the evil perpetrators who were getting their buzz without official government approval. My utter lack of interest in doing that aside, finding the patches would be difficult, at best—a few isolated plants in an isolated stretch of woods somewhere?

Which probably solved that problem, at least in terms of worrying about Norstadt siccing the DEA on every farmer around Hardwood.

Besides, it's a weed: There were certainly just as much wild and maybe less-wild plants, so to speak, around Thompsen as here.

I thought, just for a moment, about chopping down a few stalks and putting them in an evidence bag in the back of the Bronco, and, er, *discovering* said stalks in Norstadt's car if I was lucky enough to bag him speeding again, but decided against it.

The thought was entertaining though. Still . . . nah.

In one of my rare appearances at a Sunday service—I forget what David Oppegaard had used to bribe or blackmail me into coming to services that time—his sermon had digressed from the parable of the prodigal son—which, frankly, I'd never understood—into a discourse on how, if something isn't morally obligatory, it's usually easier to figure out if it's impractical before you get to the question of whether or not it's immoral, and that had made sense.

And it covered that stupid idea pretty well, and probably also covered some obvious other temptations, like handcuffing Aarsted and Norstadt to a tree somewhere out in the woods and coming back every now and then to see if they'd figured out a *modus vivendi*—as tempting as that mental image was, too.

A lot to think about while taking a piss; I zipped up, got back into the car, and headed over to Brian Gisslequist's place, although I reconsidered it for a moment when I saw his old, mainly rust-and-Bondo-colored Jeep parked next to it, which probably meant I'd have to move if and when he brought his tractor or combine or whatever was back to the shed—but decided that, what the hell, if it was good enough for Jeff, it was good enough for me.

Snake didn't object. He just curled up on the passenger seat and slept.

Traffic stops are, as I've said, easy, at least in my part of the world. It's what they call a "target-rich environment."

After going through the little silliness with the tuning forks and the logs, all you have to do is sit in the car, smoke-'em-if-you've-got-'em, and take your pick of cars zipping by, shooting them with the radar gizmo as you please.

Just for the hell of it, I shot the first ten cars that came by without doing much of anything except watching six out of ten brake lights quickly going on as the cars passed the

Bronco. The only thing not moving faster than the posted limit was Brian Gisslequist on his tractor—he was moving at a steady eight miles an hour. I had to move the Bronco out of the way and make a little polite chit-chat before he got in his Jeep and took off for town—hitting seventy-three before he was out of range, not that I did anything about it.

The next five were all speeding. The phrase "shooting fish in a barrel" came to mind.

So I did a couple of stops. When we went after them, Snake, being a dog, had to stick his head out the window on his side, and me, being a human, only put it down far enough so he could stick just his head out—which he did, even when we went over eighty, although only dog knows why.

I let the young mother with the screaming infant in the baby seat off with a warning—with a kid yowling that long and that hard, it seemed to me to make more sense for her to get back to Portland from Inkster as fast as she could, and she was only going eighty, and the screaming baby was driving me as crazy as it apparently was driving her—but ticketed the two thirty-somethings from Grand Forks in the red Porsche radar-bait penis substitute at their full rate of speed of ninety-five, which I probably would have, even if the woman—the man was the driver—wasn't on her cell phone screaming, red-faced, to what sounded like her lawyer.

Think of it as progressive taxation. Somebody who can afford a Porsche—and yes, it occurred to me, too, that Fred Honisted was also a Porsche owner; I'm a shallow kind of guy—can afford whatever the hell a thirty-miles-per-hour-over-the-limit ticket is, which a quick look at the clipboard told me was $166—$55 for the state, $111 for the town of Hardwood—and his Visa Gold accepted the $166 "bond" without a hiccup.

The guy seemed more embarrassed at her screaming than anything else. Wish she had been driving.

They sped off—well, drove slowly off, actually, with her still screaming into the phone—and I got back to the Bronco, and got the Bronco back to my perch, and let a few more go by while I had a cigarette and thought about how a thermos of coffee would probably go well about now, and wondered why Jeff hadn't mentioned that in the first place, and why I hadn't thought of it in the second place.

Back to work, such as it was.

The next candidate was a huge, formerly white semi heading east at a scant eighty-five, the vortex of its passage actually shaking the Bronco. I must have been a little too eager this time, because when I stepped on the gas the wheels of the Bronco spun, kicking up dirt and sliding me sideways before I forced my foot off the gas and made damn sure to look to my right and see that there wasn't anything coming before I got out on the highway, lights flashing.

Whee!

The truck grew in the distance, and it felt like it took forever to catch up, particularly when he didn't bother to stop at the oversized STOP sign where the road to Hatton tees off, and we were almost at the Cole Creek jog, where County 13 comes in, before I was close enough that blasting the siren made any impression.

For a moment I wasn't sure if he was just slowing to negotiate the turn, or to stop, or just because even a moron in a tractor-trailer wouldn't want to risk some other idiot running the same stop sign that he was an idiot for running.

But he slowed and pulled over halfway onto the shoulder. I stopped a couple of dozen yards behind him, reached for the microphone, and switched on the loudspeaker.

"Please just sit there for a moment, and I'll be with you in a minute or two," I said, and punched the plate numbers into the computer.

It took only a few seconds to come back fine. Ingebretsen Meat Transport—just like the painting on the back door of the trailer said—registered to a Lars Ingebretsen, who had a decent but not huge number of points on his Class III—trucker's—license. No warrants, unsurprisingly.

And no big deal; I got out of the Bronco, ticket book in hand, and as I started to walk over, he opened the door and climbed down out of the cab, a clipboard in one hand and a scowl on his face. Big guy, maybe a couple of years younger than me, and built along burly-farmer lines. His short-sleeved work shirt showed a left arm that was deeply tanned, which made his right one look pale, although it wasn't.

"Another fucking speed trap?" he asked, not particularly nicely. "Could you hurry this up, shithead?" Ah. Clearly an honors graduate of the Dale Carnegie School.

"License, registration, and insurance card, please," I said, holding out my left hand, fingers spread, to tell him to stop.

He stopped about six paces away and spat on the ground. "Sure, motherfucker," he said, reaching out with all three cards in his hand; I stepped forward to take them. "Here—just hurry it up."

I think somebody should have explained to him, at one point or another, that there are times and places to give a cop a hard time, but the side of the road isn't a real good choice. Mentioning it wouldn't have been particularly a good move, despite the obvious temptation.

"Okay. Just stay right there, and I'll—"

"Could you please fucking *move* it? In case you haven't fucking noticed, the air conditioning unit in the box stopped working, and if I don't get to Grand Forks pretty fucking quick, I'm going to have to eat all that fucking meat."

I took a deep breath and let it out. My first inclination was to take my fucking time, but, shit, a few tons of meat costs a few tons of money, and he'd only been doing eight-five, after all, and while maybe the penalty for shooting your mouth off should be more than a few dollars, if he'd gotten to his fifties without learning when and how to shut up, a roadside lesson wasn't going to do it.

So: fuck it. "Ah, just screw it. Just—"

If Snake hadn't barked at that moment, I wouldn't have spun around and ducked to the side, and the tire iron would have crushed my skull instead of bouncing, hard, off my left arm, more numbing it than hurting.

Bullshit. It fucking hurt a lot; the license and registration and ticket book went flying, and I staggered back, then backpedaled some more to avoid the second swing, and fell on my ass.

Time doesn't work the same way all the time, and neither does vision, or hearing. I vaguely remember the sound of breaking glass, I think, but I could be wrong, and it didn't seem important.

I couldn't see Ingebretsen, who must have been less than five or six feet slightly to the left of me, not even out of the corner of my eye, but the other guy seemed to be moving in slow-motion as he raised the tire iron and took an impossibly long-lasting step toward me.

He was in his early twenties, no older, although he was already starting to lose his hair: a slimmer, younger version of Ingebretsen, in the same blue work shirt, his mouth open and chest heaving, screaming something, but I couldn't hear it. It had all become irrelevant, like the distant pain in my left arm that was only a vague irritation.

Irrelevant details crowded my vision and my mind. The second button from the bottom on his shirt was open, and he had a Budweiser buckle on the belt of his faded jeans. The knuckles on the beefy fist clenched around the rising tire iron were bleeding. His nostrils flared wide, the right one visibly larger than the left, and there was a tiny bend at the bridge of his nose that spoke of an old break, badly set.

In the interval, I should have had all the time in the world to scrabble back and away, but my legs were caught in the same slow-time he was in, and the hand that was grasping for the thumb break of the pistol were caught in it, too, and there was zero, zip, and no chance that I'd be able to get it out before the tire iron fell again.

And then a blur hit him, knocking him to one side, and he was fighting a hundred-twenty pounds of German shepherd that had fastened its teeth on his arm, and was more shaking him than he was shaking Snake, and we were all out of the slow-time again, and I was sitting up on the ground, pistol in my hand, safety off, coming up, when he and Snake fell to the ground. I know Snake was snarling—I could see his chest heaving, as he shook the kid like he was shaking a rat—but my hearing wasn't working.

Ingebretsen had taken a step forward—toward me or his son, I don't know—but he stepped back, his hands held high as Snake took the kid down to the ground, not for a moment letting go of the arm that had held the tire iron.

The kid was screaming; I could see it, but I couldn't hear it. I think I was, too, although I swear I don't know what, either.

His fingers clawed on the ground and fastened on the tire iron, and my sights came up shakily.

Front sight, press. That's all it would take, but my hand wasn't working the way it's supposed to, and I couldn't get the fucking sight to hold steady on the kid's head, and I wasn't going to shoot my dog.

And then Ingebretsen kicked the tire iron out of his son's hand and turned to me, his arms spread wide, the expression on his face pleading more than the words that I still couldn't hear . . .

"Snake, *off*," I said. "Here, Snake, now."

For a moment, I didn't know how it would go, but the dog, his face covered with blood, backed off, his fur on end like a cat's, and stood there snarling, while the kid clamped his arms together over his belly and kept screaming.

There was something I was supposed to be doing, and it took me only a geological age to realize what it was. My left arm still wasn't working, and my clumsy right hand wouldn't work right with my finger still resting on the trigger.

Oh. I carefully straightened my finger and rested it along side the gun, then brought my hand up to flip the blessed cell phone open. I pushed the big red button with my thumb.

"Highway Patrol," the distant voice answered immediately.

I know I was supposed to use some sort of ten-code, the one that says "Officer Needs Help," but I couldn't remember anything for shit. "Help," I said.

That sounded like a pretty fair summation of the situation, all in all, so I repeated it. "Help."

"Sir?" She sounded annoyed. "This is—"

"Officer needs help," I said. I thought I was saying it quietly and matter-of-factly, but I've listened to the tapes since, and I was screaming it out. "County Fifteen and Thirteen. Ambulance." I was babbling something about a tire iron, about two attackers, and a lot of other shit, but she cut me off.

"Yes, Officer Hemingway," she said, her voice going all flat and businesslike. "On the way. Hold on." There was some chatter in the background. "ETA ten minutes. I say again, ETA one-zero minutes. Don't you get off the line, sir."

"Wouldn't think of it," I think I said, honestly.

"Hemingway?" Another voice came on the line; it sounded distant and crackly. "This is Phil Jennings, from Thompsen. I'll be there in two. Hang on, buddy."

I know there was something I was forgetting, but the darkness was creeping in from the edges, and it was all I could to to hold it at bay. "The dog—be careful of my dog. Don't you fucking hurt my dog," I said.

"Police dog on scene," the woman's voice said in the background. "Officer injured."

"Say again?" I heard.

"Officer injured. Police dog on scene," she repeated, slowly, carefully. "You keep talking to me, Officer Hemingway, you hear?"

Things got kind of hazy after that.

I only remember fragments of it, like the ride in the ambulance, although I remember that coming *after* I saw a guy I later learned was Phil Jennings from Thompsen getting out of his cop car, a shotgun pointed at the two Ingebretsens, and I know it didn't happen that way. Phil says Snake wouldn't let him come near me until I told the dog to lie down, and I don't think Phil would have a reason to say otherwise, but I do remember a beefy Highway Patrol guy explaining to the EMT that they were fucking taking me to Doc Sherve in Hardwood, just like I'd apparently been insisting on, and the fucking dog was going with me, and Phil's right arm, splashed with dark red blood to the shoulder, as he knelt over me, cradling the shotgun in his right arm while he was busy hurting my left arm.

I do remember the needle, though.

It hurt more than it should have, and then world went all warm and dark.

9

Bridget was smiling down at me. "Welcome back," she said.

"Umph," I said. Or something like that.

"It's going to be okay," she said.

"Wmph?" It was supposed to be "Where am I?" But it definitely came out as "*Wmph?*"

But she understood anyway.

"The clinic," she said.

I would have moved my head to look around the room, but it was too much effort at the moment. All dropped-tile ceilings look alike, anyway.

"Becky? Get Doc; he's awake."

"Mrph," I suggested. My mouth wasn't working right, and probably nothing else was, either.

I took a quick inventory. My left arm was in a preposterously large cast, and there was a steady drip-drip-drip from one of those plastic baggie things, hanging on a stand, with a tube running into my left wrist. No; I wasn't seeing double—there were three baggies hanging, all drip-drip-dripping at different speeds into a joint of some sort. A long, skinny plastic tube snaked its way down to the floor and up to my wrist.

My right arm was free, though, and I was able to raise it up two or three inches before it got to be too much effort, and I just let it drop.

Doc Sherve waddled in. "Hey there," he said. He glanced up at something over my head. "How you feeling?"

"Mrph," I said again, then forced my traitor mouth to obey me. "Like shit. How—"

He raised a palm. "It's okay. You've got a compound fracture of the humerus," he said, tapping on his own upper arm. "Came damn close to rupturing the artery, and you were an idiot to insist on coming here, and the staties were stupid to tell the EMT to bring you, and those idiots should've spun the van around and headed for Altru anyway. Lots of idiocy going around; I think it's an epidemic, myself." He took his pen out of his pocket and turned his body and leaned over so that I couldn't see my left arm. "Wriggle your fingers. Good. Now, do you feel anything?"

"Yeah. Middle finger. Pinky. Thumb. Middle finger again."

"Okay—now give me the finger."

"Huh?"

"Just shut up and give me the finger," he said, then smiled when I did just that. "Well, good. Okay. Now grip my fingers with your hand and squeeze as hard as you can without moving your arm. Okay." He turned around. "Couple of titanium pins in your humerus, to sort of hold things in place. Figure four, maybe six weeks before the cast comes off." His brow wrinkled. "You broke that arm when you were twelve or so, didn't you?" He tapped on the cast above my inner arm. "Ulna? Yeah."

I sort of nodded.

"Well, it's the same deal these days, more or less—don't get the cast wet, and when it starts to itch, be real, real careful scratching it. If—when—it starts to stink too bad, come on in and I'll cut it off, have Becky wash the arm and recast it."

"Thanks, Doc."

"Don't thank me. Moshe did the work—he's the trauma guy, not me. I just got to watch and admire, and tell him to use big stitches so you'll have a nice scar to brag about."

He kicked a stool over and climbed up to sit on the edge of the bed, then leaned over me and did a few things with a flashlight and my eyes. "You've got a few bruises here and there, and we've put enough units of blood in you that I'm having a shipment of O-pos rushed out from Grand Forks. But you're going to be okay, I think."

"And so is the dog," Bridget said.

"Yup." Doc smiled. "Although he's going to be a bit uglier than even German shepherds usually are—got a long cut on the ribcage, but it's all sewn up and he's resting comfortably. At your house, in fact." He looked at Bridget. "Fifteen minutes. Then he gets some rest. We might even turn him loose tomorrow night, if everybody plays nice. Day after tomorrow if not." He cocked his head to one side. "We'll send you home with a ton of Percocets. In the meantime, if—when—it starts hurting, just push the blue button," he said, putting it in my right hand. "Morphine is your friend. Mash it down anytime; it won't give you enough to interfere with your respiration," he said, jerking his thumb at the machine over my head, "as long as you don't have Bridge sneak you in some whiskey to wash it down with. Red button's for Becky, or you could just yell. Oh—and in case you didn't notice, you've got a catheter in your bladder, so don't go jumping around."

I hadn't noticed until he mentioned it, and even tired and woozy as I was, it took effort not to grab at my crotch.

He smoothed down the front of his doctor's coat. "Fifteen minutes," he said to Bridget.

She nodded. "Fifteen. Send Phil in, will you?"

"I don't think—"

"Just do it, Doc. The clock starts ticking when he gets in here."

He thought it over for a moment and then nodded. "Okay." He climbed down off the bed and walked over to the IV drip and made some sort of adjustment, then walked out.

The door closed behind him and Jennings walked in. He was tall and built along greyhound lines. Still in uniform, such as it was, although the shirt hung loosely on his lanky frame, and I didn't remember seeing a Hardwood PD patch on his shirt before.

"Hi, guy," he said, smiling. "Don't think we met formally before. I'm Phil Jennings. From Thompsen." I held out a hand; he took it and let me win the grip-war until I let go. "I think we're officially enemies. Even though your wife gave me a shirt of yours to wear. Hope you don't mind."

Yeah, sure; the thought of some guy wearing my shirt was exactly what I was worrying about. "You were the first one there." I didn't bother correcting him about Bridget's status.

He shrugged. "Yeah. I was closer than any of the staties."

This all felt strangely familiar. "Were you in before?"

"In here? Nah." He shook his head. "Been doing some speed stops out on County Fifteen—right near that Gisslequist place." He gave a wry grin. "Of course, being Town of Hardwood jurisdiction, that'd be utterly illegal, and all sorts of actionable, if the chief of police of Hardwood hadn't made me a volunteer reserve officer in the Hardwood PD just before he passed out." He raised an eyebrow.

I turned my head toward Bridge. "There's a reserve-officer badge in—in my desk at town hall. Could you get it and type up a letter for me to sign?"

She looked like she was going to argue, but then she just nodded and left, with a quick pat on my leg.

"Thanks. Some of the staties are in on it, too." His expression got a little grim. "It'll take a couple of days for word to get out on one-nine that there's some pissed-off cops with a low tolerance for speeding truckers along County Fifteen from Pekin to Thompson. But it will."

I could have remarked on how utterly unfair it was to punish all of truckerdom for one lunatic father-and-son team, but the rank unfairness of it all didn't bother me at the moment.

"You going to get heat from Norstadt for that?"

He shrugged. "Mike Olson's the mayor of Thompsen. I work for him. I don't know how he feels about it; I didn't ask."

Yeah. And if Olson didn't have his nose up Norstadt's butt, I was the first Lutheran—well, nominally Lutheran—pope.

"But, shit, so what?" he asked. "You and I don't know each other, and we're sure as shit on the other side of this whole Level-Three thing, but . . ." He shrugged again. "But once you're up and around, if a ten-eighty-six goes out from Thompson, you going to stop and think about how that asshole Aarsted feels about you getting in on it?"

"Probably have other things on my mind," I said.

"Yeah. Probably would have yesterday, too, I bet." He nodded and turned to leave. "See you later."

After he left, I noticed I was getting awfully sleepy again, and wondered just what it was that Doc had turned up the drip on. But then I stopped wondering anything for a while.

Life in the clinic quickly got boring, and mashing on the blue button didn't make it much less so, although it kept my arm to a dull ache. Sort of like a dull TV show with offensively bad commercials, consisting of Becka or Doc Sherve coming in to test something or other every now and then, and a little something or other being injected into my drip-drip-drip bag, only leavened by an occasional visit from Bridge and Tenishia.

I got real, real tired, real, real quick of Doc explaining to me that I should be in a real hospital.

"You need the bed that bad?"

"Well, no. The other room's empty, but—"

"If you don't think I should be here, then send me home. I'm more than fine with that."

He thought about it for a minute. "Can I have your word you'll take it easy?"

"Do I look like I've got any fucking desire to go out wood-chopping or jogging or—"

"Okay." His mouth twitched. "I'll have Becka run another quick blood test or two."

"And can you get that damned catheter out?" I wasn't impressed by the high whine that had worked its way into my voice.

"Okay." He nodded. "But if your stitches open . . ."

"I hate the sight of blood; I'll call. Promise."

"Deal."

Well, given how having a catheter taken *out* is, I'm just as glad that I was, so to speak, not around when it went in. Becka has explained that I'd feel "some pressure" when the end of the tube went past my prostate, and was businesslike and professional enough about the whole thing that I've got to admit I wasn't embarrassed. Maybe it was because I was busy being distracted.

Yeah. *Some* pressure. Uh-huh.

It was nice to be able to move around—and to be able to get up to go to the bathroom, even though my knees shook the whole time, and I seriously considered sitting down to take a leak but stubborned it out, my good hand grabbing the metal rail.

I'd kind of expected Moshe Ginsburg to check on me himself, but he didn't, and after only a little hurry-up-and-wait I was dressed—with some help; tying my own shoes wasn't on the program for a while, and we just borrowed the white-and-blue hospital robe instead of trying to figure out what to do about a shirt—and being helped by Bridget into the passenger's seat of my old Olds, with Tenishia behind the wheel.

"Don't you have school right about now?" I asked.

She snorted. "Put on your seat belt."

Well, that wasn't as easy as it should have been. My nerve endings—at least the pain nerve endings—seemed to have extended themselves into my cast, and Tenishia had to help me get it fastened.

Fuck.

Bridget climbed into the back, a cardboard box filled with my stuff in her arms, and we drove home.

The dog looked kind of funny, with his left side shaved down to that awful fish-belly-white skin, not to mention the stitches along his side that made me tempted to call him Frankendog. But his tail was wagging just fine, and he was only limping a little, and after a quick greeting he went to the back door and started wagging harder and giving meaningful glances.

Tenishia took him out, while Bridget helped me into the bedroom, and I don't really know which of those two things bothered me more.

10

Doing ordinary things with your arm in a cast isn't exactly what I'd call fun.

And it wasn't just the cast; there was something wrong with the way my body was working. I found myself feeling almost human for a while, then my knees started to shake and I had to at least go sit in the Consciousness-Sucking Chair, or, better, lie down for a few minutes.

But the main annoyance was the little things. A shower, for example, had become a major operation.

Bridget had wrapped the cast in a garbage bag, tying it off at the shoulder with a length of used-up pantyhose, so I could take a shower. It would have been nice to have one of those French-type showerheads—the ones on hoses—since there are some places that are damn hard to reach when you've got to worry about water leaking around a fucking garbage bag, and having to have somebody else scrubbing under my right armpit was just a minor indignity. It's possible, by the way, to spray Right Guard with your right hand under your Right Armpit, as long as you don't mind the Spring Fresh Smell all over your entire Right Fucking Side.

I've been known to skip running a comb through what's left of my hair, but that, at least, was something that I could handle myself, along with the shaving, so I did both.

Dressing was a thrill. I couldn't really sit around the house in shorts and a hacked off T-shirt, and my cast wouldn't fit through the arm of my robe, either, but Bridget solved that with some quick surgery on one of my work shirts—cut the arm off and carved open the shoulder until the cast would fit through the hole—and then did the same with a couple of others, promising to run them over to her mother's for a quick hemming. I was able to get into my own shorts, thankfully, with the aid of a bent coat hanger, and used the same bent coat hanger to get my jeans up, although one of those fits of weakness hit, and I was sweating bullets when I finally managed to get the pants buttoned and the zipper zipped one-handed, and I just sat down on the toilet and leaned back against the coolness of the tank until the feeling started to pass.

I needed help with socks and shoes—bending my left leg seemed to put a strain on my arm, for some reason or other—and Bridget made a comment to the effect that there was a pair of loafers in my immediate future.

But at least I felt more like a human being than a basket case when I sat down at the kitchen table to work. The work has to get done, after all.

There had been more than a few phone calls, which Bridget was intercepting. The script—*He's fine, he's resting, he's going to be okay, and yes, if you need to call 911, you'll get the Highway Patrol, at least for the next couple of days*—got boring pretty quickly, but it was kind of fun to hear her explain to her father that I was home, resting, and that if he really needed to see me, as he apparently was insisting he did, he could clear it with Doc first, then not quite hanging up on him when he didn't take no for an answer, although it amounted to the same thing.

It was just as well. While copyediting isn't, technically, a two-handed job, it sure as shit is harder to manage to hold a pile of paper steady while trying to write on it when you don't have a free hand, and using my computer was just this side of impossible, so we'd moved my operation, such as it was, out to the kitchen, with Bridget acting as caddy and research assistant, since she could pound the keys on her laptop probably faster than I could have with both arms. And it probably didn't help matters any that my head was filled with Percocet. Pain is not my friend.

You could say it was going well, but you'd have to be an idiot.

I've always been used to doing this myself, and interrupting Bridget every few minutes to have her do a quick fact-check for me was, in the medium run, not exactly going to lead to domestic felicity.

Of course, in the long run, I wouldn't have my arm in a cast or be hopped up on narcotics, it was devoutly to be hoped.

"I got an idea," she finally said. "You mind me trying some of this?"

"Huh?"

"I mean, I'm no professional copy editor or anything, but I've got a decent eye for spelling and grammar stuff, and I've been able to use a dictionary for a lot of years—and I know you've got Webster's on CD—and I can ask you if I get too lazy to open *The Chicago Manual of Style*," she said, tapping a fingernail on it. For me, it's more of a comfort object than a reference tool, these days—I've been doing this for a while, you know—but with some of the weird constructions these jokers use, I like having it handy, just to double-check. "Or you can just sit there and do the brain work while I do the heavy lifting."

"Well, it would be easier for me if you got some of the grunt work out of the way," I said, realizing how that sounded only after I said it.

She nodded but didn't seem to take offense. Being kind to the sick and injured, I guess.

Note to self: Don't push the sick-and-injured shit. Not likely to be a terribly durable routine.

So we did that for awhile, and it's damning by faint praise to say that she could make a little "1" over and a little "M" under a pair of hyphens just as well as I could. I'd already done the style sheet, and that was just as good a guide for her as it would be for the designer.

There was something kind of fun to working on it together that wasn't entirely drowned in the irritation over feeling like a spare wheel at my own job, although the tide of that kept rising.

So when the knock on the door came, and she got up to chase whoever it was away and ended up letting Dave Oppegaard in, there was a lot more sincerity in my famous hospitable greeting. His clerical collar was firmly in place, along with a professional smile.

"Hope you don't mind. Visiting the sick comes with the job."

Even when the sick don't want to be visited? I didn't ask. Must have been off my game. "Thanks for coming by."

"I came to see you in the clinic, but Doc Sherve chased me away." That would have been a sight to see. "I can only stay a minute."

"Come on in," I said. I don't do much Lutheran ritual, but I know that one. "Coffee?"

"I don't think so." He shook his head. "I'd be a bad guest if I poured about a quarter cup of that overly strong brew you make and then filled the rest of it with water. Just wanted to stop by and make sure you were okay."

"I'm fine," I said, not entirely lying. I could have been lying on a slab somewhere. "Any word on Jeff's dad?"

He shook his head. "No. Well, nothing good. Still hanging on, still hurting. I talked to Jeff last night. He sends his best, and asked if you'd give him a call when you get the chance." He frowned. "Sounds like he feels guilty about what happened to you."

"Nothing for him to feel guilty about," I said.

"Would you tell him that?"

"Sure, if you'll give me his number."

He gave me a look. "Just call his cell."

"Roaming," Bridget explained.

"Oh," I said. And: "Sure."

"I won't stay," he said. "Doc Sherve made it clear you need your rest. But I did want to stop by and say thanks."

"Thanks? For what?"

He grinned. "This chief-of-police thing. I know you didn't want to do it, but—the last couple of days to the contrary—I think it's working out. I've been hearing things—well, mainly not hearing things, if you know what I mean." He looked at Bridget, then back at me.

"It's okay. She's just as aware as I am of her dad's little games."

"Well, good. If you didn't make it a point to avoid Sunday services, you'd know that I've spent quite a few sermons, of late, trying to make some subtle suggestions about feuding not being exactly what you'd want to call Christian behavior. Those didn't seem to take."

I shrugged, then immediately regretted it. "Seems to me that a one-on-one with Bob would be more to the point."

"I tried that, too. That didn't take, either." He frowned. "Whatever you said to him at the Dine-A-Mite apparently did."

It would have been interesting to know how what I'd—fool-ishly—been thinking had been a quiet little confrontation had made its way to Oppegaard. Well, the last step was easy: his wife, Pamela. But the rest of it? Ole hadn't been paying attention, I'd thought. Becka? Or was it somebody else?

Probably didn't matter. "Well, when the Level Three matter's settled once and for all, that should be the end of that—if we get it, particularly."

He raised an eyebrow. "Really? You think an influx of hundreds of people—at least—over the next few years is going to make things simpler around here?"

"Well, not when you put it that way. What do you think I ought to do? Run for mayor?"

"Probably not," he said. "Diplomacy isn't exactly your strong suit."

Bridget chuckled.

"Well, yeah."

"Let's talk about it sometime when you're more up and around. You look like you need to be lying down, not entertaining guests."

That sounded like a good idea, and when he left I stretched out in the Consciousness-Sucking Chair rather than getting on the phone to Jeff. Just rest my eyes for a few minutes. Later.

I thought I had only closed my eyes for a minute, but the clock read 11:01 when I last noticed it, and it was well past one when Bridget was gently shaking me. "Andy Franz just called," she said. "Said he'll be here in about fifteen minutes."

Great. What now?

"Coffee?" I asked as Bridget led him into the kitchen and to a chair. He had a briefcase with him; he set it down beside the chair. "Or did you already have your second cup?"

"You remembered." His mouth twitched. "Oh, I can live large. Cups still in the cupboard over the pot?" He said, making a patting, don't-get-up motion to Bridget when she started to.

"Yeah. So? What did I do now?"

He grinned as he poured. "It's what you didn't do—got to take a report on the assault."

To be honest, until that moment it hadn't occurred to me. I'd been thinking about other things than the two Ingebretsens.

"Well, let's do it, then," I said.

"Hey, don't look so somber about it. It's not like you're going to be testifying in court, unless you really want to appear at the sentencing hearing."

"Isn't there usually some sort of trial first?" Bridget asked.

"Well, yeah." His grin widened. "There is that tradition. But, what with a confession and all . . ."

"You read them their rights and everything?" I asked, not quite realizing how stupid that sounded until it came out.

"Oh, I did better than that," he said. "And got pictures of both of them—at the hospital, before we took Lars over to the house. Except for the dog bites, not a mark on either of 'em." His brow furrowed. "You got a VCR?"

"In the living room. All modern conveniences."

"Well, can you get up?"

"Sure."

He let Bridget and me lead him down the hall into the living room, and I sank happily into the Consciousness-Sucking Chair while he fiddled with the VCR, and pulled up my hassock so he could sit next to the TV. Bridget sat down gingerly on the edge of the couch, and after a moment Cat came out of somewhere and settled on her lap.

"This is a copy—you can keep it," he said, fast-forwarding. "Thought you'd kind of like this part." He started the tape, and it showed Ingebretsen—the father—sitting across from Franz at a table. Well, it was either Franz or some other balding cop in a suit; his back was to the camera, which also caught the shoulder of a uniformed trooper standing next to him. There was a TV and a VCR on a metal stand over to the right.

"—lawyer," Ingebretsen said.

"You bet." Franz nodded. "You sure do have the right to a lawyer. I already told you that. You want me to read the card again?"

"No, but I—"

"In fact, you'd fucking well *better* get a lawyer. Much smarter than talking to me." He reached down under the table, came up with a stack of phone books, slammed them down on the table, and then reached down again and pulled up an old-style dial phone and slammed that down, too. "Get yourself a real good one, and get another one for your kid. Attempted murder of a police officer? Conspiracy to commit murder? And, for God's sake, don't try to talk the judge into a public defender. You don't qualify, and you need a real good lawyer. Shit— you're going to need Johnnie Fucking Cochrane, F. Lee Bailey, and Alan Dershowitz, and that's just to start." He reached down again and pulled out a what I at first thought was a book, but realized was a VCR tape, and put it gently on the table. "Shit, maybe you ought to get yourself some sort of film agent first, and find out what they pay on *America's Dumbest Criminals.*"

"Huh?"

He tapped a finger on the tape's label. "You shoulda smiled for the birdie, Lars," he said, getting up and walking over to the VCR. "Nobody ever tell you that all cop cars got cameras these days?"

Well, nobody had told me, and I was pretty damn sure that there wasn't one in the Bronco.

"Makes for some fucking fine viewing," Franz was saying. "Nah. Don't fucking talk to me—don't try to explain that your kid just snapped, that he's never done anything before, that you didn't know he was going to do anything stupid until he did it."

Franz got up and stopped the tape. "It's about here that I was wishing I'd talked to you before—after the kid slugged you, did Lars take a step toward the kid and the dog?"

"Yeah."

"Yup. But he could have stepped back." He nodded, then started up the tape again.

"Let your lawyer tell it to the judge, or tell your story to the jury—*after* they've seen the tape of you and your kid trying to kill him, after they've seen the pictures of Hemingway lying in a hospital bed with tubes running up his nose and out of his dick, after the prosecutor waves his bloody shirt at them. Sure—do all that. Just sit on your ass, and sit on your rights. Whatever you do, don't fucking get how sorry you are on the record, now, when I'll at least listen to you, and even tape it for the record." On the screen, he went over to put the tape in the VCR. "Oh, and in case you think I'm as dogshit-stupid as you are, this is just a copy—see this big red stamp here? It says COPY. Original's locked up in the evidence room. After you play it and call your lawyer, just stomp on it. I don't give a rat's ass." He more slammed than slipped the tape into the machine, then came back to the table and opened up one of the phone books.

"Make the fucking call," he said, shoving the phone in front of Ingebretsen. "Start at the As, or start with the guys with the big ads, or start wherever you want. You only got a right to two phone calls, but make as many as you want. You'd be a damn fool to say a word to me, and I'd rather go over to the hospital and see if your idiot kid is out of surgery and see if I can get him to lawyer up, too." He turned to the trooper. "Let's leave the asshole alone so he can talk to his lawyer. Give him half an hour, and when he's done, escort him down to holding. I want to get out of here on time for once, and— *what?*"

The "*what?*" was in response to a knock on the door. Franz opened it. "What is it?"

"Sorry, Lieutenant," a quiet voice said. "The guy in A-three says he wants to talk to you."

"Well, give me a minute to finish up here, and I'll go—shit, no, bring him *here*. I said I wasn't going to come back in here once I left, and I meant it."

Franz hit the "pause" button on the remote and turned to me. "It's not on camera, but in a couple of seconds, there's a big black guy in jeans—no shirt, cuffed behind the back, shuffling along in leg irons—standing in the door, looking all scared." He hit the "pause" button again and the tape started up.

"Officer, I—"

"Shut the fuck up. You said you wanted a lawyer; so get a lawyer. You got nothing to say to me; have your lawyer tell it to the judge. That's what his job is. He gets paid to get laughed at by judges and juries."

"Yeah, but I want to—"

"And I fucking told you that after I left the fucking room, I didn't want to talk to you anymore. You got the right to re-main silent, asshole; I got the right to not listen." He made a shooing-away gesture, then leaned out the door. "Get him down to holding," he bellowed, "and don't interrupt me with this bullshit again." He slammed the door and turned back to Ingebretsen, then took a breath and let it out.

"Sorry about that," he said, his voice all businesslike, and maybe even a little friendly. "And don't worry—you won't be in the same cell with him. 'Sides, I don't think you're his type. He likes girls." He picked up his jacket from the back of his chair and slid his arms into it. "See you in court, Lars."

"Wait."

On the screen, Franz was frowning. "What?"

"I—shit. Can I see the tape?"

"Go ahead," he said, reaching for the doorknob. "Take your time."

"No, I mean—can I, can I at least tell you my side of the story?"

"Shit." Franz didn't move toward his chair. "You sure you don't want to talk to a lawyer first? You got that right, you know."

"No, I . . . I want to talk to you."

"Fuck." On the screen, Franz sat down, and in my living room, he stood up and shut off the VCR. "And since I don't want to poison the victim's statement, let's leave it there for now."

"Camera?" Bridget asked, turning toward me. "Does Jeff's car have a camera?"

"Nope." I shook my head. "Supposed to, I think; I don't know where the paperwork is."

Franz grinned. "Well, you probably should get one. Handy thing. I kinda fibbed about that. As we all know, Sparky, cops are allowed to fib to suspects."

"I figured that out. Kind of convenient you had somebody else there, too, somebody who wanted to talk. I didn't think he was going to go for it."

"Nah. He would have gone for it—when you play the tape again, watch his face when I first start to leave—but, no, what's kind of convenient is that Dave Wilson likes playing prisoner. Hell of a lot more than I do, and we switch off, when he's catching. I didn't have time to call that off when I got up, which was the signal for the knock on the door, but it was a done deal by then. And no, I'm not a lieutenant, either—and I never did say I was—but you find that guys like to confess to somebody they think has some bulge, but not too much." He snorted. "Amateurs. A stone burglar would have laughed at me, but Ingebretsen's just an asshole amateur." He looked at me as though he was thinking, *There seems to be a lot of that going around.*

"So? You going to tape my statement, too?"

"Nah. We got some portable gear, but I think it was already checked out when left Grand Forks this morning." He looked over at Bridget. "How's your typing? And do you mind?" He pinched his left thumb and forefinger against his wrist. "Got a touch of carpal tunnel, and I'm lazy, anyway."

"I don't know if I mind," she said, stroking the cat in her lap. "And it's about forty, fifty words a minute." *And I'm not your fucking secretary*, she might as well have said.

"Shit. I can do eighty; I'd better do it. Let's use your kitchen table. You wouldn't happen to have any decaf in the house?"

"Nah. Like I told you the other night, Sparky doesn't drink it, and I haven't bothered. I could run down to the store and get some, I guess."

"If it's no trouble," he said. "Take your time. This cup should last me a while."

"Meaning you want to talk to him privately, and you figure that sending me off on some errand is better than just asking me to make myself scarce for a while?" she asked. "And if I'd said I type a hundred words a minute, would you have said you can do one-twenty?"

He started to say something, then stopped and caught his breath. "Sorry; I was out of line. Won't happen again."

"Okay."

"Now, please: Can I talk to him privately for a while?"

"Sure." She pushed the cat off her lap and stood, giving him a long look. "You really want some decaf?"

"If it wouldn't be an imposition, sure. If it would, hell, no."

"No problem. Really. Sparky's got the number; call me on my cell when you're done."

I think there was more than the usual gentle sway to her hips as she walked to the front door and closed it quietly behind her on her way out.

"Remind me not to piss her off again," Franz said.

"Don't piss her off again."

He was grinning. "She got a sister?"

"Three. I think the only unmarried one's too young for you, but she mightn't think so; I dunno. I could introduce you." I thought about it for a second. "Probably after the whole Level Three thing is settled, though? Just in case it does work out?"

"Yeah. Let's do that." The smile went away, and his expression was all professional again: disinterested but not uninterested. "Let's get to it."

"You still want to use the kitchen?"

"Sure."

Giving the statement was, well, interesting. I refreshed my memory, such as it was, with the logs from the Bronco—which had gotten itself a new window, somehow or other, although there were still a few slivers of glass on the carpet from where Snake had broken his way out. When I got to the part about how I'd approached Ingebretsen, Franz looked up from his keyboard—he was using his own laptop, not Bridget's—and gave me a look. "You didn't bring him back behind the trailer?"

"No. Pretty fucking stupid, eh?" If I'd had Ingebretsen come to me while I was still at the Bronco, the kid couldn't have gotten around behind me, not without me seeing it.

"Well, yeah." He looked at the screen for a moment. "Well, shit, that doesn't affect the facts of the case. You being a moron isn't an affirmative defense or a mitigating factor."

I would have made some smartass comment, but he had me dead to rights.

"Then again, when I was a trooper, I probably did the same thing once or twice." He shrugged. "Didn't almost get killed, though."

"No harm, no foul?" I suggested, shaking my head to show I didn't mean it.

"Yeah, maybe," he said, skeptically. He resumed typing. "Okay. 'Hemingway stated that at that point in time he was on the ground, having been assaulted from the rear, having suf-

fered what he believed to be a life-threatening injury," he said,
typing. "He stated that he then drew his service pistol because
he believed his life was in imminent danger from the assailant,
who was at the time attempting to reacquire the weapon while
struggling with the police dog, Snake, right?"

"Yeah."

He looked at me. "This is where it gets kind of handy that
Ingebretsen doesn't have a lawyer—might make kind of a big
deal over the police dog thing. No training and all."

"But he's going to be getting a lawyer."

"Sure. Who is, odds are, going to be far more interested in a
sentence recommendation than anything else, and it doesn't
amount to shit, anyway, given the confessions, but . . . okay.
You shoot?"

"You know I didn't."

"Well, I know you didn't hit anything, and I think you
might have mentioned it if you had shot at them, but you've
got to say it. Did you fire?"

"No."

"And you held your fire because—"

"Because I couldn't shoot the fucker without maybe hitting
my dog."

He shook his head as he typed "—because the perpetrator
was not, at the moment, actually able to commit further life-
threatening violence on Hemingway's person." He looked up.
"Where's the piece?"

"Bedroom," I said, "along with the rest of my cop stuff. Bottom drawer of the dresser."

"Okay—I've got to take a look at it before I leave. It hasn't
been fired since you last cleaned it, has it?"

"Nope. Had Bridge unload it, though." Loading or unload-
ing—or, for that matter, checking—a semiauto is a two-
handed operation, and I was definitely one-handed for the
time being. There's something to be said for revolvers.

"Good. Okay: Hemingway then summoned assistance, and held the perpetrators at gunpoint until other officers arrived on scene, subsequent to which Hemingway lost consciousness."

"Eventually."

He nodded. "Yeah. Okay; give me a sec." He pulled a preposterously small printer out of his briefcase and plugged the power cord into the wall and the cable into the laptop, then did a few things on the keyboard, hit a button, and the printer started to churn.

"Okay. First things first. I don't know why your cruiser doesn't have a camera, but it damn well should." He frowned.

It probably had something to do with money, and with Bob Aarsted not wanting to put yet another expensive machine in a vehicle the town didn't even own. But I didn't quite want to admit that.

"I'll see what I can do."

"Yeah," he nodded, and jerked his thumb toward the living room. "If we weren't dealing with a couple of morons, it could have gotten pretty nasty. The word of two against one, even when that one is a cop, isn't usually a good bet, but . . ." He shook his head, then leaned back in his chair and clasped his hands together behind his neck. "Say they stayed lawyered up, say they made bail—which they would have—and say they had a chance to get their story together, and forget for a minute whether or not their lawyer would come right out and help them make up a good one. Some will; some follow the rules. Either way, their story could have been something like, Oh, you did a stop and you started to get abusive—you being new to this, and not exactly overly trained and all—and you got nervous, pulled your gun on Ingebretsen, and the poor kid just was trying to defend his dad when you sicced your vicious dog on him." He gave me a long look.

"That's a story," I said.

"It could happen. Similar shit has, Hemingway. Give some guys a badge and a gun, and they start thinking with their dicks, swinging them around all over the place. Yeah, and you can thank your buddy Norstadt for me not thinking real serious about you falling into that category. Him and Rebecca Arvidson, and Robert no-middle-name Jorgenson."

"Huh?"

"Arvidson was the woman you sent in a NCIC and license check on about half an hour before you stopped Ingebretsen—she said you were a nice guy and let her go. Jorgenson—the guy in the Porsche—spent most of the time on the phone with me apologizing for his wife, and worrying that she was in some sort of trouble for mouthing off. Said you looked irritated, but just let it roll off your back. And, like I said, I thought you were pretty straight with Norstadt."

"Yeah, but I could have gone all alpha-male with a trucker where I wouldn't with a woman." My mouth tends to lead a life of its own; just because that occurred to me didn't mean I had to say it.

"But you didn't."

"Shit, no. Fact is . . ." I shook my head. It would sound stupid, and self-serving, in retrospect.

"Well, out with it."

"Seriously, just before his kid tried to knock out what little brains I have onto the ground, I'd decided that making Ingebretsen wait around while his meat spoiled in the truck just wasn't worth it, not over a speeding ticket, and not just because he was an asshole, and I was going to send him on his way. Lots of assholes in the world. Don't know that I figure I want to straighten each and every one of them out."

He gave me a long look. "You think you'd do that the next time?"

"Fuck, I don't know. Sure as shit wouldn't do it standing halfway up the trailer while somebody might be able to sneak around behind me."

"Probably not."

"So, you didn't think seriously about it, but you checked it out anyway," I said.

"Yeah. I do my job." He nodded. "And while I don't much hold with people beating up on cops, even clumsy ones, even ones that get out of line, if I'd decided you'd done just what Ingebretsen *should* have said you did, I'd be working real, real hard right now to fuck you over something serious, and given the way your mouth runs away with you, it'd be pretty easy. If I *was* going to fuck you over, I'd probably have helped you a little more with the statement, and then made you sign it before I brought up the subject." The sheets had worked their way out of the printer, and he slid them in front of me. "So read it all over again, make any corrections, and then sign it, if you want to."

Which was probably true. Just because something's true doesn't mean it isn't irritating.

"And I get the impression that you decided you needed to prove to me that you still *could* fuck me over, just the way you did Ingebretsen," I said, with probably more heat than I should have, and then added, "You going to do that?"

Snake stood up quickly.

Shit. "Snake, sit. *Down*."

"Hemingway—"

"Just hold still for a sec; it'll be okay." I wasn't watching him; I was watching the dog, who was down but not happy. "Hey, Snake, it's okay," I said, in as pleasant and low a voice as I could manage, and kept the voice pleasant and low, and kept looking at the dog as I talked to Franz. "If you're going to do something like hook me up, just give me a little warning, and I'll get the dog out of the way, okay?"

"No problem," he said. "Like I said, if I thought you'd been that kind of fuckup, I'd have handled this all differently. "No offense" meant—just a little . . . alpha-male bullshit, you said? You're not the only asshole in the world, you know."

"Really?"

"The reason I fucked the Ingebretsens over is they did it, and it's my job, and I don't think you did, and it isn't, so I won't, so if you'll just get off the bullshit, that'd be fine with me. And I sure as shit don't want to either shoot your dog or get tore up by him, either, so if you'd calm him down, that'd be just fine with me, too."

"Same here. He's just wired a little tight right now. Snake, come here. Sit. Paw." I rubbed his head, although bending to do it stretched something or other in my left arm that reminded me it was probably time for more Percocet. "We could get all complicated, dog, but you've got a dog's brain, and mine's apparently not much better, so let's just say that Andy's a friend, and you go over there and make nice, cause Andy's going to lean down now and carefully offer you the back of his hand to sniff, and after you do that, he'll make a fuss over you."

Which he did.

Franz had almost finished packing up his stuff when there was a knock on the door.

"You want me to get it?"

"Nah. I need the exercise." I struggled up from the table, bumping my bad arm and swearing a bit in the process, and went to the door.

Bob Aarsted was there, with some guy in a suit. Fortyish, maybe five-ten, slim build, nice suit.

"Hi, Ernest," he said. "Sorry to bother you, but I promised Tom he'd get a chance to meet you. Can we come in?"

Hell, no, I wanted to say.

"Sure," I said.

"Dr. Tom Hartridge, Chief Hemingway," he said, and we shook hands. "Tom's on the siting committee."

"Ah. We've been expecting you," I said. I was about to offer coffee, but Franz came out of the kitchen with his briefcase under his arm and the dog trotting along behind him— Hartridge's eyes widened a bit at the look of the Frankendog, but he didn't say anything about it, which told me he'd already been filled in.

He had to be introduced, too, and Snake insisted on being petted by his new best friend.

"We keeping you, Andy?" Aarsted asked. "Or do you need to be going—"

"I think I got time for another cup of coffee first," he said. "I'm short on my quota. If I don't get a good four cups, I tend to fall asleep at the wheel."

I repressed a smile. Pretty predictable that if Bob Aarsted wanted him out, Andy would want to stay, just to spite him. Would have worked that way for Norstadt, too, probably; he didn't have much affection for either of them.

My knees were starting to shake a little from the standing. Annoying.

"We're supposed to talk about changes in the police department if we get the Level Three?"

He shook his head. "Well, we were, but . . ." he gestured at my arm. "Perhaps next time."

"If you've got to go, we could do it another time."

"It's not that. Moshe said you got pretty banged up and should be resting." He grinned. "Your cast doesn't need changing, does it?"

"Not that I know of."

"Too bad. I'd love to watch, and give Moshe a hard time about using too many stitches." He grinned.

"Moshe?" Bridget asked.

"Dr. Ginsburg and Dr. Hartridge did their surgical residencies together," Aarsted said.

Oh. Yet another thing that he hadn't thought to mention to me. I was beginning to think that what we had was a done deal unless I fucked things up, and from the lack of expression on Franz's face, it was starting to look that way to him, too.

He gave a little shrug, as though to say, "Hey, none of my business, remember?"

I didn't shrug. Shrugging was off the list for the next month or so. "Sure. Assuming there's going to be a next time. Or we could talk now. I can't run around at the moment, but my mouth is working just fine." I gestured at the couch.

"Now would be fine," he said, sitting. Aarsted gave me a look, but sat down next to him, and Andy helped me into the Consciousness-Sucking Chair.

Franz cleared his throat. "Probably about time for me to be going."

"Got a few more minutes?" I asked. "I'd like your feedback, and I've got this hunch that you wouldn't hesitate to tell me if I'm off-base in any of this."

"No," he said, carefully, "I wouldn't."

"I think there'll have to be another visit, or several," Hartridge said. "But, if you don't mind, what do you think you need most?"

I'd read Bob Aarsted's summary, and didn't mind starting with that. "Assuming we get the Level Three, we probably need to have somebody on duty twenty-four-seven, eventually, although having somebody on call will probably work at first. Construction sites are magnets for all kinds of trouble—kids playing around, for one, and some criminal geniuses from, say, Grand Forks deciding to drive away with a bunch of building material."

Aarsted didn't quite beam.

"At the moment, I think what we need is a real cruiser—Crown Vic, probably—complete with camera rig," I said. I saw Franz nodding out of the corner of my eye.

"The town council is looking at the budget," Aarsted said. "I think we may be able to squeeze it in, sometime next year, probably. Before the ground-breaking—assuming we get the Level Three."

"No," I said. "I think we need it ASAP, Bob. I like Jeff's Bronco just fine, but it's got a high center of mass, and a sharp turn could flip it too easy. Do you want to put it on the minutes for the next meeting?"

He knew when not to call a bluff. "Done. I'll vote for it, and I'll ask the others to as well."

"But what we really need is a better-trained chief of police," I went on. "I'm not POST-qualified, and this cop stuff isn't just eating doughnuts and chasing speeders. A good helping of mature judgment is part of the picture, but there's no substitute for the classwork and the training."

"Yup." Aarsted nodded carefully. "Which is why you're scheduled to start the qualification courses in the fall."

"If it can be arranged, I'm going to start auditing the ones going on now, just as soon as Jeff's back," I said.

"I don't know."

"I know some the people involved," Franz said. "I can put in a word."

"My guess is they'll be a lot more willing if I'm all signed up and paid up for the fall, you think?" I asked.

"Make it easier," he said, looking over at Bob Aarsted.

"I can arrange that," he said. "It's already authorized when we hired Chief Hemingway. Just got to put the paperwork through and write a check, I guess."

"You got time to do that today or tomorrow?" Andy asked, gently sticking in the knife.

"Yes," he finally said.

"So, you're planning on staying on?" Hartridge asked, too casually.

"Yeah. I like Jeff Bjerke just fine, and there's a lot of stuff he knows that I don't, yet. But he's Bob's son-in-law, and I'm not sure it's worked out as well for the only town cop—or the chief of police—to be the mayor's twenty-five-year-old son-in-law.

"He's a good guy, and I'll go hunting with him anytime, but, like I say, he's twenty-five, and I'm more than twice that age, and the more I think about it, the more I think what this town needs is what they used to call a peace officer. Somebody pretty stubborn and maybe more than a little set in his ways about some things, who's more interested in making sure things go right than he is in speeding tickets. Somebody who thinks that, say, what happened with Burt Snyder and his daughter should have been caught a lot earlier, say, and would make it both a professional and personal matter to see that that kind of shit doesn't happen again.

"Somebody who doesn't really give a shit about politics, except when it means somebody'll get hurt.

"Right now, that's me. And it's going to stay me until I can't do the job. Bob's going to put in a motion for a three—no, a five-year contract for me at the next town meeting, termination only for cause, and he's going to ask the other three to vote for it. And if they don't, then they can have my badge back. I'm either going to do the job as well as I can or I'm not going to do it at all."

Aarsted had his poker face on. The only tell was how hard he swallowed. "Yes, that's what I'm going to do."

I hadn't said a word to Andy—shit, I hadn't thought this out until the words were coming out of my mouth—but he just gave me a nod.

So I just shut up. There was a lot more I could have said. I could have said that I didn't want the job, and on one level I didn't. But while Jeff had done real well at some things, he'd missed too much. He'd been too worried about what Bob would and wouldn't like, and while I'd accept that Bob doing the right thing by trying to get the Level III, the way he'd gone about it had fucking sucked rocks, and Jeff hadn't stood up to him.

I had.

And yes, I felt like shit about doing this to Jeff behind his back, and I'd try to make it up to him, but . . .

But you put first things first, and my first thing is that I take care of my own. Doesn't matter whether it's Doc and Horse and Prez and Tenishia, or Jeffie and Jeff, or Bridget—or Phil and Andy, or Bob Aarsted and Doc Sherve and Minnie Hansen or even that asshole Lars Larsen.

Don't always have to like them—and I don't always like them—but they're my people.

Me, I don't know much about a lot.

But I take care of my own.

11

My name is Ernest Hemingway. Go ahead and laugh if you want; I'm used to it. But please don't tell me any of the jokes; I've heard them all.

I have a girlfriend—who'll be my fiancée, once her divorce is final, I think (I'm sure as hell going to ask her to marry me; whatever kind of idiot I am, I'm not that kind)—and a foster daughter, both of whom irritate the hell out of me from time to time. I have a dog, too, although I know the word "have" means something a lot different with the dog than it does with the future wife and the kid, honest.

I'm the Chief of Police of Hardwood, ND. I'm on good terms with most folks in town—even the Deputy Chief, Jeff Bjerke, a term that'll probably mean more once we hire on a couple more guys, in a couple more years. I've met a few guys—and actually, a few girls—in my POST classes who just might do, but a couple of years of Highway Patrol duty first probably wouldn't do any of them any harm.

No rush.

Kind of a busy life, between family and classes and work and keeping my hand in with the copyediting, although Bridget's doing most of that these days—we haven't bothered to mention it to the editors, and they won't give a rat's ass unless they notice that the quality of the work has gone down. Which they won't; she's good and getting better, and, like I say, I'm keeping my hand in.

There's a big crew in town, clearing the ground this week for the Level-III Trauma Center, and there's going to be a lot of new people here soon.

Bridget's playing landlady on the side. One week to the day after the formal announcement was published in the *Gleaner*, she made offers on three empty houses, and is renting them out to the crew. Not quite as much of a bargain as she could have gotten before, but, well, that's my Bridget.

Some developer from Grand Forks snapped up the six others. I suspect there's a bunch of folks in town kicking themselves—either for not thinking it through, or for not having the money, or both—but Doc Sherve isn't one of them.

None of the folks on the Town Council thought it was right, even after the announcement, and while I don't think Minnie could have afforded it, I know Bob Aarsted and particularly Doc Sherve could have, and I was at the meeting-before-the-town-council meeting where that decision was made, with Bob in the lead on it.

He's not a crook, and, like I say, he pays attention, and he's watching the mail for offers from some of the hardware-store chains.

Which will come, I expect.

Some people will be moving in to staff the TC, eventually, and there isn't an empty house in town that hasn't been bought up, and a few families have cashed in and moved out—that developer from Grand Forks had money to spend.

I'm glad Minnie Hansen turned him down. I'd miss her. Wish Lars Larsen hadn't.

There will be more construction workers coming in to build, and then they'll go. Others will be coming for other things—the town's going to have one hell of a growth spurt, and a lot of folks will be moving in.

The chief construction engineer snapped up the old Snyder place the week Bridget bought her three, although there's not much for him to do, yet.

Name's Bill Addazio. Nice guy.

Dave and Ephie Oppegaard went over the day after they moved in. They brought along not just a tray of hot dishes—gotta take the bad with the good, Bill; all the neighbors brought hot dishes—but also a Catholic priest friend of Dave's from Grand Forks to introduce himself, and not coincidentally make it clear to people like that asshole Lars Larsen that there were certain kinds of problems that weren't going to happen, not in our town.

Not in my town.

Don't know if Bill's going to stay on when the work's done—he'll be able to turn a nice profit on the Synder house if he doesn't. He'll probably move on to the next job in a year or two. Hope he stays, though; he's a nice guy, and he's got a nice wife and a bunch of nice kids.

I stopped the cruiser in front of their house after dark the other night. Their lights were on, and they were all sitting around the TV in the living room, watching some sort of comedy show.

I turned off the engine and turned out the lights, and sat out in the dark with the windows of the Crown Vic open, and smoked a couple of cigarettes while I listened to the laughter pour out through the open windows.

I couldn't remember the last time I'd heard laughter come from the old Snyder place. It seemed to chase away the ghosts, at least for a little while.

I sat there until I could see again, and then just drove around for a while, and then I went home, put away my cop gear, had a stiff drink, walked the dog, and went to bed.

There'll be more people soon.

They'll be my people, too. If some of them get a bit drunk

some night, I won't give a rat's ass—although I might have to
ask them to hold it down if the partying gets too noisy; that's
part of my job. But no hassles about that—as long as they
don't get behind the wheel.

If they beat their wives or husbands or kids or fuck their
sons or daughters, they'll be given cause to regret it.

And, hey, if you're driving through my town too fast, I
might give you a ticket; I might just tell you to slow down.

We'll see.